BARON OF GODSMERE

Baron of Godsmere

The Feud: Book One

Tamara Leigh

The characters and events portrayed in this book are fictitious. Any similarity to real persons, living or dead, is coincidental and not intended by the author.

ISBN: 1942326157
ISBN 13: 9781942326151

TAMARA LEIGH NOVELS

CLEAN READ HISTORICAL ROMANCE
The Feud: A Medieval Romance Series
Baron Of Godsmere: **Book One** 02/15
Baron Of Emberly: **Book Two** 12/15
Baron of Blackwood: **Book Three** 2016

Medieval Romance Series
Lady At Arms: **Book One** 01/14 (1994 Bantam Books
bestseller *Warrior Bride* clean read rewrite)
Lady Of Eve: **Book Two** 06/14 (1994 Bantam Books
bestseller *Virgin Bride* clean read rewrite)

Stand-Alone Medieval Romance Novels
Lady Of Fire 11/14 (1995 Bantam Books best-
seller *Pagan Bride* clean read rewrite)
Lady Of Conquest 06/15 (1996 Bantam Books best-
seller *Saxon Bride* clean read rewrite)
Lady Undaunted Late Winter 2016 (1996 HarperCollins
bestseller *Misbegotten* clean read rewrite)
Dreamspell: **A Medieval Time Travel Romance** 03/12

INSPIRATIONAL HISTORICAL ROMANCE
Age of Faith: A Medieval Romance Series
The Unveiling: **Book One** 08/12
The Yielding: **Book Two** 12/12
The Redeeming: **Book Three** 05/13
The Kindling: **Book Four** 11/13
The Longing: **Book Five** 05/14

"When love has fused and mingled two beings in a sacred and angelic unity, the secret of life has been discovered so far as they are concerned; they are no longer anything more than the two boundaries of the same destiny; they are no longer anything but the two wings of the same spirit. Love, soar."

~ Victor Hugo, *Les Miserables*

PROLOGUE

Barony of Kilbourne, Northern England
Winter, 1308

"You ASK THAT we betray our liege?" Ulric de Arell scorned, though the disgust in his voice did not reach his eyes.

"And our king?" This from Rand Verdun, his disbelief seemingly genuine, though more likely he merely wished to be astonished.

Sir Archard Boursier leaned back against the trestle table and narrowed his gaze on the two with whom he had requested this meeting. Like them, he was vassal to Baron Denis Foucault of Kilbourne. Unlike them, he had little to lose.

"If we do not stand on the side of right," he said, silently amused by the tic at the corner of Verdun's mouth, "'tis England we betray."

Verdun glanced at De Arell. De Arell glanced back.

They would acquiesce. *Must* acquiesce. Despite differences rooted in jealousy and manifested in recriminations, squabbling, and the occasional crossing of swords, it was imperative the three ally.

"A betrayal for a betrayal," Verdun said with accusation.

Archard pushed off the table. "You were there. You heard what Foucault told and yourself advised he stand with the earl and the baronage against the king and that miscreant he calls *friend*." The insufferable

— 1 —

Piers Gaveston, who had been named England's regent in the king's absence.

Archard shifted his gaze to De Arell. "You said the same. Do you now claim you were wrong?"

"I do not!" De Arell barked, then grunted. He did not like being led to bait—worse, sinking his teeth into it.

Floorboards creaking beneath his weight, Archard crossed the candlelit room of the inn he had procured for their meeting. He halted a stride from the two men, nodded at the purse on De Arell's belt. "Still you will deliver the missive to the king?"

The man's nostrils flared. "I am pledged to Foucault."

Archard drew a deep breath, grimaced at air fouled by travelers who paid to sprawl upon flea-infested pallets in this chamber. But not this night. This night, only three gathered here, noblemen all. And not to sleep, but to decide loyalties that would not be without betrayals.

"Just as Foucault is pledged to the earl," Archard reminded both men.

Verdun opened his mouth, but before he could state the obvious, Archard did it for him. "Dare not say the earl owes anything to a king such as that, or I shall knock the words back down your throat!"

As Verdun's mouth twitched with greater zeal, Archard stared at this one whose face women sighed over, a face with which Verdun's young son was also gifted—or cursed, if one asked this man who aspired to be better known for his valor.

"So like De Arell," Archard said, "you will aid Foucault in betraying the earl?"

Verdun's jaw shifted. Of the two men, he would be the most difficult to turn. Though a worthy adversary, he was more honorable than most—at times, dangerously so.

"Or will you stand with me?" Archard pressed.

Of a sudden, De Arell stepped forward, causing the one he encroached upon to ready his head and hand to wield his blade.

"In all this," De Arell said, "what has *The Boursier* to lose?"

Though others titled Archard such, it was with reverence for his skill at swords and fists. In this instance, it was a taunt embedded in a question meant to remind him he was but a knight, unlike these two whom Foucault had made castellans. "What have I to lose?" he said between his teeth. "Certes, not what should have been mine."

The man's eyebrows arched into the hair upon his brow. "Is that why you ask this of us? To see us reduced to landless nobles the same as you?"

Hold! Archard counseled the hand that ached for the hilt. It would take more than the word of a knight to convince the earl that Foucault betrayed him. At the least, the missive was needed. At the best, the accord of De Arell and Verdun.

Archard jammed his fingers into his palms. "What do you think will happen when the earl discovers his baron has gone the side of the king?"

"*If* he discovers it," De Arell submitted.

"He shall. Be it a fortnight, be it a year, he shall learn of Foucault's faithlessness. Then you may find yourself as landless as I."

The arrow struck, bleeding a long silence. Not that the two men had not considered such an event, for they were not fools.

"If Foucault is stripped of his title and lands," Verdun was the first to speak, "what will become of his son?"

The baron's heir. Though the young man had earned his spurs five years past, Simon Foucault had yet to return from France despite his father's insistence that he take his place upon the barony of Kilbourne. Instead, he remained in service to the count who had fostered him during his knight's training. As for refusing his obligations, Simon was clear on that. Why sacrifice his desires when Archard Boursier could better serve in his absence and would one day serve the son as he had served the father?

Fresh anger coursing through him, Archard said, "He will find his own way."

"What of Baron Foucault's daughter?" Verdun asked.

She who was besotted with Archard, marriage to whom might have seen him awarded lands of his own. However, Foucault had refused to yield to her pleading to wed one who was landless—and too valuable in his current position.

"As her mother will likely return to her family in Scotland," Archard said, "she will surely accompany her."

Verdun heaved a sigh. "Mayhap we shall yet convince Baron Foucault—"

"Have we not tried?" Archard snapped. When their liege had told of the noblemen who had united to seek the banishment of Piers Gaveston under threat of revolt, De Arell, Verdun, and Archard had all agreed it was best for England. Foucault had not. Though he had taken the oath alongside the other barons and put his name to the Declaration of 1308, he intended to warn the king of what the baronage intended and, henceforth, serve as the crown's eyes and ears.

"What do you hope to gain, Boursier?" De Arell asked with a sly smile. "The earl's favor?"

Archard glanced at the single window with its filthy oilcloth that glowed from the light of torches outside. "I want what was first promised to me, but given to you, De Arell. I want what was next promised to me, but given to you, Verdun."

De Arell laughed.

Narrowing his gaze upon the man, Archard spread the strings on his purse, reached inside, and touched gold. However, when he withdrew his hand, it was dirt upon his fingers—the color of daub that held together peasants' homes. Still, it was as gold to him. Baron Foucault had given him a handful ten years past as promise Castle Mathe would be his, a second handful six years past as promise Castle Kelling would be his, a third handful a fortnight past as promise the castle to be raised to the east would be his. But just as the first two promises had been broken, the last would come to naught.

As senior household knight and adviser, he had ensured the barony's workings and revenues all these years, and Foucault needed him to remain in that position. Thus, promise after promise Foucault had made lest Archard Boursier pledge himself to another.

You should have! he admonished. *What fool you were to cling to the belief you would be rewarded for your faithful service.*

Even so, despite the longing to pass something worthwhile to his young son, perhaps he could have accepted being overlooked, but Foucault's decision to stand against the baronage was an offense upon which he could not turn his back. Nor could De Arell and Verdun if they had a care for themselves and their families. And England.

Archard broadened his shoulders. "Regardless of my gain—if there be any—you know this is right, that if the barons do not prevent the king and Gaveston from grinding England underfoot, all will lose."

The muscles of Verdun's face jerking—a tic here, a tic there—he strode to the door and came back around. "This I know!" He looked to De Arell. "As do you."

De Arell considered him, then moved his gaze to Archard and inclined his head. "Very well, I am with you—providing I have your word. Should the earl reward us, you shall support my bid for the barony. As will you, Verdun."

Archard nearly laughed. "You? Baron of Kilbourne?"

"There is none worthier."

That could be argued, but it was a waste, especially since the height to which De Arell aspired was impossible for any of them to attain. Though much of Kilbourne was wooded and uncultivated, it was a barony of good proportion and prospect. If the earl removed Foucault, a mere castellan would not replace him. Still, it behooved Archard to agree.

"And *my* reward, De Arell?" he asked.

"As I shall take Foucault's residence for my own, you shall have that which I now keep—Castle Mathe." He smiled wide enough to reveal a gap where a back tooth had been pulled. "A lord at last, Boursier."

Vassal to De Arell. Laughable.

"What do you propose for me?" Verdun asked, though Archard was certain that neither did he believe the earl's gratitude would extend to elevating a castellan to a baron.

De Arell's hesitation was pretense, of that Archard was certain. Before the man had arrived at the inn, he had known exactly what he came for. But if his plotting resulted in the earl learning of Foucault's betrayal, England would be in the hands of the baronage. And, God willing, the earl would show his appreciation by granting Archard his own lands.

That would be enough, he assured himself. Even if his reward was an obscure demesne in the north, all that mattered was a home for his motherless son, Bayard.

At last, De Arell answered Verdun. "Though my eldest son is betrothed, a worthy husband my youngest son will make your daughter."

Verdun took nearly as long to respond, but finally said, "So be it."

"So be it," De Arell repeated and looked to Archard.

Silently cursing them both, Archard jerked his chin. "So be it."

Thus, a pact was made between three men who loathed one another, none of whom could guess that the earl would split Kilbourne into three lesser baronies and reward the betrayers by naming each a baron in his own right. Of greater surprise was that which was bestowed upon Archard Boursier—Foucault's residence, the prized and impregnable Castle Adderstone.

1

———∞∞∞———

York, England
Early autumn, 1333

RAGE HURTLED UP Bayard Boursier's throat, but before the emotion could cast itself across his tongue, the king leaned near and warned, "Make your sacrifice an honorable one, Boursier."

Bayard glared at England's third Edward—all twenty and one years of him to his vassal's thirty and one. Golden hair sifting in air that wafted the scent of summer's end, the whelp arched an eyebrow.

Ignoring the danger in which he placed himself, Bayard bit, "Honorable? 'Tis my enemy you ask me to wed."

Edward spread his hands on the chess table between them. "Ask? 'Tis not a request, Boursier."

Then if Bayard refused, there would be forfeiture to pay—the barony passed to him by his father ripped away as surely as the barony of Kilbourne had been torn from Denis Foucault years ago. Of course, it would be the same for Bayard's enemies should they reject the king's solution to the warring between the three families.

"Methinks the Verduns and De Arells will like it no better," Edward fed into Bayard's head, "but they shall do as commanded."

Bayard did not doubt it. To retain lands awarded to their fathers twenty-five years past when the three men had united against their

— 7 —

traitorous baron and the king, the latter having fathered this Edward, they would yield.

Bayard dragged patience up from his depths as Father Crispin would counsel. "Six weeks," he said in a barely level voice. "Grant me that, Sire, and I shall end this warring." Somehow.

Edward scowled. "Six weeks when twenty-five years could not resolve your petty differences?"

Bayard nearly protested the pettiness of those differences, for there was nothing trivial about pillaging villages, burning crops, and slaughtering cattle. However, pettiness did play a role, for jealousy and bitterness were at the root of the offenses. Ulric de Arell, denied his desire to become baron of all, had been dealt another blow when Castle Adderstone was awarded to Archard Boursier. Thus, he had struck at Boursier, and Boursier had struck back. When Verdun would not side with one or the other, his lands had been attacked, and he had attacked back—a three-pronged vicious circle they had passed to their sons.

"Nay," Edward said. "We will not tolerate further raiding and plundering. The marriages will be made."

Bayard tightened his hold on the chess piece he had captured before Edward's announcement of his plans to ally the families. Feeling the imprint in his palm, he opened his fingers and looked down. Though it was but a pawn, the ivory piece had been destined for greatness in the form of an exchange that would have returned Edward's queen to the board. However, as Bayard was not one to willfully lose, even to a king, he had taken the piece. But still Edward would have his pawn—and its name was Bayard Boursier.

The king settled back in his chair and surveyed the lavish garden into which Bayard had been admitted an hour past. A smile hitching up his mustache, he said, "Though it cannot be said our father held your father in high regard, Boursier, that is all the more reason I look fondly upon your family."

It was putting it kindly to say the feckless Edward II had not thought well of the Boursiers—or the De Arells and Verduns. After all, they had

turned against Foucault who had forfeited his life along with the barony of Kilbourne when he had taken up arms against his liege, the earl.
Fortunately, as with most things to which Edward II had aspired, the king
had been largely unsuccessful in retaliating against the three families,
including his attempt to have Foucault's son, Simon, claim his father's
title. However, that particular failure was a result of the young man's
death during a skirmish in service to his French lord.

And now Edward II was also dead. Forced to abdicate to his
estranged fourteen-year-old son nearly seven years past, he had been
murdered shortly thereafter—if the tale was to be believed. And it was.

"Thus," the third Edward continued, "we have decided to grant you
first choice of wife, which will determine the other alliances."

The honor made Bayard want to spit. Five years ago, he had committed the mistake of wedding one of his enemy—and it had cost him
an eye. Clenching his fingers to keep from reaching to the patch, he
silently cursed the woman to whom he had been granted an annulment
of marriage.

"What think you?" Edward prompted. "The widow, Elianor of
Emberly, or the half-noble, Thomasin of Blackwood?"

One choice was no better than the other. The niece of the wife who
had cuckolded him? Or the niece of the man who had been his wife's
lover? Struggling to control his emotions, Bayard set the pawn among
the other pieces he had captured. "Your move, Sire."

Edward's lids narrowed, but he returned his gaze to the board. As
he considered his pieces, the herald who had earlier announced Bayard's
arrival reappeared.

"Your Majesty, Sir Francis Cartier requests an audience."

Bayard knew the name, though never had he met the mercenary
who held royal favor for aiding in the demise of Roger Mortimer, the
divisive lover of this Edward's mother.

"Cartier!" The king beckoned to his visitor.

Bayard looked around at the older man who, despite an unimpres-
sive height, was of good build. A moment later, he was grateful he had

heard tale of that one's heavily scarred countenance. The lower half of Cartier's face down to the skin visible above the neck of his tunic was broadly cratered and thickly ridged. According to rumor, the flesh had been ravaged by fire when he sought to free commoners locked in stables set ablaze by brigands.

Bayard shifted his gaze to the upper half of the man's face that was smooth but for the grooves that two score and a dozen or more years had cut into it. And found the knight's dark eyes upon him. And so they remained until Sir Francis halted before the king and bowed, causing the tail of the gray hair bound at his nape to shift over one shoulder.

Edward swept a hand to the bench beside him, the farthest end of which was draped with a rosebush. "Join us."

As the knight lowered himself, the king said, "Baron Boursier, you and Sir Francis are acquainted?"

"We are not, Sire."

"Ah, now 'tis remedied." Edward turned his regard upon the other man. "Once more you are returned to us. How long this time?"

"A sennight, unless Your Majesty requires more. As ever, I am yours to command."

"And I am ever grateful, Sir Francis."

Mouth pursing amid his cruel disfigurement, the knight jutted his chin at the chessboard. "I have interrupted your match."

"More than a match. Baron Boursier and I have come to an agreement under which his family shall retain their lands."

Inwardly, Bayard seethed.

Outwardly, Sir Francis frowned.

"Did I not discuss the matter with you, Sir Francis?" Edward asked.

The man's brow smoothed. "The Boursiers, the De Arells, and the..." He raised a hand that had also fallen victim to fire, jabbed the air with a finger. "...Verduns." Mouth curving with what seemed an attempt at a smile, he reached to the side, cupped a hand around a rose, and stroked its flaccid petals. "What is your determination, Your Majesty?"

"Peace by way of marriage."

The petals spilled from the knight's hand and fluttered to the ground. Frowning over them, he said, "You are beneficent, Your Majesty. Had I vassals and did my coffers suffer from petty disagreements, I would make a quick end to it by declaring their lands forfeit."

Until that moment, Bayard had felt only a stirring of dislike for the man.

Sir Francis looked to him. "You do not like that, Boursier. But then, neither will you like marriage to your enemy." He raised his eyebrows. "Of course, from what I hear tell, your second wife will be no more amenable to bearing your name than the first."

Bayard clenched his jaws. Though he had long borne the renown of one who had beat his wife and been made a cuckold, such reminders made his blood run hot.

Sir Francis sighed. "Methinks I would forfeit ere marrying one I loathed for the privilege of holding little more than dirt."

Now Bayard clenched his hands, longing to feel the smack of flesh and bone.

As if searching his memory, Sir Francis raised his gaze, causing sunlight to reveal gold in brown eyes so dark they were almost black. "I have heard tale of a household knight who weighted his purse with dirt in hopes it would one day turn into land." He chuckled, shook his head.

The hair on Bayard's neck rose. His father had carried soil given him by Baron Foucault as promise that one day he would be granted lands of his own—a promise twice made lies.

"But such is the foolishness of grasping men," Sir Francis concluded.

Edward cleared his throat, reminding the two men in whose presence they sat. "A true knight errant you are, Sir Francis."

Knight errant. From what Bayard knew of the man, it was a pretty way of identifying him as that class of soldier who sold his services to the highest bidder regardless of ethics. A mercenary.

"Your leave is granted, Boursier," the king said.

Dismissed. Of no more import than the abandoned chess game. Though Bayard knew Father Crispin would disapprove, he said again, "Your move, Sire."

Annoyance flickered across the king's face, but he advanced his piece as expected. Several moves later, the color of anger seeped into his face.

"Checkmate, Your Majesty." Bayard stood, bowed, and pivoted. He had taken barely two strides when a clatter evidenced the chess pieces had been swept from the board.

"Boursier!"

He turned. "Sire?"

Having gained his feet, the king pressed his palms to the chess table. "Two months I give you to choose between the Verdun and De Arell women. Wed by the last day of autumn or forfeit all."

Insides boiling like water over a roaring fire, Bayard inclined his head.

"Checkmate, Boursier," Edward loosed one last arrow, "and no game, this."

2

Barony of Godsmere, Northern England
Autumn's end, 1333

To stop the wedding, she would have to kill the groom. Or so Agatha sought to convince her.

Peering up from beneath the ragged edge of the thick shawl she had drawn over her head, Elianor of Emberly considered the man who approached astride a destrier blacker than the dregs of her ink pot. Though Bayard Boursier was fairly complected, he seemed no less dark than his mount. From his perspiration dampened hair that flipped up at the nape to his unshaven jaw to the merciless heart that beat beneath an ebony tunic, he was kin to the night.

El ground her teeth over the king's plan to ally the bitterest of enemies. Had Edward learned nothing from the mistake of five years past when her aunt had been made to wed into the Boursiers—one that had turned the families' hatred more foul?

"A pox on you, Edward," she muttered as she glared at the king's agent of misery, a man whose appearance hardly improved the nearer he drew, one made worse by the black patch covering his left eye.

A fearsome groom he would make for Thomasin de Arell whom, it was told, he had chosen to take to wife and would do so within the next six days to avoid forfeiture of his lands. But providing all went as planned, *The Boursier*, as he was better known—as if the whole of him could not be contained within his given name—would not have the De Arell woman. Nor would he have El, though until three days past, she had feared he would choose her. Thus, she had laid plans to avoid a sacrifice possibly greater than that offered up with her first marriage.

Despite the shawl's heat that was too much for a relatively warm day, she shivered as memories of her husband crawled over the barriers erected against them.

She shook her head. Murdoch Farrow, to whom she had been wed five years ago at the age of sixteen, was dead. And, God forgive her, she had nearly danced to be free of him. Just as Thomasin de Arell would rejoice in being spared marriage to Bayard Boursier.

As he drew closer, she lowered her gaze. But one peasant among the many who thronged the market in the town outside Castle Adderstone's walls, she feigned interest in the foodstuffs offered by a merchant—an old man whose bones and joints were prominent beneath a thin layer of skin. A moment later, his hands shot up and, in concert with his voice, expressed annoyance over his dealings with a stout woman whose heavily loaded cart evidenced she was from the castle kitchens.

El slid her gaze past unplucked chickens suspended by their legs to the riders who skirted the gathering, and hazarded another look at The Boursier. She groaned. Having only seen him from a distance when he had brought his men against her uncle's, he was larger than thought. Beneath a broad jaw, his neck sloped to expansive shoulders, chest tapered to sword-girded hips, bulky thighs gripped his destrier, hosed calves stretched long to stirrups.

Curling her toes in her slippers, she assured herself she could do this. Though he had chosen Thomasin de Arell, still her family—the Verduns—must ally with the loathsome Boursiers, meaning it fell to her uncle to wed this man's sister. However, if El's plan succeeded, the Boursiers would be expelled from these lands, as might the De Arells.

Pricked by guilt that the De Arells might feel Boursier's wrath for that which would soon be worked upon the latter, she reminded herself of the raid upon Tyne five months past. A dozen villagers' homes had been burned with half their crops, and all evidence suggested the De Arells were responsible for the atrocity visited upon the Verduns' people.

The flick of Boursier's reins drew El's gaze to tanned hands that appeared twice the size of her own. Familiar with the cruelty of which a man's hands were capable, she told herself this one would not get near enough to hurt her as her departed husband had done. Still, her heart pounded with emotions she had struggled to suppress since her wedding night when she had realized Murdoch found her tears pleasing.

Boursier was less than twenty feet distant when the sun came out from behind the clouds, and she was surprised to see his looks lighten. She would have said his hair was deepest brown, but sunlight revealed it to be darkly auburn. And the one visible eye was pale, though she could not tell if the gaze he swept over the town folk was blue, green, or gray. Regardless, his soul was black.

Doubt prying at her purpose, she silently beseeched, *Lord, can I do it?* Not that she believed God would condone her plan, but neither was she certain he would condemn her.

She shifted her regard to the diagonal scar above and below Boursier's eyepatch. Though deserved, he surely loathed the Verduns and De Arells for an affliction without end.

When he was nearly upon the stall behind which El stood and his gaze settled on her, she forced herself not to react in any way that would attract more attention—all the while praying the shawl provided enough shadow to obscure her face. Not that he had ever seen Elianor of Emberly.

Though questioning disturbed his brow, he urged his destrier past.

She eased the air from her lungs, swung around, and hastened to the hooded one who awaited her near a stall piled high with cloth.

Despite broad shoulders that fifty years of life had begun to bend, the woman who looked down upon El had something of a regal bearing. It was also present in high cheekbones and the dark, sharply arched eyebrows Agatha raised to ask what need not be voiced.

El glanced beyond her at the great fortress that flew the red and gold colors of the House of Boursier, and nodded. In the guise of a kitchen wench, she was ready to steal into Castle Adderstone. Or so she prayed—or should have.

Six days she must hold him. Then, for his refusal to wed his enemy, his lands would be forfeited. Unless she failed.

I shall not, she promised herself.

Even now Boursier was likely feeling the effects of the draught she had slipped into his drink a half hour past. That had been no easy task, one nearly rendered impossible when the cook had approached her. Blessedly, as she tensed for flight, someone had called him to the storeroom.

In his absence, she had stirred Agatha's preparation into the cup that was to be delivered to Boursier's bedchamber, the lord of Castle Adderstone's habit of wine before bed having remained unchanged since Agatha had endured a year in his household.

"'Tis just ahead," Agatha said low, raising the torch to burn away the cobwebs blocking their passage.

El peered around the older woman at stone walls laid not by man, but by God. Here was the place to which Boursier was destined. Carved out of the bowels of the earth outside his own castle, the shaft with its branching passages had been dug by Verduns and De Arells twenty years past when, for several months, they had joined against the Boursiers. El's own grandfather had assisted with the undermining that had brought down a portion of the castle's outer wall—a short-lived victory.

Months following the thwarted siege, she had visited Castle Kelling and bounded onto her grandfather's lap. Only one arm had come around her. Bayard Boursier's father had taken the other.

"This is it, my lady," Agatha said as she turned left off the passageway onto another, at the end of which lay an iron-banded door with a grate at eye level.

El considered Boursier's prison. "It will hold him?"

Agatha fit one of several keys into the lock and pushed the door inward. "'Twould hold three of him."

El accepted the torch offered her, stepped into the chill cell, and grimaced. The stone walls were moist with rainfall that seeped through the ground above. To the right, a rat scuttled into shadow. Ahead, three sets of chains and manacles hung from the walls. Were Boursier of a mind to be grateful, he would be glad he had only to endure this place for the six days remaining of the two months given him to wed his enemy.

As El turned out of the cell, she wondered again how Agatha had learned of the passage formed from the mine of that long ago siege, the entrance to which was a cavern in the wood. More, how had she obtained the keys? Unfortunately, the woman's secrets were her own, but El would not complain. While wed to Murdoch, she had benefitted from those secrets in the form of sleeping powders.

Meeting the gaze of the one in the doorway, she said, "Aye, it will hold him."

Agatha drew from her shoulder the pack that would sustain Boursier and tossed it against the far wall. "You are ready, my lady?"

"I am."

With a smile that revealed surprisingly white teeth, Agatha turned to lead her into the devil's lair.

"I know what you do."

Bayard had wondered how long before she stopped hovering and spoke what she had come to say. He returned the quill to its ink pot and looked up at his half sister who stood alongside the table.

Jaw brushed by hair not much longer than his, she said, "You will not sacrifice yourself for me."

He wished she were not so perceptive. Though she had attained her twentieth year, she regarded him out of the eyes of the old. Yet for all the wisdom to which she was privy, she was a mess of uncertainty—the truest of ladies when it suited, a callow youth when it served. And Bayard was to blame, just as he was to blame for her broken betrothal. Had he not allowed her and her mother to convince him it was best she not wed, the king could not have dragged her into his scheme. Of course, it truly was advisable that she not take a husband.

"Pray," she entreated, "wed the Verdun woman, Bayard."

He would laugh if not that it would be a bitter thing. "I assure you, one Verdun wife was enough to last me unto death." He curled his fingers into his palms to keep himself from adjusting the eyepatch.

Her brow rumpled. "Surely you do not say 'tis better you wed a De Arell?"

He shrugged. "For King Edward's pleasure, we all must sacrifice."

Her teeth snapped, evidence it had become impractical to behave the lady. "Then sacrifice yourself upon a Verdun!"

Never. Better he suffer a De Arell woman than Quintin suffer a De Arell man. Of course, he had other reasons for choosing Thomasin. The illegitimate woman was said to be plain of face, whereas Elianor of Emberly was told to be as comely as her aunt whose beauty had blinded Bayard—in more ways than one. Then there was the rumor that Elianor and her uncle were lovers and, of equal concern, that she had given her departed husband no heir. He would not take one such as that to wife.

"Hear me," Quintin said so composedly he frowned, for once her temper was up, she did not easily climb down from it. "As Griffin de Arell already has his heir, 'tis better that I wed him."

Feeling his hands begin to tighten, he eased them open. Regardless of which man she wed, regardless of whether or not an heir was needed, she would be expected to grow round with child.

He forced a smile. "'Tis possible you will give Verdun the heir he waits upon." And, God willing, she would have someone to love through what he prayed would be many years.

Quintin drew a shuddering breath. "I will not give Magnus Verdun an heir."

He sighed, lifted his goblet. "It is done, Quintin. Word has been sent to De Arell that I ride to Castle Mathe four days hence to wed his daughter." Though the wine was thick as if drawn from the dregs of a barrel, he drank the remainder in the hope it would calm his roiling stomach and permit a fair night's sleep.

He rose from the chair. As he stepped around his stiff-backed sister, he was beset with fatigue—of a sort he had not experienced since the treacherous woman who was no longer his wife had worked her wiles upon him.

"Make good your choice, Bayard," Quintin warned.

He looked across his shoulder. "I have made as good a choice as is possible." Thus, she would wed Verdun, and the widow, Elianor, would wed the widower, De Arell, allying the three families—at least, until one maimed or killed the other.

"You have not," Quintin said.

Pressed down by fatigue, he stifled a reprimand with the reminder she wished to spare him marriage into the family of his darkest enemy. "If I give you my word that I shall make the De Arell woman's life miserable, will you leave?"

She pushed off the table. "*Your* life, she will make miserable." She threw her hands up. "Surely you can find some way around the king!"

He who demanded the impossible—who cared not what ill he wrought. Though Bayard had searched for a way past the decree, it seemed the only means of avoiding marriage to the enemy was to vacate the barony of Godsmere. If he forfeited his lands, not only would Quintin and her mother be as homeless as he, but the De Arells and Verduns would win the bitter game at which the Boursiers had most often prevailed. Utterly unacceptable.

"I am sorry," he said, "but the king will not be moved. And though I have not much hope, one must consider that these alliances could lead to the prosperity denied all of us."

Her jaw shifted. "You speak of more castles."

He did. When the immense barony of Kilbourne had been broken into lesser baronies twenty-five years past to reward the three families, it was expected licenses would be granted to raise more castles. However, the gorging of their private animosities had made expansion an unattainable dream.

"Accept it, Quintin."

She opened her mouth, closed it, and crossed the solar. The door slammed behind her, catching a length of green skirt between door and frame.

Her cry of frustration came through, but rather than open the door, she wrenched her skirt loose with a great tearing of cloth—their father's side of her. Later, she would mourn the ruined gown—her mother's side of her.

Though Bayard had intended to disrobe, he was too weary. Stretching upon his bed, he stared into the darkness behind his eyelid and recalled the woman at the market. Not because of the comely curve of her face, but the prick of hairs along the back of his neck that had first made him seek the source. In her glittering eyes, he had found what might have been hatred, though he had reasoned it away with the reminder that his people had suffered much amid the discord sown by the three families. And that was, perhaps, the worthiest reason to form alliances with the De Arells and Verduns.

Curiously aware of his breathing, he struggled to hold onto the image of the woman. As the last of her blurred, he determined it was, indeed, hatred in eyes that had peered at him from beneath a thick shawl. A shawl that made a poor fit for a day well warmed by sun.

3

THE SQUIRE MADE a final, muffled protest and slumped to his pallet.

"Now The Boursier," Agatha said, pulling the odorous cloth from the young man's mouth and nose.

For the dozenth time since slipping out from behind the tapestry, El looked to the still figure upon the bed. Though the solar was dark, the bit of moonlight filtering through the oilcloth showed he lay on his back.

El crossed to the bed. "Does he breathe?"

"Of course he does." Agatha came alongside her. "Though if you wish—"

"Nay!" She was no murderer, and holding him captive would accomplish what needed to be done.

"Then make haste, my lady." Agatha tossed the coverlet over Boursier's legs so they could drag him down the steps of the walled passage. And drag him they must. Though the older woman was relatively strong of back and El was hardly delicate, there was no doubt Boursier would still outnumber them.

El put her knees to the mattress and reached to the other side of the coverlet upon which he lay. As she did so, her hand brushed a muscled forearm. She paused. It should not bother her to see such an imposing man laid helpless before his enemies, but it did. Of course, once she had also pitied Murdoch. Only once.

Returning to the present, she began dragging the coverlet over his torso. When she reached higher to flip it over his head, his wine-scented breath stirred the hair at her temple and drew her gaze to his shadowed face.

By the barest light, something glittered.

She gasped, dropped her feet to the floor.

"What is it?" Agatha rasped.

El backed away. "He..." Why did he not bolt upright? "...looked upon me."

Agatha chuckled. "It happens." She pulled forth the cloth used upon the squire and pressed it to Boursier's face. "But let us be certain he remembers naught."

Would he not? Of course, even if he did, the glitter of her own eyes was surely all he would know of her. Heart continuing to thunder, El watched Agatha sweep the coverlet over Boursier's head.

"Take hold of his legs," she directed.

El slid her hands beneath his calves. Shortly, with Agatha supporting his heavier upper body, El staggered beneath her own burden. Boursier seemed to weigh as much as a horse, and by the time they had him behind the tapestry, he seemed a pair of oxen. Perspiring, she lugged him through the doorway onto the torchlit landing.

"Put him down," Agatha said as she lowered his upper body.

With a breath of relief, El eased his legs to the floor.

Agatha closed the door that granted access to the keep's inner walls and jutted her chin at the wall sconce. "Bring the torch."

El retrieved it, and when she turned to lead the way down the steps, a thud sounded behind. She swung around.

Agatha had hefted Boursier's legs, meaning his head had landed upon the first of the stone steps. "Nay!" she protested. "We must needs turn him. His head—"

"What care you?" Agatha snapped, lacking the deference due one's mistress. But such was the price of her favors.

Still, El could not condone such treatment, for a blow to the head could prove fatal. "We turn him, Agatha. Do not argue."

"My lady—"

"Do not!"

Agatha lowered her eyes. "As you will."

El assisted in turning Boursier and, shortly, Agatha gripped him about the torso. His feet taking the brunt of the steps, they continued their descent. At the bottom, Agatha dragged him through the doorway that led to the underground passage.

"Give me the key, and I will lock it," El said.

Continuing to support Boursier, Agatha secured the door herself.

Trying not to be offended, El led the way through the turns that placed them before the cell.

When Agatha dropped Boursier inside, once more having no care for how he fell, El glared at her.

From beneath a fringe of hair that had come loose from the knot atop her head, Agatha raised her eyebrows.

El held her tongue. She supposed the rough treatment was the least owed one whose grievance against Bayard Boursier was great. Agatha had spent a year in his household serving as maid to his wife who had also been El's aunt. For one long year, Agatha had aided Constance when Boursier turned abusive, and comforted her when he took other women into his bed. Given a chance, it was possible she would do the baron mortal harm.

El fit the torch in a wall sconce, then aided in propping Boursier against the cell wall. She tried not to look upon him as she struggled to open a rusted manacle, but found herself peering into his face. And wishing she had not.

She returned her attention to the manacle and pried at it, but not even the pain of abraded fingers could keep from memory her enemy's dimly lit face—displaced eyepatch exposing the scarred flesh of his left eyelid, tousled hair upon his brow, relaxed mouth. All lent vulnerability to one who did not wear that state well.

"Give it to me." Agatha reached for the manacle.

El jerked it aside. "I did not come to watch," she said and glanced at Boursier's other wrist that Agatha had fettered. Wishing the woman would not hover, she pried until the iron plates parted, then fit the manacle. As she did so, his pulse moved beneath her fingers—weak and slow.

Alarmed, El asked, "How long will he sleep?"

"As I always err on the side of giving too much, it could be a while. Perhaps a long while."

"But he will awaken?"

Agatha shrugged. "They usually do."

Murdoch always had.

"And most content he shall feel," Agatha added.

As Murdoch had felt, which had many times spared El his perverse attentions, just as what she did this night would spare the De Arell woman Boursier's abuse.

El extended a hand for the keys and, at Agatha's hesitation, said firmly, "Give them to me."

The woman's nostrils flared, but she surrendered them.

El met the upper plate of the manacle with the lower. It was a tight fit, one that might make it difficult for blood to course properly, but she gave the key a twist. As she rose, she looked upon Boursier's face and the eyepatch gone awry. She struggled against the impulse, but repositioned the half circle of leather over his scarred eyelid.

Behind, Agatha grunted her disapproval.

El considered the pack of provisions. There was enough food and drink to last six days, after which she and Agatha would release Boursier.

Though she wished she did not have to return to this place, Agatha was of an uncertain disposition—not to be trusted, El's uncle warned. Not that the woman would harm the Verduns. She simply did not take direction well, firm in the belief none was more capable of determining the course of the Verduns than she. Thus it had been since Agatha had come from France eleven years past to serve as maid to El's aunt.

"We are finished," Agatha pulled her from her musings.

El knew they should immediately depart Castle Adderstone, but something held her unmoving—something she should not feel for this man who had stolen her aunt from another only to ill treat her. "What if he does not awaken?" she asked.

"Then death. And most deserving."

Once more unsettled by Agatha's fervor, wishing it had been possible to take Boursier on her own, El frowned in remembrance of how quickly the woman had agreed to help—and how soon her plans had supplanted El's. Grudgingly, El had yielded to Agatha, who was not only conversant in this place, but had possessed the keys that granted them access to Castle Adderstone.

"Do not forget who he is," Agatha said, eyes glittering in the light of the torch she had retrieved.

El peered over her shoulder at Boursier who was no different from Murdoch—excepting he was mostly muscle whereas her departed husband had been given to fat. And that surely made this man better able to inflict pain and humiliation.

Lord, what a fool I am! she silently berated herself for feeling concern for one such as he. *It is no great curiosity that Murdoch made prey of me.*

"Never shall I forget who he is," she said.

Agatha lowered her prominent chin, though not soon enough to obscure a childlike smile.

Telling herself she did not care what pleasure Agatha took in Boursier's suffering, El stepped from the cell.

As Agatha pulled the door closed, she beckoned for the keys.

"Nay," El said, "I shall hold to them."

The woman's lids sprang wide. "You do not trust me, my lady?"

El longed to deny it, but said, "Forgive me, but I do not." She locked the cell door.

Feeling Agatha's ire, she followed the woman from the underground passage, taking the light with them and condemning Boursier to utter darkness. A darkness that would not lift for six days.

All of him ached.

With a breath that tasted foul and a groan that bounced back from walls that seemed too near, he opened his eye and blinked in an attempt to fathom the bit of light provided by torches lit about the inner bailey. But no glow penetrated the window's oilcloth. All was black, as if he were blind.

He wrenched a hand toward his right eye and jerked when a rattle resounded around the room and metal links struck his forearm.

Disbelief slammed through him, then anger. Shouting above the clatter of chains, he thrust his arms forward. If anyone was near, they would know he had awakened from whatever had rendered him senseless.

A memory—there one moment, slipping away the next—stilled him. Was it something he had seen before whatever had drugged him had taken full effect? Something heard? Felt?

He groped backward, but that which he dragged forth had little form due to the darkness in which it was bred. There *had* been a glimmer as of one whose eyes gathered bare light. And a scent. But that was all he had of the one who had stolen him from Castle Adderstone. How—?

The wine! After all these years, had Agatha returned to make good her threat of ruin?

Forgetting his aches, he bellowed and strained against the manacles, but no one came to part the darkness that was so complete it returned him to the question of his sight. Had the last of it been taken from him? Was there light upon his face he could not see?

He touched his right eye. It was there, but in the presence of light, would it yet see him through the world?

He clenched his hands. Had Agatha stolen him from his bed? Likely. But it might also be Griffin de Arell who would not wish his daughter wed to a Boursier, regardless that his illegitimate offspring could not be dear to him. Then there was the possibility this atrocity involved both Agatha and the De Arells. Though the woman was occasionally seen on Verdun lands, Bayard's men had caught sight of her on De Arell's barony. Thus, Bayard was likely imprisoned at Castle Mathe.

He pressed his palms to the wall at his back and groped along the slick surface, but that beneath his fingers revealed nothing of the place at which he was held. His right hand brushed something. Another prisoner? If so, either dead or unconscious to have not been awakened by Bayard's raging.

Grudgingly grateful for the length of chain that permitted movement on both sides, he felt a hand across what turned out to be a pack. He dragged it onto his lap and tossed back the flap. The first bundle he pulled out smelled of dried fish, the next was a loaf of bread, and there were two large skins of wine.

Provisions? Meaning none would be coming for him soon? Meaning he was not meant to die? Why? For the suspicion his death would cast upon the De Arells? For how long—?

"Six days!" he shouted and continued to shout until his throat felt as if sliced through.

He dropped his head back. If he did not escape before the last day of autumn, he would not wed the De Arell woman and Godsmere would be forfeited.

"Lord!" he called upon the one to whom Father Crispin would counsel him to turn. Even so, it was more a cry of anger and frustration than an appeal for aid.

Perhaps I should have chosen the Verdun woman, he silently seethed. It was as Quintin had pressed him to do. Quintin who was alone except for her needy mother. Quintin who did not always act upon the wisdom gifted her.

Staring into darkness, Bayard ignored the voice that told him to pray and, instead, vowed that the De Arells would answer for what they had done. Then he cursed them, strained against his chains, and felt one give.

4

"For an hour, you have told all that has gone in my absence," Magnus Verdun said, "yet naught have you revealed of your own absence."

Seated opposite her uncle at a work table in the cavernous kitchen, El fit bewilderment onto her face. "My absence?"

He scowled. "Do you play with me, I vow it will make for unsatisfactory sport."

She lowered her gaze to the bread and cheese platter that had been prepared for him upon his unexpected return this eve. Though grateful he had not arrived home on the night past, which would have placed him here while she was yet at Castle Adderstone, still someone had discovered and reported her absence. Who?

"Elianor?" Magnus spoke her name in full as he did when seeking to impress upon her a matter of great import.

Returning her regard to the darkly handsome man who was only seven years older than she owing to the sixteen years between him and El's mother, she said, "Forgive me, Uncle—"

"*That* will gain you naught." He grimaced. "Too, it makes me feel old."

She nearly smiled. Though in private, she was *El* to him, and he was *Magnus* to her, she reverted to his title of kinship when circumstances called for cajoling. In this instance, the tactic had failed.

"Forgive me, Magnus. I am tired."

He chose a piece of cheese from the platter, chewed it, and followed it with a draw from his tankard. "Where were you, El?"

There was one thing that might get past him—the abbey to which her aunt had been sent years ago to await the annulment of her marriage to Bayard Boursier, and where she had remained with the exception of a visit to Castle Kelling that first Christmas. Since El had come to live here following Murdoch's death, she had visited Constance at the abbey a handful of times, and always came away hurting for the woman whose vow of silence and mournful eyes made their time together painful. Bayard Boursier had done that to her aunt, lending truth to what Agatha had told upon being ousted from Castle Adderstone for aiding Constance in battling her husband's brutality.

El met Magnus's gaze. "I journeyed to Ellesmere Abbey."

He frowned. "To visit Constance?"

She hated deceiving him. But he was honorable, and what she had done was without honor, though it *was* deserved—providing Bayard Boursier had awakened.

Chastising herself for continuing to worry over their enemy, she said, "To pray for the sacrifice the king demands of us."

She felt his pity sweep her, knew he hated that she must suffer another loathsome marriage. But it was no less than he would suffer if she failed.

He rose, came around the table, and laid a hand upon her back. "I fear your prayers are not to be answered."

When she looked up, his steel gray eyes awaited her. "You have not asked after my progress with the king."

"I do not have to." Though she had shaken herself from bed upon word of his return, she had not been so muddled she had missed the weight upon his brow. Thus, she had distracted him by rushing into an accounting of the affairs of the demesne.

He dropped his hand from her. "No matter the cost to our families, King Edward will have his barons exactly where he wants them."

She ached for him. Though what she had done would free the Verduns from the Boursiers, still there were the De Arells. "I am sorry, Magnus."

A tic started at his right eye. For as long as she could remember—since she had been a little girl and he a boy of ten—the spasming had presaged the fires beneath a usually calm exterior. Would he contain these?

He slammed a fist on the table, causing the platter to jump and its clatter to resound around the kitchen. "Would that I could have done something!"

"You tried," she said softly.

For a long moment, he did not move, and then he drew a deep breath. "The only hope we have hinges upon the one Boursier chooses for a wife."

Then he did not know of the missive she had shared with Agatha, had not learned elsewhere of Boursier's decision.

He shifted his jaw. "Mayhap he would rather forfeit than wed his enemy."

Though he spoke it, she knew he did not believe Boursier any more capable of forfeiting than he was himself. Thus, when Boursier was released, would any believe he had been abducted? She prayed not, that all she had done would be of benefit to her family.

"Soon, we shall know," Magnus said and turned away.

"Already we know."

He halted, slowly came back around. When he spoke, his voice was chill. "What have you not told me, Elianor?"

Elianor again. She slipped off the stool and clasped her hands at her waist. "The Boursier has chosen Thomasin de Arell."

He closed his eyes, and when he opened them, there was relief in their depths. "Then you shall wed Griffin de Arell. Hardly a prize, but it could be worse."

She felt a surge of affection for this man who had worried over what marriage to Boursier would do to her.

"Thus," he said, "it falls to me to wed the Boursier woman."

El knew she should say nothing, but she had to reassure him. "It is possible The Boursier will not go through with the marriage."

"Methinks only by God's intervention would he yield up his lands." Once more, fire flared in his eyes, and she knew he loathed that he was not the master of his fate. "Our course is set, El." He started across the kitchen.

"Magnus, how did you know I was gone from Kelling?"

He looked over his shoulder, the turning of his lips causing a groove to appear in his left cheek. "I may oft be absent, leaving you to manage the demesne in my stead, but I refuse to be uninformed as to what transpires while I am away."

"Tell, Magnus," she pressed.

He stepped into the corridor and called back, "I warned you about Agatha."

As he went from sight, she gripped the table's edge. The woman had betrayed her? It made no sense, for Agatha also wished Boursier to forfeit.

El laid a hand to her thumping chest. Magnus would not mislead her. Would he? Perhaps he knew—

She shook her head. If he knew what she had done, he would have confronted her.

She cinched the belt of her robe. Though it was the middling of night, Agatha would receive her.

Shortly, having traversed the torchlit bailey beneath the curious regard of men-at-arms, El tapped on the door of the hut that stood alongside the candle maker's shop.

The door creaked inward and Agatha's sharp face appeared. "My lady?"

"I must needs speak with you." El put a foot forward and, after a hesitation, the woman opened the door wider.

El stepped into the gloom cast by a flickering candle that was little more than a puddle of wax. As the door closed behind her, she settled her gaze on Agatha's work table and considered the items upon it—mortars, pestles, flasks, vials.

"For what do you seek me at this hour?" Agatha asked, though it sounded more like a demand.

El swung around. "My uncle is returned."

Lips puckering as if to suppress a smile, the woman stepped around El. "'Tis fortunate he did not return earlier," she said and settled on a stool at her table.

"What did you tell him, Agatha?"

The older woman raised her dark eyebrows. "I?"

El crossed her arms over her chest. "Speak, and do not be false with me."

Agatha reached to a jar from which a handle protruded and pulled it toward her. As she peered into it, she began to hum. It was always the same song—a pastorela that told of a nobleman's longing for a shepherdess. Sometimes the humming progressed to lyrics, other times not.

"Girl, said I, charming thing," Agatha engaged her tongue, "I turned away from my path to keep you company; for a young peasant such as you should not, without an equal companion, herd so much cattle, in a place like this, alone."

"Agatha!"

The woman chortled and drew the spoon from the jar. When it came free, dripping honey, she said, "Woe to you, little fly. Now you know that which is sweetest is often deadliest." She picked the bug from the honey, smeared it across the table, then stuck the spoon in her mouth and began to suck at the sweetness responsible for the fly's death.

Struggling for patience, El said, "I wait."

The woman pulled the spoon from her mouth and licked it, then returned the spoon to the jar. "I have not spoken to your uncle, my lady. He told you I had?"

"He implied you had revealed I was gone from Castle Kelling."

Agatha slowly nodded. "'Tis deceit he works upon you. Deceit to cover for the one he has set to watch over you."

"But—"

"Think, my lady! For what would I reveal we were gone from Kelling? I know your uncle would not condone what we did." She turned her palms up. "Just as you know I want the same thing you want."

El delved the austere face and small, intense eyes of the one who had aided her.

Agatha sighed. "Worry not, my lady. You shall have what you seek." She rose, crossed to the other side of the table, and peered into a jar. "Providing you are cautious—and more so we must be now that your uncle is returned."

"What say you?"

She picked up a pestle and began grinding the contents of a mortar. "Certes, you are watched, my lady. Thus, there are two things you might do when it is time for us to return to Castle Adderstone."

"Speak."

Agatha peered into the mortar. "Do you know what this is, my lady?"

"What two things might I do?" El pressed.

"'Tis that which I shall burn to put The Boursier to sleep. In this way, he may be released without peril."

"Tell, Agatha!"

Her tormentor looked up. "Either I go alone to release The Boursier, or neither of us goes."

El glowered. "I will not let him die."

"It might be necessary."

"I will not allow it!"

Agatha set the mortar on the table. "You are weak, my lady."

"I care not what you name me. I will not be responsible for a man's death."

"And yet you would steal all he holds dear, all that makes him a man. Is one not as bad as the other?" She gave a sharp laugh. "Truly, you would do The Boursier a mercy to leave him where he is."

"Nay."

"My lady, 'twould be believed he chose forfeiture and—"

"That he left all behind? His sister, stepmother, destrier, sword, armor? With nary a word?"

Agatha sighed. "The king has told that if Boursier does not wed by the appointed day, no excuse will be tolerated."

El crossed the space separating them. "He *will* be released."

The woman lowered her gaze. "As you will, my lady." A moment later, her hand rose between them, palm up. "At least allow me to be the one to release him so it may be done without your uncle's knowledge."

Give her the key—she who would feel no remorse over Boursier's death? Through the material of her robe, El felt the ring suspended from her girdle. Had Agatha lied about telling Magnus of her lady's absence from Kelling?

"You have my word that whatever you bid, I shall do," Agatha said. "Now, let me aid you as I did with your husband."

The offer was tempting, for all could run afoul were El followed from Kelling.

"My lady?"

El shook her head, started for the door. "I shall accompany you."

"Do we fail"—anger sharpened Agatha's voice—"'tis upon your head."

El swung the door open. "So be it."

5

THE BOURSIER WAS missing, as told by the friar who paused at Castle Kelling on a morning so chill the frost on the ground seemed more a veil of snow. But on the morrow, the Baron of Godsmere would reappear, his *defiance* of King Edward sealing the Boursiers' fate.

Though El endeavored to be of good cheer for what she had accomplished, a noose fashioned of guilt continued to tighten about her throat.

She glanced at Magnus where he leaned near the friar. The more he conversed with the man, the greater the doubt he exuded. If he could not be convinced to even consider the possibility Boursier had chosen forfeiture over marriage, would any others?

Lord, I pray Magnus never learns what I have done.

She lifted the lower edge of the tablecloth and wiped the juice of an apple from her fingertips. It was time to join Agatha who made preparations to ride to Castle Adderstone once all were abed.

El stood and met the gaze Magnus turned upon her. "Pardon, my lord, but I have tasks to which I must attend."

He inclined his head.

Adjusting her wimple, she stepped from the dais and crossed to the corridor that led to the kitchens. Bypassing that doorway, she continued to the one that handed her into a shriveled garden that evidenced autumn had been hasty in yielding to winter.

She shuddered. Though grateful for the sideless, fur-lined gown she had earlier donned atop her lighter, close-fitting cotehardie, she wished she had a mantle about her shoulders. Unfortunately, Magnus would question her if she returned abovestairs to fetch one. How she wished he did not watch her so closely!

Passing through the cloud of her breath, she traversed the path to the gate and entered the inner bailey. Shortly, she was admitted to the hut that was warmed by the fire beneath a hanging pot.

Agatha gestured El to a stool, then crossed to her work table. "A warm honey milk to chase away the chills, my lady?"

Though El occasionally shared a drink with her, she'd had her fill while breaking her fast. "I thank you, but nay." She lowered to the stool.

As if El had not declined, Agatha tipped a pitcher to the rim of a cup, poured, and returned with the vessel.

El shook her head. "I have had my fill."

"You are certain, my lady? 'Tis just made."

"I am certain."

As Agatha returned to the table, El asked, "All is ready?"

The woman picked through her containers. "'Tis," she finally said and met El's gaze past the vial she lifted before her.

El eyed it. "That is it?"

"Aye. Five minutes of smoke, and he shall be out."

Long enough to unbind him and leave him to discover he was imprisoned beneath his own castle.

"Regrets, my lady?"

El was surprised to find Agatha standing over her, the pitcher at her side. "Regrets?"

"For The Boursier."

"Why would I have regrets?"

Agatha bent, bringing her face level with El's. "Despite all your departed husband did to you that I could not prevent, your heart and resolve are weak."

El tried not to be offended. "Lest you forget, Agatha, 'twas I who first determined to undoThe Boursier. I who shall see it through to its proper end."

The woman straightened and stepped past El. "I do not forget, my lady, which is why I must do this."

Before El could make sense of her words, pain crashed through the back of her head. She cried out, fell from the stool, and collapsed on the dirt floor.

Struggling to remain conscious, she rolled onto her back and squinted at the dimming figure who stood over her with pitcher in hand.

"Forgive me, my lady," Agatha said from the other side of a dark tunnel, "but you should have accepted the honey milk."

No matter how much he roared, no matter how often he slammed his chains against the stone walls for how many ever hell-bent days and nights passed, no one came. But someone *would* come, for the provisions signified he was not meant to die. And when they came, it would be to a man no longer a baron.

If not that his throat was painfully hoarse, he would roar again.

Bayard raised his manacle-clasped wrists and drove his hands into his hair. Such fools his captors were to think a man bereft of all would not spend his last ounce of life seeking retribution. And a bloody retribution it would be.

He dropped his arms. The rattle of chains meeting with the ground causing a bitter smile to rise, he felt a hand down one to the end that had come free from the wall. It was the same with the other chain, the rust of years and the fury of a wronged man having freed him that first day.

He stalked across the dark to the door that would not budge regardless of his raging. Dragging a scraped and scabbed hand over the grate, he assured himself that his enemies would soon bring a torch to peer at him. And he would be waiting.

El heard a groan but only realized it came from her when she creaked her lids open.

She thrust up to sitting and gasped at the pain at the back of her head. Cupping a hand over the swelling, she looked around the hut. How long gone was Agatha? How near to murdering The Boursier?

She struggled to her feet and, gripping the stool, squeezed her eyes closed and drew deep breaths. When she finally steadied, a cool sweat covered her, causing her cotehardie to cling.

She released the stool. A peasant's mantle could easily be had from Agatha's trunk, the same that El had worn to steal upon Boursier's demesne, but what of a horse to more quickly deliver her to Castle Adderstone? For certain, one did not await her in the wood as Agatha had arranged the last time. Could a mount be obtained from the stables without anyone gainsaying her? Mayhap she should go to Magnus...

"Nay," she breathed, "this I will do myself." Providing, of course, Agatha had not gained too much of a lead and no ill befell El on a journey that boded ill for a woman without an escort. And a fairly imposing escort Agatha had been the last time, her height and sturdy build giving none cause to question whether her hooded figure was that of a man or woman.

El slid a hand to her girdle and touched her meat dagger, the only weapon she possessed. Praying she would not have to wield it, she crossed to the trunk near Agatha's pallet. Inside was the mantle she had worn before.

"Dear Lord," she prayed as she fastened the aged garment around her shoulders, "I repent all. Stay Agatha's hand, preserve Boursier's life. Amen." She pulled the hood over her head and stepped outside.

Finding the day beset by the gentle flurry of an unusually early snow on this, the last day of autumn, she whispered, "Surely it can get no worse."

6

―⚬⚬⚬―

B AYARD DROPPED HIS head back against the wall and stared at the grate as the glow without crept within. Though it was slow to invade his darkness, his eye ached for having been too long without light.

Heart pounding as if beat into shape upon an anvil, he listened across the distance to determine how many he would face.

Only one set of footfalls.

Foolish confidence, he mused. *Easy prey.*

Maintaining the appearance of being chained to the wall, keeping still lest the clamor of metal alerted his captor, he squinted at the increasing light and hoped he would not be blinded by its brilliance if the torch was brought within.

The one outside the door halted, and the thrust of light against Bayard's eyelid evidenced his captor peered into the cell.

Come, he silently entreated. *Step inside so you might see how harmless I truly am.*

There came the sound of the torch being fit into a sconce, then the scrape of a key.

The door groaned inward, but Bayard subdued the impulse to lunge to his feet. Easing his lid open, he focused on the shadow that moved across the floor as the mantled figure crept forward with a dagger in hand.

Never had waiting been so torturous, but at last his prey was too near for any outcome other than that which he'd had days to plan. With a crash of chains, he thrust upright, causing the one before him to gasp and stumble back.

The glare of torchlight in the passageway denying Bayard the satisfaction of looking upon the miscreant's terror, he swung an arm and was satisfied when the meeting of chain and flesh roused a cry of pain. He swung the other arm and was further satisfied with metal striking bone.

His captor-turned-captive wheezed and toppled.

Chest heaving as if he were hours into a battle rather than moments, Bayard looked upon the still figure that wavered in and out of his vision, squeezed his eye closed, opened it wide. Catching the flash of silver near his prey's hand, he swept up the dagger, then thrust a booted foot to the man's side and flipped him onto his back.

A groan evidenced the miscreant lived despite the blood upon his visage that ran into dark hair drawn back from his face.

Though tempted to further bloodletting, Bayard focused instead on the slack, prominent jaw, sharp cheekbones, and high brow. When the features came together, he was not truly surprised to discover they did not belong to a man.

He stared at the one who had tainted his wine to aid Griffin de Arell in this abomination—just as she had tainted it years past to aid Bayard's wife, Constance. Remembering the day he had discovered Agatha of Mawbry's treachery and ejected her from his lands, he recalled her cold, still gaze, heard her vow that one day she would take all from him. And so she might have.

Stoked by hatred of a depth he had denied himself for years—so destructive its unleashing could as easily turn on the one who unleashed it—he struggled against the longing to end this now. To end *her*.

Gripping the dagger so tightly the crack of his knuckles echoed around the walls, he talked the terrible, black emotion down by telling himself it would be better if Agatha suffered long just as he had done.

After retrieving the keys from the door's lock, he dragged the groaning woman to the wall and fit her with one of two remaining sets of manacles. She would live—for however long he allowed it. As for the chains, they were more firmly in the wall than his own had been. Thus, they would hold her.

He straightened. Bitterness but one of many foul tastes in his mouth, he set a key to the manacles binding his own wrists and was shaking with anger when the links hit the floor.

He looked one last time at Agatha and turned away. As he did so, he heard more footfalls. De Arell's? Nay, the step was too light for a man of his size.

"Agatha!"

A woman's voice. De Arell had sent two women to do his bidding? It lacked sense. Griffin de Arell was a man who, with his own hand, returned thrust for thrust, blow for blow, ruin for ruin.

"Do not!" the voice came again.

Bayard strode to the wall alongside the door and, dagger ready, mused that there would be a use for the remaining set of chains.

A mantled figure sprang inside. Moisture upon hair of a dark blond color, the ends of which were tucked into a wimple fallen down around her neck, the woman halted halfway across the cell.

El stared at the one slumped against the wall. Lax arms fit with chains, chin resting upon a chest marked with blood, the only movement about Agatha was the slight rise and fall of her chest.

As El took a step toward her, a fearsome sensation skittered up her spine.

Dear Lord, he is within!

Back crawling over the wrathful gaze upon it, she strained for sounds of movement. But The Boursier was as still as one whose prey was without recourse. Though she knew she was lost, she determined she would not yield without whatever fight she could summon from limbs battered by wind and snow that had turned fierce the last half hour of the ride.

She slid a hand beneath her damp mantle, with chill-stiffened fingers pulled her meat dagger and silently entreated, *Lord help me.*

She swung around.

Head bare inches from the ceiling, gaze lit as if by the fires of hell, he did not move.

El glanced at the dagger he wielded, gripped her own tighter. Were she granted a chance, where should she stick her blade? His gut? But if she managed that, would the short blade gain her freedom?

It would not. She knew it as surely as she had known Agatha had come to murder him. Soon she would be The Boursier's.

He stepped forward. "I find the smell of your fear pleasing," he said in a ragged, hoarse voice.

Just as Murdoch had liked the fear she had stubbornly denied him. She swept her dagger forward. "Come no nearer!"

He slid his own dagger beneath his belt, advanced on her.

Despite the longing to back away, she swung her dagger when he came within reach.

As if swatting a fly, he caught her wrist in a manacle wrought of bone and muscle, and dragged her toward him.

El bit back a cry, lost her breath when she fell against him. When she finally filled her lungs, she wished she had not, for he reeked of nearly six days of close confinement.

"A meat dagger!" he scorned.

Drawing air through her mouth, she followed his gaze to the short blade protruding from her fist. When she returned her attention to his face, she shuddered. His features were sinister, as much for the glitter in his single eye as the eyepatch with its scar above and below and a sennight's growth of beard.

A muscle in his jaw convulsing, he pried her fingers from the hilt. "A fine dagger for a wench. Stolen, I wager."

He thought her a commoner, not only as evidenced by Agatha's tattered mantle, but that no lady would do as she had done. It was better this way, though, for it would keep his vengeance from Magnus.

He jerked her nearer, delved her face. "'Twas you who came to my solar. You I saw."

She gasped. Agatha had assured her he would remember nothing of what he had seen, but he did.

"You at the market," his foul breath spilled upon her face.

Then she had not been as deeply in shadow as she had thought.

"You and the witch will pay for all," he rasped. "And your lord, De Arell."

Of course he believed the Baron of Blackwood responsible for this. As Boursier had meant to take Thomasin de Arell to wife, it followed her father would try to prevent the match.

Though relieved it was not Magnus's name spoken, El cringed at placing blame elsewhere, even if it was on the deserving Baron de Arell.

"What day is it?" Boursier demanded.

She put her chin up. "A day too late for you." At least, past the middling of night it would be. But no matter how swift his destrier, he could not reach Castle Mathe in time to wed Thomasin de Arell.

He bared his teeth. "Then too late for you, wench."

El summoned her own anger. "I am not afeared of you, Bayard Boursier."

"Nay?" His lips curled amid the dark growth of beard. "You shall be."

Already she was. Everything she had suffered while wed to Murdoch would not likely compare to what this man would do to her, for he possessed what her husband had not—vengeance. But she would die before allowing Boursier to bask in her fear.

"Where is De Arell?" he demanded.

"I vow, he is unaware of this."

"You lie. Tell me!"

She glared. "I *have* told you."

Boursier thrust her toward the wall where Agatha was chained. "Then I have vengeance aplenty to wreak."

He snatched up the third set of chains to do to her what she had done to him. But there would be no provisions for Agatha and her. And their imprisonment would not be limited to six days.

He pulled her around to face him and began to fit the manacle to her wrist.

Though she knew it was futile to resist, she brought her knee up with as much force as she possessed. And found her target.

He grunted but did not bend to the pain.

"Do you still like the smell of my fear, Boursier?" she taunted.

He dropped the chain, gripped her throat, and pushed her back against the wall. His body followed, pressing against her so she could not unman him again.

Brow moist, the muscles of his face twitching, he growled, "Accursed woman!"

"Miscreant!" she returned on the bit of air allowed her.

Chest rising and falling against hers, he stared at her, then stepped back. If not that he continued to hold her to the wall, she might have slumped to the floor.

Something drew his gaze lower and made him frown, then she felt his hand on her chest.

She yelped and renewed her struggles.

Unaffected, he pushed the mantle off her shoulders. "A lady's dagger," he murmured. "A lady's garments."

Dear God, she silently beseeched, *spare Magnus my stupidity.*

The Boursier arched an eyebrow. "Lady Thomasin, I presume?"

El did not know whether or not to deny it. She swallowed against his calloused palm. "I am not a lady."

"I will not argue that." He lifted the wimple that had come down around her shoulders and considered the fine material. "But you are Thomasin de Arell. My betrothed."

A peasant woman with blood cut by that of the nobility. Was there any gain in allowing his assumption to stand? Middle ground, she determined. "No more your betrothed, my lord. You missed by a day."

His gaze hardened further. "I ask again, where is your father?"

She gained a full breath past his grip. "And I say again, Griffin de Arell knows naught of what I have done."

"I am to believe you and that witch"—he jerked his chin at Agatha—"did this alone?"

"I know it must pain you to be bested by women, but 'tis so."

Bayard stared at the woman who continued to test his anger though he held her life in the squeeze of a hand—the same woman he had chosen to wed though she was not plain of face as told.

"You should have…" a strained voice spoke from below.

Bayard looked down.

Agatha's bloody face was turned up, gaze upon her mistress. "…should have let me kill him."

"You are unwell, Agatha?" Bayard scorned.

Her lids fluttered, but when they lifted again, her gaze was hard. "All you have lost, Boursier. Thus, I have made good my vow."

"All?" he snarled. "But I have you and De Arell's daughter."

The woman startled so hard the back of her head struck the wall.

Bayard showed his teeth in what he knew was an ugly smile. "Aye, I know who she is."

The frown upon her face faded. "Do you?" She shifted her gaze to the one who had aided her.

"I do." Though he had intended to chain the younger woman alongside the older one, her identity changed all. He released the De Arell woman's throat, gripped her arm, and dragged her toward the door.

"Agatha!" she cried as he pulled her into the passageway.

"God preserve ye, my lady!" the woman called.

God! Bayard silently scoffed. *As if Agatha of Mawbry knows anything of that divine being!*

He slammed the door. Though he had grown accustomed to the muted light within, the torchlight in the passageway was so glaring it felt as if a shard of glass had been driven into his eye. He squeezed it closed and opened it several times before seeking the key that would seal Agatha inside.

"Do not do this!" Thomasin de Arell beseeched. "You cannot leave her—"

"Can I not?" He thrust his face near hers and was momentarily distracted by how much more comely she was in full light. If this was plain of face, Elianor of Emberly must be radiant.

He turned, cranked the key in the lock, and reached to the wall sconce.

"At least leave the torch for her!"

"As 'twas left for me?" He swept it to hand and began pulling her down the passage. A moment later, he ground to a halt. "Almighty!" he shouted, rage turning his hands into fists as he stared at walls he had not looked upon in years. Such sacrilege to have been imprisoned in his own home!

A whimper at his side returned him to Thomasin de Arell, and he saw she had dropped to her knees. The reason for her collapse was his white-knuckled fist around her wrist. It surprised him that her fine bones had not snapped.

He eased his hold enough to allow her to catch her breath, then pulled her to her feet.

She stumbled after him into the main passage that ran from the keep to the wood. As he unlocked the door that accessed the keep's walled passages, he paused at the further realization Agatha had possessed keys to Castle Adderstone's secret defense. How had she come by them? How long had he been vulnerable to her?

He thrust the door open, pulled the De Arell woman through, and locked the door. "Now let us see what ruin you have made of my household, *Lady.*"

"No more *your* household," she hissed.

He turned to her. "Until someone risks their life to take it from me, 'tis mine."

She tilted her head, causing hair the color of ripe wheat to fall across her brow. "You will tell that to the king?"

He leaned near, breathed the scent of her that sharply contrasted with his reek. "Lady, deprive a man of all, give him naught to lose, and a beast you shall unleash." Especially if ill had befallen his sister. "As Agatha told, you should have allowed her to kill me." He frowned. "Why did you not?"

In her silence, he sensed what seemed unease, but then she said, "That you might suffer longer."

He should not be surprised.

As he pulled her up the first flight of stairs, it struck him that the steps were likely the source of his aches and bruises. If it was true the De Arell woman and Agatha had acted alone, they would have had to drag him from the solar. But it was not to the solar they now returned.

At the first landing, he turned left and, shortly, halted before a door hidden by a tapestry on the other side. He thrust the torch in a sconce, pressed the catch, and opened the door.

The noises from within the hall evidencing a meal was in progress, Bayard pulled Thomasin de Arell out from behind the tapestry—to the gaping surprise of retainers and servants, the former being scarce in attendance. Most noticeably absent was his sister, Quintin.

The steward jumped up from the bench alongside the lord's chair. "My lord!"

Father Crispin was the next to gain his feet. Something like a smile tugging at the corners of his mouth, he closed his eyes, crossed himself, and moved his lips in silent prayer.

As for Quintin's mother—Bayard's stepmother—when there was finally movement about Lady Maeve, it was in the drop of her spoon to the table.

Bayard yanked his captive across the dais and halted before the steward. "Where is my sister?"

The man dragged his gaze from the De Arell woman. "Gone, my lord."

"Gone?" Bayard's shout lifted the man's sparse hair off his brow.

"In search of you, my lord."

Bayard growled. "If I have to reach down your throat to more quickly gain an explanation, I shall."

"My lord," the man said, "three days was all we could keep her from her foolishness. Two days past, despite our protests and those of her mother"—he glanced at the lady who now pressed a hand to her chest as if to calm her heart—"she took to mount and told she alone would search you out if none accompanied her. Thus, Sir Victor amassed a score of knights and thirty men-at-arms."

Fifty to protect her. At least in that, Bayard's senior household knight had been wise. "Rollo is with her?" The man-at-arms whose duty it was to accompany Quintin when she left the castle was surely at her side, but he needed to hear it, for there was none better to hold her safe.

"I fear not, my lord."

"What?" It took every crumb that remained of Bayard's self-control to not shake the man.

"His mother was ailing, and Lady Quintin gave him leave to go to her two days ere she departed to search you out. Certes, had he known what she intended, he would not have left her side."

Bayard drew a deep breath. "Were her escort well provisioned?"

"Aye, my lord, lest the weather turned foul."

"Their destination?"

"Castle Mathe upon the barony of Blackwood, my lord."

Then Quintin also realized his disappearance stank of De Arell. For five days had—

Only five days had passed? This, the sixth day? He looked to the windows set high in the walls. The first of night shone through the oilcloths, meaning hours remained before all was forfeit. Hours, and here was his unwilling bride, and here a priest.

Bayard wavered. Though Quintin had surely reached Castle Mathe and was under the able protection of Sir Victor and those he commanded, he did not like that his sister was out there, especially considering how headstrong she could be when she felt she or her family had been wronged. Aye, he would go after her, but as it would take time for his men to prepare for the journey, there was no reason to not make right what the passing of one more night would have made wrong. When he departed Castle Adderstone, it would be as a married man.

He looked around the hall. "You!" He jerked his chin at the nearest man-at-arms, then a dozen more. "We ride to Castle Mathe this eve."

"But my lord," the steward protested, "to ride through the dark in the midst of a storm—"

"Storm!" Bayard barked.

"Aye, my lord. You do not know?"

Bayard pulled the De Arell woman from the dais and started across the hall. At his advance, the porter opened the door, admitting snow that billowed across the hall and ruffled the rushes.

Bayard stared out into the white tempest that whipped chill flakes against his face. Though he had seen moisture upon Thomasin de Arell's hair when she had entered the cell, he had been too full of wrath to understand its significance. But that anger hardly compared to what gripped him now, filling him so full his muscles began to quake.

"It appears you are without recourse, my lord," said the woman beside him.

Did she not sense his anger? Feel it in his hand upon her? See it upon a face so heated it was surely livid? "Am I?" he growled and caught up her chin. "But I have you, Thomasin de Arell—recourse enough to satisfy me until the snow lifts."

How gratifying it was to see fear in her eyes, even if only for an unguarded moment. Accepting the challenge that replaced her fear, he turned her back into the hall. "Don your robes, Father Crispin. This night, I wed Lady Thomasin de Arell."

His pronouncement was met by cries near and far—the first that of his bride-to-be, the second that of his stepmother who stood so abruptly she nearly upended her chair.

As Bayard drew a straining Thomasin toward the stairs, Lady Maeve descended the dais. Four years past, following the death of Bayard's father, her figure had begun to grow plump, slowing her movements. Now, she was quick on her feet and reached him before he could ascend the stairs.

He halted. She did not need to speak for him to know what she wanted—that she would have him jeopardize his life and the lives of his men to ride to Quintin's aid. And he would if he believed his sister was in mortal danger. But though he worried for her, he did not believe her life was at risk. Even were she huddled in a tent outside Castle Mathe's walls, her demands for her brother's release unanswered, she was protected by the men of Godsmere.

"Bayard!" Lady Maeve gripped his arm. "You waste time wedding this…" Her upper lip hitched and she shifted her gaze to Thomasin. "…De Arell." She looked back at him. "You must needs ride on Castle Mathe."

He understood her sense of urgency, for Quintin was her only child and precious to her. "If I could do so without endangering the lives of my men, I would, Lady Maeve, but snow is upon us as much as night, and I am certain no ill will befall her while Sir Victor is at her side."

Dark eyes desperate, she dug her fingernails into his flesh. "And if he is not at her side? If ill has befallen him?"

Bayard did not know from which well he drew patience, for he would have thought them all dry. "Then she has another fifty men to ensure her safety."

She released him and shoved hands into her hair. "Dear Lord, if anything happens to her…anything…"

Bayard cared for his stepmother, but for this he was often grateful she had Quintin who, for four years now, was more mother to Lady Maeve than daughter.

He motioned two men-at-arms forward and pushed his betrothed toward them. "Deliver her to the far chamber abovestairs and keep watch over it. And know this—if she is not there when I come for her, your punishment will be dire."

The men inclined their heads and took hold of their charge.

With a backward glance, Thomasin de Arell allowed herself to be guided up the steps.

Now to deal with yet another woman with whom he was not fit to deal.

7

ONLY DEATH OR forfeiture would stop the wedding, and as he was relatively whole and had no intention of yielding up his lands or his soul, vows would be spoken this eve.

Grinding his teeth, Bayard considered the ring pinched between thumb and forefinger. The gold band was wide but plain, the oblong jet stone engraved with an odd symbol resembling an eye.

Though there was nothing to suggest Lady Maeve should have been loath to relinquish the ring as she had been—indeed, were it not of such small diameter, it might have been made for a man—it would serve his purpose since the wedding ring that had first been his mother's and was now his stepmother's did not belong on the hand of a woman like Thomasin de Arell. As for Constance's discarded ring, it boded no good to bind his new wife to him with that which had not kept his first from cuckolding him.

Bayard dropped the ring into the purse on his belt, gripped the stone mantel with both hands, and stared into the fire. Though its blazing heat had sufficiently warmed away the underground chill, it made him reek all the more.

"Almighty!" he choked. He could rail night and day against the treachery of the De Arells, but who would believe him when all he had to show for his imprisonment were two women—one a lady, the other a conniving commoner? And that was not the only barrier. Just as unscalable was the revelation that he, a man of the sword, had been easily felled. Thus, there was nothing to do but wed. Or was there?

He considered Thomasin's protests when he had called for Father Crispin to don robes. If she refused to speak vows, it would be her family that forfeited. But would they alone forfeit? The king had said he would accept no excuse if Bayard was not wed by this day, and even if Edward reconsidered, it would likely mean marriage to the Verdun woman. Of course, alongside Thomasin, Lady Elianor was no longer without appeal.

But Thomasin it would be, for she was present and would wed him under threat of forfeiture. Hence, the bargain proposed to Quintin nearly a week past would come to pass—to make the De Arell woman's life miserable. More than miserable should ill befall his sister.

What had Quintin planned? To play the lord and demand her brother's return from outside the walls? Or be the lady and, by guile, gain entrance to the great hall?

He pushed off the mantel and, as he stepped back, cursed his men for following her. They should have—

Nay, they could not have. Had they refused her, she would have stolen away, putting herself at greater risk once she stood before Griffin de Arell.

Bayard frowned. Was it possible the man knew nothing of his daughter's foul deed? Though it seemed only Lady Thomasin and Agatha had entered into the underground, it was hard to conceive they had planned their enemy's undoing without aid. But it was harder to believe Baron de Arell had entrusted the endeavor to women, especially one his daughter.

Whatever the answer, Bayard would take no chances. Through the fall of snow, he had led his men to ensure no others lurked about the entrance to the passage in the wood. There they had come upon the horses that had carried Agatha and Lady Thomasin. Lest he leave himself vulnerable again, Bayard had set men-at-arms in the passage until the entrance could be sealed with stone and mortar. As for Agatha, his men were under orders to ignore her cries. How long before death quieted her?

Behind, the door whispered on its hinges, but Bayard kept his back to it. By the quick-legged strides over the rushes, he knew it was Squire Lucas. And the young man was not alone, as told by the whisper of other feet.

"What is it?" Bayard demanded.

"A bath, my lord." The squire's voice was strong and even as he had been taught it should be. A thump behind evidencing the lowering of the tub, Lucas continued, "Whilst the water is being carried abovestairs, I shall scrape the beard from your face."

Bayard pulled in a breath of the tainted air about him, knew others suffered more for it than he. It would not do for a man so vilely attired to speak marital vows. Or would it?

He turned. "You!"

The women halted in the doorway.

"Gain your beds," he said.

Their eyes widened, and Squire Lucas spluttered as he had *not* been taught. "But my lord, a bath—"

"Can wait." Bayard jerked his chin at the women and they scurried into the corridor.

When next his squire spoke, he was once again the young man who aspired to knighthood. "As you wish, my lord." He lifted the razor from his side. "This can also wait?"

"It can."

"Anything else, my lord?"

Bayard adjusted his eyepatch. "I would know what happened the night I disappeared."

A flush crept up the young man's face, and Bayard knew he suffered for not having come to his lord's aid. "I remember little beyond awakening foul of head to the prod of your sister's foot." His color heightened further, for he did not look at Quintin without the sickness of love upon his countenance. He set the razor on a nearby table and stepped forward. "Your sister knew it was Baron de Arell who seized you from your bed, my lord."

Bayard was not surprised. And he could imagine Quintin's frustration and anger at being unable to convince Adderstone's men to leave the castle vulnerable in order to search out their lord with nothing more than her convictions to guide them. If only they had found some way to contain her!

He crossed to a chair and dropped into it. "Your leave is granted, Squire."

"Neither would you change your garments, my lord?"

Bayard looked down his soiled tunic. "I would not."

Without gape or splutter, the squire crossed the solar.

Bayard watched closely as he neared the table upon which he had laid the razor and was pleased when the young man retrieved it. A few more years, and he would be ready to assume the responsibilities of knighthood.

The squire glanced over his shoulder.

Bayard nodded. "Lest my new wife determines to shave me herself."

The young man frowned. "Surely she is not so bold, my lord?"

Though all knew it was Thomasin de Arell who had vilely trespassed against the Boursiers, Bayard had not revealed what, exactly, had transpired. "Surely she is, Squire. And do not forget it."

"I will not, my lord." He pulled the door closed behind him.

"Aye," Bayard muttered, "surely she is." Thus, he would allow her another quarter hour in which to search out a means of escape, then he would take the shrew to wife.

Agatha. Magnus. The Boursier woman.

El rubbed the heels of her hands against her eyes.

"Lord, I have made a botch of it all," she whispered to the one who seemed to prefer the role of observer to that of participant. "Is there no way to set the board right—to return the pieces to where they were ere I toppled them?"

Though angered by Agatha's betrayal, she could not abandon the woman to that dark, putrid pit. Then there was Magnus. If not this eve, by morn he would discover her absence. What would he do? And what of Boursier's sister who was trying to recover her brother from a man who did not hold him? What if ill befell her in the snowstorm?

Feeling like a small animal in the claws of a beast, she dropped her arms to her sides and looked around the small chamber to which she had been escorted by Boursier's men. The window was barred, the battered chest was locked, and the wall behind the tapestry lacked an entrance to the walled passages. As for the door, it was guarded from without and there was no means of securing it against any who wished to come within. And, eventually, The Boursier would come within.

El stifled a whimper. She could not declare her true identity, for Magnus would suffer dishonor alongside vengeance, and it would not stop Boursier from taking her to wife to secure his hold on Castle Adderstone. Nor could she claim to be other than Thomasin de Arell, for if believed, she would rejoin Agatha in the underground.

There was only one thing for it, and it made her shudder. She must consent to a marriage that could see her excommunicated were it discovered what she had done. When Boursier came for her, she would wed him and, hopefully, escape him in the days ahead. By the time he learned his marriage was invalid for having wed a woman who was not Thomasin de Arell, his lands would be forfeit. And if she could not escape him? She would surely wish herself chained in the underground. Of course, there was yet the night ahead when The Boursier brought vengeance to the marriage bed.

El drew a deep breath, told herself she had survived before and would survive again. Memories loosed from the graves she had dug them, she rubbed her hands over her sleeves to warm away her chill. Unfortunately, Agatha's mantle would be of no use until it dried.

She glanced at where she had draped it over a chest, silently cursed the lock that would not give. What was inside? Something that might hand her and Agatha out of this place?

She returned to it, but after further prying, she was no nearer to breaching the lock. Tears stinging her eyes, she started to turn away, but the front corner of the lid drew her gaze. She curled her hand around the warped edge, jammed her fingers into the narrow gap, and heaved. The wood bent. She heaved again.

With a resounding crack, the wood split, and she stumbled back and landed on her rear. Catching the sound of murmurings outside the door, she glanced at the shard of wood torn from the lid and would have tossed it aside had it not so closely resembled a blade.

She hastened to her feet, tossed up her skirts, and thrust her makeshift weapon into the top of her hose. If not for the creak of the door, she would have yelped when a splinter slid into her thigh.

Dropping her skirts, she spun around as a man-at-arms put his head around the door.

"What do ye, my lady?"

El stepped to the side to block sight of the damaged chest. "I wait," she said. "And wait."

"We heard something."

She shrugged. "What do you think 'twas?"

He swept narrowed eyes around the chamber, grunted, and pulled the door closed.

El dropped to the chest. Despite the splinter's burn, she returned her attention to the lid from which she had gained her weapon. The enlarged gap was too narrow to fit a hand into, and she did not dare attempt to further rend it.

Would a blade of wood keep Boursier from ravishing her? As with her previous attempts to defend herself, it did not seem possible, but there was one thing her future husband could not take from her—her will. Whatever he gained, it would be by way of thieving.

Wishing for a fire to warm away her chill, El hitched up her skirts to examine the splinter driven into her thigh.

"My lord!" a voice came through the door.

She jumped up, repositioned the mantle over the chest, then set her teeth against the burn of the splinter and clasped her hands before her.

The door opened, and there stood The Boursier, none the better for the time afforded him to look the groom. Had he decided against wedding her?

"Come," he bit, "the priest awaits."

Then he would defile the lord's chapel with his stench and ignoble appearance, showing no respect for God?

Telling herself she was not surprised, she stepped forward, the movement making her more aware of the splinter—surely punishment for the sin committed in taking another's name to speak false vows.

Sending up a prayer that one day she would be forgiven for what she had done and was about to do, she crossed the room and halted before Boursier who stood inside the doorway, his singular gaze promising ill.

Sarcasm a defense none could wrest from her, and which she had used to strike at Murdoch those times she had dared, she said, "A most handsome groom you make, my lord. To my end days, I shall hold dear the sight of you come for your loving bride."

That grim smile again. "A wise woman would pray her end days would not be long in delivering her from such a husband."

His words fell like a lash, but El tempered them with a like response. "Or that her *husband's* end days not be long in delivering her from him." As she had prayed while wed to Murdoch. A prayer answered, though at the time, two years of marriage had seemed an eternity.

Boursier glowered.

El forced a laugh. "Does my wit exceed yours?"

His hands convulsed at his sides, as if he longed to feel her throat beneath them again.

She raised her chin higher. "The priest waits on us, my lord."

With a sound low in his throat, Boursier stepped to the side to allow her to pass. There was not enough room to do so, and her pierced flesh brushed his thigh as she exited the chamber.

Tears rushing forth, she lowered her face so he would not see her discomfort.

"The end of the corridor," he said.

El looked past the men-at-arms to the far doorway from which flickering light shone. Before the chapel stood the priest, to the right those who would bear witness, including the renowned Lady Maeve of whom it was said Bayard Boursier's father had wed to atone for his sins.

A hand gripped her forearm. "But two hours remain ere middle night," Boursier rasped and drew her forward.

Every step forcing the splinter deeper where her makeshift knife rode against it, El bit her lip harder.

The scent of Boursier further assailed her when he bent his head near. "What was the sound my men heard from within your chamber?"

She looked up into his dark face, sighed. "But a failed attempt. It seems your walls are no longer pregnable."

His nostrils flared. "Fair warning I give, *lady,* cause me further grief and you shall rue the breath you breathe."

Continuing forward, she shifted her gaze to the priest. "You think I do not already?"

Boursier straightened. "I am pleased," he said, voice as if born of the storm outside. "But it *can* go worse for you."

She knew that. Had she not survived worse and worse with Murdoch? Though that reminder was meant to strengthen her, something within her bent so deeply she feared it might snap. Head beginning to spin, she halted, causing Boursier to arrest his progress.

"I have no time for this," he growled.

Feeling the stares of the others, she settled her gaze on the priest who stood ready to feed her words that would make of her a blasphemer.

She drew a long breath, met Boursier's gaze. "If I do this, will you release Agatha?"

"If you do not," he said, "your father's lands are forfeit."

Or so he believed.

"Do you understand, *lady?*"

"Aye, *Lucifer,*" she answered as once she had answered Murdoch, "I understand." Just as she understood that speaking thus might draw the same punishment her husband had dispensed. By her hair and before his entire household, he had dragged her from the hall. What had happened next upon the stairs...

The fire in Boursier's gaze razed the memory, and for a moment she was grateful.

"I am Bayard," he said, "but if you wish the devil at your side, 'twill be no trouble to accommodate you."

Why did he not now? Murdoch would have—even before a chapel, regardless of witnesses.

Boursier urged her forward, his far-reaching stride causing the splinter to be more deeply felt.

This eve, then, El realized. Whatever kept him from retaliation would be overcome once a bed was at her back. Squeezing her arms against her sides, she wished for a swift horse beneath her.

She blinked, glanced at Boursier. "What of our horses?"

"They are in my stables."

And would not easily be gotten from there.

As they neared the chapel, Lady Maeve came forward. "Are you certain of this, Bayard? There is naught else to be done?"

"As already discussed, I am without choice, my lady. Thus, I must needs wed this woman so your daughter does not return to a home no longer hers."

Tears brightened the woman's dark brown eyes, but she jerked her chin. "You know what is best, my son."

To El's surprise, The Boursier squeezed his stepmother's shoulder. "Quintin will be at your side again soon. Now, vows must needs be spoken." He released her and drew El to where the priest waited.

Up close, the man was younger than he had appeared in the hall—a bit older than his lord, perhaps thirty and five. Though he could not be said to be attractive, his head too round and large atop a slender body, nose long and hooked, there was something captivating about his eyes despite the disapproval there.

"Proceed, Father Crispin," Boursier said.

"My lord, surely you..." The man cleared his throat. "'Tis God's house to which you come. Could you not don more suitable garments for the speaking of vows?"

"I could. Now marry us."

Father Crispin's mouth twitched as if he might argue, but he inclined his head.

Struggling to contain her trembling, El heard the drone of the man's voice that did not seem to match the movement of his lips. And when he looked to her and spoke Thomasin de Arell's name, she could only stare.

"You are without choice," Boursier rasped.

"Again, Lady Thomasin de Arell," Father Crispin said, "do you freely give yourself in marriage?"

She inclined her head. "If I must."

Beside her, Boursier stiffened further. Before her, Father Crispin slowly shook his head. "My lord—"

"'Twill suffice, Father. Continue."

Next came the recitation of duties she must perform as the wife of Bayard Boursier. God willing, by the time the snow lifted, she would find a way to free herself.

When he released her arm and raised her hand, El startled over his scraped and scabbed wrist that contrasted with her pale, smooth flesh.

The manacles, she realized and imagined how he must have strained to wrench them from the wall. Truly, few would fault him for whatever form his vengeance took. Not that he was undeserving of the ill he had suffered. Merely, she understood the anger of his debauched soul.

El winced over her quaking fingers, knew The Boursier felt her discomfort and took joy from it.

Lord, will I never again be warm?

Next came the vows. Boursier spoke them first, each word thick with resentment. By the time the priest turned to El, her legs were almost too weak to support her.

"Lady Thomasin," Father Crispin began, "are you prepared to pledge your troth?"

Teeth chattering, she said, "I am."

Boursier grumbled something and looked behind. "Squire Lucas, fetch my bride a mantle ere she shakes herself apart."

El muffled her surprise. Why did he care? For fear she might collapse and be unable to finish her vows?

After a tense silence, the squire returned with a mantle that Boursier draped over her shoulders.

As the fur lining settled around her, she sighed. Though such a fine garment surely belonged to the lord of Castle Adderstone, what mattered was its warmth.

"My lady?" the priest prompted as The Boursier once more lifted her hand.

In a haze, she repeated the vows fed her. The ring was next, its appearance surprising her. But regardless that it looked as if made for a man, it would serve its purpose of marking her as being passed, like so much chattel, into the coffers of a man.

After the priest's blessing of the ring, Boursier slid it onto her finger, and it was then she looked near enough upon the jet stone to see its face was carved—a half circle inside which two vertical, off-center lines reached from the straight base to the arch.

El shuddered over the finality with which the ring settled on her. Despite its loose fit, it felt more final than the tight-fitting band Murdoch had placed on her hand.

Catching a sound of distress, El followed it to Lady Maeve and saw the woman's eyes were fixed on the ring. Because it symbolized her stepson would ever be tied to a woman of whom she did not approve? Or had the ring been hers—adorning her hand when she had wed Archard Boursier?

Nay, it had not, for Lady Maeve yet wore a ring upon that finger.

"You would kiss your bride, my lord?" the priest asked.

El caught her breath, looked up at Boursier.

He looked down at her. "There shall be time aplenty this eve," he said.

"Then let us continue with the nuptial mass." Father Crispin turned into the chapel that was golden amid the light of numerous candles.

Boursier turned El opposite. "It is late, Father, and the act is well enough done."

"But 'tis unseemly, my lord!"

As Boursier pulled El down the corridor, she pressed a hand to the wood concealed beneath her skirts.

"My lord, a proper wedding—"

Boursier halted, swung around. "If you did not notice, this is no proper wedding, Father."

"Indeed, it is not!" the priest snapped, his show of anger—both in tone and brightly colored visage—surprising El.

"Is the lady not now my wife and I her husband?" The Boursier demanded.

"That she is, but—"

"Then 'tis done."

The priest's nostrils flared, and when next he spoke, his voice was strained as if it took great restraint not to shout. "My lord, if not a mass, at least do not take the lady to your chamber without the blessing of the bed. 'Twill bode ill otherwise."

"What about this marriage does not bode ill?" Boursier retorted.

The priest strode forward and set a hand on his lord's arm. "You require the blessings of the Church."

Boursier hesitated, then pushed El toward him. "A quarter hour. No more." He motioned to the men-at-arms who had stood watch outside her chamber and nodded them toward El. "I shall be belowstairs drinking my fill in hopes it will blunt King Edward's decree," he said as he strode away.

As if *he* would be made to suffer this night! El pressed her lips together, but what swept across her tongue would not be contained. "You are sure you would not like me to prepare that wine for you, my lord?"

The priest drew a sharp breath, but her eyes were all for Boursier who did not falter as he continued toward the stairs. But he had heard her, as evidenced by the turn of his hands into fists.

El squeezed her eyes closed. Now to survive the marital debt she would be required to pay this night.

8

———

"THE TIDINGS I deliver will not surprise you, my lord," Father Crispin said as he stepped off the stairs into the hall.

Of course they would not, Bayard brooded as he met the priest's gaze over his goblet. But he would have to hear it—the least owed this man for his troubles.

As Father Crispin neared, Bayard lowered the goblet. "Tell," he said.

The man halted before the dais. "She will not be put to bed."

Bayard dropped his feet from the table and stood. "Then it falls to me to do it."

Father Crispin, more than a priest, sometimes a friend, entreated, "Have patience, my lord. She wished this marriage no more than you."

Less than he—little enough to see him dead.

Bayard descended the dais. "On the morrow, you shall send a missive to the king informing him that vows were spoken."

"I shall, my lord."

Bayard inclined his head. "And now I must see to my *wife*."

Father Crispin stopped him with a hand to the arm. "'Twould not do to beseech you to be of good cheer that it is not the Verdun woman, but still it is a thing for which to be grateful."

Bayard nearly resented his encouragement, but it was understand-able. The man was well-acquainted with Constance Verdun's sin, for he had witnessed it himself. And for it, he had aided his lord in obtaining an annulment.

Bayard adjusted the eyepatch. "One is likely as bad as the other," he said, thinking a man would be wise not to give any woman his back, regardless of whether she was a Verdun or a De Arell. On the heels of that thought came another, one fed by the priest's presence in the hall. Though men-at-arms kept watch outside his solar, Thomasin was alone in the lord's chamber. Would she dare the walled passages knowing the access to the underground was locked? If she possessed another key, and it was possible, she might try. Not that she would get past the men posted below.

Bayard pivoted and ascended the dais.

"My lord?" the priest called.

Bayard thrust aside the tapestry and released the door's catch. Still the torch burned in the sconce where he had set it before bringing De Arell's daughter into the hall.

As he was familiar with the passages and preferred not to alert his *wife* to his presence until he was upon her, he eschewed the torch, descended the steps, and halted before the door that let into the underground. It was locked. Still, he turned a key in it and opened it wide.

The man-at-arms on the other side lowered his sword when he saw it was his lord.

"All is quiet?" Bayard asked.

The flickering torchlight behind the man showed the shadow of a grimace. "If quiet is the howling that comes from yon passage, my lord. Fortunately, it let up a short while ago."

Meaning Agatha either slept or had lost her voice. Bayard inclined his head, closed the door, and secured it.

Was Thomasin yet abovestairs? Or might she lurk in one of the passages?

After assuring himself all were clear, he halted before the door behind the tapestry in his solar. He listened but caught no sound. Pleased the hinges did not creak when he opened the door, he looked out from behind the tapestry.

She stood in the center of the room facing the door beyond which his men-at-arms kept watch. And behind her back she gripped a stick—its jagged point meant for him.

Teeth clenched, he glanced at the bed. The coverlet and sheet were turned back, doubtless by Father Crispin who would have blessed the bed all around. But it was unlikely any blessings would come of this marriage.

Further embittered, he returned to the door and closed it loud enough to alert Thomasin to his presence. Now the game could commence.

When he stepped from behind the tapestry, she faced him, eyes large, hands behind her back.

"You disappoint, Lady Wife."

Her eyebrows rose. "How so, Lord Husband?"

"I expected to find you in the passages."

"I considered them, but it seemed a waste of time since I have no key with which to deliver me free of you."

"Indeed." He stepped toward her. "The priest tells that my wife refuses—"

The door opened, causing her to jump and angle her body in an attempt to keep hidden what she held behind her back.

"Now what are you about, Lady Thomasin?" the man-at-arms asked a moment before he caught sight of his lord.

"Take your leave," Bayard said. "Your watch outside my solar is no longer required."

The man nodded, closed the door.

Bayard continued toward the new lady of Castle Adderstone. "The priest tells that my wife will not be put to bed."

She took a step back. "I am not afeared of you, Bayard Boursier."

He smiled. "As you seem fond of boasting in the midst of retreating—and trembling."

She glanced down her front as if seeking evidence of such. It was there. "You mistake a chill for fear."

He halted a stride from her, glanced at the hearth that throbbed its heat around the chamber. "Do I?"

Her pale face paled further. "You are not the first man whose attentions I have suffered."

Her words jolted him. It was bold to admit to having had lovers, and surprising that her father had not kept a closer watch on her—a woman-child of ten and seven. Or was she? She appeared to be several years older. But then, the commoner's life she had led until recent years more quickly aged a person.

"You are not a maiden, then," he said and wondered why he was disappointed.

She blinked as if only then realizing what she had revealed. "I..." She put her chin up. "Many there were before you. Many there shall be after you."

Pain shot through Bayard's jaw, a warning that if he ground his teeth any harder, they would crack.

Cuckolded once, but never again, he silently vowed, *even if I have to lock her into a girdle of chastity.* As he should have done with Constance.

"Of course," she continued, "'tis for you to decide if you wish to risk the diseases with which I am afflicted."

She went too far—so far he knew she lied. Numerous lovers she had not had, perhaps none.

Bayard thrust a hand forward. "Give over to me."

Her gaze wavered. "What?"

He breached the space between them, and she jumped back and swept the jagged piece of wood toward him.

Bayard sighed. "You think to fare better with that than you did with a dagger?"

"Upon my word, I will sink it into your flesh!"

"One should not make promises one cannot keep. It renders them a fool." Though he could easily have wrested the stick from her, he was not ready for the game to be finished. Thus, he skirted her, forcing her around so her back was to the bed.

She sliced the air again.

He sidestepped and advanced, and once more she retreated. And so it went until she trod upon his squire's pallet and came up against the mattress.

"Fool," he said and snatched her wrist.

She strained backward, fell onto the bed that had been blessed for the consummation of their marriage, cried out as she sank into the mattress.

As he fit himself atop her to prevent her from unmanning him again, she stared at him with wide-thrown eyes, and her trembling transformed into violent quaking.

Though Bayard told himself fear was his due, the enormity of it that could be both felt and seen disturbed him. The possibility of death or some other terrible violence warranted such a reaction, not anything he would do to her. Warring between outrage that she believed him to be so wretched a being and shame that he frightened her so much, he began prying the crude weapon from her fingers. It was not easily achieved without snapping her bones, but finally he had it from her.

"Be assured," he said, "I am no ravisher. Just as I will not suffer your sharp little stick, you will not suffer my attentions this night." He pushed up off the mattress.

As he straightened alongside the bed, her eyes remained upon him as if she thought he meant to spring something on her.

Choking down another dose of shame he had no cause to feel, he stepped back.

Her quaking eased, but she continued to stare at him, and if she breathed, it was in no way obvious.

He pushed a hand through his hair. "All that remains to settle is whether or not you must be bound."

Finally, she drew breath, a sharp thing that told she feared what he might do to her were she so incapacitated. It nearly made him curse. Doubtless, Agatha had filled her pretty head with lies about his relationship with Constance.

"Since you must remain here so none can declare our marriage unconsummated," he said, "I speak in terms of gaining my rest, Lady Thomasin. And that I cannot do if you do not seek your own."

As she slowly pushed up to sitting, he strode across the solar and around the tub and tossed the stick onto the fire.

El stared at his broad back. She did not understand why she had reacted so strongly when he had pinned her. It was not as if she had not been pinned before. And all those times when she had been forced to pay the marital debt, she had survived. But then, Murdoch had not had Boursier's advantage of strength. Though few were the struggles she had won against her first husband, she had not been entirely without recourse. Thus, more than once he had borne the marks of her aggression for all to see—as opposed to the hidden marks he had left upon her.

Hating the uncertainty of not knowing if Boursier intended the same and would be upon her the moment she showed relief, she said, "I do not understand you."

He turned, met her gaze. "I would have it no other way."

Frustration flew through her. It made no sense that he would not exercise his husband's rights. Regardless of how weary he must be, surely he would put forth the effort, for the marriage must be consummated. If not—

"I know what you are thinking," he said, "that an unconsummated marriage can be annulled and my lands declared forfeit." He smiled grimly. "But know that you are mine, and when I can stomach having you in my bed, all will be consummated. And in that bed, you shall bear our sons and daughters."

Those last words making her lower her chin for fear of what her face would reveal, her eyes fell upon the ring he had placed on her finger. Though it was as poor a fit as the one with which Murdoch had shackled her, Boursier's was loose enough that it could easily be lost, whereas her first husband's had been so tight that its removal following his death had required a fine saw.

El yanked herself back to *this* husband and the children he expected to get on her. Were she Thomasin de Arell, it was possible she would bear heirs, but she was Elianor of Emberly who had wed Murdoch Farrow and borne no children in the two years she had been in *his* bed—and not all because of the relief Agatha had provided. Of course, it was possible El's constant prayer that she not swell with the child of a man who would make as loathsome a father as he made a husband, could be responsible for her barrenness. Perhaps in that, God had answered her.

"Now," Boursier said, "will you behave or must I call for rope?"

She lowered her feet to the floor. As she straightened, she was reminded of the splinter. It had gone too deep to yield to her efforts to remove it once the priest had withdrawn from the chamber. Blessedly, it had not pained her when Boursier's great body had pressed upon her. Because her mind had been otherwise occupied with that which would cause greater pain? That must be it, for it certainly tormented her now.

"Answer me, Thomasin," Boursier demanded.

"Very well. I give my word you need not fear me through the night."

He glowered. "'Tis not an easing of fear I seek, but rest."

She put her chin up. "If you keep your distance, rest you will have."

He came around the tub. "Then you will take my squire's pallet, and I shall have my bed."

So near? She glanced at the chairs before the hearth. "I prefer a chair."

He advanced on her, and it took great resolve not to retreat.

"'Tis obvious you fear me, Thomasin." He halted before her. "But there is one thing you need not be anxious about. The word I give is the word I keep. As told, I will not lie with you this eve."

She wished to believe him, but such promises she had heard before and, to her detriment, had believed those first few times. "You are mistaken," she said, crossing her arms over her chest. "'Tis not fear that gives the chair appeal. It is your scent. It could drop a man dead."

Though the turning of his mouth was not a smile in the truest sense, neither was it grim. "And *your* scent"—he lowered his head, breathed to the left and right of her—"I would know anywhere."

The rumble of his voice did something to her insides that had little to do with fear.

He drew back. "Since that night when first you came to my bed, it has stayed with me."

When she and Agatha had stolen into his chamber and she had caught the glitter of his gaze.

He gave a bitter laugh. "Even through all the days of my imprisonment."

When he lifted a hand toward her face, she jumped back and, once again, came up against the mattress.

He had lied, would now do to her what he had said he would not. The only good of it was that she had not been fooled.

"You will have to get used to my touch"—his calloused fingers slid over her throat, reminding her of when he had gripped it—"for once you are in my bed, I intend to touch you often."

As the vows she had spoken gave him every right to do, time and again extracting the marital debt, regardless of her own desires.

As she cast frantically about for a way to delay the inevitable, it struck her that this time his hand on her was different, almost gentle, and when his fingers curled around her nape and pushed up into her hair, a peculiar sensation swept over her scalp and sank down through her.

"Breathe," he said.

She gasped and, mortified by the traitorous sound, flung her gaze back to his.

"At least you are not frigid," he murmured.

Was she not? Of course she was—detested the mere thought of him going near her dread woman's place as much as she had detested Murdoch going there…hurting her…

She snatched her arm up, pushed Boursier's hand off her neck. "You flatter yourself when all that can be said of you is that your stench steals one's breath."

His eyebrows rose. "When 'tis time to consummate, we shall know for certain, hmm?"

"Only if you are, indeed, the ravisher you say you are not."

"I assure you, 'twill not be by ravishment I have you."

Hating that the bed remained at her back, she said, "Your word I would have on that." Of course, it would only be for the satisfaction of flinging it at him when he proved it a lie.

"My word I give," he said, then stepped back and nodded at the pallet alongside the bed. "Gain your bed whilst I extinguish the torches."

She waited until he turned away, then slid her feet out of her slippers and started to lower to the pallet. The splinter dug deeper, causing pain to tear up her thigh. Pressing her lips tight, she eased onto her side and dragged the blanket over her.

A few moments later, there was only the glow of the hearth to light the solar. Then came the sound of garments being shed.

When Boursier's dark figure drew alongside the bed, she tensed. However, he stepped over her and settled on the mattress.

"I sleep light," he said, then added, "that is, when my wine has not been fouled by Agatha's hand."

"By *her* hand 'twas not fouled," El corrected him.

He was silent a long moment. "Then she used you well."

"Or I her."

More silence that made her regret she had not kept her spiteful thoughts to herself.

Lord, let him keep his word, she silently prayed as she turned the ring on her finger. *At least this night.*

And it seemed he would, for a quarter hour later, his breathing deepened.

9

ACCURSED SNOW! STILL it fell, though not as thickly as on the night past.

Bayard shuttered the window, pulled a black tunic over his head, and adjusted his eyepatch.

The only good of the new day was that he was clean, having washed away the filth of his six days of imprisonment. Though he had longed to sink into a hot bath, he had made do with a basin of chill water, soap, and a hand towel, for there was much to set in motion. More, it would not do for the maids who carried water to see his bride upon his squire's pallet. And that thought reminded him of the need for proof of consummation.

Dragging a hand across his bearded jaw that he would have Squire Lucas scrape clean later this day, he stepped around the bed and halted at the foot of the pallet where Thomasin lay on her side.

Though her brow was bunched as if she suffered unpleasant dreams, she was undeservedly lovely. Blond hair that was not as dark as previously thought, and which knew neither curl nor wave, fell across her face, over a small nose, and lifted gently at the breath come from a mouth that required no rouge.

Plain of face! Whoever had said that suffered poor eyesight.

She moaned softly, parting her lips to allow a glimpse of teeth, then rolled onto her back. Her eyes popped open, and she startled to see him standing over her. "Oh, this dream is not much better than the other."

"Worse," Bayard drawled and retrieved his sword belt from atop the chest and began fitting the metal-trimmed leather around his waist. "Unfortunate for you, I am quite real."

She slid her gaze down him. "You are certain? The man from the night past looked more a beast."

"The man you remember, Lady," he said, buckling the belt, "spent nearly six days and nights in a hell of your making."

"And has finally bathed." She sat up, but though she lowered her face, he heard her breath catch.

"You are ill?" he asked.

She shook her head. "I must...relieve myself."

Berating himself for the show of concern that was surely born of a fair face, he said, "See to it," and lowered to the chest to drag on his boots.

She thrust the blanket aside and stood, but when she stepped forward, she favored her right side.

Had her leg cramped? Reminding himself he did not care, he pulled on the second boot as she closed herself in the garderobe.

He stood and considered what mischief she might make while he was belowstairs. The walled passage and the iron-banded chest presented the only threats. With keys from the purse on his belt, he secured both, then turned to the rumpled bed and reached for his dagger.

If not for Thomasin's muffled moan, he would have himself provided proof of consummation.

He crossed to the garderobe, but before he could demand to know what ailed her, she muttered, "Oh, 'tis deep."

The garderobe shaft? Surely she did not think to escape down it. No lady would—

Neither would any lady do what she had done to him. Though Griffin de Arell had titled his daughter, she remained far too common.

Bayard wrenched the door open.

Standing in the bit of light that shone through the narrow slit in the wall, Thomasin snapped her chin up and dropped her hitched skirts— but not before he glimpsed a shapely thigh marked by angry red flesh.

"That you dare!" she cried.

"Without apology." He pulled her from the garderobe to the bed. "Show me!"

Face flushed, she glared at him.

Though he knew he should not concern himself with the wellbeing of one whose only concern for him was that he forfeit his lands, he said, "Do it, else I will toss up your skirts."

"I have taken a splinter, 'tis all!"

He caught a fistful of her cotehardie and yanked it high.

Though she tried to sidestep, he held her firmly as he looked upon the swollen flesh. It was a splinter—three inches lodged beneath the surface of her skin.

"Sit," he said.

"I will not!"

He pushed her onto the sheet and, when she tried to scramble off, pressed a hand to her chest. "Cease, Thomasin!"

She dropped onto her elbows.

Bayard pulled her skirts higher and confirmed the flesh of her thigh was infected. "How came you by this?"

She pressed her lips tight.

"That piece of wood you thought to put through me," he concluded, then said, "The splinter must needs be removed."

"As I endeavored to do ere you trampled my privacy! Are you done?"

He frowned. "You would leave it to fester deeper?"

"I would not have *you* touch it."

Why did he think to do so? That she might tremble for fear that such an intimate view of her would incite him to claim his rights over her? Though he was tempted to convince himself it was what he wanted, he did not. Regardless of his past sins, regardless that he had once before wed a lady who had not wanted him in her bed, he was no ravisher.

He straightened. "I shall leave you to it." He strode to the door.

"Have you a physician in your household?"

Bayard turned, saw that she had risen from the bed. "Castle Adderstone has a physician, but he is gone. Do you know where?"

"Of course I do not know!"

"He accompanied my sister to the barony of Blackwood."

She looked down. "Oh."

Bayard nearly left her then, but there was the question that kept running through his mind. "If 'tis true Griffin de Arell knew naught of my imprisonment, how was it accomplished?"

Her lids lifted. "Upon my word, 'tis true. Whether you wish to believe it or nay, you were bested by women, Bayard Boursier." She took a step forward, winced.

The splinter pained her, and not even for ease of it would she ask for his help.

"Though most of what I know of Griffin de Arell is from a distance," he said, "it would be a changed man who would allow his daughter to do what you did."

She thrust her chin forward. "As I did not wish interference from one who would refuse to allow me to do what needed to be done, I did not ask for permission."

"I am to believe a woman-child of but ten and seven capable of working such ill?"

"I am twenty and—" She snapped her teeth closed.

Unsettled, Bayard said, "Twenty and what?"

In that moment, El almost wished Murdoch had cut out her tongue as he had threatened to do when she had used it as a sword upon him. Holding her gaze to Boursier's, she said, "Twenty and some months." Not that it was much of a lie, for she was but a year older than that.

Whether or not her deception passed, she could not know, for he shuttered his face.

Pressing her shoulders back, she tried not to think about the wretched splinter. "'Twas I who determined to abduct and imprison you.

My—" She had nearly said *uncle*. She shifted her weight opposite her aching thigh. "My father knew naught of my plan."

Boursier crossed the solar and once more placed himself over her.

There was barely a foot between them and she had to tip her head back, but El held. And wished she had put more distance between her and the bed. Wished he smelled as he had done on the night past. Wished his auburn hair waving off his brow did not look so clean and crisp. Wished she did not still feel the touch of his fingers upon her thigh. Most of all, she wished the gait of her heart was all fear.

She crossed her arms over her chest. "*I* did it."

His scarred eyebrow rose above the eyepatch. "If 'tis true it was done without De Arell's knowledge, it was surely at that witch's counsel."

"Her name is Agatha, and though she aided me, she did so because I asked it of her." From what had happened in the underground, did he know Agatha had turned on her lady so she might work her own plans against The Boursier?

His blue-green eye glittered. "It was *Agatha* who came to kill me."

El swallowed, not only for the lie she would tell but to distract herself from her throbbing thigh. "She did as she was told. Thus, your vengeance should fall upon me alone."

"Then"—he looked down her—"the only question is how best to extract payment from one's wife."

Though he had vowed he would not ravish her, the threat ran through El on wanton feet.

He lifted her chin. "Of course, until I ride on Castle Mathe, I shall not know the extent of what is due me."

When would that be? Had the snow let up? Might he attempt a ride this day? If so, his absence from Castle Adderstone could mean her escape—and the sooner the better, if there was any hope of freeing Agatha.

"But this I vow," he continued, "if ill has befallen my sister, you shall wish I had left you in the underground with that beastly woman."

She stepped back, only to whimper when pain shot through her thigh.

Boursier turned steel around her forearm. "Fool," he said and pushed her down on the bed and dragged up her skirts.

Something about the bend of his head and his hand upon her thigh prevented her from struggling.

He looked up. "You would have me draw it out or nay?"

She jerked her chin. "Pray, do."

He pulled a dagger from his belt, and she flinched at the sight of the keen edge. "What do you intend?"

"Be still." He gripped her thigh and lowered the dagger toward it.

Grabbing up handfuls of the bed coverings as his blade opened the thin layer of flesh, El squeezed her eyes closed to keep tears from spilling.

"'Tis out," he said.

She looked at the bloody splinter between his fingers, breathed, "I thank you."

He considered her, then set the splinter on the bedside table.

"Hold," he said when she started to rise, then swept up the sheet and, with an impersonal touch that shook El in ways it should not, wiped the cloth across her blood-smeared thigh.

Regardless that she told herself she was as repulsed as she had been by Murdoch's touch, this was different. And it made her shudder.

Boursier's gaze captured hers, and something passed between them that stopped her breath and caused his nostrils to flare. "Why?" he said softly. "Why when you do not wish it any more than I?"

Neither did she understand it, nor would she discuss it. "I do not know of what you speak."

He lowered his gaze to her lips, and of their own accord, they parted for him as El stared into a face that, despite its bearded jaw, was more attractive than previously thought.

He drew nearer, and she did not know what possessed her, but she lowered her lids.

She heard his breath, felt it on her lips, caught the faint scent of mint.

"Aye, Wife," he rasped, "you will soon come to my bed."

She sprang her lids open and, awash in self-loathing, said, "For what would I willingly lie with a man so undesirable he could not hold his first wife?" It was cruel, but it cleared the satisfaction from his face, and so she pressed on. "Rejection is what comes to one who takes that which does not belong to him."

His gaze darkened. "Pray tell, Lady, what comes to one who *fails* to take what does not belong to her?"

As in Elianor of Emberly who had tried to steal his birthright. She narrowed her lids. "I suppose that would be marriage to a one-eyed beast."

Slowly, he drew back. "Enjoy your sharp teeth whilst you have them, Lady, for I will pull them."

Though she knew she ought to leave it there, once more she did not heed her inner voice as so many times she should have done with Murdoch. She dropped her feet to the floor and stood. "Possible only if you can hold me as you could not hold Constance Verdun."

He merely smiled. "Some women are not worth holding onto. Indeed, had your fool uncle realized that, he would yet possess his sword arm."

Uncle Magnus? What——?

Nay, it was Thomasin's uncle, Serle, of whom he spoke—the man who had dared to reclaim the woman lost to Bayard Boursier. Though a betrothal had been made between Griffin de Arell's younger brother and Constance Verdun while they were children, Bayard Boursier's offer for El's aunt had presented too much temptation. Magnus and Constance's father, Rand Verdun, had broken his word and wed his daughter to the Baron of Godsmere whose rank outdistanced the landless Serle, thereby condemning Constance to marriage to a man she had not loved and who had made her suffer.

If not for the burn of El's thigh that reminded her of the aid this man had given her, she would have retorted that were *he* not so fool, he would yet possess the eye lost to Serle de Arell's sword. But she had already pushed him too far.

Boursier yanked the sheet from the mattress and glanced at her blood upon it. "And I had thought I would have to bleed myself," he murmured.

Her frown fled when she realized it was consummation to which he referred. And, as Murdoch had done after that brutal night following their wedding when he had displayed her virginal blood, this man would display what would pass as such. It was custom, but still it offended.

She thrust her shoulders back. "Virginal blood when I have had lovers?"

His brow lowered. "Lovers you shall have no more." He dropped the sheet over his arm, said, "I have preparations to make," and turned away.

He meant to ride on Castle Mathe? Meaning the snow had let up?

He flung open the door, looked around. "Do not grieve my men-at-arms."

Then he would again post them outside her door. The lady of Castle Adderstone—false or otherwise—remained a prisoner.

The door closed.

As the sound of Boursier's booted feet faded, El pulled up her skirts and considered her inflamed thigh, then touched where he had touched, splayed her hand where his had splayed, felt again feelings never before felt.

"Dear Lord," she entreated, "what have I done?"

10

THE DAY COULD not have drawn itself out any longer. No matter how often El tossed back the shutters, the snow did not cease. The morning meal was delivered, next the nooning meal, and before long there would be supper.

After the first hour of searching for something to aid in her escape, all that was left to her was to peer out at the snow and worry over Agatha and Magnus. Certain the older woman faired reasonably well, having been imprisoned only a night and a day, Magnus worried her the most. Hopefully, the snow would keep him from searching her out. If not, he would likely journey to the abbey. And then?

Turning the ring on her finger, she moved her gaze from the torch-lit snow beyond the shutters to the tapestry behind which lay the door that would not give. Next, she considered the door across the solar beyond which stood Boursier's men-at-arms. Hopeless. But it could not be thus forever. There had to be a way around Boursier. Or through him.

She cringed in remembrance of when she had set aside defiance to gain from Murdoch something otherwise unattainable—mercy for her maid when the woman trod upon the chausses he had left amid the rushes, permission to stroll the garden where Agatha passed powders to her like those used to imprison The Boursier. How she had hated bending to Murdoch, but she had been given no choice. Just as it appeared she was given none now.

You can do it again, she told herself. And, God willing, Boursier would prove as susceptible as Murdoch and she would not be made to suffer his attentions as she had suffered her husband's. Not that she had freely given herself to Murdoch. Merely, when she had needed something badly, she had not fought him.

"Lord," she prayed, "let not Boursier lay me down."

Of course, that was the stuff of naiveté.

She turned back to the window, considered the red and gold banners flown on either side of the portcullis set in the inner wall, then lowered her gaze to where false testament of her lost chastity flapped in the swirling snow. The sheet had been set above the entrance to the great hall, thereby proclaiming Boursier was—and would remain—Baron of Godsmere. Just as it was meant to ensure that when he was gone from this world, all would pass to a child sown of his loins.

El touched her belly, sent up a prayer of thanks that no babe had ever taken hold. Once she had dreamed of little ones about her skirts, of loving them and watching them grow, but she had been grateful that with each violation of her body, she had given Murdoch no heir. Of course, he had blamed her and she had been punished accordingly.

She bowed her head, clasped her hands beneath her chin. "If I cannot escape Boursier, let me be no more fruitful than I was with Murdoch."

She opened her eyes, parted her hands, and looked upon slim fingers tipped with nails just long enough to rake a man's flesh. She curled them into her palms. For whatever gain there might be toward escape, she would keep them to herself, hold her caustic tongue, and defer to Boursier as much as she could bear.

She laid a palm to the place beneath her skirts around which she had wound the linen bandage that had earlier been delivered with salve. She grimaced. Boursier's squire had spoken no word, and she had known he knew she was responsible for his loss of consciousness the night she and Agatha had breached the solar. No ally there. Yet.

A fair face God had given her, surely that it would be of some use. Of course, guile was not likely what the Lord intended.

When a knock sounded, she smoothed a hand over her hair, pushed it behind her ears, and swept her tongue over her lips to make them glisten. "Enter!"

A tray in hand, the young man stepped through the doorway.

She smiled. "Once more, you deliver me from hunger, Squire."

Silent still, he set the tray on the table near the hearth where, this morn, the tub had sat. Neither had the maids who had removed the tub spoken to her. Not that she had given them reason to converse, but from this moment forward, all must change.

She crossed the solar and placed herself in the squire's path as he turned to leave. Smiling wide to summon the groove in her cheek that made her face more becoming, she said, "You are most kind, Squire...?"

She glimpsed a spark of interest, but he stuffed it behind a glower. "Squire Lucas, and it is not out of kindness I bring your supper. 'Tis by order."

"Nevertheless, I am grateful. Will my lord husband be joining me?"

"Baron Boursier takes his meal in the hall with his men, my lady."

"Oh, I had hoped..." She sighed, stepped to the platter of viands, and touched the rim. But though she waited for the young man's sympathetic response, he gave none.

She turned and saw he appeared unmoved. Worrisome, for if she was unable to pluck a chord of sympathy from him, what hope had she of Boursier believing her acquiescence?

She pressed her shoulders back. "Would you carry word to my husband that I would be pleased to share my meal with him?"

His eyebrows gathered. "You would?"

"I would."

His lips pursed, then stretched to a mocking smile. "I shall carry word." He gave a curt bow and departed.

El groaned as the door fit into its frame. All did not progress well.

She schemed.

Once more granted an opportunity to observe his conniving wife while she slept in the chair opposite, Bayard rubbed a palm across his jaw that Lucas had scraped clean earlier this eve—rather, yestereve, for it was now two hours into the dark of a new day. His squire's recounting of what had occurred when he had delivered Thomasin her meal had tempted Bayard abovestairs to determine what game she played. Instead, he had kept her waiting the same as he kept Father Crispin waiting, though the latter could not be more obvious that he wished an audience.

Bayard grunted. This one sought to corner him to work further deceit upon him. That one sought to corner him to offer counsel and prayer that, at the moment, was unwelcome. Though he knew the priest would speak truth in attempting to bring his lord back to the place from which Thomasin's offense had caused him to stray, Bayard was not ready and did not know when he would be. Indeed, if he lost his home and lands and the ability to provide for his family and people, he might never be ready. Thus, it was best that Father Crispin not waste his breath until more was known of what this woman had wrought.

He moved his gaze from her softly seamed lips to lashes that fluttered with the movement of eyes that followed the images of dreams. What did she see? Of what did a commoner turned noblewoman turned abductor dream?

A small sound escaped her and her eyebrows gathered. "Do not," she whispered, then spoke something else that came apart before it made it across the space between them.

She grabbed a breath. "I shall..."

Bayard stepped around the chair he had leaned against these past minutes.

"Certes, I shall," she hissed.

He strode forward, settled his hands on the chair arms on either side of her, and leaned in. "Shall what?" he asked in a voice yet hoarse from the abuse to which he had subjected it while imprisoned.

As if noting the intrusion upon her dream, she frowned, but her lined brow did not mar her loveliness. In fact, she was more comely up close, unlike many women who looked best from a distance. Her skin was unblemished, cheekbones brushed with warm color, lips flushed and full as if recently tasted and found to be to a man's liking.

Bayard growled. For what had the Lord set such beguiling creatures in men's paths? To undo them? For certain, Constance Verdun had undone him. To test them? That, too. To curse them? Especially so, as evidenced by his singular gaze and facial scarring that had swept asunder that which had once found adequate favor with women.

"I shall!" Thomasin spat.

"What?" Bayard asked again.

"Kill you."

He leaned nearer. "You think so?"

"I know so!" Her eyes opened, and for a moment it seemed she looked through him. But the hatred darkening her green gaze receded, and she said with what sounded like relief, "The Boursier."

As he was known—as had been his father. Though he was accustomed to the impersonal title, he resented her use of it. "Bayard," he bit, "your husband. Now tell, how do you intend to kill me?"

From the rapidly fading dream, Murdoch's face lunged at El, and she realized she had been talking in her sleep as she sometimes did according to her maid. Determinedly, she let the rest of the dream—which had once been terribly real—slide away so that all she saw was Boursier's freshly shaved face above hers.

"Tell," he said on a breath entwined with wine.

Reminding herself of the deception she must work, she said, "Ease your worry, Lord Husband, for you are not the man of my dream. That one is dead." As soon as she spoke that last, she wished she had not, resented that he was too close and sleep was yet too near for her to think clearly.

"By your hand?" His eyebrow arched above the patch.

At least a dozen times she had killed Murdoch, though only in her heart. If not for Agatha's powders, how much nearer might she have come to the deed?

She shook her head. "I am no murderer."

"Are you not?" Blessedly, he straightened. "Yestereve, you wished me to believe you were capable of such. This eve not?"

She had forgotten about that—when Agatha had bemoaned that she should have been allowed to kill him and El had retorted she had not done so in order to ensure he suffered.

"I know what you want, Thomasin," he said, "but you shall not have it."

El sat straighter. "What do I want?"

His lips curved, though they did not much resemble a smile. "Abandon hope. For as long as King Edward requires it, you shall remain Thomasin Boursier." He turned and strode to the hearth.

She might have abandoned civility along with hope were it not all she had. She pushed up out of the chair. "Think as you will," she said and started toward the pallet. She halted. Was it still her place, or would he prove himself a liar this night?

She turned toward his broad-shouldered back.

Dear Lord, let him be too weary.

"Tale is told," he said without looking around, "De Arell's daughter knows well how to turn servants to her cause. That she readily becomes one of them to work her guile. That with ease, she steals from the castle and hies to the villages to distribute her ill-gotten gain."

El had heard as much and envied the young woman who defied her father to ease the lives of those she yet considered her people. For this, it was said, she always returned to Castle Mathe. Did Griffin de Arell beat her? Likely, for he was nearly as great a fiend as Bayard Boursier.

"What else is told of me?" El asked, thinking there might be something she had not heard that she ought to know as long as she claimed that woman's name as her own.

He turned, and his gaze pierced her. "That you spit and curse, and with great purpose chafe your father with rustic speech though much effort he expends to make of you a noblewoman."

She nearly balked. Not that she was unaware of those tales. Rather, she was appalled she had not thought to use them to better behave as one whose roots had unfurled in the soil of the peasantry.

"Aye, I know who you are and what you want," he said, mistaking her silence. "Be assured that those who serve me also know and shall not succumb to your schemes. No aid will they give you in escaping me." He strode forward and placed himself over her as he seemed fond of doing. "You are at my mercy."

Though she strove to hide her reaction to words with which Murdoch had often threatened—and acted upon—she felt the emotions jump off her face. Worse, she staggered back a step, earning herself Boursier's frowning regard.

Weakness! all of her cried at allowing him to see into her. She settled her face, forced her breath deeper, and searched for a distraction. She found it in the question that remained unanswered. "Why did you choose me over the Verdun woman when your hate is greater for my family?" She narrowed her gaze on his eyepatch and decided to see how much farther he could be pushed. "After all, 'twas my uncle, Serle, who took your eye."

His lips thinned and his glare was so keen it slashed. "As I took his arm."

Something the Boursiers seemed fond of doing, his father having taken the arm of El's grandfather during that long ago siege upon Castle Adderstone. "Then for revenge you chose me, Thomasin de Arell?"

Bayard stared at the woman who dared where others did not. None spoke of the eye he had lost, and certainly none drugged him and imprisoned him in his own home. And yet, when he had warned she was at his mercy, she had reacted as she had on the night past with far more fear than was warranted for one who so greatly dared.

"Was it for revenge?" she asked again.

"Certes, I shall have satisfaction for the ill you worked upon me and any that befalls my sister, but it was not revenge that made me choose you."

"What, then?"

He was tempted to refuse her an answer, but he said, "Having been wed to a Verdun, I determined one beautiful harlot of deceitful bent was enough to last me a lifetime. Thus, I chose you as I was told you were plain of face, which you certainly are not, that you were ten and seven and a maiden, which you tell you are not, that you might provide me an heir, which Elianor of Emberly did not provide her now departed husband, and I did not think you could be as deceitful as my first wife, which you have proved false."

Thomasin averted her gaze, but when she returned it to him, her eyes glittered. "Mayhap you give women good reason to deceive you," she said, her pretense of civility boiled down to anger. "You assuredly gave Constance Verdun little choice."

Certain she referred to Agatha's tale that not only had he beaten his wife but fouled the marriage bed with other women, Bayard curled his fingers into fists.

"As for your first wife being a harlot," she continued, "that is a matter of opinion."

Struggling to keep his hands at his sides, he said, "The opinion of a man cuckolded."

She snorted. "I would not brag on that, *Husband,* lest it reflect upon your prowess in bed and put me in the same mind as your first wife."

Bayard was acquainted with the color of anger, though he had only experienced such crimson, fiery flashes during life-threatening hostilities and combat, as when he had awakened to find himself chained to a wall...as when he had come upon Serle de Arell with Constance. But though he told himself that no moment of this was life-threatening, he was moved to react as Bayard Boursier did not react.

He grasped Thomasin's shoulders and pulled her toward him. When she yelped and landed against his chest, he nearly came back to himself. But the gaze she tossed up at him brimmed with challenge, taunting him just as her words had done.

He pulled her up to her toes, felt his hot breath deflect off her brow. "'Tis time you took your place at Castle Adderstone, the only place you shall have whilst you darken my home."

When he lifted her into his arms, she bucked, kicked, and tried to rake his face, but no flesh did he give as he carried her to bed.

"Pig!" she cried. "Miscreant! Poltroon!"

He dropped her onto the feather-filled coverlet.

Immediately, she sprang opposite, but he caught her back and dropped atop her.

When she once more came at him with hooked fingers, he pinned her arms to her sides.

"Ignoble beast! You gave your word!"

He met her wide-eyed gaze. "As told, the word I give is the word I keep. 'Twill not be by ravishment our marriage is consummated." Now to seduce his wife...

He lowered his head.

She jerked hers aside.

It suited him, for it was not her lips he sought. He wanted to taste her, but not there. Not yet. He put his mouth to the smooth flesh between neck and shoulder, tasted the sweetest salt touched with rose water.

She stiffened.

He kissed his way to the hollow of her throat, breathed her in.

She shivered.

He moved to her jaw.

She released her breath on a single word, "Oh," drawing it out long enough to be several words.

He put his lips to the corner of hers, past which her breath was coming fast and shallow, then released her arms and cupped her face. As he closed his mouth over hers, her eyes found his, and in hers was a mix of desire and fear, as of oil and water—in one another and yet not.

When he deepened the kiss, her lids fluttered closed.

He reached down and raised her skirts.

One moment her body was soft and yielding, the next not. She wrenched her mouth from his. "You gave your word!"

The desire that had coiled through him began to loosen as he wondered when he had last longed for a woman as much as he longed for this one who had sought to see him stripped of all he possessed. Unfortunately, the answer was close at hand—the night he had come to his marriage bed and Constance had been waiting for him. Though there had been no love in her eyes, she had opened her arms to him.

But not even that little would Thomasin yield.

Determining he must move slowly with her, he pulled his hand from beneath her skirts and drew it up her side. She jerked, and when he returned his mouth to the place between neck and shoulder, she hissed, "I do not want this. I vow I do not!"

Feeling her erratic pulse beneath her soft skin, he murmured, "You do not want to want this. There is a difference."

"Is that what you told yourself when Constance Verdun pleaded that you not ravish her?"

Bayard stilled as he was dashed against memories of that other woman. He saw her again in his bed, felt her curves, heard her husky words of desire. And all the while, inside her beautiful head, she had plotted his end.

He drew back. "Constance Verdun was a harlot, a woman who, in the same day, gave herself to husband and lover."

His new wife's gaze wavered, but she blinked and it was firm again. "Were she a harlot, it was not for being with a man she loved. Nay, only were she with a man she did not love and freely gave herself to him, might she be named such."

Serle de Arell, the man Constance had loved. Bayard Boursier, the man she had not loved. "A harlot, then," he said.

Her eyes flashed. "Speak false if it eases your conscience, but know this—by ravishment only shall you have me. I am no harlot."

The discrepancy of her words nearly slipped past him. Not surprisingly, Thomasin de Arell was no different from those whose blood had dripped nobility into her commoner's veins. "One moment you claim you are capable of murder," he said, "the next you deny it. One moment you prate of lovers, the next tell you are no harlot. What is the truth?"

El berated herself for the missteps she continued to make that would see her exposed were she not more careful. The quiet, painless years since Murdoch's death had weakened her ability to speak and keep lies, providing far too little practice in Magnus's household.

"So deep are your falsehoods you do not even know yourself," Boursier scoffed, then rolled off her and onto his back.

El was too surprised to move. If it had been Murdoch who had tossed her on the bed, nothing would have stopped him from doing whatever perverse thing he wished to do—not pleading, not tears, not anger, not teeth and nails, not fists and knees, not even the appearance of a maidservant who would suffer for interrupting her lord's sport.

Nay, El corrected, there was one thing—one person—who had been able to stop him. Though Agatha could never be dear, during those times Murdoch had been at his most dangerous, she had provided El with relief from his attentions.

When Boursier turned his head toward her, she resisted giving him her gaze. "The marriage will be consummated as it must be," he said. "If not this night, then another—and soon."

She stared at the ceiling. "Then you will prove you are more of a liar than I."

"There will be no lie, Thomasin. You *will* give yourself to me."

She loathed that he was certain of it. But then, she had given him reason to be when his attempt to seduce her had delivered results. She had not struggled. Rather, she had floated upon the peculiar, breathtaking sensations roused by his touch. And nearly drowned when he had laid his mouth upon hers.

So *that* was a kiss. Gently coaxing, almost reverent. Slowly deepening, the need for breath forgotten. And that sweet tug straight down the center of her, promising something other than the pain inflicted by the grinding of a mouth against hers.

Promising. Only promising, for as Murdoch had taught her, the promises of men were made to be broken.

At her continued silence, Boursier prompted, "You will yield."

She knew she should hold her tongue, but she turned her face to him. "Ergo, you seek my love?" She smiled tightly. "Only *that* might induce me to yield to one such as you."

His jaw convulsed. "One does not seek what one neither trusts, nor requires. And should you ever think to deliver unto me such feelings, false or otherwise, I vow to reduce them to ashes."

She did not doubt it. Were it possible to love a man like him, it would be at the cost of one's soul.

Slowly, lest he spring upon her, she sat up and pushed her skirts down. "We are of the same mind, then," she said and lowered her feet to the rushes.

Not until she straightened from the bed and he made no further attempt to detain her did she allow herself the indulgence of relief. He was different from Murdoch. Of course, that did not mean he was better. If she was unable to escape him, he would eventually ravish her—and do far worse when he learned she was not the woman he believed he had wed.

El looked across her shoulder, saw Boursier had laid a forearm across his eyes. She bit hard on regret, wishing she had been able to maintain a pretense of acquiescence. For all the hours since her capture, she was no nearer her release or Agatha's. If only the snow would cease long enough to send Boursier after his sister!

Tomorrow, she prayed as she lowered to the pallet. *Tomorrow.*

11

LIGHT SWEPT IN, next a chill that made her hunch her shoulders, then a dread voice that reminded her this was no dream.

"Arise, Thomasin!"

El opened her eyes, looked up. Though the flickering torchlight evidenced it was not yet morn, Boursier was dressed for a journey—boots, thick hose, tunic and undertunic, sword and misericorde, mantle. Meaning her prayer was answered. The snow had let up.

"Godspeed," she murmured and reached behind to retrieve the blanket he had tossed off.

Boursier closed a hand around her forearm and hauled her to her feet. "I give you a quarter hour."

"For what?"

"You are to accompany me to the barony of Blackwood."

Dear Lord...

He released her. "Surely you did not think I would leave you behind to work your trickery upon my people?"

Surely she had. El dropped to the mattress edge, nearly buried her face in her hands. Was there nothing in this world she could make right?

"More," Boursier added, "if your father does hold my sister, he will sooner release her if you are at my side."

Were she Thomasin de Arell.

El joined her hands, felt the press of the ill-fitting ring that did not a marriage make. If not this day, then the next, her deceit would be laid bare. Perhaps it was better to tell Boursier now, for the longer she led him down this path, the greater his fury when he was shown to have seriously veered off course. But then her fate would be sealed and she would have no chance at all.

She clasped her hands opposite, stared at her crossed thumbs. There was always the possibility of escape during the ride. "I shall accompany you, then."

"There is no question of that." He pivoted.

El stood. "I have a boon to ask of you."

He turned. "Do you truly expect me to grant one?"

"I expect only a yea or a nay."

He considered her. "For what do you seek a yea?"

She squared her shoulders the better to bear the weight of his refusal. "I would see Agatha ere our departure."

He narrowed his gaze, lowered it to her left hand.

Only then realizing her thumb once more turned the gold band around, she closed her fingers into her palms.

The Boursier returned his gaze to her face. "Better you spend your time with ablutions and tending your leg."

She stepped forward. "Agatha has been down there two days."

"And there she shall remain." He opened the door, stepped into the corridor. "If you do not see to your injury, I shall," he said and closed the door.

El stared at it, wished her eyes capable of piercing wood and striking him down. The stuff of fluff, her mother would have reprimanded were she alive—just as El's tears of frustration were the stuff of fluff.

Though she longed to defy Boursier, it would gain her naught. Setting her jaw, she crossed the solar and lifted the hand towel from beside the basin of water.

Darkness is her name, the voice of Archard Boursier wound through his son as he turned into the passage that led to the cell.

When Constance had brought her maid, Agatha of Mawbry, with her to Castle Adderstone five years past, something about the woman had bothered the ailing Archard who had warned Bayard to keep a watch on her. Bayard had, though not enough. Thus, Agatha had time and again tipped powders into his wine to keep him from his wife's bed. Now, four years after banishing the witch, she had come again, this time with Thomasin de Arell.

"Aye, darkness is her name," he muttered, "and plague, and malice, and all things loathsome and twisted."

He halted before the cell door, adjusted his eyepatch, and turned the key in the lock. Pushing the door inward, he thrust the torch in ahead of him. As expected, the woman's chains held. But though there was no movement about her and a quarter hour had passed since last she had tormented his men with her howling and cursing, he sensed she was awake.

"Agatha of Mawbry," he said.

Not a hair stirred, not a breath moved her shoulders, not a twitch enlivened her hands.

He settled to his haunches and considered her downturned face that was too defined and severe to evidence it had ever been pleasing to the eye. Then there was her build, so tall and sturdy it was easy to overlook the feminine features that differentiated her from the opposite sex.

Bayard pulled the sack of food and drink from his belt. It would suffice for several days, ensuring none need tend the witch in his absence. And when the task of sealing the underground passage was completed a day hence, none would further suffer her ranting. He tossed the sack onto her lap.

"I am not done with you," he said, "but when I am, you shall bedevil the Boursiers no more."

She remained as still as the dead.

He straightened. "I shall deliver your well wishes for a fruitful marriage to my wife." He turned and crossed to the door.

"Foolish Boursier," she drawled, "you know not what you have done."

The torch in one hand, the keys in the other, he peered over his shoulder and saw her head remained bowed. "You know not what *you* have done, witch."

With a slight pitch of her shoulders, she expelled a laugh. "I know more than you," she spoke into her chest and began to hum—the same accursed song he had often heard when she had dwelt at Adderstone.

When she started in on the lyrics, Bayard turned away.

"Sir, said she, whatever I may be, I can tell sense from folly. Keep your acquaintance, Lord—"

He slammed the door and fit the key, but as he strode opposite, she cried, "Bedevil the Boursiers!"

He did not falter.

"Bedevil the Boursiers!"

He clenched his jaws.

"Bedevil the Boursiers!"

He ground his teeth.

"Bedevil the Boursiers!"

12

<hr>

EL HUDDLED INTO the mantle she had worn the night of her marriage to Boursier, breathed hot air down her chest. Unfortunately, it did little to vanquish the chill that claimed nearly all feeling in her down to her toes. For hours, their horses had plodded through melting snow that slowed their journey, and though she had earlier prayed for a lengthy ride so she might find a way to free herself, now she almost wished it was done regardless of what awaited her. But with day quickly setting into night, they would not likely reach Castle Mathe on the barony of Blackwood until the morrow. Of course, were Magnus's demesne their destination—as it was hers—a turn east and another few hours would deliver them there.

She looked to where The Boursier rode ahead. So rarely did he glance around that, if not for his men at her back, she could have slipped away. But perhaps she would find an opportunity to flee if they paused for the night.

A half hour later, they turned into the wood and Boursier set his men to lighting fires and pitching tents. As his tent was the first to be raised, it was not long before El left the warming fire she shared with the watchful Father Crispin. Not that she preferred Boursier's tent, but she would be away from prying eyes and, hopefully, find a means of escape.

Passing through the mist of her breath, she tossed back the flap and glanced over her shoulder at Squire Lucas who had followed her. She entered and dropped the flap. Hoping the young man's duty did not extend to the privacy of his lord's tent, she waited and, when he remained outside, lowered her hood.

She gazed through the muted light at the cramped confines. The snow had been cleared from the ground, leaving the sodden leaves of autumn underfoot. In the far corner, a fur lay atop a pile of blankets. Opposite, one of Boursier's packs leaned against the tent wall. As she eyed that last, light at her back brought her around.

She raised the tent flap, and there stood Squire Lucas with a lantern.

"Baron Boursier commands that you keep this lit whilst you are within." He reached it to her.

She stared at it, resented that her shadow against its light would keep those outside apprised of her whereabouts lest she attempted to escape out the tent's backside.

"You may tell your lord I am not afeared of the dark," she said.

He glanced behind, and she followed his gaze to where men cleared snow to erect another tent. Boursier stood in their midst facing her, and she felt his warning gaze across the fire-lit dusk.

"If you like," Squire Lucas said, "I shall summon Baron Boursier so you may tell him yourself, my lady."

Grudgingly, she accepted the lantern and dropped the flap. Uncomfortably aware she could make no move without being seen, she turned back into the tent.

"Well, then," she muttered, "how will you do this?" Even if she could retrieve her horse, she would not likely get far before Boursier brought her back. But on foot...

It did not bear thinking about, but it was her only chance. Better she succumb to the night's chill or a hungry beast than Boursier's fury. But how?

Doubtless, she would not find any weapons in his pack, and the blankets were of no use. That left only the lantern.

She caught her breath. Dare she?

She did. But not until dark was fully upon them so she might better her chance of escape. She crossed to where the blankets were piled, lowered to them, and settled in for her vigil.

A great gust rent the air, followed by a burst of light.

Drawing his sword, Bayard swung around. But no mortal came against him.

"Thomasin!" he shouted.

As he and the others ran to the pyre that hardly resembled the tent it had been moments before, Squire Lucas tossed back the flap that had yet to be consumed.

Would the young man reach her in time? If not, would he give his own life alongside hers?

Cursing himself for sending her the lantern, Bayard stretched his legs long one last time, but as he made to dive into the disintegrating tent, his squire burst from it. Sleeve aflame, he dropped to the ground to put out the fire in the moist earth.

"Do not, my lord!" he cried as Bayard lunged into the tent.

Fiery breath struck him across the face as he swept his gaze around the wall of flame moving toward him. Though he longed to deny that nothing could live beyond that, were Thomasin not yet dead, in the next moment she would be.

Something sharp driving itself through his chest, he sprang from the tent as it came down. He hit the earth amid a shower of brightly burning embers, rolled onto his back, and stared at the ravenous flames.

Squire Lucas rose alongside him. Though the sleeve of his tunic was charred, it appeared the flesh beneath was spared. "Forgive me, my lord." He shook his head. "All was aflame. I could not even see her."

As Bayard shoved upright, something bothered the back of his mind. He dragged it forward and looked to the others gathered around. "You heard no scream?"

They answered with apologies and shakes of the head.

No cry for help, though minutes earlier Thomasin's shadow had revealed she sat as she had done for the past half hour. She had not been caught unaware. Had not fallen victim to flame and smoke.

Relief swept him, only to disappear beneath a wave of anger. The woman had set his tent aflame as a diversion to allow her to slip out the back.

"I am sorry I could not reach her, my lord," Squire Lucas choked.

"That is because she was not within!"

"What?"

So heated that his brow beaded, Bayard jerked the mantle from his shoulders and tossed it at his squire. Pivoting toward the two dozen horses corralled between a spread of trees, he shouted, "Master of the horses!"

The man stepped forward. "My lord?"

"Are all mounts present?"

He took a quick count. "They are, my lord."

Then she had gone on foot, though surely the commotion had tempted her to risk stealing a horse—as Bayard was tempted to leave her to the wood. But it would be the death of her on a night such as this. More, if De Arell held Quintin, Thomasin's presence would aid in gaining his sister's release.

"I shall bring her back," he announced and touched his sword hilt, next his misericorde.

"My lord?" Father Crispin called.

Bayard shook his head, causing the priest to halt his advance. "Later," he once more put off the priest's attempt to counsel him and almost wished he had denied the man's request to accompany his lord to Castle Mathe.

He turned away. Thomasin could have no more than five minutes on him, and if she believed it was enough to escape him, she was more the fool. As a horse would sooner alert her to his pursuit, he stalked past the tent's remains.

Easy prey, he told himself. A woman alone. Hindered by skirts. The dark of night. The cold of winter. And there, distant from the heat of the fire, he found footprints in the crisp snow that showed she moved toward one of the three who guarded the camp's perimeter.

Bayard would have smiled were it possible to work such an expression onto his mouth. He followed her footprints as the dying fire of her guile cast a path for him, then continued onward by the light provided by the bit of moon. Reliant more upon instinct than sight, he paused often to listen to the wood, and finally caught the sound of branches snapping underfoot.

Setting his dagger before him lest he encountered a beast of the wood, he lengthened his stride. And cursed when he caught sight of the knight who guarded this portion of the wood. Where had Thomasin gone?

El hugged the trunk tighter, carefully shifted her weight on the branch from one numb thigh to the other as she glanced through the barren trees at the knight who witnessed his lord's anger.

When she had trod the branch beneath the snow, its snapping had crackled across the chill air and she had known it must be heard. Thus, she had climbed the nearest tree—a difficult feat. She had scraped her palms, the backs of her hands, her cheek, and for all that had gained only five feet above the ground.

Broken fingernails, a scratched wrist, and a torn skirt had seen her up the last ten feet she had managed before The Boursier appeared, crushing all hope it would be believed she had perished in the fire.

Praying the warmth generated by fear and flight would outlast Boursier's presence where he stood thirty feet out, El lowered her chin and gave her heated breath to her chest.

"My lord!" the knight hailed. "Something is awry?"

"Lady Thomasin has gone to the wood."

The dark figure of the knight halted before Boursier's formidable bulk. "I have seen naught of her, my lord."

"And heard naught?"

El held her breath.

"I heard something, and for it left my post."

Having hoped Boursier would assume the sound was made by the knight and the knight would think it made by his lord, El inwardly groaned.

"She is near," Boursier said.

A breeze stirred the barren branches of the surrounding trees, and she knew the shudder that went through her was as much of fear as the cold piercing her garments.

"Return to your post and remain alert," Boursier ordered.

"Aye, my lord."

Barely breathing, El watched Boursier who stood unmoving—doubtless listening.

Lord, let me not be had, she prayed. *Let him not look to the tree tops.* After all, no lady would scale a tree. Would she?

His chin rose, though not high enough to carry his gaze to the branches. "Lady Thomasin!" he called. "It shall go worse for you if you do not yield now."

He did not know what *worse* was, but come the morrow, *she* would know if she surrendered. Pressing her teeth into her bottom lip to keep from scratching at the itch crawling her spine, she waited for Boursier to resume his search.

He did not, as if he knew she was within reach, as if he had but to wait for her to come to him.

The itch nearly unbearable, she squeezed her eyes closed and tried to imagine scratching it, but the vision did nothing to lessen the prickle of her flesh.

"Now!" Boursier shouted.

She flipped her lids up and picked out his dark figure just as he raised his head.

Hugging the tree tighter, sending up a fervent prayer that her dark mantle against the night sky would keep her from sight, she swallowed her breath. At last, he turned and stalked opposite.

Mother of mercy! she silently gave thanks.

She bore the itch until he was out of sight, then loosened an arm and swept it beneath her mantle to scratch at the crawling place. In doing so, she gave the branch she straddled more weight. With a crack that seemed to echo for miles, it lurched beneath her.

She gasped, wrapped her arms around the trunk, and clasped her hands. A moment later, the branch broke and fell away.

El slammed against the trunk. Clinging to it, she struggled to get her thighs around it, but her skirts fought her. The muscles of her arms screaming, she slid a foot down the bark.

"Loosen your hold!" Boursier commanded.

"Dear Lord," she breathed, though at that moment He was hardly dear to her. Indeed, she questioned if such a deity existed outside the teachings of the Church, just as she had questioned His existence during those endless nights beneath Murdoch. She had needed God, or at least a sign that if there was to be no end to her suffering there was some purpose. But silence had been her answer, her only savior Agatha with her powders—Agatha who was chained in Boursier's underground, who could not be helped as she had helped El, and who could not aid her mistress now.

Chest compressing her anguished heart, desperation and helplessness giving rise to anger, El peered over her shoulder. Boursier's arms were outstretched, inviting her to trust that he would catch her, promising to deliver her from one deadly fate so she might suffer another.

Shoulders burning, tears blurring her vision, she continued to cling to the tree and struggle to get her legs around it.

"You are had!" Boursier shouted.

At least he did not make pretty lies of it. Still, she continued to dangle, her arms jerking and trembling.

"God's patience!" he spat. "Let go!"

And she did, though not because he demanded it. Arms failing her, she cried out as she plummeted and felt a rush of fear so intense it swayed her consciousness. A moment later, she was jolted by arms that wrapped around her back and thighs and carried her downward.

Feeling Boursier's breath against her tightly closed lids, smelling smoke on him, she opened her eyes upon the glowering man whose anger was every bit as keen as the day her captive had become her captor. And at whose mercy she was—all because of an itch. But she also knew anger, its hooked fingers yearning to rake him and King Edward.

"So it goes worse for you," Boursier rasped.

Determined that he would not see the tears gathering in her eyes, she twisted around. The ground was a foot below, Boursier having carried her weight down to his haunches to lessen the impact. To her surprise, he made no attempt to restrain her, but when she stumbled to her feet and swung around to face him, the pale moonlight across his face told all. He feared his own anger—unlike Murdoch Farrow who had gloried in it. How strange that he should prove less a beast than the man to whom she had been wed. Of course, all would collide this night—and again on the morrow.

Face cold and still, hands flexing in and out of fists, he straightened. "I nearly lost my squire to your deceit!"

The young man had gone into the fire after her? Though she tried not to care, she did. She had been certain no one would risk their life to save hers.

"Fortunate for you," Boursier continued, "he escaped unharmed."

She nearly thanked the Lord, but there was little evidence her voice was counted among those to whom He listened. *If* he listened.

Beneath her mantle, she grabbed up handfuls of her skirts. Above it, she set her chin high. "I did not expect any to come for me. After all, would you not think fire a fitting end to the woman you did not wish to wed?"

His hands flexed again as if he imagined her throat between them. "Not as long as you benefit me."

He referred to his sister. But not even for Quintin Boursier would he, himself, have gone into the fire to bring out his hated wife. Why that should make her ache, she did not know.

She pushed her shoulders back. "Do what you will and be done, Boursier. I am tired."

He took a step toward her, but as she braced herself, a voice sounded from behind.

"My lord!" his knight called.

"I have her!" Boursier answered. "Return to your post."

"Aye, my lord."

Boursier narrowed his gaze on her. "What I intend to do is a dish best served in one sitting. Thus, until I am able to savor every moment, I shall wait."

Just as Murdoch had sometimes done, postponing punishment as a means of swelling her fear. And those instances of retaliation—every pain inflicted planned—had been worse than his usual fare.

Though dread sought to overthrow anger, El pushed it down. "As you wish, but do not think I shall suffer more for fear of what awaits me."

Bayard stared at her. He had not considered such, but he would not dissuade her. "Aye, you shall suffer more," he said and grasped her arm.

As the anger he could feel pulsing through her was tempered by the fear he also felt despite her efforts to conceal it, he did not expect her to resist, but she wrenched free.

"Unless you intend to work your revenge now, do not touch me!" Her eyes challenged him, seemingly unaware he was not closed to the emotion she held beneath such a face. It was nearly enough to make him pity her many failures. A husband she did not want. A husband she had. Forfeiture of Boursier lands she wanted. Forfeiture she did not have. Escape she sought. Escape she did not find. For all of her guile, she had gained worse than nothing.

That last easing his own emotions, he gestured her forward. "Come."

She whipped the hood up over her head and stepped past him, only to swing around and thrust a finger against his chest. "I am not"—she thrust again—"afeared"—another thrust—"of you!"

She knew not the waters in which she flung herself. Fortunately for her, he knew, just as he was aware that this pitiful show of hers was more an attempt to convince herself she was unafraid than to persuade him. Just as he knew his threats of retribution had provoked her fear beyond what was necessary. Rather, what *should* be necessary.

Feeling tenfold more tired than before she had led him on this chase, he grasped her wrist and drew her near.

She snapped her head up, causing the hood to once more settle around her shoulders and moonlight to reflect in wide-flung eyes that portended further argument and scorn.

"Cease, Thomasin," he said. "I am angry, and I think even the Lord would agree you have given me much cause to be, but no matter the lies told of me, no matter the words I wield against those you wield, I will not beat you."

Her finely arched eyebrows drew near.

"Forsooth, there shall be consequences," he continued, "but only those that will, at worst, frustrate and anger you. Hopefully, they will also deter you from engaging in further dangerous behavior."

She tilted her head farther back, and he noted scratches across one side of her face that were surely the result of her ascent of the tree. "I do not believe you."

"Doubtless, I have Agatha to thank for that," he murmured, and possessed by something he knew he should examine before acting upon, lightly touched her cheek.

She drew back, tugged to free her wrist, and gave a sharp gasp.

It was then he felt the stickiness against his palm. Shifting his gaze to her hand, he saw the back of it was raked with blood. Too, several of her fingernails were torn. Guessing her wrist also bore evidence of her escape attempt, and for this she was pained, he released her. "Apologies," he said. "I did not mean to hurt you."

He expected her to quickly put space between them, but she went very still, the only movement about her a deepening frown.

He traveled his gaze over the curves of her face and once more wondered at the lie that she lacked comeliness. She was not just lovely, she was beautiful. And when her lips parted, he forgot the vow he had long ago made himself, forgot the danger inherent in desire born from the shallow depths of beauty, and lowered his head and put his mouth to hers.

For one moment while surprise held her unmoving, he tasted the woman he had taken to wife. Over the next several moments, while surprise gripped him, she tentatively and with quick sips of breath, tasted him.

"Ah, nay!" she cried and stumbled back.

Bayard loathed being at a loss for anything, but as he moved his gaze from her bent head to her heaving shoulders, he knew there was no way to make light of what he felt.

He stepped forward. "'Tis cold, Thomasin, and the morrow and whatever trials await us will soon be upon us." He turned a hand around her upper arm and, when she did not resist, drew her against his side and urged her forward.

Though neither spoke as they started back to camp, Bayard felt her spirit stir in the air about them, next the surety of her step, then the lengthening of her stride. By the time they gained the camp, he was not surprised that anger had once more settled over her.

Beneath the glares of his men, she pulled free and went to stand before the smoking remains of his tent.

Bayard accepted the blankets his squire brought him, crossed to Thomasin's side, and thrust them at her. "You shall bed before the fire."

She hooked an arm around the blankets. "I expected no better."

As he turned away, he caught sight of Father Crispin where he stood to the left. Bayard acknowledged him with a nod and knew from the man's glance at Thomasin and the push of his eyebrows that he sought permission to speak with her.

It would likely be of no benefit, Bayard knowing from his own circumstances that one must be receptive to counsel for it to do more than graze one's conscience, as evidenced by his willful resolve to have Constance Verdun for his own and her determination that never would she belong to him. Still, he inclined his head and, as Father Crispin approached Thomasin, withdrew to the bordering trees to observe their exchange.

The priest halted alongside Thomasin. When she did not acknowledge him, he asked, "For what did you work this foul deed, my lady?"

She turned her face to him. "You know why I did it."

He nodded slowly. "Just as I know you must needs repent."

Her expression tightened. "For trying to escape a marriage I do not want?"

"My lady—"

"Nay!" Her raised voice gained the attention of the few who did not already watch her. "I am not your lady. Nor your lord's lady. And never shall I be."

Bayard's muscles bunched, but though she dishonored him before all, he checked the desire to drag her into the trees. After what had happened in the wood, it was best not to be alone with her.

Father Crispin laid a hand on her shoulder. "The baron but fulfilled the king's command, Lady Thomasin. Thus, as what has been done cannot be undone, for the good of all, you must resign yourself to being a Boursier."

Though the priest did not seem to notice what his words wrought upon Thomasin, Bayard saw it and strode forward.

She shrugged off Father Crispin's hand. "I am not a Boursier!"

He took a step nearer. "Pray, make your peace with this marriage."

"'Tis not a marriage!" She whipped her gaze to Bayard. "I am not his—"

Her teeth snapped closed. Still, she had revealed enough to alert Bayard to her plotting.

He halted alongside Father Crispin and looked down at his wife who intended to present lack of consummation as grounds for an illegitimate marriage, who had surely lied in telling she had taken lovers on the chance he would be more inclined to leave her virtue intact. Thus, when she was examined, it would be revealed that she had never been with a man.

Still, Bayard tried to talk himself down from the inevitable by telling himself King Edward would not declare Boursier lands forfeit, that he would but order the marriage consummated. Unfortunately, the assurances did not stick, for the whims of kings often transcended logic and one would be foolish to lay such a risky bet.

"You have done all you can, Father," Bayard said as he held Thomasin's gaze and wondered if she realized what must happen this eve. "Find your rest."

"'Tis imperative you and I speak," the priest said low.

"And so we shall. Later."

With a sound low in his throat, Father Crispin turned away.

Bayard leaned near Thomasin. "Not a marriage? You are right, but this night it shall be." He took the blankets she clasped to her chest and pulled her across the camp.

13

"Your word!" El gasped. "You—"

"Seek your beds," Boursier ordered his men who feigned disinterest in their lord and lady. "Sir Miles, my wife and I shall avail ourselves of your tent."

The man nodded and caught the blankets tossed to him.

Boursier halted before the tent set farthest from the others, shoved aside the flap, and pushed El in ahead of him.

She swung around. "What of your vow?"

He straightened as much as was possible beneath the low-ceilinged tent. "It stands. However, as recently demonstrated, you are not averse to my touch, and so we have all night to gain your consent."

"I will not give it."

"I believe you will."

"And if I do not?"

"Then you shall have another day in which to plot against me, as I shall have another day in which to seek a means of seducing my wife."

El fought the impulse to find a way past him, logic dictating it would be a laughable endeavor.

Boursier stepped forward. "Now let us see how long ere you once more return my kisses."

How she wished that was a lie, but when his mouth had covered hers in the wood, there had been something almost pleasant—never before known to her—in the feel of his lips. Only his lips. No restraining hands or weighty legs pinning her. For however long it had lasted, and she could not know if it had been a moment or many, she had forgotten the source of the pleasure that moved through her. When she had come back to her senses, she had feared herself almost as much as she feared Boursier, and a return to anger had seemed the only means of regaining control. Unfortunately, she had worked herself into such a frenzy she had not thought through the words she had flung at the priest. Words that could have revealed the truth of her but had, instead, been perceived as a threat.

Boursier put a hand beneath her jaw, lifted her chin. "And so we begin," he said.

There was not enough light to see him clearly, but she saw his head lower and felt his breath across her face.

"You need not do this, not now," she pitched her voice low so those outside would not hear. Such was her pride—born from humiliation earned in Murdoch's household when, as a new bride at the age of ten and six, she had pleaded for aid in subverting his cruelty. Her efforts had earned her the pitying regard of women servants and the taunts and sly glances of Murdoch's men. "I give you my word that my virtue is long gone, that were I examined, no maiden would be found."

His mouth brushed hers, and he pushed the mantle off her shoulders.

"Bayard!" she gasped.

The hand that searched up her side laces stilled. "Now I am Bayard to you?"

"Bayard," she said again, hoping her concession would give him pause long enough for her to convince him to further delay consummation.

He laughed, then swung her up against his chest and strode to the rear of the tent where he lowered her atop a pile of blankets.

Finding herself on her back and unable to rise for the man above her, she tried to roll to the side, but he returned to the place between neck and shoulder that, on the night past, had done something nearly as devastating as his kiss had done this eve. And it was happening again, easing the tension from her and loosing her breath on a small, voiced sigh.

In that moment, she knew the traitor in her would yield. And in the midst of the pain to come, Bayard Boursier would gain indisputable evidence there was nothing virtuous about her. But proving him wrong could be bittersweet if the blame for her barren womb was Murdoch's and she found herself with child—she who was not Thomasin and, thus, not truly wed to this man.

The hopelessness of it caused her eyes to pool. Alarmed, she squeezed them closed, for tears had never served her well with Murdoch. Indeed, he had liked them so much that one of her first acts of defiance had been to wield their absence against him. It had not stopped him, just as her struggles had little effect, but there had been some satisfaction in lessening his enjoyment.

Still more tears squeezed from beneath her lids, evidencing the past three years under her uncle's protection had been too kind. Then a sob slipped past her lips.

Bayard lifted his head. "Thomasin?"

Wondering at the concern in his voice, she struggled to keep further sounds of distress from escaping, but her chest convulsed with another sob.

He drew back, asked again, "Thomasin?"

Was it possible a woman's tears affected him in a way they had not affected Murdoch—that rather than rouse him, they stayed him? If so, had her aunt made use of them?

Continuing to suppress her own misery, she tried to fathom Bayard's face above hers, but it was too dark to determine if anything in his expression reflected what was in his voice.

Deciding she had little to lose and, perhaps, much to gain, she did not hold in the next sob, nor ease the tremble in her voice when she said, "Pray, do not do this. As God is my witness, I have no innocence left to plunder."

In the silence, she was struck by the thought that even a woman wed twenty years who had birthed a handful of children would have more innocence about her than the one who had been Murdoch's wife for only two years.

"I am tired, Thomasin," Bayard said. "More than I want you, I want my rest, and could we do this another night, we would." His sigh warmed her face. "But you are my wife, you are a Boursier, and no matter if we battle 'til the end of our days, ours *is* a marriage. It lacks only proof you are no longer a maiden."

Then tears would not dissuade him.

He lowered his head, and his mouth touched hers so gently it nearly made her forget she was trapped beneath him and would soon be reacquainted with pain such as she had not known in years. Nearly.

Panic welled, and she thrust her hands to his chest, causing his mouth to loosen. "There is proof aplenty I am no maiden," she said and should have stopped there, but she could not contain her desperation. "In the most unholy manner, I have been defiled. Time and again and again!"

Bayard drew a deep breath. "Let us be done with——" He jerked as the meaning of her words unfolded. Though earlier she had boasted of numerous lovers, this was no boast. This was dark. And ugly.

Which was the lie? Or might both be lies? Both true? He had heard that before her mother dispatched her to her noble father three years past, Thomasin had labored in the household of a great lord. And some nobles believed it was their right to bed women who served them, willing or otherwise, even those as young as Thomasin would have been. Had that been her fate? One ravishment after another?

Anger roused by the possibility she had suffered such, he searched backward through his experiences with her and stopped upon what she had spoken on the night past when she had come up out of her dream threatening to kill the one who stalked her behind her lids.

You are not the man of my dream, she had said. *That one is dead.* And rather than regret, she had exuded something between relief and satisfaction.

If it was true she had been abused, not merely another attempt to secure forfeiture of his lands, it would explain much about her—so much he was inclined to believe her. And it made him feel like a cur for trying to seduce her so the vanquished might yield up what she feared to yield. Indeed, what she might ever fear to yield if he did not more carefully handle this woman with whom he was destined to spend his life.

Peering at her face below his, he wished there was enough light to make out her features. "Thomasin?"

He heard her swallow, felt her chest quake.

Easing his weight off her, he lifted a hand to her face and felt moisture upon her cheek. "I did not know," he said, then slid an arm beneath her, rolled onto his back, and pulled her atop him.

She gave a little cry and tried to scramble off, but he held her there, and after some moments, she rasped, "Wh-what are you doing?"

"Taking a risk in giving you time to become accustomed to my person and my touch."

"Then you will not...I will not be made to pay the marital debt?"

"Marital debt," he muttered with distaste. "Nay, not this eve."

Where she lay trembling atop him, head raised as if she might better peer into his face than he had been able to peer into hers, he felt suspicion spring up alongside fear, and he was fairly certain of its source.

"Agatha and her lies have no place between us," he said gruffly. "Leave her where she is."

Hearing her teeth click, hoping it was from chill and not fear, he reached to the side, grasped the blankets they lay upon, and pulled them over her. "Sleep, Thomasin."

"If I must lie with you, can it not be at your side?"

"So you shall, but this is where we begin."

"I do not understand."

"As told, you must become accustomed to me, and I can think of no better way to accomplish that and gain your trust than this." At least, for as long as he could bear being so near her. Were he not fatigued—more, disturbed by what she had revealed—it might be unbearable now.

After some moments, she scooted down him, causing him to grit his teeth, and gingerly settled her cheek against the hollow of his throat and her hands to his shoulders. Not unbearable, but close, especially with the mussed hair atop her head tickling his chin and her breath feathering his collarbone.

Determinedly, he turned his thoughts to the one who had committed the atrocity against his wife such that she viewed lovemaking as no more than what the Church named the marital—or conjugal—debt. How would he render justice were the man not dead as told? Such brooding proved a good distraction until Thomasin pulled him back to an awareness of her body against his.

"I know you hate Agatha," she whispered, "but she has been good to me. Indeed, I may even owe her my life."

He doubted that.

"You will not let her die, will you, Bayard?"

Deciding it best not to discuss the woman, he said, "Go to sleep."

"But—"

"To sleep, Thomasin."

For what seemed hours, he stared at the canopy overhead and twisted his thoughts around the one who had defiled her. Throughout, she remained tense, evidencing sleep also eluded her—until he removed his arm from her waist to draw the blankets closer against the chill winter air.

The breath shuddered out of her. Though he had intended to hold to her throughout the night, he lowered his arm to his side. Minutes later, her breathing turned slow and deep.

Wondering if he would ever be able to intimately touch her as a husband ought to be able to do, he joined her in sleep.

14

―❦―

SOMEONE WAS SIGHING.

Wonderfully warm, happily muddled, El wondered if it was her. The next softly voiced breath confirmed it. But what was so pleasurable that she was sighing in this space between sleep and awakening?

That you are safe, said the soothing voice it had taken a year to come near to believing. *That you are alone in your bed. That there is no threat of Murdoch coming to you. That all you need do is rest and float and worry not what lies in wait. Safe, El. Now and evermore.*

"Evermore," she whispered, and frowned when her lips brushed something. Or had something brushed her lips? The latter, she realized as it lightly traced the lower curve, then the bow above.

Not safe, a voice railed against the soothing one. *Not alone. What cruel game does Murdoch play?*

"Thomasin, I must needs rise."

This time a sharply indrawn breath sounded from her. Not Murdoch. Not her name spoken.

She lifted her head. In the bit of light that told the new day had dawned, she met the gaze of the man who lay beneath her.

All that had been forgotten in sleep tumbled back. Though she was hardly safe and certainly not alone, she nearly laughed with relief to see it was Bayard Boursier with whom she shared a bed. "Oh," she said, becoming aware of the sounds of an awakening camp. "Is it over?"

"Over?" His frown was more heard than seen.

She moistened her lips. "Your attempt to accustom me to your person."

"Aye," he drawled, "for now—though my *attempt,* as you call it, proved most effective."

She was afraid to ask, but said, "How is that?"

"You are still here, are you not? And without me holding to you throughout the night."

There was no disputing that. Though she had awakened to his touch upon her lips, she was not anchored to him in any way—had made of him her pillow the whole night. Discomfited, she said, "Certes, I was tired."

"And content," he said, this time with what sounded like a smile.

"I was not!"

He chuckled, a sound she did not expect. "Where are your arms, Thomasin?"

Up around his shoulders, hands clasped behind his neck.

"Though you made yourself quite comfortable," he continued, "such comfort was denied me. Despite giving me little reason to rejoice in taking you to wife, it cannot be said you are undesirable. For that, I attempted to move you to my side partway through the night, but you would have none of it."

"I do not believe you." She hated herself for the retort that was pitifully disproved by the fact she had yet to loosen her hold on him.

"I assure you," he said as she slid her hands from his neck to his shoulders, "I am not in the habit of torturing myself."

She pushed off him, dropped to her knees beside him, and shed the blankets as she rose to her feet.

Boursier was nearly as quick to rise. As he straightened, he gripped his right shoulder and began kneading the muscles. "Unfortunately, I am the one who shall pay for your lesson."

Guilt rushed through her, but she turned from him.

"Remain within," he said and stepped away. He tossed back the tent flap, letting in a gust of chill air that made her shiver. "Thomasin?"

El looked up.

"Do not inconvenience me by making me chase after you again."

Inconvenience. That *was* all her efforts had amounted to. Thus, this day he would learn the truth about the woman he had not truly wed. If there was any good in it, it was that there would be no further opportunities for her to humiliate herself by clinging to him through the night and returning kisses she did not want.

She sighed. "I shall aspire to take myself in hand."

He glowered, dropped the flap, and left her to her dread.

How her conscience recoiled—so much it angered her. She should not feel remorse for the blow Boursier would be dealt this day, not after what he had done to her aunt. And yet...

The man who could have worked such wicked things upon her, and justified them to himself, had time and again pulled back from that edge, almost as if it was one with which he was unfamiliar. Or, perhaps, he no longer was. But people did not change that much, did they?

Tell him, her cautious side urged. *It will not bode well, but it will be far worse if you hand that honor to Griffin de Arell.*

She released a billowing breath, glanced over her shoulder at where Boursier conversed with his knights.

She should tell him. But what if, by some miracle, she were able to escape and save Magnus the misery of her recklessness? Even if it could be proved he knew nothing of her plan, as her guardian he would also pay a price.

"I cannot tell him," she whispered and caught the sound of footsteps amid the clank and jangle of armor.

She did not need to look around to know it was Boursier. Though she had avoided his gaze since exiting the tent a short while past, she looked across her shoulder as he drew alongside.

"'Tis time," he said.

El stared at what the light of day lit that the dark of night had not. His eyebrows and the hair at his brow were singed as if he had drawn near a flame.

"The fire!" she blurted. "You did come for me."

His lips thinned. "You are my wife."

Hating that he did not make it easy to loathe him, she murmured, "I am grateful, and I..." She drew a breath. "I am sorry my behavior placed you and your squire in danger."

He raised his eyebrows. "Dare I hope that means you will not behave rashly in future? Or is that too much a part of you, Thomasin?"

Not Thomasin, as he would soon learn. Elianor, as he would also learn unless she somehow kept her identity hidden. Regardless, great anger and dishonor he would know when he once more found himself reduced to a fool.

Tell him, the voice came again. *Tell him while there is still time.*

Leaving his question unanswered, she lowered her gaze down his figure that was outfitted for battle should the drawing of blood prove necessary to bring his sister home. But even in the absence of so much plate and chain mail armor, he was imposing, his presence alone commanding respect.

Respect that will be trampled when he learns of his error, the voice came again. *For a man such as The Boursier, that could prove a fate worse than forfeiture of his lands.*

El struggled to stay the course, but regardless of his past sins, she could not ignore that he had not added to them since divesting her of her role as captor, though she had certainly given him good cause to sin against her. There was nothing she could do about his lands, but she could at least spare him the public humiliation of having been duped by a woman.

"I will help you mount," he said and turned away.

"Bayard?"

He looked across his shoulder. "I am pleased I am still that to you."

Her use of his Christian name had not been intentional, and she wished it did not come so easily. "There is something I must needs tell you. Something that will spare you looking the fool."

His gaze narrowed. "What do you play at now?"

"Naught. When you captured me, you assumed I was Thomasin de Arell, and I did not set you right." She swallowed hard. "I should have."

He stared at her, growled, "I am full up with your games. Like it or nay, this day your father learns who is your lord."

El pulled a hand from beneath her mantle and closed it around his forearm. "I vow, De Arell is not my father, and if you attempt to present me as such, all you will gain is scorn and laughter." She shook her head. "I would not have that."

A muscle in his jaw jerked. "I am to believe you have a care for me—for my pride?"

"I should not, but I do. Your lands may be forfeit, but there is no reason to make matters worse by presenting to De Arell a woman who is not his daughter. Nor your wife."

His nostrils flared.

"'Tis true, Bayard. The marriage is invalid, for it was not Thomasin de Arell with whom you spoke vows."

"Then who?" he demanded, though his singular gaze told he did not believe her.

Inwardly, El squirmed. She knew escape was less possible now, but there was nothing to gain and could be more to lose by revealing she was Magnus Verdun's niece. She raised her chin higher. "Not Thomasin de Arell."

He pulled her hand from his arm and lifted it before her face. It was the ring he showed her. "Aye, Thomasin *Boursier*. And there is naught you can do to change that. As long as the king demands it, my wife you shall remain."

El stepped nearer him. "Pray, Bayard—"

"Enough!" He pulled her toward his men who were ready to ride. Though they cast their gazes elsewhere, they would be blind and deaf to not know of his displeasure as he lifted her onto her horse.

El held in the tears that aspired to her eyes, accepted the reins he thrust into her hands, stared after him as he strode toward his destrier.

"I can do no more," she whispered.

"You can be the wife the Bible commands you to be," the priest said as he urged his mount nearer hers.

She looked around. "*Were* I his wife."

Father Crispin sighed. "He deserves better than you. Better than that Verdun——" He slid his eyes heavenward as if to ask forgiveness for what he had nearly named her aunt. "That Verdun *woman*," he finished and applied his heels to his horse.

As the animal carried him past, El wondered at his words that sounded more like those of a friend than a priest. Next, she considered Bayard's men. None looked her way, containing their curiosity as they had done when she had stepped from the tent this morn.

Though she had expected sly glances and crude asides following her night with Bayard, there had been none. She had heard a lord's men were a reflection of himself, and as it had proved true with Murdoch, so it was true with her uncle whose men, for all their ferocity, showed courtesy and respect off the battlefield. To wit, Bayard's men ought to be as repulsive as Murdoch's, perhaps worse. They were not.

15

⎯⎯∽◉∽⎯⎯

THE MEN QUINTIN had taken with her were outside Castle Mathe's walls, smoke from the fires of their encampment casting gray shadows against white-washed stone.

Bayard glanced at the sky. From the sun's position, it could not be more than two hours since he and his men had left the encampment. Expecting Quintin would ride out to meet him, he spurred his destrier ahead of his knights.

Soon, three riders appeared—all men, meaning Quintin was inside the castle since nothing would keep her from accompanying those who rode to greet their lord.

Feeling the storm within seek the surface, Bayard reminded himself he was not without recourse. He had Thomasin regardless that she proclaimed otherwise. Providing De Arell had a care for his daughter, the man would relinquish Quintin to protect Thomasin from retaliation—not only Bayard's, but that of the king who would now order Quintin to wed into the Verdun family.

As Bayard had done throughout the ride, he pondered Thomasin's pleading that her lie be believed. So genuine she had seemed. Because she feared her father? Feared him more than the one who was now her husband?

"My lord!" called Sir Victor, a man as dry as dry could be.

Bayard reined in. Moments later, his senior household knight halted his destrier.

"For what did you allow my sister to enter De Arell's walls?" Bayard demanded.

The man settled his hands on his saddle's pommel and slowly leaned forward as if nothing in the world were urgent. "As Lady Quintin is wont to do, my lord, she did not listen. Thus, though De Arell denied holding you, your sister was determined to enter and see for herself."

"You could not turn a *woman* from such a reckless quest, Sir Victor?"

The knight shrugged, though it was not from lack of deference. Simply, it was who he was—a man who allowed little to settle too long upon his shoulders. A good thing in many circumstances, but not this. "As your father oft noted, my lord, Lady Quintin would have fared better had she been born a man."

As those who had accompanied their lord reined in behind him, Bayard said, "Tell me what happened."

"De Arell invited your sister to his table. When we were unable to convince her to decline, five others and I accompanied her within. Your lady sister sat at De Arell's side and, throughout the meal, demanded to be told where you were held. He refused her."

"Because he did not hold me!"

"'Tis most obvious now, my lord."

Bayard dragged patience up from his depths. "Continue, Sir Victor."

"De Arell should not have laughed at her, though I cannot say her response would not have been the same had he not mocked her." He heaved a sigh. "I saw what was coming but could not reach her quickly enough to prevent it. She drew her dagger upon De Arell and laid the blade to his throat."

Bayard clenched his hands, looked to the castle, imagined his sister imprisoned in one of the towers whose banners boasted the green and black of De Arell. Providing the Baron of Blackwood had not harmed Quintin, she would be pacing.

"And when still he would not tell," Sir Victor continued, "she cut him."

Bayard heard his knuckles crack. He was not surprised at what his sister had done, for though she was a fine lady when it suited, she was far less a lady when it did not. He returned his gaze to the knight. "How badly did she injure De Arell?"

"Only deep enough to anger him."

Bayard turned a hand around his sword hilt in anticipation of the blood he would shed. "I assume she was subdued."

"Aye, as you know, she may think herself a warrior, but she has not the skills."

And she had not had her man-at-arms, Rollo, there to defend her. "What harm did De Arell do her?"

"He landed her upon the table and took the dagger from her. That is all."

All he had seen. "Where were you and the others?"

"We were all present, my lord." The knight drew a long breath. "Unfortunately, we were unable to aid your sister, for De Arell's men drew around us."

What fool thing were you thinking, Quintin? Bayard silently took her to task.

"We were turned out." Sir Victor glanced over his shoulder. "Thus, we know not where your sister is held."

Had she been abused? Ravished? The ache in his teeth warning that if he did not cease their grinding he would break a tooth, he eased his jaws. "This day, De Arell will deliver my sister to me." He looked behind to where Thomasin had reined in.

She met his gaze, slowly shook her head to refute his claim.

He swept his arm forward and called, "Ride!"

Amidst the thunder of hooves, Bayard led his men across the meadow that had shed a good deal of its snow.

Those who had accompanied Quintin to Castle Mathe gathered as their lord neared and greeted him with calls and raised arms. Still, their faces were anxious. And for good reason. Though it could not be said

Bayard Boursier was harsh, neither did he tolerate senseless errors. Thus, in the midst of winter when most were wont to pass the season in idleness—out of the chill wind—they would train. And train hard.

"Archers, mount up!" Bayard shouted, causing a dozen men to run for their bows and horses.

As El allowed her mount to be carried forward with the others into the smoke of numerous campfires, she considered the imposing fortress lorded by Griffin de Arell. A man-at-arms stood in each embrasure between battlements, and more soldiers were atop the gatehouse.

If De Arell was not among them, he soon would be, and then the lie Bayard believed she had told would be made truth amid the grind of his humiliation.

Bayard slowed and led his men past the tents and across the stretch of land before the castle walls. A hundred feet back from the drawbridge raised against him, he dragged on the reins. "De Arell!" he shouted.

El halted her mount amongst those who flanked her and resettled her hood upon her head. Not that its cover would keep her from being revealed, but it was of momentary comfort. As she waited for the Baron of Blackwood to show himself, she pressed a hand to her roiling belly.

"Boursier!" a voice assaulted the silence.

El returned her gaze to the gatehouse. The bearing of the man who appeared there proclaimed him the lord of Castle Mathe, though not his age. She had imagined that the one who was to have been her husband had Bayard wed Thomasin would have more years about him—at least two score and five. However, he appeared to be younger by ten or so years, meaning it was in his youth he had sown Thomasin upon a commoner.

"I have come for my sister!" Bayard shouted.

De Arell smiled. "For what do you think I would give over my prisoner—a woman who, in the presence of all, tried to murder me?"

Bayard looked around and found El's gaze in the depths of her hood, then turned his destrier and guided the animal toward her.

"Thomasin," he said as he drew alongside.

She peered up at him, doubted the shadow cast by the hood hid the distress upon her face.

He set a hand to her forearm and leaned near. "You are my wife now and under my protection. No harm can he do you."

Though jolted by his concern, of greater note was that he believed she—rather, Thomasin—feared her father. "I am not frightened of De Arell. There is naught he can do to me. Indeed, he will likely thank me for suffering you a fool and sparing his daughter marriage to The Boursier. Thus, the only protection I require is that which will save me from your anger."

His gaze glittered darkly, hand dropped from her. "You truly think me a simpleton."

"Nay, merely deceived."

He reached up, yanked the hood back, and looked to the gatehouse. "I have your daughter, De Arell. Now deliver my sister to me!"

El met De Arell's gaze, tensed in anticipation of his denial.

He stared, shouted something to his men, and strode from sight.

"My lord!" called the knight named Sir Victor.

El fastened her gaze on him. Brow furrowed, he hurried his mount toward Bayard.

He knew. After all, he had been in De Arell's hall. Thus, he must have seen the man's daughter. The realization frightened El, but she was grudgingly grateful the man might save Bayard from further humiliation.

Sir Victor halted before his lord. "Surely you do not say this is—"

"Lady Thomasin Boursier," Bayard said.

The way he said it—low and threatening, as if daring the knight to gainsay him—made her tense further. Now the truth would be told.

Darkness welled through Bayard as he stared at his man whose only failing was Quintin's ability to maneuver him where he should not go. For that, he had surely assembled the garrison to ride in search of their lord. But in the matter of Thomasin, did he also fail? While in De Arell's hall, had he been presented with another of that name?

Almighty, he called to the heavens, *if this woman is not De Arell's daughter, all is lost.* And he would be left holding a fool's cap. But it made no sense. Did it?

His breath sounding like a wind in his ears, he searched backward through these past days—Agatha's reaction in the underground when he had threatened De Arell's daughter, Thomasin's unwitting divulgence that she was not ten and seven, Agatha's warning yestermorn that he knew not what he had done, Thomasin's fervent avowal to Father Crispin that hers was not a marriage, her revelation this morn that she was not Thomasin.

But who else would dare what this woman had done other than one who did not wish to wed him? There was yet Thomasin's father, but it made no more sense today than it had days earlier that De Arell would send women to work his ill, especially his own daughter. Had he sent another?

"You say this is not Thomasin de Arell, Sir Victor?" he demanded.

The man leaned in. "I but question whether it is truly she."

Bayard refused to indulge in the relief that sought to seep through him. "Then you have not laid eyes upon Lady Thomasin?"

He shook his head. "She was not present in her father's hall, my lord, but her father told that she was abovestairs."

To conceal the absence of his daughter? Bayard began to smile, while beside him Thomasin groaned. Her deception was undone. Still, a nag of uncertainty remained.

The drawbridge began to let out its clattering chains, drawing Bayard's gaze past Sir Victor.

De Arell was coming out. And to assure their lord's safety, archers appeared between the battlements, arrows nocked, bows drawn.

Bayard's archers responded in kind.

"My lord?" Sir Victor pressed.

"Soon we shall know the truth of it," Bayard said and looked to the woman at his side. "You had best pray you *are* Thomasin de Arell."

Her smile was sorrowful. "No amount of prayer can change that I am not."

Why did she persist? He returned his gaze to the drawbridge that slowly lowered to reveal a mounted rider beyond the bars of the portcullis. Shortly, the massive wooden structure met the ground with a reverberating crash, and the portcullis began to rise.

Resenting the loss of his eye that forced him to turn his head to fully assess what he stood against, Bayard considered the archers on the walls. A slip of the finger was all that lay between him and an arrow to the heart.

"Come, Thomasin," he said as De Arell guided his horse onto the drawbridge.

"Bayard—"

"Say naught!" he commanded, then seized her reins and guided her forward.

De Arell halted his destrier near the end of the drawbridge and eyed Thomasin.

With displeasure or questioning? Displeasure, Bayard determined, though still he was nagged. He reined in twenty feet distant from the man.

Hands light upon the pommel of his saddle, the corners of his mouth curling slightly, the lord of Castle Mathe shifted his regard to Bayard. "Tell me, Boursier, are your lands forfeit or nay?"

"Nay."

"Then you spoke vows with my daughter?" He glanced at Thomasin.

That the knave did not otherwise acknowledge her caused the claws of that which crept up Bayard's back to more deeply pierce his flesh. "As ordered by the king, the alliance was made."

"Bayard," Thomasin tried again, "he—"

"Now you will release my sister."

De Arell shook his head with mock regret. "I would, but should the king, through some beneficence, honor your marriage, it will fall to me to wed Lady Quintin."

Disavowing all he implied, telling himself De Arell and his daughter made sport of him, Bayard leaned forward. "It falls to you to wed Elianor of Emberly."

Once more, De Arell looked upon the woman who had to be his daughter. "That is no longer possible, is it, my lady?" He arched an eyebrow. "I am right about you, am I not?"

Thomasin inclined her head.

"I cannot say I am displeased." This time his smile showed teeth. "Word came early this morn that you had gone missing from your guardian's demesne. Thus, he has ridden to Ellesmere Abbey to search you out." He looked back at Bayard. "Mistakenly, of course."

Her guardian. Ellesmere.

How the flesh of Bayard's neck stung! "What game do you play, De Arell?"

"Not I, though your *wife* makes my family part of hers by taking the name of one dear to me." He peered over his shoulder. "Show yourself, Thomasin!"

16

FEELING THE POUND of his heart, Bayard followed De Arell's gaze to the gatehouse roof.

An archer stepped back, and a woman appeared between the battlements.

"There is my daughter, Boursier. Younger than your *wife* by several years."

Though distant, there was no mistaking the woman was more a girl than the one at Bayard's side, nor that she was plain of face as was told.

Everything slammed together—every godforsaken piece—but still he denied it. Denounced it. Rejected it. Not only for the loss that would be his family's, but for the pity and attraction he had felt for the woman who had wrought his downfall, the same for whom he had allowed himself the smallest hope they might make peace enough so all the days of their lives would not be cursed.

Admit it, he told himself. *The Boursier who suffers no fools has been made one—worse, in full sight of his enemy.*

Anger taking a long stride through him, he bitterly accepted that what De Arell told with such satisfaction was as true as when Bayard had come upon the man's brother with Constance. Just as his first wife's beauty had exposed the vein in his neck, his second wife's beauty flayed him wide open.

What he could not yet see for the emotions nearly blinding him was the identity of the one who was not De Arell's daughter. Knowing he ought to know, he swung his gaze to her.

Though what shone from her eyes looked like regret, he named it deception.

"At last," De Arell said, "the mighty Boursiers, ever taking what is not rightfully theirs, brought to heel."

He referred to the barony of Godsmere and Castle Adderstone to which his sire, Ulric de Arell, had aspired, and Constance Verdun whom his brother, Serle, had pursued even after she was wed to another.

Bayard loosened a fist in anticipation of his sword hilt.

"And by a woman, no less," Griffin de Arell struck again.

Bayard closed his fingers around cold steel.

"Bayard," the woman at his side entreated.

Reason edging aside rage—assisted by the long shadow thrown by the archer whose arrow was trained upon him—he released the hilt.

De Arell made a sound of approval and turned his attention to the woman. "You took my daughter's name."

"As 'twas assumed I was she," she said softly, "I did not dissuade Baron Boursier. I had to protect my family."

He returned to Bayard. "I knew something was afoul when you did not come for Thomasin—that never would you forfeit. Thus, it came as no surprise when your sister told that you had been taken. The only surprise is the one who took you." He looked to the deceitful woman. "For all you tried to do, Lady—and I thank you for it—I doubt your uncle will be pleased."

Inwardly, Bayard jerked. Here was the reason it was not possible for De Arell to wed Elianor of Emberly. Already she was wed. Falsely so.

The guile! The cunning! The same as Constance!

Feeling as if his insides were twisting out, he narrowed his gaze on her.

"I tried to tell you," she whispered.

He bared his teeth. "When you were without choice."

De Arell shifted in the saddle. "What do you think the king will do with this?"

What *would* he do? Even when told of what had transpired—further degrading Bayard—would he waver on his word that he would accept no excuse were an alliance not made by the given day? Would Godsmere truly be forfeit? Quite possible, for what liege wished to number among his vassals one so heinously duped?

De Arell sighed. "You know not how I yearned to shout from the battlements 'twas not my daughter you held." He shrugged. "Though it would hardly please my brother that I did not, still I am satisfied."

Bayard wrenched his sword from its scabbard.

"Bayard!" the treacherous one cried. Had she not grasped his arm, he would have put heels to his destrier to meet at swords with the one who mocked him.

De Arell did not set his own blade before him but threw up an arm to command his archers to stand down. "Enough, then." He glared at Bayard. "I have my bit of flesh, and 'tis sufficient."

Bayard's chest heaved with an emotion so staggering it returned him to the desecration of his marriage bed. Determinedly, he dragged himself back to this moment and set his gaze to the hand upon him. "Pray hard, Elianor of Emberly. For yourself and your accursed uncle."

Her eyes widened further. "Magnus had naught—"

"Another lie?" He made no attempt to temper how dark his soul was in that moment. "Regardless, your family *will* suffer."

She released him.

He lowered his blade. "I will take my sister now, De Arell."

"She is not yours to take." The man's destrier shifted, tossed its head, and was settled with a pat to the neck. "Your sister attempted to slay me"—he lifted his chin to reveal the scabbed gash beneath—"and for that none will deny my right to hold her. Thus, until such time as I determine what to do with Lady Quintin, she remains." He frowned. "Of course, she is not much of a lady, is she?"

Bayard could not remember another time he had felt so powerless. Regardless of the sieges, skirmishes, and raids waged between their families, the Boursiers had more often prevailed, and whatever their losses, it was never even close to ruinous. Now to find himself at the mercy of another! And all for the treachery of Elianor of Emberly, the foolishness of Quintin, and the audacity of Griffin de Arell.

He tightened his grip on his sword.

It will benefit Quintin none if an arrow is put through you, he told himself and, with effort, returned his sword to its scabbard. "A pity my sister did not kill you."

"I would not be surprised if that was her intent," De Arell said. "But worry not. As long as daggers are kept from her, she need not fear me."

"I would see her."

"I will allow it. Indeed, with day soon to fade, 'twould be ill-mannered of me not to offer you a night's lodging."

It was hardly a sincere offer, but Bayard would accept it since the nearer he drew to Quintin, the greater the possibility of bringing her out of Castle Mathe.

"Of course, the invitation is extended to your wife as well." De Arell once more flashed his teeth.

Bayard seethed. The man took far too much enjoyment in eschewing Elianor of Emberly's name in favor of her false marital status.

Bayard glanced at where she sat once more working the ring around her finger, her gaze upon the gatehouse roof where Thomasin de Arell stood. "As it would be ill-mannered not to accept," he said, "we shall avail ourselves of your hospitality."

"Then come." De Arell started to turn his mount.

"Surely you do not think I would enter your lair without a watch upon my back?" Bayard said.

Annoyance flickered across De Arell's face, but he said, "I know I would not," and swept a hand toward Bayard's men. "Choose a half dozen if it pleases you."

"Three shall suffice." Squire Lucas, Sir Victor, and the priest—the latter should a witness of high repute be needed. Bayard looked to Magnus Verdun's niece. "Remain here."

As it hurt too much to gaze upon his hatred, El continued to watch Thomasin de Arell whose curiosity brimmed over the wall and wished she had not tried to avert King Edward's decree. Too, how much better had she never glimpsed in Bayard a man different from the one who had worked ill upon her aunt.

When he spurred his horse back toward his men, she looked to Griffin de Arell.

He watched her out of eyes the color of rough seas—darkest blue, almost black. And intense, as was the rest of him. His dark blonde hair was cropped close at the sides, the crown longer and lighter as of one who is often out-of-doors. His face was passably handsome, but the growth of beard that was several days too long made him appear coarse. Too, though he was not near to being an old man, there were lines in his face that would not likely be found in Bayard's for another dozen years, though the latter was only three years younger.

"So, you aspired to rid our families of the vile Boursier," he said.

Resenting the easy manner in which he spoke, as if they were allied against a common evil, El retorted, "Be assured, Baron de Arell, had it been possible to rid my family of yours as well, I would have."

His eyebrows jumped. "Mayhap marriage to you would *not* be preferable to marriage to the Boursier woman."

El tipped her chin up. "Assuredly not, for I would have cut your throat." It was a lie, but he could not know that.

He snorted. "Your threat falls short of its mark, my lady. Were you capable of such, Boursier would not have gone missing from his bed. He would have been found dead in it."

How she resented being so easily known!

"As already told," he said, "I thank you for sparing my daughter marriage to Boursier, for even your uncle is a better choice than what might have been."

As if Magnus were foul! "Better for your daughter," she snapped, "not Baron Verdun."

His face darkened. "If you believe Quintin Boursier a better match for your uncle, you cannot have met the termagant."

El knew this was not the direction she ought to go, but her churning emotions pushed her onward. "'Tis not necessary to meet her to know—"

"You believe my daughter is unworthy of your uncle?" There was something dangerous in his eyes.

She had not meant to imply that, had only been intent on arguing away her feeling of helplessness. But it seemed the enemy before her was not entirely without honor, for if she correctly interpreted his reaction, he cared for the young woman born into a common life.

She shook her head. "I did not say that, nor would I." She felt momentary relief at the sound of approaching horses, and almost laughed. Griffin de Arell could flare his nostrils and glare all he liked, but she was safer in his company than Bayard's.

"Take me to my sister, De Arell," Bayard said when he once more gained her side.

The Baron of Blackwood turned his mount and started back across the drawbridge.

Though El longed to fall in behind Bayard with the three who had joined him, she urged her mount to keep pace with his. "You wish to know why I did it?" she asked.

He continued to stare after De Arell.

She dragged her teeth across her bottom lip. Gone was the night past when he had laid no cruel hand upon her, when he had shown concern for her fear, when he had made himself her pillow so she might become accustomed to him.

As they passed beneath the portcullis into the outer bailey, the wall walks of which teemed with garrison, El drew a deep breath. "I am sorry, Bayard."

He looked around, and his singular gaze was so sharp she felt a pain in her chest. "Not yet you are."

She believed it, though only long enough to recall his past threats. Before he could once more deny her his gaze, she said, "You forget that I am acquainted with your revenge. You will not harm me."

He slowly smiled. "All has changed."

More than his words, his tone shook her confidence, for it was frighteningly familiar. The last time she had heard a voice tainted with such was the eve of Murdoch's death when he had cornered her in the solar and demanded to know of the pouch of powders that had fallen from her sleeve. She had told him it was to ease the pain of her monthly flux, but he had not believed her and—

She blinked away the memory and came back to Bayard who watched her through a narrowed lid.

"All has changed," she concurred with a sickening turn of the heart. She could only hope and pray Magnus would not be made to suffer as well.

"Thomasin!" Griffin de Arell called.

El followed the man's turn of the head to the steps that descended from the gatehouse.

Stepping off them was the young woman who had exchanged stares with El from between the battlements. No mantle about her shoulders to ward off the chill, Thomasin snatched up her skirts without regard to her show of ankles and ran forward. Her lack of propriety reminded El of her youth. Of course, she had been no more than ten winters aged when last she had committed such an error.

De Arell halted his horse, and though his back was turned to El and the others, his stiffening shoulders evidenced he was displeased by his daughter's advance. But though she should have noted it herself, she did not drop her skirts until she drew near.

He stretched out a hand to bring her astride, but she continued past him.

"Thomasin!"

She threw a glance over her shoulder. "I would see who is me."

"She is Lady Elianor of Emberly," her father said.

She gasped and clapped a hand to her mouth. A moment later, she halted beside El. When she dropped her hand, a broad smile lit her face so completely that one could no longer call her plain. Still no beauty, but lovely in an easy way.

Thomasin glanced at Bayard and wrinkled her nose at his grim countenance. "Oh, Lady, that ye dared—and against The Boursier!" She laughed. "You must tell all!"

El ached for the humiliation that caused Bayard's wrath to convulse in the space between them. And yet, she did not think it innocently inflicted. Thomasin de Arell's eyes sparkled too much. She might be years younger than the one who had taken her name, but she knew what she did.

"Thomasin!" De Arell called.

She rolled her eyes. "We shall speak later," she said and swung away.

El looked at Bayard. He was as still as stone, the only movement about him the muscle in his jaw as he stared at the one who had driven the shard of humiliation deeper.

Once Thomasin was seated before her father, they continued across the second drawbridge toward the keep.

El peered up the edifice that stood at the center of the inner bailey. On the summer past, it had surely been white washed, for the paint yet shone fresh and bright. Even the outbuildings had received a fresh coat.

Before the steps that ascended to the keep's great hall, De Arell dismounted and lifted his daughter to the frozen ground. She turned toward El, but her father caught her arm.

"Make quick to the kitchen and tell Cook there shall be five more for supper." He nudged her toward the steps.

Thomasin gave a huff of discontent and mounted the steps as a young knight of handsome proportions descended them.

De Arell acknowledged him with a nod, then turned to the lad who had taken his destrier's reins. "Aid Lady Elianor in her dismount."

"Squire Lucas will tend her and keep watch over her in my absence," Bayard said and swung out of the saddle.

"As you wish."

El watched as Squire Lucas stepped to his lord's side to receive instructions. Though she could not hear what was said, she guessed Bayard was warning the young man against her.

Shortly, Bayard strode toward De Arell and demanded, "Where is she?"

His host made him wait while he conversed with the knight who had descended from his hall. The man nodded once and again, then remounted the steps.

"Your sister is in yon tower." De Arell nodded at the wall of the inner bailey.

"My lady?" Squire Lucas called to El.

She looked at where he had come alongside and leaned toward him.

As he lifted her down, she watched De Arell and Bayard, followed by Sir Victor and Father Crispin, stride opposite.

The moment her feet touched the ground, the squire released her.

Beneath her mantle, El clasped her hands and silently prayed her actions had not caused Quintin Boursier to suffer.

"Come, my lady." Squire Lucas gestured for her to precede him up the steps of the keep.

A short while later, the knight who had introduced himself as Sir Otto, threw open the door of a chamber and motioned El to enter.

She stepped past him to the center of the room, turned, and asked, "Where is Baron Boursier to bed, Sir Otto?"

His eyebrows arched above darkest brown eyes. "With his wife, of course."

Remembering the tone with which Bayard had threatened her, El swallowed hard and glanced past him to Squire Lucas who remained in the corridor. Forcing a smile, she said, "I thank you, Sir Otto."

He inclined his head. "I am pleased to be of service, my lady." He retreated, and as he drew the door closed, added, "Baron de Arell has ordered a bath delivered to your chamber to ease the labor of your journey."

Alone, El considered the chamber that was of good size and well furnished, and was surprised that De Arell had not placed Bayard and her in a room better suited to one's enemy.

She advanced on the bed and halted at the realization of what she did. Though tempted to sink down upon it, she would not have Bayard find her there. Because of her deceit, he was no longer the man of the night past, and though part of her did not wish to believe he would truly harm her, that credulous side of her had not seen his face, nor his hands that had flexed as if to feel her neck between them, nor heard his voice vowing vengeance.

El nearly pitied herself that she would once more suffer a man's cruelty, but no good would come of it. Somehow she would survive as she had done with Murdoch. However, for all her self-assurance, she shuddered at the prospect of another long, torturous journey.

17

⊷

THE DOOR BANGED against the wall, and there Quintin stood, a scowl on her face, arms folded over her chest. But the moment her gaze lit upon him, her defiance dissolved, and she ran forward.

"Bayard!"

He stepped into her prison, opened his arms, and wrapped them around her. Though he was still in the grip of anger, and some of it was her due, he allowed her to cling to him. After all, who knew what ills she had suffered? And Griffin de Arell would pay for every one of them.

She tipped her face up. "He has freed you?"

He shook his head. "Never did De Arell hold me, Quintin."

Like a pond disturbed by a pebble cast to its center, her brow rippled. "I do not understand. If 'twas not that vile mis—"

"'Twas not this vile miscreant," De Arell drawled.

Quintin lurched sideways to peer past Bayard. "Aye, miscreant," she said.

Bayard released her, stepped to the side. Though relieved she showed no signs of bruising or abrasions, it did not mean her garments did not hide marks of aggression. He looked to De Arell in the doorway. "I would speak with my sister alone."

The man settled a shoulder to the door frame. "I await your apology, Lady Quintin."

She put her chin in the air. "How gratifying to know you shall wait forever."

A smile tilted his lips. "That is not so long—at least, not for one who has the freedom to spend his days and nights as he pleases. You, however…"

She expelled a breath of anger.

He slid his gaze down her, the appreciation with which he did so causing Bayard to struggle against the impulse to set upon him. Then the man pushed off the door frame and gripped the door handle. "A half hour, Boursier. That is all."

Bayard longed to demand more, but he stayed his tongue. He had only three men with him, and one a priest. Now was not the time to challenge De Arell. That would come later.

Catching Sir Victor's gaze past the Baron of Blackwood, Bayard inclined his head to remind the man to remain alert.

When the door closed, Quintin demanded, "If not De Arell, who?"

"Elianor of Emberly."

Her head jerked as if he had slapped her. "Magnus Verdun's niece? She who makes of herself his leman?"

"The same you wished me to wed."

"But—"

"What harm has De Arell done you, Quintin?"

Annoyance flashed across her face. "He is arrogant, ill-tempered—"

"He struck you?"

"He would not dare!"

Then De Arell had not used his fists on her. Still, there were other ways to do harm. Bayard drew a deep breath. "I would know all that befell you."

"The knave took my dagger!"

Lord, grant me patience, he silently beseeched. "After you cut him, I presume."

"Would that I had cut him deeper!"

"What else did he do?"

She gestured at the room. "Know you how many days I have suffered this place?"

"Quintin!"

She frowned. "What?"

"Has De Arell abused you in any way?"

Her eyebrows rose. "Did the baron beat me? Toss up my skirts and do unto me deeds most foul?"

"Quintin!"

She crossed to the bed and dropped to the mattress. "Griffin de Arell is a churl, a knave, a miscreant. But nay, those things he did not do."

Bayard experienced such relief that he momentarily felt light of body. By the divisiveness of a woman, Godsmere might be lost, but at least Quintin would not bear the brutal scars of that loss. But that unsettled him in a different way. De Arell was a formidable enemy who ought to show no compunction against striking at the Boursiers through Quintin—even in spite of the king's decree that the three families ally.

"You should have sent for Rollo that he might accompany you," Bayard said.

"As I am sure you were told, his mother was ill. And 'tis not as if I did not have an impressive escort."

The difference was that the man-at-arms would have stood behind her while she dined with De Arell and likely would have prevented her from attacking her host. However, it was of no benefit to point that out.

"Now tell, Brother," she said, "how did Lady Elianor do what she did? More, why?"

"The answer to the first is Agatha of Mawbry."

Her eyes widened. "Agatha."

He knew she was remembering the severe woman who had been put out of Castle Adderstone. Lest her thoughts moved on to Constance who had introduced the witch into their home all those years ago, he hastened to distract her with the answer to her other question. "As to why the lady did it…" He paused, recalling Elianor of Emberly's offer of an explanation that he had ignored. But he knew. "'Tis the same as our families have always done—sabotaging one another. In this instance, the hope that what appeared to be defiance of the king's decree would result in forfeiture of our lands."

Quintin mulled this, then patted the mattress. "I wish to hear all of it."

And she did—*nearly* all of it.

"Lady Quintin remains," De Arell pronounced and leaned back in his chair.

Bayard stepped nearer and pressed his palms to the table between them. "Your purpose, De Arell?"

"*That* we have already discussed, Boursier." He clasped his hands across his chest. "It has not changed, nor shall it, unless the king determines otherwise."

Bayard knew the path the man led him down, but though the likelihood of such an occurrence barely existed, he said gruffly, "Speak."

De Arell nodded at the chair his squire had placed opposite his own. "Seat yourself."

"I shall stand."

The man shrugged, as seemed his habit. "If Edward permits the delay in marrying my daughter, I shall return Lady Quintin to you—my new son-in-law."

Aye, this path Bayard's thoughts had traveled while he was in the tower room with his sister, but he did not believe the king would permit it any more than De Arell believed it.

"However," he continued, "if he orders a legitimate marriage between you and Lady Elianor..." He allowed the remainder to dangle like a trap set for prey—on a path Bayard had *not* been down.

Even Quintin had not gone there between her pacing and fuming, for it was surely as unthinkable to her as it was to him that he would willingly take to wife the one who had levied such dishonor upon him. But it was possible Edward would remedy the ill by ordering such. After all, alliances he sought, and alliances he would have.

"Thus," De Arell said, "if Edward determines the house of Boursier should join with the house of Verdun through you and Lady Elianor, your sister and I shall wed shortly."

Bayard seethed over the possessive glitter in the man's gaze. "For what do you think my lands will not be declared forfeit?"

De Arell leaned forward. "Consummation, which was once said to make a marriage—providing both parties consented."

Consummation that had not been had despite it being professed the morning after the wedding when Bayard had given the sheet to be hung out. *That* he could not disavow, though it was now known that the woman with whom he had exchanged vows was a widow whose virgin's blood had been shed long ago.

A light entered De Arell's gaze. "I wager you have had Elianor of Emberly to bed."

Bayard pressed his palms harder to the table to keep from lunging across it.

"You know Edward will conclude the same," De Arell said. "And though 'tis true I would be satisfied to see you forfeit, I know you will not do so willingly—as I would not. Hence, Lady Elianor has handed me an opportunity I gladly accept. I shall suffer marriage to your sister providing my daughter does not suffer marriage to you."

Bayard's innards churned. His enemy had come to the only conclusion to be had outside of forfeiture. If the Boursiers had any chance of holding their lands, it began and ended with Elianor of Emberly. But that left Quintin with this man, the only hope of it that she had suffered little thus far. And once more he was nagged by the lack of retaliation against her. It revealed the man was not entirely without honor as was expected of one sprung from the loins of Ulric de Arell who, doubtless, remained ensconced abovestairs.

But perhaps the son merely exercised caution lest harm done to Quintin brought the king's wrath down upon the De Arells...

Of course, one should not forget that Quintin was desirable, endowed with loveliness that, upon first acquaintance, disguised a heart not cast from the same mold as most women's. She liked being a lady, liked the finery of such, but she also liked being in control.

Bayard almost smiled. Despite what Quintin had done to De Arell, the man could not know what awaited him. But he might soon learn.

He straightened. "If Edward does as you believe he shall, I wager you yourself will regret choosing my sister over forfeiture."

De Arell's brow lowered.

"I shall take my men with me when I depart," Bayard said, "but I will depart only if Sir Victor remains behind to keep watch over my sister."

"No harm will she suffer."

"Let us be certain, hmm?"

After a moment, De Arell said, "Very well, he may remain."

"One more thing." Bayard loathed what he must ask of him. "As you bore witness to Elianor of Emberly's deceit, I would have you add your words to those Father Crispin will compose to inform the king of what transpired that caused me to wed one other than your daughter."

Griffin de Arell smiled. "It would be my pleasure."

Of course it would—a chance to heap further humiliation upon his enemy.

"Now," Bayard said, "I must speak with my *wife*."

18

THE BATH GREW cold, the steam that had risen from it following the delivery of bucket after bucket of water having dissipated.

Kneeling alongside the tub, forearms on its rim, El dipped a hand in the water. Lukewarm. Even so, it would be lovely to sink into—if she dared. She did not.

Whether it was a moment from now or hours, Bayard was coming, and for nothing would she be caught unclothed and more vulnerable than she already was. Thus, using a towel wet in bath water, she had cleaned away all evidence of these past days, including the dried blood beneath the bandage she had removed from her thigh.

She lifted moist fingers to hair that would benefit from a good washing—or, at least, a good brushing. Instead, she had set it aright by raking fingers through the tangles.

When the sound of footsteps and voices slid beneath the door, she hastened to her feet and hoped it was not Bayard outside the chamber. That hope scattered when his voice came through.

She wished she could blame her quaking limbs on the cold, but fear was responsible. It would be hard for a woman to do worse to a man than what she had done to Bayard. He had been drugged, imprisoned, compelled to speak false vows to save lands that might now be forfeit, his sister had been taken prisoner, and he had been made a fool in front of his enemy. Had ever a man been so ruined so swiftly?

The door opened to reveal Bayard's face that, unsurprisingly, evidenced anger. And most terrible it looked alongside his eyepatch.

He stepped inside, closed the door, and strode toward her.

She curled her toes in her slippers. She would not run. Would not give him the satisfaction, just as she had denied Murdoch the satisfaction of casting her in the role of pitiful prey.

Immediately, she regretted allowing her thoughts to go in that direction, especially under these circumstances that hearkened back to those with which she had lived night in and night out. Her long dead husband rising before her, a memory so vivid it was as if Murdoch's head were set upon Bayard's shoulders, she silently entreated, *Hold, El! You held then, you can hold now.*

But despite past experience, her knees softened so suddenly she had to catch hold of the tub's rim to remain upright. Hearing her breath, she dropped her chin and tried to bring her white knuckled fingers into focus.

"Thomasin!"

She saw the toes of Bayard's boots a moment before she felt his hand on her arm—several moments before she realized it was not her name he spoke. She would set him right on that as soon as she set herself right.

She forced her breath slowly in and out until her legs firmed up, opened and closed her eyes until the blurred edges sharpened.

Seeing Bayard's long fingers around her forearm, she raised her chin and was grateful for the absence of compassion in his glowering face. It made it easier to gather anger about her.

Bayard stared into Elianor of Emberly's pale face, the only color to be found that of her green eyes. Despite seething that had bred upon itself during the meeting with De Arell, her reaction to his entrance into the chamber had caused his fury to falter. As much as he longed to dismiss her weakness and trembling as a means of maneuvering him into exposing his back, fear had a feel and scent all its own. And it filled this room.

Though he had shown restraint these past days while he believed his captor-turned-captive was Thomasin de Arell, it seemed the impostor expected him to beat her. Fortunately for her, Bayard's father had taught him to be a man, not a coward who demanded respect and obedience while landing fists to a woman and planting a foot upon her back.

Even when Constance had cuckolded him and she and Serle de Arell had sought to slay him, he had not lost control enough to do such a thing. Instead, his revenge was had in the flesh he had taken from De Arell and, later, annulment of his marriage and inducement of the Church to impose penance upon adulteress and adulterer by committing the first to a convent, the second to a pilgrimage. It had sufficed.

"Do not call me that," Constance's niece hissed. "I am *not* Thomasin!"

So she once more sought to hide fear behind anger.

"Habit only," he bit. "I know well who you are, Elianor of Emberly, just as you know well to cower and tremble for what your conniving has wrought." He would not bruise or break her, but there would be consequences.

"Cower and tremble?" she scorned. "I am not afeared of you!"

It was true she no longer cowered, but he could feel the tremble beneath his hand upon her. "No matter how many times you proclaim such," he said, "it will be no smaller lie."

She glared.

"Do you think because I have only one eye, I am blind? That I could not see you nearly collapsed when I entered? That I cannot feel the fear writhing beneath your skin? Were I to release you, methinks your knees would seek the floor."

She tensed, and he thought she meant to prove him wrong by trying to free herself, but she said, "If my knees did seek the floor, it would be from fatigue and hunger since I have hardly slept or eaten these past days. That is all."

Bayard knew he should let it be, but the woman pushed him beyond good sense. "That is *not* all," he said and pulled her toward him.

She gasped and threw up a hand to ward off a blow.

"And there is your lie laid wide open," he said and drew her stumbling after him to a chair to the right of the tub. "Sit!"

She glanced behind, back at him, slowly lowered herself.

Though Bayard had come abovestairs to discuss an entirely different matter, he said, "Tell me who did it."

Her hands on either side of her gripped the seat's edge hard as if in preparation to thrust upright. "'Tis the truth I have told," she said. "Magnus had naught to do with it. Had he known what I intended, never would he have——"

"I speak of the one who beat you, Elianor."

She swallowed so hard he was certain the sound of it could be heard from the other side of the room. But just as she denied fearing him, she denied this with a shake of her head. "I know not of what you speak."

He clenched his hands to keep from slamming them to the chair arms. "No more lies. Who was it? The same who stalks your dreams—the one you vow to kill?"

She released her hold on the seat and crossed her arms over her chest. "Neither do you know of what you speak."

If he did not, he was near to knowing. Deciding it was best to put distance between them, he pivoted, strode to the tub, and peered into its clear, unsullied depths from which no heat rose.

Though baths were a luxury one did not shrug off, Elianor of Emberly had let this one turn tepid—doubtless, rather than risk him happening upon her unclothed. Understandably, she would not place herself in a vulnerable position that could tempt a man, especially considering what she had revealed last eve.

In the most unholy manner I have been defiled, she had said.

Then he knew. She spoke true that she had not been beaten—not in the usual sense. But she *had* been abused. By her uncle? He did not think so, for she was too quick to defend and protect him. Her departed husband?

A memory of Murdoch Farrow, whom Bayard had encountered at a tourney years past and whom he had later learned Constance's niece had wed, sprang upon him. A castellan upon a barony a day's journey from Castle Adderstone who enjoyed his food to the detriment of the destrier that bore his weight, Farrow had preened and bragged and beat his mount after it stumbled during a joust. Afterward, during feasting in the great hall, his behavior had turned more foul. Doubtless, that loud, irascible miscreant had done things to Elianor that caused her to fear a man's touch.

He turned toward her. "It was your husband who abused you."

Color bloomed in her face, and her gaze sharpened with what seemed resentment. And hatred. For him? Farrow? If the latter, might his death be attributed to her? If he had defiled her, and Bayard did not think she lied in that, she had good cause to seek his demise. Had she sought it? The night Bayard had made her his captive and he had asked why she had not allowed Agatha to kill him, she had retorted that she had wished him to suffer longer—a slow death. Later, however, she had claimed she was no murderer. Considering the depth of her deception, he knew he ought to believe her capable of taking a life, but he could not accept it.

Still, he said, "Tell, Lady, how did Farrow die?"

El knew what he asked, and there was no reason not to answer. "The swine choked. Blessed day, that." A hundred times she had wished such upon Murdoch, and half as many times she had repented of such evil thoughts. Regardless, she had been denied her freedom—until that last time.

She set her chin higher. "He did not always chew well ere swallowing. So, nay, I did not murder my husband." She narrowed her lids. "Though it was not for lack of longing."

His gaze pried at her as if to see into places she did not wish him to go. Lest he succeeded, she looked down and plucked at her skirts.

She felt him watching her, and when she finally lifted her chin, that which she glimpsed in his gaze caused her anger to churn. She had long suffered the pitying glances of women servants in Murdoch's home, and yet few had tried to aid her for fear of Murdoch. Her only hope had been the occasional relief given by Agatha who passed powders to her—that and the possibility Murdoch would one day break his neck, his heart would give out, disease would grip his gut, he would choke...

Hating that Bayard knew her shame, loathing that memories of Murdoch had revealed her fear, she snapped, "Do not pity me!"

His jaw shifted. "I do not. I but wish to know so I might determine the wisdom of giving you my back."

Then she had read his gaze wrong? He was concerned only for himself? Though she told herself she was pleased, it hurt. Especially as *she,* who knew never to pity a man—who had once pitied Murdoch and been cruelly repaid—had pitied Bayard for the humiliation and loss she had dealt him this day.

She pushed up out of the chair and took a step forward. "Then you have yet to determine the wisdom of trusting the woman responsible for your forfeiture? For heaping humiliation upon you? For causing your sister to be imprisoned?" She shook her head. "You are not very quick, Boursier."

His nostrils flared, and she hated that she should feel his struggle. Indeed, she almost wished there were no struggle—that he would prove he was the same as Murdoch. It was so much easier to hate one's enemy than to—

What?

When he strode toward her, she held her feet firm to the rushes to keep from running.

He halted before her. "Trust you, I will not, Elianor of Emberly, but properly wed you, I shall."

Her feet came unstuck as if the roots she had sent down through the floor were cut. She took a step back and came up against the chair. "Wed me? For what do you wish to do that?"

"It has naught to do with what I wish, all to do with Godsmere."

"But 'tis too late. The day given to speak vows is past."

"And yet our marriage could still be deemed valid, the speaking of vows but a formality that can be attended to this day."

El shook her head. "Pray, explain yourself."

"As our host, De Arell, has noted, consummation was once said to make a marriage—providing both parties consented. Thus, the king may bend on this."

She gasped. "As well you know, there has been no consummation!"

His smile was tight. "The sheet was hung out that all might bear witness, and they did."

She pressed a hand to the thigh that had provided evidence of consummation.

"Your blood, Elianor," he said, "and that is enough."

"Blood a widow does not shed!"

"Regardless, all of Castle Adderstone accept that we are husband and wife."

"That does not mean the king will."

"It does not, but if anything can save my lands, it is proof of consummation and the speaking of vows with Elianor of Emberly, and that last we shall do this day."

How she loathed being trapped between him and the chair! Though he came no nearer, it felt as if he had set himself over her. And around her. As if she might never escape him. And she would not if she did what he demanded of her.

"And if I refuse to speak vows with you?"

"You will not." It was said wearily. "Regardless of whether or not your uncle was aware of what you did, the Boursiers shall not be the only ones to forfeit. Indeed, though you made a fool of me, methinks King Edward will more likely forgive my trespass than your family's."

And Magnus would pay for sins not his own.

Helplessness beating through her, El closed her eyes. There was no way out. She would be made to suffer endless years of Bayard's loathing, perhaps even his fists. With dread, she accepted her fate. With desperation, she prayed his lands would not be forfeit, for if King Edward did not accept their marriage, the long years with this man would go all the worse for her.

She looked up. "Then I must needs wed you."

He inclined his head. "Father Crispin is in the chapel."

How certain he had been! But it was not as if she had a choice. This day, and every day hereafter, she would be Elianor Boursier. Once again, unhappily married. Once again, reduced to chattel used and disposed of as a man saw fit.

Quintin Boursier was not pleased.

Her eyes sought to burn holes in El's back as surely as the one caustic muttering she had been allowed had burned El's ears.

Suppressing the impulse to return the glare, El forced herself to focus on the priest who seemed even less pleased than when he had first recited vows for Bayard and her. They repeated them, one after another until El feared the scream inside her would leap out and further desecrate the proceedings.

Finally, it was over. The ring she had returned to Bayard before the ceremony once more loose upon her finger, her husband turned her out of the chapel.

Thomasin fell first to El's regard, her twinkling eyes unable to match the serious set of her mouth. Clearly, she was amused. And she could afford to be, for she was not the one made to suffer an unwanted marriage. But soon she would, for if King Edward accepted the vows spoken this day, Thomasin would wed Magnus. And a peculiar match that would be—the handsome, refined Baron of Emberly wed to the simple, misbegotten daughter of Griffin de Arell.

Enjoy your amusement whilst you can, El silently warned, *for a proper lady Magnus will expect you to be.*

Braving Quintin Boursier's stare where she stood alongside Baron de Arell, El lifted her chin as Bayard guided her past his sister and wondered again how it was possible for a woman to be so lovely without benefit of long tresses. Her hair was much too short for a lady—

El swallowed. Her own had been shorter once, a rebellious gesture for which she had paid dearly.

Do not think there, she told herself as she descended the stairs along-side the man who was now, truly, her husband. *This day has its own worries.*

Shortly, she lowered beside Bayard at the lord's table to settle into a semblance of a feast that seemed to mock the alliance between the Boursiers and the Verduns. Staring across the gathering, she wished she were not so alone and resented the powerlessness girding her head to toe.

"I have sent word of your marriage to your uncle, my lady," Griffin de Arell announced.

She looked past Bayard.

The man raised his goblet. "Of course, such tidings will not likely give him ease." He glanced at Bayard, smiled, and put the goblet to his mouth.

His words pricked, and before El could think better of her own, she retorted, "As it gives *you* ease to know you will soon wed a Boursier?"

Darkness crept across his face.

Two seats down, Lady Quintin gasped.

Beside El, Bayard stiffened.

"'Tis unfortunate for all, Lady Elianor," De Arell rumbled, "that we are forced into such marriages."

She narrowed her gaze on the Baron of Blackwood. "Marriages that would have been unnecessary had you not laid ruin to six months of peace by raiding and burning the village of Tyne."

His nostrils flared. "Still, I maintain that was not the work of me or mine."

It was as he had claimed in the missive sent to her uncle five months past, but she believed it no more now than she had then. She opened her mouth to respond, but Bayard leaned toward his host, blocking her view of De Arell.

"As you maintain you had naught to do with burning my crops last summer, De Arell?" he clipped.

The man sighed. "I did that—after you slaughtered a score of my cattle."

El heard Bayard's teeth grind. She had been told of the cattle found gutted, and that Bayard had denounced the accusation leveled at his family. Would he do so again?

With a breath that broadened his shoulders, he turned from De Arell.

But El was not done with their host. However, as she leaned forward to further prod him, Bayard's grimly set face gave her pause.

"You would do well to put your mouth around food, rather than words, *Wife*," he growled, then stabbed a chunk of venison in the trencher between them and thrust it in his mouth.

Do not say it! El counseled, but out it came. "And you would do well to chew your food in full."

He stared at her, then swallowed and said low, "I am not Murdoch Farrow. It will take more than an ill-gotten bite for you to rid yourself of me."

El feigned a sigh. "And for that, did I not steal you from your bed and imprison you?"

"Aye, and now Agatha suffers for your trespass."

The reminder jolted her. Did Agatha still suffer? Might she have managed to escape? More likely, she was dead or near death. And that realization—the weight of its responsibility—caused her anger to ebb. She looked down and away, swept her gaze over the castle folk at the lower tables who were more intent upon their meals than the petty affairs of the nobility. They led a hard but simple life, and in that moment she wished hers was as simple.

An hour later, she followed the stiff-backed Father Crispin up the stairs to repeat the ritual of putting the bride to bed. And as he had discovered the first time, he would find her no more receptive now that she was Elianor Boursier.

19

⚬⚬⚬

"WE LEAVE AT dawn," Bayard said, closing the door behind him.

El settled deeper into the chair and sank her chin into the coverlet she had taken from the bed as Father Crispin, tight-lipped and shaking his head, had withdrawn from the chamber.

Considering the night past when Bayard had unbalanced her by abandoning his seduction to give her time to become accustomed to him, she could not begin to guess what this night held for her. What she did know was that, however he went about consummating their marriage, this time he would. But though resigned to it, she had not been able to lie upon the bed as the priest had entreated her to do.

Hoping to delay the inevitable, she asked, "What of your sister?"

He came around the tub of chill water. "She has been returned to the tower. On that, De Arell will not be moved."

And the fault was El's. Telling herself it was of no use to wallow in regret, she said, "As neither would you be moved regardless of the reason for my transgression against you."

He stepped nearer, and she tensed in anticipation of a show of intimidation, but something flickered across his face and he halted. "I know the reason you did what you did. I know why you transgressed."

She clenched her hands beneath the coverlet "Why did I?"

"You took me from my bed for what you believe I did to your aunt. You did it for my death so that you and yours would be free of the Boursiers."

She started to protest that last, but he continued, "You did it for Magnus Verdun so he would not be made to wed my sister. And you did it for yourself that you might more easily hold to your uncle through the young, simple Thomasin de Arell."

The rumor. Until that moment, El had refused to allow it to more than bother her as if it were a fly pestering her shoulder. Now it mortified her that he believed her relationship with Magnus was of a carnal nature.

"I would not have thought you one to indulge in rumors, Bayard Boursier, especially one so far-fetched."

He raised an eyebrow. "If a rumor is persistent enough, eventually it finds an audience. Naturally, as you are now my wife, I would like you to dispel it."

Though part of her balked at accommodating him, she knew her silence would serve no good thing, that it might even make the night ahead more difficult.

"'Tis true I seized and imprisoned you for what you did to my aunt, and that I did it so my uncle would not suffer marriage to your sister. But though I let you believe I sought your death, there is no truth in that, just as there is none in what is said of Magnus and me—"

"If it was not my death you sought, then what?"

"As told, forfeiture. I had only to imprison you past the day you were required to wed and the Boursiers would hold Godsmere no more."

His head tilted. "You wish me to believe that afterward you would have released me?"

"That was my intention."

"You did not worry about reprisal?"

She looked down. "'Twas not for you to know who had imprisoned you."

"Then you were certain I would believe De Arell was responsible, he who did not wish his daughter to wed me."

Regret washed over her. "I guessed you might."

"Thus, not only would you remove the Boursiers, but possibly the De Arells."

She pulled her teeth over her bottom lip. "After all these years of conflict and raids and burnings...I did not believe I would regret it much."

His regard was so intense it felt as if his patched eye bore through her. "What of Agatha? You cannot tell me she was not of a mind for murder."

She could not. And could there be any reason to dissuade him now that death was likely upon the woman and there was nothing from which to protect her? Though a bit of the lump on El's head remained as a reminder of Agatha's deception, she had to defend her. After all, Agatha would surely be far from Godsmere had she not agreed to her mistress's scheme.

"Agatha but tried to aid me, to prevent happening what did happen."

His lid narrowed. "You are certain that is all she aspired to do?" El's hesitation raised a grim smile to his lips. "Even if you did not seek my death, and I would be more a fool to easily accept that, what of your uncle and you? 'Tis told you are lovers."

She set her chin higher. "'Tis told you are a beast, but that does not make it so."

"Does it not?" His lips thinned. "You say that, and yet this day you cowered for fear of this beast."

El shook her head. "'Twas not fear of you that moved me. It was fear of—" She stopped her words, causing him to arch an eyebrow above the patch. She had already revealed enough of herself and her first marriage to allow him to guess Murdoch had abused her, but as there was too much to deal with in her present without reaching back into her past, she would reveal no more.

"There is no truth to that wagging of tongues about my uncle and me," she returned to the topic from which she had veered.

He delved her face. "I am to believe you?"

"Lovers we are not, have never been, shall never be. I feel for him as one feels for a brother. For that, I wished to spare him marriage to Lady Quintin."

"My unladylike, debauched sister? She who dared ride upon Castle Mathe and take a dagger to De Arell's throat? Not quite as unsavory as one who imprisons a man to steal his lands, but still unworthy of your beloved Magnus."

He was right. Who was she to judge Quintin Boursier? Though El's encounter with the disagreeable woman gave her more reason to not wish her uncle to suffer marriage to a Boursier, what Bayard's sister had done did not compare to what she, herself, had done.

"Now that we have come to the end of that—for now," Bayard said, "tell me what you fear."

His return to that of which she did not wish to speak stirred the memories. Lowering her chin, she struggled to find something with which to weigh them down. Anger always worked, but before she could draw upon it, Bayard stepped near, hooked a finger beneath her jaw, and raised it.

"What do you fear?" he asked again.

Feeling the ache of tears, she tried to drop her chin, but he drew it higher.

"*Whom* do you fear?" His deep voice, no longer hoarse from days in the underground, caused something strange to sing through her.

She swallowed the tightness in her throat, only to wish she had not, for the next draw of breath she spent upon the words, "Not you." And unlike the other times she had tried to convince him he did not make her heart aspire to flee her chest, there was nothing defiant or challenging in her speaking of them.

His eyelid flickered, mouth softened. "What did Farrow do to you?"

Say no more! she silently commanded, and yet...

"Not what you do to me," she whispered to the one who, despite being much too near, did not alarm her as much as he should.

He drew closer, slid a thumb across her lower lip. "And what is that, Elianor?"

As with each time he called her by name since learning she was not Thomasin, something fluttered in her breast. From childhood, she had preferred the simpler, affectionate *El* when propriety did not require her name in full. But how she had come to loathe *Elianor* while wed to Murdoch!

Not only had there been no one in his household with whom she could draw close enough to be called *El,* but Murdoch had taken all the beauty out of her given name by placing more emphasis than was necessary on the first part of it, most notably when displeased. In contrast, Bayard made four notes of her name rather than three. Stranger yet, the first was mostly breath, emphasis placed on the second note such that her name upon his lips sounded more like *Lianor.*

"Tell me," he pressed.

She did not know what he did to her, only that it made her speak what she should not and stay when she should flee. And that *did* make her fear him, though not in any way to which she was accustomed.

"Naught," she lied. "You do naught to me, and that is not a bad thing."

She could not be certain, but she thought he flinched. "You compare me to Farrow."

"I will not discuss him with you."

He drew a deep breath of what she hoped was patience, released her chin, and straightened.

Gathering her courage, El pushed the coverlet off her shoulders and stood. "I know the debt that must be paid this night." As she peered up at him and he peered down at her, she struggled against the longing to clasp her arms over her chest. "Let us be done with it."

Annoyance lit his face. "*It,*" he growled. "Hardly the way to rouse a man to passion. Is that how you kept Farrow from your bed?"

If only it had been that easy. Clenching her teeth, she sidestepped and started toward the bed.

Bayard pulled her back around. "I would know about Farrow."

She wished his gaze did not reflect concern he should not feel.

And surely does not, she told herself. *He but seeks to know your vulnerable places that he might exploit them for the humiliation you visited upon him.*

"Elianor," he pressed.

Hating that her tongue tensed and lips quivered as if to form the words, she drove her fingernails into her palms.

"What did that miscreant do?"

*Miscreant...*As if, in spite of the ill she had worked upon Bayard, he had determined she was the victim. As if she were worthy of championing. As if she were precious to him.

She was not. Still, a longing to be more than chattel pierced her, and it so confused her that she once again spoke what she should not. "You make it sound as if you care."

His gaze narrowed.

"But as that cannot be," she hastened to add, "I can only conclude you wish to know how broken I am. Unfortunate for both of us, now that we are bound one to the other, it can serve no good to know the state of my first marriage. And as already told, I will not speak of it."

"Then I must needs discover the truth myself," he said. "Now to bed, Elianor."

She suppressed the instinct to defy him and tried to ease the tension that came so naturally to her. Though she knew he had abused her aunt, her experience with Bayard these past nights indicated his abuse was not of the ilk to which Murdoch had subjected her. Thus, until she knew whom, exactly, she had wed, it was best to let him do with her as he would.

She turned away and, consoling herself that whatever awaited her would aid in teaching her how to battle him for however many years she must suffer his attentions, crossed to the bed.

As she slid beneath the coverlet, Bayard moved around the chamber extinguishing candles.

Once the room was draped in darkness with only the far corner vaguely lit by moonlight hard-pressed to penetrate the oilcloth covering the window, she heard Bayard's feet upon the rushes on the opposite side of the bed. Then came the sound of a buckle sliding off leather, followed by the rustle of garments.

Dear Lord, she sent heavenward, *grant me courage.*

Amid the silence that evidenced Elianor held her breath, Bayard tossed his tunic to the foot of the bed. Next, he dragged off his boots and left them where they fell.

Though he knew he ought to set about seducing his fair wife, his instincts once more prevailed as he settled into the mattress.

It was no good thing for a woman not to want the man to whom she was wed. It was something much worse for her to so revile his touch that the air vibrated with her dread. Still, he should at least pull her close as he had done on the night past. And he would have if not that the thought of being so near her called to mind this morn when, beneath the spell of sleep, she had held to him and sighed as if content. It had made something clenched inside him begin to loosen.

He knew it was foolish and weak to care that a woman wished to be in his arms—that in spite of all, he wanted what Constance had refused him. However, as Elianor had said, they were bound to each other for life, and even if Boursier lands were declared forfeit, this woman and he would likely remain together until their end days. Thus, since the lie of consummation was far preferable to the truth of seduction that might make her regard him as not much better than her first husband, he would leave her be.

"Bayard?" she whispered. "What do you?"

"I would think it obvious." He despised the resentment in his voice. "Good eve."

She was silent so long that were he not attuned to her unease he might have thought she drifted toward sleep. "But..." she finally spoke. "Then you will not...I thought..."

"As did I," he growled. "But I do not want you, Elianor. Not this night."

"I do not understand."

And he did not wish to explain it. But it seemed he must were he
to know any peace. "I have had one marriage made of obligation, and if I
must have another, so be it. But first let us see if you will lie with me out
of want rather than the obligation of paying the marital debt or the hope
of overcoming your fear of the unknown."

She swallowed hard. "So once more you risk—"

"You are a widow. There is proof aplenty of consummation. But
know this, I will speak false if you gainsay me. And do not doubt I will
be more believed than the woman who sought to steal my lands. Now
sleep."

"Here?"

She wished to know if she would be allowed to cling to her side of
the bed or once more made to lie atop him. "There."

He heard the breath go out of her. When she replenished it, she said,
"I thank you."

It was good that the depth of her relief should so offend, for it
helped to temper the desire roused by the sensual strain of her voice
across the dark.

The only sound about them the air they breathed, they lay there.
Neither stirring. Neither speaking. Neither sleeping.

Despite all he had told, she did not trust him, and for that was surely
fending off fatigue that could leave her vulnerable.

Though frustrated that she refused to speak of her marriage to
Farrow, Bayard pitied her for whatever had been done to make her thus.
And he supposed he ought to pity himself. If she was truly broken—
though she had proved she was not entirely averse to his touch—he was
the one who would have to live with the jagged pieces of Elianor of
Emberly.

With the morrow's ride to Castle Adderstone drawing near, he
turned his back to her and, after some minutes, made a conscious effort
to breathe deeply in the hope of easing her worry sufficiently to allow her
to sleep. It was not long before he felt the mattress give as she cautiously

rolled away from him onto her side. A short while later, her breathing deepened.

Unfortunately, his own rest was not as easily found. His mind was too crowded with all that had passed since the night the witch and Elianor had drugged and imprisoned him—the night all had changed. Surely for the worse.

Minutes mounted, and he knew at least an hour had passed when Elianor's breathing quickened. Was it another frightening dream like that which had made her vow to kill the one who visited her behind her lids?

He dropped onto his back and peered across the space between them. It was too dark to more than make out her shoulder that sloped toward her waist.

"Elianor?" he rasped.

She whimpered, then there came a scraping sound as of fingernails clawing at the sheet she lay upon.

He set a hand on her shoulder, and she jerked. "Elianor?"

Utter silence. Utter still. Then something between a sigh and a moan sounded from her and she quaked.

"He can hurt you no more," he murmured.

Her body continued to convulse, and Bayard considered pulling her atop him so she might sleep content as she had done on the night past. However, not only would he once more find himself tortured by temptation, but were she yet caught up in the dream, she might prove unreceptive.

"You are safe," he said and lifted his hand from her.

She gasped and clapped a hand over his, pressed it back to her shoulder and held it there. "Lianor," she said with desperation. "Lianor."

Bayard wondered what caused her to speak her own name—rather, a semblance of it.

"Aye," she whispered, "Lianor." Minutes later, her breathing eased, and the fingers gripping his relaxed.

Bayard could have slid his hand from beneath hers, but he did not and thought how wrong it seemed to feel any compassion after all she had done.

Shifting his gaze to the dark ceiling, he silently called upon the one whom he had pushed to the farthermost reaches of his consciousness alongside Father Crispin whom he continued to deny a private audience.

Lord, what am I to do with this woman? How am I to make a life with one such as this? More, perhaps, how is she to make a life with one such as me?

He did not expect an answer, and there was none forthcoming. And yet he felt—or did he hope?—he was heard.

20

THE WINTER WEATHER was warming. Though the reprieve would be temporary, it was welcome. But it also meant they would reach Castle Adderstone well before nightfall.

Despite the warmth that had moments earlier made her consider parting her mantle, El shivered, hunched her shoulders, and looked across the field over which their mounts sped.

Bayard rode at the head of his men, setting a pace on his black destrier that jarred her head to toe and made her long for the bed in which she had awakened this morn.

This morn...

She gripped the reins tighter. When she had opened her eyes, dawn had begun to press its face against the oilcloth. It had not been necessary to look around to know her husband occupied the bed, for his hand had been on her shoulder. More disturbingly, her hand had pressed his to her as if she welcomed his touch.

Though she could not recall her night travels, she knew it likely she had dreamed aloud. And it had shamed her nearly as much as it had disquieted her to know the man who had no cause to comfort her had done so.

Cautiously, having long ago learned how to negotiate a bed without disturbing its other occupant, she had turned onto her back, causing Bayard's hand to ease from her shoulder. She would have risen immediately had she not been captivated by the countenance of the man who yet slept. He had looked almost boyish in repose, hard-set mouth no longer in evidence, lashes casting shadows upon his broad cheekbone. Though she had told herself it was only the dim light that made him appear approachable, she had been tempted to lay a hand to his stubbled jaw.

When he had awakened a quarter hour later, he had found her in the chair on the far side of the chamber. He had not spoken of what had caused him to reach to her in the night, and she hoped it meant he was unaware of having done so. Still, it gave her much to ponder about what it told of his character, once more calling into question the man whom she had believed him to be. Where was evidence of the one who had abused her aunt?

Bayard had donned his clothes while she averted her gaze, saying very little beyond ordering her to ready herself for departure. And depart they had, following a tense farewell between Bayard and his sister, the latter having been permitted the reach of the inner bailey and, throughout, made to remain at Griffin de Arell's side. Unfortunately for Bayard, the Baron of Blackwood was no fool, for El did not doubt her husband would have spirited away his sister given the opportunity.

How he must hate me in this moment, she thought, *if not in every moment.*

She returned her gaze to him and was struck by the desire to ride at his side where his horse kicked up sprays of melting snow that caused the air to sparkle as if angels had set themselves around Bayard.

A short while later, she feared he might need those heavenly beings when a score of riders appeared on the rise ahead.

Bayard dragged on the reins, raised an arm, and shouted something to his men.

The beat of El's heart doubling, she slowed her mount to a trot amidst her husband's men. Who came? Brigands? Nobles traveling to—

She caught her breath. They came from the direction of Ellesmere Abbey in the west. If they continued their southeastern course, they would be at Castle Kelling within a few hours. Was it Magnus returned from searching her out?

The ring of metal announcing the drawing of swords, El tapped her heels to her mount. "Mayhap 'tis my uncle," she said as she came alongside Bayard.

He narrowed his gaze on those who had halted atop the rise.

She touched his sleeve. "Methinks—"

"I know what you think—what you hope." He looked around. "Do you truly believe I would be at ease if 'tis so?"

She blinked. "We are wed, Bayard. There is now an alliance between our families."

His eyebrows drew close. "Is there? You forget you are not the first Verdun with whom I have spoken vows."

"This time, it shall be different," she said before she could think better of her words.

Whatever crossed his face, it was quick to turn bitter. "Aye, *this* time I am fully aware of what the Verduns are capable of."

So he was, and she was to blame. She shifted her gaze to the riders opposite. "If 'tis my uncle, there need be no crossing of swords. I will speak to him and—"

"You will not!" He took the reins from her. "You will do as told and no more."

"But—"

A movement on the rise drew their regard to the single rider who approached.

"At the ready!" Bayard shouted as El strained to determine the colors of the tunic worn over armor that glinted with day's light.

Bayard also waited for the colors to reveal themselves. Moments later, dark blue and silver identified the one who ventured forth as being of Emberly. But they did not come from that direction, meaning if Verdun was among these men, De Arell's missive informing him of the marriage had yet to come into his hands. Had Verdun ventured out into winter's bite to search for his niece? Did he care that much for her?

She gasped. "He *is* of Emberly!"

Bayard was provoked to see such joy upon her face.

"And 'tis Magnus!"

The fervor with which she spoke her uncle's Christian name further riled him. Though she denied that Verdun and she were lovers, he would be stretching himself in a dangerous direction to believe her.

"Then let us not keep him waiting." Bayard returned his sword to its scabbard, looked to his men, and thrust a staying hand in the air. Then, gazed fixed on Verdun, he guided his and Elianor's mounts forward.

As his enemy's countenance took form, he wondered why God had made such a man to be so right of face. A man whose looks, like those of his father, Elianor surely found more appealing than those of the *one-eyed beast*.

Gut roiling, he looked to her and saw her eyes sparkled above a bowed mouth. He had thought her lovely before, even when she glared and spat, but now...

Lord, he silently beseeched, *if You could not make Elianor of Emberly uncomely, could You not have made her only passing pretty? You know my weakness, and yet you wedge this beauty into my life—so tightly her deceitful person is now one with me.*

Her smile broadened further, revealing for the first time she had all of her straight, white teeth and causing Bayard's hand to cramp upon the reins. If it was true she wanted Magnus Verdun as Constance had wanted Serle de Arell...

Though he tried to convince himself it was fury he felt, the emotion flooding him had more depth and reach. Knowing the best way to fortify the walls to which Elianor had laid siege was to properly name this emotion, he acknowledged it as jealousy. And warned himself that if he did not stamp it out, it would blind him as it had once blinded him to Constance's guile.

He pulled the reins.

As Verdun continued his advance, Bayard felt Elianor's gaze jump between her uncle and himself. However, he kept his gaze upon Verdun, for it was poor judgment to turn one's attention from a Verdun or a De

Arell. Of course, Elianor was also a Verdun and had done worse to him than ever her uncle had done.

Magnus Verdun reined in, urged his destrier sideways, and looked from Bayard to Elianor. "How fare thee, El?"

El? Bayard ground his teeth.

She inclined her head. "I—"

"The proper form of address is Lady Elianor *Boursier*," Bayard tread upon her words.

Not even the surprise that swept across Verdun's face marred his looks. But was it only surprise? Or also dismay for what would never again be his?

Verdun reset his expression. Still, his voice was almost choked when he said, "'Twas told you chose Thomasin de Arell for your bride."

"So I did. And I would have wed her if not that your *niece*"—a reminder of all she would be to him henceforth—"imprisoned me past the king's appointed day in the hope my lands would be declared forfeit."

In that moment, there could be little doubt Verdun had been unaware of Elianor's plans. Lids wide, mouth slack, he shone disbelief upon her. "Elianor?"

Bayard glanced at her, saw she had lost her smile.

"'Tis true," she said. "I—"

"Agatha!" Verdun growled. "It was that woman."

Elianor shook her head. "'Twas at my bidding she aided me."

"So you think!" His harsh words surprised Bayard who remembered him as a squire whose refined voice had spilled upon one's ears as easily as his looks spilled upon women's eyes. However, what did not surprise was the tic that started at the corner of his right eye and foretold the truth of one who appeared in control. *That* Bayard had seen when Magnus Verdun had been a prisoner at Castle Adderstone and, years later, when he had protested his father's decision to break word with the De Arells and, instead, wed Constance Verdun to Bayard. Such a pity—in hindsight—that Rand Verdun had not heeded his son's argument.

Magnus Verdun looked over his shoulder to where his men awaited his signal. Were he wise, and if he controlled his impulses, it would not be forthcoming.

He drew a deep breath, returned his regard to his niece. "I fear I cannot help you, El"—he shot his gaze to Bayard—"other than to give warning, Boursier. Do you harm her as you harmed my sister—"

"Regardless of what your sister and that witch tell," Bayard said, "never did Constance suffer the back of my hand or my fists."

Verdun's mouth tensing further, tic more evident, he looked to Elianor. She shook her head. "I vow, Bayard has done me no harm."

"And yet he tells you imprisoned him."

"I did." She scraped her teeth over her lip. "Forgive me, Magnus. Could I change what I have done, I would."

Why her words should disturb him, Bayard did not wish to ponder. If she could, indeed, change what she had done, he would be returning to Castle Adderstone with Thomasin. And he ought to want that—at least, more than he wanted Elianor.

"I thought you had taken sanctuary at Ellesmere," Verdun said.

Then it was that place from which he returned, Bayard realized— had surely gone there to bring her back so the Verduns would not forfeit.

"You should have, El," Verdun surprised Bayard.

Should have? Then he cared more for her than that his lands would have been lost? Once more stabbed by jealousy, Bayard struggled to get out from beneath its weight. However, the thought of Elianor intimate with Verdun would not allow it.

"Nay, Magnus," she said, "I would not have you lose Emberly. That I would not do."

Bayard bared his teeth. "But you would do it to a Boursier."

Before she could respond, Verdun said, "She *did* do it to a Boursier— *The* Boursier."

"And failed," Bayard retorted. Of course, had Agatha not returned to murder him, all would be different.

"Where is Agatha?" Verdun demanded.

Hating that the man's thoughts ran with his own, Bayard said, "She is my prisoner, and so she shall remain."

"Providing she yet lives," Elianor said, her tone a mix of accusation and guilt.

Though Bayard owed her no explanation or easing of conscience, he said, "She lives."

"But she has been in the underground for—"

"She was provided for ere we departed Adderstone."

Her eyes widened, and for a moment he felt as if she saw in him what should not be seen.

He returned his gaze to Verdun. "It seems you shall wed Thomasin de Arell—unless the prospect is as undesirable as your niece speaking vows with me."

Though the smile that lifted Verdun's mouth was forced, it made the devil more handsome. "I will not forfeit."

"I did not expect so."

"Where are you taking my niece?"

"To Castle Adderstone, the only home she shall know henceforth."

The man's brow furrowed. "Whence do you come?"

"Castle Mathe, where we were wed on the day past."

The man surely tried to contain his startle. "You are only just wed? Then—"

"The marriage will stand," Bayard said, and silently prayed the king would allow it. "Lady Elianor and I were first wed on the eve of the king's day, though then I was led to believe she was Thomasin de Arell."

Verdun's eyes flashed to Elianor. "Elianor?"

"'Tis so," she said.

"All was remedied at Castle Mathe," Bayard continued. "For the deception your niece worked upon me, I do not doubt the king will be satisfied his demands have been met once he receives the missive sent by Father Crispin and witnessed by Baron de Arell."

Elianor caught her breath. "The king is to be told what I did?"

"Your treachery cannot be hidden, Elianor," Bayard said, holding his gaze to Verdun whose destrier pranced sideways and snorted, evidencing its rider's agitation.

Verdun urged the animal forward. "I would hear the tale in its entirety, Boursier."

"Only if you intend to accompany us to Adderstone. Day wanes and there are many leagues to cover."

Verdun peered over his shoulder at his men. When he looked back around, the derisive smile on his lips was also in his eyes. "Then I shall accompany you."

Bayard glanced at Elianor and begrudged the hope brightening her countenance. "That was not an invitation, Verdun."

"It sounded one to me. What think you, El?"

She looked to Bayard. "What harm, my lord? He *is* now your uncle."

The reminder that Verdun was once again kin was not welcome, and it chafed more that the man was now cast in the role of an older relation though he was younger than Bayard by several years. "As once he was my *brother*," he rumbled.

Verdun hitched an eyebrow. "On the joyous occasion of bringing home your new bride, methinks it best not to venture there, Boursier."

Hatred struggling to rise up and express itself through bloodletting, Bayard held his gaze firm to the other man's. As evidenced by all the days since his imprisonment, what had been mostly dormant for years owing to Father Crispin's patient counsel had reawakened, first with Agatha, then with Elianor who pretended herself to be Thomasin, next with De Arell, now with Verdun. Fortunately for those who roused his wrath, he knew better than to loose it, for to do so could prove satisfying enough to tear his soul.

Thus, he must accept that, as things had stood between Verdun and him while he was wed to the man's sister, it would stand between them now that he was wed to the niece—neither liking or trusting the other.

"Then we shall leave your sister at Ellesmere Abbey where she belongs, Verdun." Bayard turned his destrier and Elianor's mount. "We ride!"

21

CASTLE ADDERSTONE. IMPRESSIVE. Imposing. But not entirely impregnable.

As the drawbridge completed its descent, its timbers creaking and groaning, chains clattering, El considered the breath-stealing edifice she had last looked upon in a much different context.

And so I return not as one who wishes to breach these walls, she mused, *but as one who should not wish them breached—as Bayard's wife in truth. No more Elianor of Emberly. Now, and mayhap evermore, Elianor Boursier.*

"To have and to hold," she whispered, warming in remembrance of when Bayard had held her, though he had yet to have her in the truest sense of marriage.

"For better, for worse," she breathed, aching over the possibility the latter would govern their lives.

"Till death do us part," she mouthed, shivering at the thought he would leave her a widow and fearful of looking near upon why that disturbed her. There had been no such worry with Murdoch.

Riding several horse lengths ahead as he had done through the town outside Adderstone's walls, Bayard reined in his destrier short of the drawbridge that, having firmly settled to the ground, invited them to pass over it into the outer bailey. He urged his horse sideways, met El's gaze as she came alongside, and looked to the others.

Beyond the bulk of his approaching men was her uncle's entourage who had slowed their advance considerably, creating a sizable gap between the two parties. However, such was not the case with those who came behind Magnus's men.

Upon crossing the border into Godsmere, Bayard had ordered a dozen of his knights to take up the rear, thereby hemming in those who had been forced to ally with the Boursiers. Though it could not have come as a surprise to Magnus, and the precaution was justified considering the history between the families, El knew her uncle had taken offense. But she also knew he was honest enough to acknowledge he would do the same were this the barony of Emberly.

She pulled the ties that had prevented the air stirred by their ride from casting off her hood and eased the woolen fabric down around her shoulders. "You will let them all in?" she asked, certain Bayard questioned the wisdom of allowing a score of men who were too recently his enemy to enter his walls.

Without moving his gaze from them, he said, "Ought I, Wife?"

Was he consulting her? Or baiting her? "Though 'tis with grudging my uncle accepts our marriage," she pitched her voice low, "he knows there is naught to do but abide by what the king decreed. Thus, I do not believe you have anything to fear from him."

"Never have I had anything to fear from a Verdun. Simply, I do not care to be inconvenienced." He turned his face to her. "Rather, never has a Verdun of the male line put fear through me. I have certainly known fear at your hands, Elianor—that I would lose my lands. And may yet lose them."

If the king did not accept their belated marriage.

As El stared up at him, she remembered again awakening to the warmth of his fingers beneath hers and upon her shoulder. "I pray you do not, Bayard."

The eyebrow above the patch rose. "Do you?"

She inclined her head. "I know there is little hope for a marriage neither of us wanted, but I would not war with you all the days of our lives."

"For that only you would not have my lands declared forfeit? You do not also see the wrong of what you wrought?"

She looked at those who had drawn rein to await her husband's determination, picked out Magnus where he and his retainers sat their horses in the midst of Bayard's men. "Ever I have known the wrong of it," she said, moving her gaze past her uncle to a hooded rider over his left shoulder, then beyond to Godsmere's knights who were to become more familiar to her than those of Emberly.

Returning to Bayard, she said, "But knowing it and wishing a different outcome other than that which King Edward seeks..." She raised and dropped a shoulder. "I did not heed my conscience, and I regret I am not the only one who must pay the price for what I did."

He probed her face so deeply that her cheeks that had grown numb during the last hour of the ride began to warm. "Mayhap the price will not be as high as thought," he said and lifted an arm and swept it toward the outer bailey, signaling all to enter.

As she passed beneath the raised portcullis behind him, she looked to the ring upon her hand and pondered what he had said. Though she found hope in it, she warned herself to be slow to embrace it lest she find it torn from her. And yet...

Lord, do You hear me? Is it possible Bayard and I can make a better show of marriage than he and Aunt Constance made of their union?

Providing her husband had truly gained control over the abusive expression of his wrath, which was possible considering he had dealt her no blows, their marriage might not be without substance. But surely a better chance it would stand if he did not refuse to acknowledge the harm done her aunt.

Bayard halted his destrier before the stables, spoke briefly with the man who hastened forward to receive his orders, then motioned for El to continue on with him to the inner bailey.

As she urged her horse ahead of his squire's and Father Crispin's, she glanced around and saw her uncle's men and Bayard's were dismounting at the stables—a precaution, since gladly received visitors usually remained astride all the way to the keep, at which place squires and grooms led their mounts back to the stables. Another slight over which

Magnus would take offense. Hopefully, he and his men would not also be required to relinquish their weapons.

At the keep's steps, Squire Lucas was the first to dismount. Thus, when Bayard and the priest swung out of their saddles, the young man was there to gather the reins passed to him.

Bayard came alongside El. It seemed natural for his big hands to grip her waist, for her to descend the length of his body and settle her feet between his. And as she stared at the damp earth beneath her slippers, she mused that only once had Murdoch assisted in her dismount—the day his bride had been delivered to him. Afterward, there had been no call for aid in dismounting, for he had rarely allowed her outside the keep, and never outside the castle's walls. She had thought she would suffocate, more even than when Bayard had held her to the wall with a hand to her throat.

"And so you are home, my lady," he said.

She lifted her face. "So I am. Will I ever...?"

His eyebrows rose. "Ever?"

Having nearly asked if she would be allowed outside Adderstone's walls, she was grateful she had breathed the words back in, for they would give him more cause to pry into her relationship with Murdoch.

She summoned a smile. "You will take me riding, will you not?"

His eyelid narrowed, and she felt suspicion roll off him.

"Bayard!"

He looked around at his stepmother who descended the steps with such haste it appeared she might trip and tumble to the bottom. Immediately, he released El and bounded past the priest and up the steps.

"Quintin?" Lady Maeve demanded when he took hold of her arm. "Where is my daughter?"

"She remains at Castle Mathe, my lady."

Despite the din that rose from the outer bailey, the sound of the woman's indrawn breath descended the half dozen steps to where El clasped her hands at her waist.

Then Lady Maeve's eyes fell upon her stepson's wife and something flashed in them. Anger? Disbelief? "Why did Quintin not return with you?" she demanded.

"I will tell all," Bayard said, "but now is not the time."

"Not the time—?"

"I assure you, Quintin is safe under the watch of Sir Victor."

"But—"

"Suffice it to say," Bayard spoke above the outer bailey's din that further encroached upon the inner bailey, "Griffin de Arell will not relinquish her lest she makes it difficult for him to take her to wife. Which he must now do."

The grooves in her brow deepening, Lady Maeve said, "I can make no sense of you. As you have wed De Arell's daughter, 'tis for him to wed the Verdun widow."

"So it was, my lady," Father Crispin interceded where he peered up at them from the base of the steps, "but it is not possible now that Baron Boursier is wed to Elianor of Emberly."

"Elianor?" The lady swept her regard from the priest to the woman who stood to his right, lowered her gaze down the younger woman. "This is not Thomasin de Arell?"

"It is not." There was impatience in Bayard's voice, but it was gone when he said, "Forgive me, Lady Maeve, but an accounting of what has transpired must wait, for this eve we have guests."

She opened her mouth as if to press him further, but closed it when the voices and tramp of those who had stabled their horses swept into the inner bailey.

"Methinks it best that you await me in your chamber," Bayard said.

She gasped. "You leave your sister at the mercy of a De Arell and think to put me away like a pair of old boots? I will not tolerate it!"

He set his jaw. "As you will, but I vow you will like this even less whilst you remain ignorant of the situation."

She put her chin up. "I shall stay."

He took her arm and led her down the steps.

Grateful it was Bayard who came alongside her, rather than his stepmother, El turned toward the inner walls as her husband's squire led the great destrier and the priest's horse beneath the portcullis. Moments later, Magnus and his men, flanked by those of Castle Adderstone, passed beneath that same portcullis. Mantles riding their shoulders, the thick woolen garments all of a length that fell below the knee, the hoods of most having been lowered, they advanced on those before the keep. And visible with each parting of their mantles amidst far-reaching strides were the weapons of which they had not been divested.

"They are of Emberly," Lady Maeve hissed from the other side of Bayard.

"Aye," he said. "Lady Elianor's uncle, Baron Verdun, and his men."

"What are they——?"

"We shall discuss it later."

The procession halted before them and Magnus curtly bowed. "We thank you for your hospitality, Baron Boursier."

It was grudgingly spoken, and there was no more warmth in Bayard's clipped response, "You are welcome at Castle Adderstone."

"Baron Boursier," Magnus said before Bayard could give him his back, "ere we proceed, there is something you must needs know."

"Speak, Baron Verdun."

Magnus turned sideways and reached behind.

A hooded figure stepped forward, parted its ground-sweeping mantle with a fine-boned hand to reveal it was not men's chausses worn beneath, and gripped the hand Magnus offered.

El stopped breathing. *Pray, nay,* she sent to the heavens, though she knew this moment was so fully upon them it could not be returned to its narrow-necked bottle.

As something painful fell through her, she heard the priest exclaim, "It cannot be."

But it was, as further evidenced by the release of the hood down around the shoulders of the beautiful woman who had returned to a place that had been her home well before it had become El's—a place where she was not and would never again be welcome.

Her. At Adderstone. Again.

Amid the gasps, none of which carried as far as that of Lady Maeve who stumbled and snatched hold of her stepson's arm, Bayard stared at the woman who had been his first wife—she who had reluctantly spoken vows with him, distantly accepted and returned his embraces, made of him a cuckold, and sought his death.

Though outwardly he did not move, not even when she raised her gaze to his eyepatch, his every muscle bunched in preparation to draw sword and spring upon Magnus Verdun for stealing that woman inside Adderstone's walls.

"Bayard?"

Above the pound of blood that made it feel as if his heart might break free of his chest, he heard his name. For a moment, he thought it was *she* whose lips it had crossed, but the full mouth that had enticed him years ago remained seamed.

Elianor's voice, then. Elianor's hand upon his arm. Elianor at his side. Elianor, his wife.

But then and now and evermore, niece to this brother and sister, he reminded himself. *She who believes the ill of you told by these two and Agatha.*

Still, though the part of him given to rage wanted Elianor gone so he might yield to his baser side, she was a balm to the deepest of wounds. He did not understand how it could be, but he was grudgingly grateful for her presence, without which he might suffer one more regret. And the king's wrath.

He shifted his regard to Constance's brother who looked neither amused nor satisfied. Indeed, his stance was wary, the angle of his right arm beneath his mantle evidencing his other hand was on his sword hilt. It was the same for Verdun's men and those of Adderstone.

"My lord," the priest entreated, "let us speak—"

"Not now, Father!" Bayard needed none to warn him of how little it would take for the king's decree to run red. Despite how far he had come in the years since Serle de Arell and he had flung the other's blood upon the floor, tapestry, and walls of the solar, Bayard was still the man who had borne witness to his wife's cuckolding—whose mind eagerly dredged up images best held down by the weight of less lethal memories.

He did not look to Elianor, but returned his focus to the feel of her hand upon him. He drew a slow breath, and in a voice so tight he did not recognize it, said, "What is this, Verdun?"

"Most awkward, I allow, but had I revealed my sister accompanied me home to Kelling, I believe you would have denied us entrance to Adderstone."

"You believe right. Hence, what does *she* do outside the abbey?" Bayard knew that in directing the question at Magnus Verdun he slighted the woman to whom he had been wed, but considering their parting, he was certain few would fault him. Too, if the vow of silence she had taken upon entering the convent held—a vow he resented since she hid behind it to keep alive the belief he had abused her—no answer would have been forthcoming.

"Blessedly," Magnus Verdun said, "the abbess was convinced that, with our niece gone missing, her charge should be allowed to return to Castle Kelling. Fret not, though. 'Twas agreed that, regardless of what ill had befallen Elianor, my lady sister would return after Christmas. Hence, your vengeance remains intact."

Bayard would not argue that vengeance was a concern, though he might have if not that he now stood before the one who had defiled their marriage bed. He had thought himself much recovered, that these past years of prayer and Father Crispin's good counsel had moved him beyond the place he had found himself the day blood coursed his face as his wife's lover clasped a sword-bitten arm to his chest. But he was back, and though not overwhelmed by a thirst for revenge, he longed to strike—to send the Verduns out into night that was coming fast and frigid as told by the graying of day and the breeze stirring toward a wind.

Control thyself, he heard words spoken by the priest time and again over the years. *Think as God would have you think. Act as God would have you act. Be as God would have you be. Forgive as God would have you forgive.*

That last, he rejected. At this moment, it asked too much of one made of flesh and blood-red memories. And for that, he was almost grateful when Lady Maeve leaned more heavily upon his arm, muttered, "I feel terribly ill," and collapsed.

He caught her up in his arms and, amid the murmuring, berated himself for not considering how deeply Constance's reappearance might affect her, especially after learning Quintin was held captive.

"My lady?" he asked.

Her eyes opened so narrowly that only the brown of them could be seen. "Forgive me," she whispered, "but I cannot bear to remain in that one's company."

Bayard turned toward the steps, remembered his duty, and came back around to fix his gaze on Elianor. "My lady wife," he emphasized the title Constance had spurned, "as you are now mistress of Godsmere and I am otherwise occupied, I would have you see to our *guests.*"

She inclined her head. "I shall."

Noting she did not respond in kind by according him the title of *husband*, telling himself he must never forget she was first a Verdun, he shifted his regard to the Godsmere knight who was second only to Sir Victor. The man awaited his nod, and Bayard gave it. Elianor, her kin, and those in service to the Verduns would be afforded every courtesy due them. It would be no great imposition, though, for the only courtesy they warranted was that of being kept under close watch.

He glanced at his stepmother whose brow was pleated as if she were pained, then turned his back on all of them.

El watched her husband, followed by Father Crispin, ascend the steps to the great hall. She did not understand what twisted and knotted in her chest, was afraid to make sense of the indignation she had felt upon realizing Magnus had brought Constance here in such a way Bayard was unprepared. Perhaps more, she feared the emotion that had risen through her when her husband had looked upon Constance. It stank of jealousy that she had no cause to feel.

"El?" Magnus touched her shoulder.

When Bayard carried his stepmother from sight, she looked around. "Ah, Magnus, for what did you do this?"

"I would have had it be otherwise," he said low, "but I could not leave you to Boursier without being assured you are truly safe."

"You should have sent your sister on to Kelling."

"I tried to, but she refused."

El glanced past him. Her aunt's gaze was more direct than ever it had been. Was it the quickening cold that made El shiver? Or those still, probing eyes?

"*Are* you safe?" Magnus asked. "You can speak true now."

She nodded. "My answer does not change in the absence of my husband. Bayard has done me no ill. Indeed, his behavior puts one in mind of a changed man."

Censure darkened his gaze. "Or a more cautious man."

Was that it? El did not think so. But she should. After all, one could not truly know another in so short a time. And yet...

Despite having severely tested one said to have abused his first wife, she herself bore no bruises—visible or otherwise—and time and again Bayard had shown self-restraint that even Magnus would be hard pressed to bestow upon one who did to him what she had done to The Boursier. Too, until her uncle's appearance, there had been little cause for Bayard to exercise caution.

Hating that her mind was wracked with uncertainty, El said, "'Tis possible, but let us discuss it later that we might sooner see you and Aunt Constance settled in for the night."

She turned and, as she led the way up the steps, felt the kiss of ice upon her cheek before her warm skin melted it away. Overhead, sparse clouds gathered. If they continued to increase their ranks, they might lay down enough snow to prevent Magnus and his entourage from departing Adderstone in a timely manner. Doubtless, had

Bayard an inkling of that possibility, he would have been less inclined to admit his old enemy.

When El entered the hall, she faltered at the realization that the first time she stepped foot in Adderstone as its lady in truth, she did so in the company of the one who had last bore the title—a woman Bayard had wanted as opposed to one he did not want.

It is well, she told herself. *So long as he does not prove himself to be another Murdoch, it is well.*

22

"My lord?"

Bayard knew what was asked of him, just as he knew what his answer ought to be, but his emotions were too clawed to venture where he was not ready to go.

He did not want to resent Father Crispin's lack of subtlety. He did. He did not want to be offended by the many attempts to counsel him. He was. He did not want to curse the man for lingering outside Lady Maeve's chamber. Oh, the temptation!

Pulling his stepmother's door closed, he said, "Not now," and strode around him.

Father Crispin hastened after him, passed him, and placed himself in Bayard's path. "As well you know, my lord, 'tis even more imperative that we speak."

Beset with one more temptation, that of thrusting the man aside, Bayard nearly lost the battle. However, as if noting his lord's struggle, Father Crispin reverted to his old self that had been neither biddable nor eloquent.

"Ah, wee Boursier," he drawled, the same as he had done when he was a lad of twelve and Bayard only six, "never will ye gain that horse's back if ye are not willing to risk a bit of throwin' and kickin'."

Twenty-five years past, it had truly been a horse to which Crispin referred, hoping to goad the son of Baron Foucault's knight into once more braving the mare that had sent the boy flying and nearly trampled him. Now he referred to peace, the *throw* and the *kick* being counsel and prayer.

The harsh words behind Bayard's teeth retreated, and he lowered his lid. Though it made him feel weak-hearted to wish himself back to easier days when his greatest obstacle was mounting a testy horse, it was of comfort. As well his old friend knew.

Bayard returned his gaze to Crispin. The man's eyebrows were hitched above a hooked nose in a very round face better suited to a very round body rather than the slender frame to which not even his habit could add weight.

The man shrugged shoulders from which tension had eased and smiled just enough to resurrect a mischievous light in eyes more often solemn as befit his profession.

On such rare occasions, Bayard selfishly wished Crispin were not constrained by holy vows, that his counsel was more practical than biblical, even if the advice proved the same. But the man was what Archard Boursier had made him—a priest. And contentedly so, it seemed. Most of the time.

The former stable boy had an eye for women, and though he did not act upon his desire, at times his regret over that forbidden him was almost tangible.

"I am sorry," he said, the light slipping to the corners of his eyes and going from sight. "I know you are pained at seeing her again, especially on the occasion of returning to Adderstone with your new wife."

Bayard nearly scoffed. To be pained, he would have to have feelings for the woman. He did not. He was offended by her presence, and it was that which had caused anger to tear at him.

"What I am," he said, "is deeply resentful. What I want is that woman gone."

"Understandable." Crispin folded his long-sleeved arms over his chest. "As difficult as 'tis, my son, methinks there may be good in Lady Constance's arrival."

Bayard's ire resurfaced, nearly as much a result of Crispin once more assuming the role of God's voice as his pronouncement. "Good?" he barked.

The man's eyes widened, and he glanced toward Lady Maeve's chamber.

Chagrined over the necessity of being reminded of his stepmother's much-needed rest, Bayard lowered his voice. "There is no good in having her here, and do not think to convince me of it with scripture. I am not of a mood for it."

The man's expression wavered, and for a moment Bayard thought his old friend might reappear, but it was the man of God who said, "Pray, listen. Lady Constance could have continued on to Castle Kelling, but she insisted on returning to a place where she also knew pain." He held up a hand in anticipation of Bayard's protest. "Aye, pain that was much her own doing."

It was true it was not all her own doing, Bayard having long ago accepted his culpability when he had conspired to break the betrothal between Constance and Serle de Arell. But for that, he had all the more reason to believe vengeance had brought her inside his walls.

"I will not allow her to wedge herself between Elianor and me."

"Ah." A bit of the glint returned to the man's eyes. "I had begun to wonder about your feelings for the lady, Elianor."

"Feelings?" Bayard snapped.

"Having had occasions to observe you in the company of women, I have only ever known you to be as affected by Lady Elianor as you were by her aunt. Can it be..." There, a bit of a smile. "...you esteem this marriage forced upon you?"

Bayard had his denial at the ready, but instead asked, "With whom am I speaking—Crispin or *Father* Crispin?"

The man sighed. "It ought to be the latter, but I am here as well, my friend."

Though Bayard did not want this conversation with either of them, he said, "Then to the latter, I say: I am determined this marriage shall not end the same as the first. To the former, I say: I am hopeful it shall be better than the first." He started to step around the man.

Crispin caught his arm—as ever, a strong grip that belied a body more given to bone than muscle. "Give me leave to finish a thought that may make the Verduns' presence more tolerable."

"Speak."

"In returning here, 'tis possible Lady Constance seeks forgiveness."

Bayard would not argue that. What he would argue was the terms of her quest to be forgiven and, in turn, forgive him, terms with which the priest was acquainted.

However, before the man could be reminded of the missives that had arrived one each year since Constance's departure, Crispin amended, "I, of course, speak of true forgiveness."

Among his favorite topics, and at which Bayard did not excel. But Crispin had good reason to hold that virtue dear, for its bestowal had saved his life years ago. Baron Foucault, suspecting his attempts to keep the crown informed of the baronage's plans were being thwarted by one close to him, had enlisted the stable boy to report Archard Boursier's goings and, when possible, follow at a distance.

Crispin's discovery at a wooded meeting between Archard and the earl, days before the latter moved against Foucault, nearly earned the boy a noose. Being fond of Crispin for the kindness shown young Bayard, Archard had forgiven him and reasoned that he had no choice but to do as Foucault bid. The earl had granted mercy, contingent upon Crispin covertly serving him as he had served Foucault. And so he had.

Unfortunately, upon Archard's award of Adderstone, there had been enough resentment from Foucault's former retainers that the stable boy had come under threat of maiming for his role in overthrowing the old baron. Thus, Archard had sent him away and borne the cost of training him into the priesthood. Years later, following the death of Adderstone's old priest, Crispin had returned.

"Therefore," the man continued, "the question must be asked if you believe yourself capable of forgiving Lady Constance."

Might she seek true forgiveness? Grant true forgiveness? Or, as ever, would she hold hostage the truth of that day behind her vow of silence?

Slowly, Bayard shook his head. "I fear you delude yourself in thinking this time she will not lay out the terms of peace between us. But were it true forgiveness..."

Crispin waited. And waited. Then he sighed heavily. "We will speak again this eve. In the chapel, aye?"

Grudgingly, Bayard nodded. "This eve," he said and left the priest to be about his prayers.

It was unusual that the lord and lady of Adderstone and their noble guests eschewed the great hall at the evening meal, but when Bayard sent word to El that he had other matters to attend to, she had concluded it was best that all dine in their respective chambers. Thus, while the Boursier and Verdun retainers sat down to a light repast in the hall, platters of viands were delivered to those abovestairs.

As one was carried past El into the solar outside which she stood, she caught back the words she had been about to speak to Adderstone's steward whose willingness to assist the new lady of Godsmere had surprised her. Above all, she appreciated his aid in providing accommodations for Magnus and Constance—the former given a chamber belonging to the absent Sir Victor, the latter a chamber usually occupied by two household knights.

Once the unburdened woman servant exited the solar and hastened down the corridor, El summoned a smile for the steward. "I thank you, Edgar. You have been more kind than you surely believe I warrant."

His mouth quirked. "I am a practical man, my lady. Regardless of how you came to be my mistress, I see no reason to be at odds with one who now has my lord's ear. Thus, as long as you give the baron no cause to throw you off as he did his first wife"—his eyes darted to a door farther down the corridor—"I will give you no cause to regret or undermine my place at Adderstone."

Practical *and* candid. "Then methinks ours shall be an agreeable relationship."

"I pray so, my lady." He bowed.

Certain he meant to depart, El asked, "I would have my husband join me at meal. Do you think he is still with his stepmother?"

When Edgar looked up, she directed her gaze down the corridor to the chamber he had earlier told her belonged to Lady Maeve.

"I would not think so, my lady. Nor would I suggest you seek him there."

Though El might have been tempted to tap on the door, she was not sure she would have done so, and now she would not. She did not yet trust Edgar, but his words confirmed her own belief that it would be unwise to approach Lady Maeve.

"Good eve, my lady." The steward stepped past her, halted, turned back around. "I am not wont to give advice so early in an acquaintance-ship, but I shall chance it."

She feared she would not like it, but that did not mean she should not hear it. "I thank you."

"Lady Maeve is a fine woman—a good woman—but when she is in one of her turmoils, as she has good cause to be with her daughter held captive and Lady Constance beneath her roof, 'tis best to walk wide around her. Times like these…" He raised his palms. "She remembers who she was ere she was a Boursier."

A woman who would have lost all had Bayard's father not taken her to wife. "I understand."

"I fear you do not. But now you are informed." He pivoted and, his bit of hair lifting in the chill draft that meandered along the corridor, strode toward the stairs.

When he went from sight, the tension that had climbed through El began to ease, and she yielded to the impulse to lean against the door-frame. She closed her eyes, savored the quiet, and as she settled into it, breathed, "There now."

The groan of a door brought her eyes open, and she turned toward the chamber midway down the corridor. "El?" Magnus said, his brow troubled as he strode toward her.

She pushed off the doorframe and met him partway.

Gripping her shoulder, he searched her face. "Are you well?"

"I am but tired. And you? How do you find your accommodations?"

He scowled. "Do not be distant with me. Regardless that you are now wed to Boursier, I am your kin and shall ever be."

She nearly protested, but it was true. She *was* distancing herself, but wisely so considering what some believed of their relationship. "Apologies, Magnus." She squeezed his hand on her shoulder—and once more revisited memories of this morn when it was Bayard's hand beneath her own.

She lowered her arm to her side. "All is strained," she said, "and though much of that is of my own doing, with Constance here..."

He sighed. "I should have insisted she continue on to Kelling. But when she would not be dissuaded, it occurred to me there could be gain in her accompanying me."

"I do not understand."

"It seemed a good means of testing Boursier—pushing him to lose control in my presence to reveal his true character."

That surprised her. Though she knew Magnus was astute, she had not thought him so cunning. "He did not lose control," she said.

"In that you are right, though surely you felt the edge upon which he teetered?"

She had, but she could hardly blame Bayard for going so near it, especially as he had not done so on his own. Magnus had as good as flung him there.

He raised his eyebrows. "Truly, you feel safe with The Boursier?"

She looked down, hated that she was ashamed to admit as much and that Magnus would think her more a fool. "Certes, Bayard is no Murdoch."

A finger beneath her chin returned her gaze to his. "I am glad, but he does not have to be a Murdoch to be treacherous, El."

Years ago, she had reconciled herself with what her uncle had learned of her marriage when she, widowed and homeless, had accepted his offer to live at Castle Kelling. Though she had Agatha to thank for his generosity, the woman having informed him of his niece's need, there had been a price to pay. Without a care for El's pride or modesty, Agatha had revealed much of what those two years with Murdoch had cost her lady, though even she could not know the full extent. Magnus and El never spoke of her abuse in more than general terms, but it always made her insides writhe.

"Bayard is not treacherous—not anymore," she said, while inside she whispered, *If ever he was.*

"I am pleased you think so well of me, my lady," her husband's voice sounded from the solar.

El spun around. He was not in the doorway, but he was inside. How? The hidden passageway.

"If you are done with my wife, Verdun," he called, "I have need of her."

"El?" Magnus rasped.

Keeping her expression clear of anger over Bayard's eavesdropping, she peered over her shoulder at her uncle. "Worry not," she whispered and crossed to the solar.

Lit by the fire that had cast off much of the chamber's chill, Bayard sat in one of two chairs before the hearth alongside the table upon which the servant had placed the tray of viands. Though El could not be certain where he directed his gaze, for his patched eye was in profile, his attention appeared to be on the goblet he cupped in the hand draped over the chair's arm.

How long had he been there? She knew he had not been present during her conversation with his steward, for she would have heard his entrance from where she had stood alongside the door. But when Magnus had come out of his chamber, she had moved away from the solar. How much of the exchange with her uncle had Bayard overheard?

As she reached to close the door, he looked across his shoulder. She expected censure. Thus, its presence on his face did not unnerve her. What did catch her unawares was Magnus.

"Forgive my intrusion, Baron Boursier." He put a foot over the threshold. "Though the day has been long for all, I would speak to you of what has transpired—and has yet to transpire."

Bayard considered Magnus with the same censure he had shone upon El. "We shall speak of it on the morrow, Verdun." Despite his relatively placid face, his tone told there would be no argument. "Good eve."

Magnus eyed him, then El.

She inclined her head. "Good eve, Uncle."

He sent her a look that told he would be near should she require aid, then strode down the corridor.

When El heard the thump of the door in its frame, she closed the solar's door and turned toward Bayard. "How does your stepmother fare?"

"She is resting now and will likely be recovered come the morrow."

"I am sorry she is distressed."

"She has cause to be." He frowned. "Do you know of what cause I speak?"

El clasped her hands at her waist, in doing so was made more aware of the loose fit of her wedding band. "Doubtless, she detests that you were made a cuckold and sustained the injury you did."

"There is that, but more, there is Quintin. She was also injured the day I found your aunt and Serle de Arell abed." He gestured with the hand that held the goblet, causing the wine within to spill over the rim and onto the rushes. "*That* bed."

El glanced at where her marriage had yet to be consummated, alongside which she had slept on a pallet those first two nights before they had departed for Castle Mathe. "I did not know. What happened—?"

"Now you do know, as you should know 'tis no easy thing to have Verduns or De Arells beneath our roof."

And now there were three Verduns here where there had been none for years.

"Just as it is no easy thing to happen upon one's *current* wife alone with another man," he added.

El stiffened. In previously titling her as the woman to whom he was bound for life, there had been bitterness and regret in his tone, but the addition of the word, *current*, put more distance—and accusation—between them.

She stepped forward and halted before Bayard. "Magnus and I were only conversing, as well you know."

"Aye," he drawled, "conversing."

Did he insinuate there might have been more to their encounter had he not alerted them to his presence?

"Is it your habit to steal upon others and listen in on their conversations?" she demanded.

Bayard stared at the woman he had riled as he had not intended to do. Jealousy would have to answer for that. And Constance, her sudden appearance having torn memories from his darkest recesses that had trampled the hope extended when he had told El the price of what she had done might not be as high as thought. But perhaps that was good. Perhaps the more painful the reminders of Verdun treachery, the less vulnerable he would be to their schemes.

And the more likely those memories will eat you through, Father Crispin spoke as clearly to him as if he stood here, a reminder that Bayard ought to be in the chapel.

"Is it your habit?" Elianor pressed.

He glanced at the goblet he had taken from the tray, and once more pondered the dark red contents that had yet to pass his lips. "'Tis not," he overruled the argument that he owed her no explanation. "When I came upon my steward and he relayed your wish to dine with me, my use of the hidden passageway was a matter of expediency, not a means of stealing upon Verdun and you. Thus, the only thing of which I am guilty is of not sooner making my presence known."

She blinked, and the anger that had tightened her expression eased. "Why did you not?"

"Having happened upon a conversation in which I found myself under discussion, I saw little cause to weigh the right and wrong of gaining insight into matters that concern me."

"And what insight did you gain?"

"That my unwilling bride feels compelled to defend me. Just as surprising, that her uncle knows more about her relationship with her departed husband than is known to the man to whom she is now wed."

"You think it evidence my relationship with Magnus is of a carnal nature?"

Jealousy concurred, though the instinct he dared not trust told otherwise. "You say it is not so, but what you shared with one you claim is naught but kin seems much too personal."

She shook her head. "'Twas not I who told Magnus——" She drew a sharp breath, averted her gaze.

The Elianor whom Bayard wanted to know better once more retreating, he set the goblet on the tray, rose from the chair, and took the stride to her side.

He lifted her chin. "Do not deny me, Elianor. As your husband, I have the right to know that against which you seal your lips—that which makes you fear my touch even whilst you wish it."

Her lids fluttered, and he found himself holding his breath throughout her struggle, but just when he thought she would refuse him, she said, "It was Agatha who revealed the truth of my marriage to Magnus when she appealed to him to take me in following my husband's death. I would not have had her do so, but..." She momentarily closed her eyes, and when she opened them, they were moist. "'Tis true that Murdoch abused me, and ever in such a way it could not be known were one to gaze upon me." A sharp laugh cast her warm breath upon his jaw. "He placed too high a value on my looks to spoil them."

Though Bayard had guessed as much, his insides convulsed with anger of a depth last felt while he had been chained to a wall. But whereas

then it was the barony of Godsmere slipping away from him, now it was
Elianor. How was he to put together the pieces made of the one who,
God willing, would be mother to his sons and daughters? And how was
he to quell this longing to wreak vengeance on a man who, also God
willing, now dwelt in the pits of hell?

He returned Elianor to focus, knew from her wide, searching eyes
she sensed something of what moved beneath his skin.

Lord, he silently entreated, *I should be on my knees—better, my face.*

"Bayard?" she said softly.

In a gruff voice, he said, "There are not many men who would consider themselves fortunate to be dead, but I wager Murdoch Farrow does."

She winced, drew her chin out of his grasp, and took a step back.

Knowing it best to not further inquire after the miscreant, Bayard
let the matter be. However, there were other things that needed answers.
"You say 'twas Agatha who asked your uncle to take you in. For what did
she do so?"

Elianor's shrug was hesitant. "She has a care for me—is the only one
who did whilst I dwelt with Murdoch. If not for her..."

"What?"

"She passed powders to me that rendered him unconscious with
little remembrance of the time before. Though I dared not use them
often lest he become suspicious, when he was at his worst—drunk or in
a rage—I stirred them into his..."

"The same powders you slipped into my drink the night Agatha and
you stole me from my bed," he said low.

"Aye."

"The same powders Constance gained from her and used upon me
whilst we were wed."

She blinked. "That I did not know."

He should not be so quick to believe her, but he did. "For that, I cast
Agatha out of Adderstone, hoping that once Constance was no longer under
her influence, a better marriage we could make." He drew a deep breath. "I
do not know what that witch is about, Elianor. I know only that she is poison."

She folded her hands at her waist. "And I know only that I owe her."

"Methinks you are wrong. Like King Edward who makes pawns of our families, she has made a pawn of you." When she opened her mouth to argue it, he held up a hand. "Regardless of what you believe you owe her, *I* owe her naught—certainly naught of good will. And I have no intention of allowing her to further befoul my life or the lives of those dear to me."

"What will you—?"

"—do with her? I have not decided. And do not ask me to, for this day has put me in no state of mind to sensibly determine that one's fate."

"I understand," she begrudged. "But tell me, is she well?"

Bayard counseled patience. "I have not seen her, but it was reported that though she rages less, she is as loud as ever. And that is all I will speak of her, Elianor." He turned and reached for the goblet to quench his thirst. But the witch was too near in thought, and he once more hesitated over the wine's red depths.

"'Tis not tainted." Elianor stepped alongside him. "I vow, it is not."

He looked down at her and saw in her eyes what seemed desperation. That he believe her?

"Would you have me drink from it first?" she asked.

He lifted the goblet and drained half its contents. "I will leave you now," he said and set the vessel on the tray.

Elianor laid a hand on his arm. "You will join me at meal?"

"Father Crispin expects me, and I have kept him waiting long enough." He lifted her hand from him and brushed his lips across the backs of her fingers. "Good eve, Wife."

El watched him go, wished he would not. Wished...

What do I wish? She looked to the bed. *I wish Constance had never been there. I wish she were not there now. I wish Bayard free of their past. I wish her presence did not have the power to send* my *husband away from me.*

But she had been. She was. He was not. And she did.

Marveling that not so long ago, never would such thoughts have come upon her and cause her eyes to prick with tears, wondering if, perhaps, she was ill of mind, El stared at the foodstuffs.

Out of duty to her hungering belly, she snatched up a piece of cheese. She ate it and several more, took a swallow of wine, and began extinguishing the candles.

Once the chamber was dark except for firelight, she was reminded of that first night when she and Agatha had stolen within—when she had bent near Bayard and seen the glitter of his gaze, when unbeknownst to her, he had taken in her scent. It seemed so long ago they had dragged him from his bed and through the hidden passageway to imprison him in that place to which Agatha was now subjected.

"Agatha," she whispered, and was tempted to go behind the tapestry and try to find a way into the underground so she might assure the woman to whom she owed much that she would convince Bayard to release her. But that could prove a lie if he refused. Would he? The man she had believed him to be would, but the man he was proving himself to be, the same she wished here with her now—

She shook her head, stepped toward the bed, and halted. She pondered the pallet where she had slept when last she was here, wondered if that was where Bayard expected her to sleep.

She shed her gown. Clad in her thick chemise, she turned back the bed's fur-lined coverlet and lay down, claiming her place where Bayard would find her when he returned. But how would he feel to look upon her here, where once he had looked upon Constance in the arms of another man? The thought nearly made her scramble onto the pallet.

She pulled the coverlet over her, turned the ring on her finger, and whispered, "'Tis our bed now. Ours," and yielded to sleep.

23

A GATHA OF M AWBRY hummed. And the nearer the footsteps sounded, the louder she hummed. It was not The Boursier come to her, for the tread belonged to a woman—else a timid man. Regardless, neither ought to be here. Happily, either would serve.

When the torch was lifted to the grate in the door, the dim light that had entered the cell like a slow-moving fog spewed itself against the walls and upon its single occupant.

Pain pricking eyes blinded by days of darkness, Agatha ceased her humming and squinted to see who peered within, grunted, and jerked her face aside. "I am not dead," she barked out of a throat that felt as if ripped through. "Now get thee in here!"

There came the rattle of iron testing iron. When the correct key engaged the lock's innards, the resulting click fell as sweet upon Agatha's ears as honey upon the tongue.

Honey, she mused. *How I miss it, but soon I shall coat a spoon with it, suck it clean, and again and again until I decide how best to hurt those whose hurts are due me.*

The door swung inward, and the feet of one far too long in coming stepped inside with hesitation that bespoke fear. Deserved fear. But depending upon that one's identity, forgiveness might be granted—for a time.

Eyes slitted against light too potent to allow Agatha to clearly see the one who would loose her upon the Boursiers and the others who could not know they were next, she said, "Is it you, Lady Elianor?"

The one in the doorway stepped to the side and fit the torch in a sconce.

"Elianor?" Agatha asked again, though the continued silence made her fairly certain this one was not the one named.

In shoes that scraped the earthen floor almost as if the feet resisted being drawn forward, the hooded figure traversed the cell.

"Not Elianor," Agatha pronounced as her savior crouched beside her.

"It is not," that one said and dropped the hood around shoulders so lax they stank of defeat.

It took Agatha a moment to recognize the voice, a moment longer to focus on the face. Delight nearly made her crow, but after all she had endured, anger held greater sway.

"You could not have come sooner?" she demanded.

Her savior swallowed, the dry sound of tongue, palate, and throat too little of a balm to keep Agatha from aching to feel that one's throat between her hands—rather, *hand*, for it would be some time before she regained use of the less dominant one.

"It was not possible to free you ere this day," the pitiful one said. "But I am here now, and though 'twas a difficult undertaking, I have secured the keys for your release."

Agatha thrust her manacled hands forward, and her savior leaned near and gasped at the sight of the left hand that hung limp from one set of iron bands. "Dear Lord, what have you done?"

"Struggled and fought as you have not done. Now make haste!"

As the keys jangled between trembling fingers that searched for one that fit, Agatha considered her bruised and scraped wrist, next its broken hand. Determination had done that—perhaps even a touch of madness. In an attempt to free herself, she had broken several bones, but her hand was too large to slip from the manacle, and the pain too great to wreak further damage. Too, belatedly she had realized that even were she able to free the broken hand, the other would also require breaking and leave her more helpless.

"This one!" her savior exclaimed. Shortly, the manacle fell from the broken hand. As the key was fit into the other, Agatha continued to stare at her maimed limb.

Further proof of the sins of the Boursiers, she told herself and felt a spasm of pride. The hand would never be right, but the other would serve as it had always done, and this one would heal sufficiently to be of some use.

With another click that once more turned Agatha's thoughts toward the sweetness of honey, the second manacle released.

"Ah." Agatha raised both hands before her face. In silence complete except for her savior's shallow breathing, she pondered the differences that were as day to night...right to wrong...good to evil...life to death.

That last summoned a smile to lips so unaccustomed to bowing in that direction that the muscles pained her. But she must become accustomed to smiles, for there would be many more in the days to come. Days that would be dark for the Boursiers. And the De Arells. And the Verduns.

Laughter leapt from her, so coarse she snapped her mouth closed against further expressions of merriment. She was no crone, would not be for many years.

"Agatha?"

She looked back at the one whose face reflected wariness. Once more attempting a smile, Agatha lifted her good hand and patted that one's jaw, the skin of which had no right to be so soft. Unfortunately, the one who had come for her was a necessary ill—or *had been.*

Agatha wavered, but though tempted to make the underground this one's final resting place, such a death might reveal what should not be revealed. Yet.

Her savior drew back, started to rise. "Come. The sooner you depart Adderstone, the better."

Agatha wrenched that one back down. "First, I must know what has gone whilst I have been in this accursed place."

"But—"

"Tell!"

And so her reluctant savior did, eliciting from Agatha sprays of spit, barks of anger, and curses so blasphemous Agatha was time and again beseeched to attend to her soul.

Fortunately, all that had gone afoul could be put to rights, Agatha assured herself. For years the three families had suffered loss at her hands as she dwelt amongst them, biding her time while the one who would reap all was groomed to grind them underfoot. But though the plan had been to wait a time longer, and she would have been content to do so, the King's meddling had changed all. Thus, the end was near. And would be sweeter than the sweetest honey sucked from a spoon.

What sounds were those? Whence did they come? Inside a dream?

As it was darkness El stared into, she reasoned the hiss of voices and rasp of footsteps could not issue from a dream. The corridor, then.

She lifted her lids and swept her bleary gaze around the chamber. Nothing moved in the faint, golden light that was all that remained of the warming fire, and when she turned her head on the pillow, she was as alone as when she had lain down. But surely the sounds were of Bayard—of him returning to share the bed with her.

She looked to the door, but as she waited for it to open, she realized the sounds came from the hidden passageway. Had Bayard ventured into the underground to check on Agatha? And with whom did he now speak?

El told herself to wait—to ask him when he entered—but the voices and footsteps were receding. She turned the coverlet back, rose from the bed, and crossed to the tapestry and slipped behind it.

Pressing an ear to the door, she listened. As thought, the sounds were moving away. Fairly certain she would find the door locked against her, she gasped when her release of the catch caused it to swing inward. Fortunately, it did so without creak or groan.

The keep's inner walls were lit by a torch, and when she leaned in to peer down the passageway, she saw the light was held aloft by one of two figures moving opposite.

Though tempted to call to Bayard, she knew he would not like that she had breached the passageway. Too, it was possible neither of the figures was her husband. Indeed, they did not look tall or broad enough, and since they had ceased speaking, their identity could not be known from their voices.

El pulled the door closed, only to give rise to a screech of protest. But it was not the hinges that betrayed her. It was the rodent who wriggled free of the door's pinch.

Before El could retreat, those at the far end spun around.

"Bayard?" El ventured.

The one in front snatched the torch from the one behind. Flame flickering full upon a face that was familiar despite the damage done it during Bayard's escape from the underground, El gripped the door's edge to steady herself.

"Aye, 'tis me, free of my prison," Agatha said in a grating voice similar to that with which Bayard had been afflicted the first few days following his escape from the underground. "And I have not you to thank, have I?"

"How…?" El shook her head. "How did you…?"

"Stay!" Agatha commanded the one behind as though he or she were a dog, then traversed the passageway with labored steps that evidenced discomfort.

Though El longed to retreat to the solar and slam the door closed, she owed Agatha too much. Thus, she stepped forward and closed the door lest Bayard chose this moment to return to the solar.

From the steps that descended toward the underground, a draft of chill air fluttered the hem of her skirts and swept up the backs of her legs. Shivering, she pressed her arms tight to her sides and peered beyond the woman advancing on her to the one surely responsible for Agatha's release. But that one's identity could not be known at this distance, it being hooded.

Agatha halted. Holding the torch to the side, though near enough that it warmed El's cheek, the older woman lowered her gaze down her lady. "You look well, Elianor. Indeed, too well for one wed to The Boursier."

This was not the first frisson of fear El had felt in the woman's presence, but this one was not as easily dismissed, clambering up her spine and sinking teeth into her neck. Still, she stood firm—until Agatha lifted between them a hand that hung obscenely limp from its wrist.

El stumbled back. "What happened?"

"The Boursier, *that* is what! And you did naught to aid me. Too busy warming his bed, eh?"

"I—"

"You no longer believe what he did to your aunt. Do you?"

At El's hesitation, she smiled a frightening, broken-toothed smile. "You are of no more use to me, Elianor of Emberly."

"Agatha—"

"Not Agatha!" she rasped. "Aude!"

One moment, the heat of the torch was upon El's face, the next, its flame was hard upside her head.

She strained to hold her feet firm to the floor, reached for something to turn her hands around, felt air slip through her fingers. Too much air. Too far to fall.

Her cry echoed off the walls, threw itself back at her as she twisted around and threw her hands up to break her fall. The hard landing on her side. The terrible sound of something breaking. The shock that numbed her—though only for a moment. Before she could voice the pain tearing at her insides, darkness descended, the relief it offered so great she could not bring herself to try to hold to her place in the world.

"That is a broken neck," Agatha's voice came to her as if from the mouth of a long tunnel whose light was a mere pinprick. "A fairly satisfying end to a Verdun, do you not think?" Then she began to hum.

24

His knees were sore, joints stiff. However, despite time spent with Father Crispin and at prayer, he could not keep his emotions from lurching each time his thoughts lit on Constance who should not be upon the barony of Godsmere...within the walls of Castle Adderstone...just down from the chamber that now belonged to Elianor and him.

Bayard halted before the solar's door, considered his squire who had made his bed to the left of it, gripped the handle—and stilled as he questioned the wisdom of going in to his desirable wife. Not only was he determined to give her time to become accustomed to him, but the thought of consummating marriage to his second wife whilst the first slept so near was unsettling.

Telling himself his fatigue would quickly put him to sleep regardless of whether or not Elianor had taken her place in his bed or once more huddled on the pallet, he entered the chamber.

The glowing embers upon the hearth revealed she was not on the pallet nor the bed, though the turned back covers of the latter evidenced she had been there. Certain she must have lost her courage and curled up in one of the chairs, he closed the door and started toward them. She was not there.

"Accursed woman!" he growled and strode to the tapestry she had surely gone behind. Next, he cursed himself for leaving the door to the inner walls unlocked when he had earlier come through and overheard his wife and Verdun's conversation. Not that Elianor could reach Agatha since the door that accessed the underground was locked, but she would try.

As expected, he opened the door to chill air. What he did not expect was darkness, certain she would have taken a candle with her. Guessing she must have heard him and put it out, he called, "Elianor!"

Silence.

"Enough!" he snapped. "Now!"

Still nothing.

Did he underestimate her again? Was it possible she *had* gained the underground? Or, thwarted, did she explore the passages in hopes of finding another means of reaching the witch? Of course, there were only two ways to access that cell—the stairs to the left and the cavern in the wood.

Being well-versed in Adderstone's inners walls, Bayard did not return for a candle but briskly descended the steps. As he neared the landing, he halted. Elianor's scent was here. More disturbingly, the scent that always called to mind iron and earth. Blood.

Gripped by fear of a sort he had known in a time so distant he could not recall the occasion, he caught a sound from below. Though faint, it was of breath.

"Elianor?" Cautiously, he descended the last steps lest he trod upon her. When he reached the landing and his foot nudged something, he dropped to his haunches and let his hands discover that to which darkness blinded him.

Knowing that how severely Elianor was injured depended on how far she had fallen and what part of her had taken the brunt of the fall, he cautiously worked his hands up her cold, still form where she lay on her side against the wall—bare feet, lower legs, chemise-entangled upper legs.

When he reached her hips and she remained unresponsive, his fear stepped back in deference to a greater anger than that which he had felt upon discovering she had gone into the passageway. "All for that witch!" he growled.

She moaned.

"Elianor!"

Her breath caught sharply as of one either slow to return to consciousness or incapable of a better response.

Praying it was the former, he continued his exploration, feeling a hand up her right arm and shoulder, across her throat, and up into her hair on the left side of her head that rested on the floor.

She drew another sharp breath when his fingers found the swollen gash above her ear—the source of blood.

Wary of moving her until he knew the extent of her injury, he said, "Awaken, Elianor."

She whimpered, whispered, "Bayard."

A good sign. Thanking the Lord, he wiped his bloodied fingers on his chausses, then cupped her icy face in his hand. "What hurts?"

"All," she croaked.

"Is anything broken?"

Her swallow sounded painfully dry. "Not my neck." A sob escaped her. "Though she wished it so."

He nearly probed her meaning, but her injuries were more important. "What, then?"

"My..." Her teeth clicked as of one chilled. "...arm."

The left one, doubtless thrown up to break her fall. He slid his hand down her neck to the shoulder she lay upon, next the arm. She tensed as he probed its upper reaches, cried out when he moved to her forearm.

"Anything else?" he asked.

"I do not know."

Aching for however long she had been down here, which could be as many as three hours, he said, "I must needs lift you. When I do, your arm will pain you more."

Her hesitation was brief. "Be done with it."

He nearly called her brave, but lest anger's preference for *impetuous, defiant,* and *deceitful* usurped his tongue, he said no more.

He eased her onto her back, and the first note of a scream escaped her before she closed her mouth on it. Thus, further expressions of pain sounded from behind her lips. But there was nothing for it, there being no other way to free her broken arm to position her to be carried up the steps.

He settled the injured limb atop her torso, and when he lifted her, she was limp. Grateful she found relief in unconsciousness, he carried her up the steps and into the solar.

"Squire!" he bellowed as he came out from behind the tapestry.

The door swung open as he lowered Elianor to the bed. "My lord?" The sway in the young man's body revealed sleep yet clung to him.

"Send for the physician," Bayard ordered. At Lucas's hesitation, he roared, "Now!"

The squire ran, but before the sound of his retreat was lost in the turning of the stairs, a door was thrown open farther down the corridor and far-reaching footsteps revealed Elianor's uncle would soon fill the doorway.

"Bring a torch within, Verdun!" Bayard shouted and turned back to his wife. Though more illumination was needed to know the extent of her head injury, the remains of the fire showed blood upon her dark blond hair.

As he reached to draw the fur-lined coverlet over her, light rushed into the chamber.

"What goes?" Magnus Verdun demanded. A torch in one hand, a dagger in the other, he shifted his gaze from Bayard to Elianor. "God's teeth! What have you done to her?"

Bayard reached for his sword, but he had unbelted it for prayer and left it in the chapel. Taking his dagger to hand, he strode forward to intercept the other man. "Hear me, Verdun!"

The only alternative was for the man to start slashing, and that would be of poor effect while he held a torch that, if loosed, would catch the rushes afire. "Upon my word, Boursier," Verdun said where he halted three feet distant, "I shall spill every drop of your blood."

Bayard's pride bucked at having to defend himself, but for Elianor's sake, he said, "I did not do this. The blood is from a head injury she sustained during a fall."

"What fall?"

It was almost laughable that neither the savage glint in the man's eyes, nor the sneer of his mouth made him a frightening being. He was too blessed with good looks. However, there was power in being so misread, for those who did not know him surely mistook him for an unworthy adversary.

"She stole into the inner passages to aid Agatha," Bayard said. "I found her at the bottom of the stairs that access the underground where the witch is held."

"Bayard," Elianor choked.

Dismissing Verdun's dagger, he returned to her side and, seeing she trembled, drew the coverlet over her.

As he tucked it around her, she gasped, "Do not, Magnus!"

Bayard jerked his chin around and found her uncle much too near, dagger at the ready. But before he could move to defend himself, a sob pushed past Elianor's lips, followed closely by, "My husband did not... do this."

Verdun narrowed his gaze. "You are saying you did take a fall?"

"By Agatha's hand."

Bayard startled. "Agatha?"

"She struck me...with a torch."

"Fool woman! You release that witch and she nearly kills you!"

Elianor shook her head on the pillow. "I did not let her out."

She lied. Had to, for no others would free Agatha.

"I give you no cause to believe me," Elianor said in a voice strained with tears, "but the Lord knows I did not do it."

"If 'tis true Agatha is no longer in her cell," Bayard said, "I can think of no other who would release her." In the next instant, he corrected himself. This night, within his home were many who were too recently his enemy. If Agatha had, indeed, been freed—a seemingly implausible

feat for any who lacked knowledge of the inner walls and, more, keys—
Magnus Verdun or one of his men could be responsible. Or Constance.

He ground his teeth. Aye, she whose servant Agatha had first been
and who had been well served by the witch, who knew the passages and
had once had access to keys that had let Serle de Arell within.

"I heard voices in the walls," Elianor continued. "I thought 'twas you,
Bayard."

"Voices?" Verdun stole the question from Bayard. "Who was with
Agatha?"

When she spoke again, her voice was thready as if consciousness
once more slid away. "I know not...did not draw near enough."

Bayard struggled against his warrior's sense that warned he should
not linger here, that what he had learned was sufficient to rouse his men
and lead a search of the castle. If the witch had not already gone from
Adderstone, every moment that passed drew her nearer escape. But
first, the physician. Once Elianor was in his care and guards were posted
to ensure her safety, he would search out the accursed woman—and
whoever aided her.

"Elianor," he said, "do you know if that other one was a man or a
woman?" If the latter, it could have been her aunt.

She shook her head, and when she whimpered as though pained,
there was an answering sound of distress.

Bayard looked past Magnus Verdun to where Lady Maeve gripped
the doorframe. Eyes wide, she stared at the beautiful woman beside her
who was wrapped in a robe, hair down around her shoulders and bare
feet upon the threshold.

"Do not!" he growled, then more loudly, "Dare not step foot in
here!"

Constance shifted her gaze from him to her niece, then to her
brother. An instant later, Magnus Verdun strode toward her—wisely so,
shielding her not only from Bayard's wrath but that of Lady Maeve who
had never looked so inclined to loose her teeth and nails upon another.

"Leave the torch!" Bayard ordered.

The man thrust it in a wall sconce alongside the door, then drew his sister down the corridor, leaving Bayard's stepmother the only occupant of the doorway that, hopefully, would not be absent the physician much longer.

"Lady Maeve," he said, "light the candles."

She startled as if slapped, with obvious reluctance stepped inside.

"How bad is it?" Elianor croaked.

Bayard looked back at her. Though her lids were tightly closed, tears spiked her lashes. "The physician will soon be here and set your arm aright," he said, anger once more rising at the possibility both promises could easily be transformed into lies.

"I cannot feel all of it."

For now, a blessing, but later...

"Agatha thought 'twas my neck. Ere all went black, I heard her say—" She sobbed.

The blood slamming through Bayard's veins made him long to be inside the walls, outside the walls, wherever the hunt for the witch might take him.

He glanced at the empty doorway, and as he silently vowed that if the physician did not appear in the next minute he would shout down the castle, Elianor's uncle strode inside.

"Rouse your men and mine, Verdun," Bayard barked. "If that vile thing is yet near, we shall root her out."

Verdun halted, nodded, and withdrew.

Forcing a breath deep to calm himself, Bayard lowered to the mattress edge and laid a hand to Elianor's cheek. "What did Agatha say?"

The convulsions upon which her sobs were borne eased, and she lifted her lids enough for the light in the chamber to sparkle in her eyes. "She saved me from the worst of Murdoch. I thought she was...Not my friend. Something else."

Something else, indeed, Bayard seethed. "Tell me."

"I heard her tell that other one 'twas a satisfying end to..." She swallowed loudly. "...a Verdun."

Then that other one who had freed Agatha had not been a Verdun? Not Constance?

"Why does she hate me so?" She bemoaned. "She must know I would have freed her were it possible. Why?"

"Because that one is evil," Lady Maeve said, coming alongside the bed with a candle whose flickering light revealed Elianor's hair was singed near her left temple where the torch had struck her. "Ponder it night and day, but ever the answer shall be that there are some whose only excuse for the ill they do others and themselves——" She wrenched her words to a halt.

Bayard looked to her and saw she had tightly closed her eyes. But before he could express concern, she turned aside, set the candle on the table, and continued, "The only excuse for the ill they work is the devil in them. Certes, Agatha of Mawbry is among those into whom the infernal one has poured his foul breath."

He understood his stepmother's feelings, for she also believed Agatha was as much at fault for the cuckolding as Constance. That act of infidelity had led to the bloody confrontation into which Quintin had inserted herself and paid an unseemly price—a price that could prove even greater once she wed.

"I am a fool," Elianor said softly.

"Nay," Bayard said, "you are not."

"I am. After what she did the night we were to release you…" Once more her lids lowered. "I should have run when I saw she was the one inside the walls."

Bayard glanced at his stepmother who had not moved from alongside the bed and whose gaze was upon Elianor.

"What did Agatha do that night?" he asked, loathing that as she once more teetered toward unconsciousness he must push for further insight to aid in bringing the witch to ground.

Elianor's lids fluttered. "Her hate was so great, I did not trust her to release you."

Her words further muted by sounds upon the stairs—blessedly, the physician's high-pitched, nasal voice among them—Bayard leaned closer. "Aye?"

"I insisted on accompanying her…she struck me senseless…took the keys."

That night was still near enough that he remembered its every detail. Now he understood the reason Agatha alone had appeared before him in the cell, Elianor's belated arrival that was preceded by her urgent cry for the witch to cease, Agatha's lament over not being allowed to kill him while it was still possible.

"Her hand," Elianor said so low he was not certain he heard right.

"Aye?"

"Broken."

Then the witch had snapped her bones to try to free herself. He was not surprised. After all, rats gnawed off limbs to escape traps.

"She said…not Agatha."

He frowned. "I do not understand."

"Aude?" Elianor slurred.

Before he could ask her meaning, she drew a sharp breath and said, "I will come back to you, Bayard?"

Wondering what caused his heart to feel as if wrenched from his chest, he said, "Soon, Elianor," and brushed his mouth across hers. "Now rest."

He lifted his head and, finding she had slipped away, assured himself that whatever course the physician prescribed, it was better done with her unawares.

"You care for her," Lady Maeve said with aggrieved wonder. "A Verdun. How can it be?" Her eyebrows gathered nearer. "After what Constance—"

"She is not Constance." He straightened and stepped past her.

She caught his arm. "Of course she is! Once again you succumb to beauty and the pleasures of the bed, forgetting all that—"

"Cease!" Bayard pulled free, only to pause over the hurt that flashed across her face. Despite the circumstances under which his father had taken her to wife, she had done her best to be a good mother to him, and she had certainly been a good mother to Quintin—until Archard's death when the confident, charming lady of Godsmere had begun to crumble and cling, and more so following the bloody confrontation between himself and Serle de Arell.

"Forgive me," Bayard said, "but I have matters to attend to." As evidenced by the entrance of the physician and Squire Lucas who were followed by Verdun. While the latter ordered the knights and men-at-arms with him to remain in the corridor, Bayard motioned the physician forward.

The man lowered his bag to the bed, carefully examined the gash above Elianor's ear, then her arm.

"What say you?" Bayard asked.

"Her head is not as bad as it looks, and methinks her broken arm is to thank for that—that it took much of the fall. I believe it can be properly reset, but I make no promises."

Bayard was tempted to demand his word that she would come out of this whole, but he was well enough acquainted with the man's considerable skill to know it would be a lie forced out of him.

"I leave her in your hands," he said and strode past his stepmother. In the corridor, standing alongside Verdun, he quickly assigned men-at-arms to hold watch over the solar, as well as the chambers of Lady Maeve and Constance.

Not surprisingly, Verdun protested that last.

"For her safety as well," Bayard said, though it went beyond that, and from Verdun's expression, he knew it.

"*My* men will keep watch over my sister," he said.

"As you will." Since Adderstone's men would share guard over the corridor and be of greater number, it was no onerous concession.

"And now we hunt," Bayard said.

Empty-handed. All the harder to accept when one's blood thrummed with vengeance. And if Magnus Verdun's bearing and facial tics were to be believed, neither was he pleased with the hours-long search that had yielded little evidence that Agatha of Mawbry had ever been within Castle Adderstone.

All they had found were fresh footsteps in the snow banked against the outer curtain wall where she had escaped by way of the postern gate. If not that much of the snow before the castle had melted earlier in the day, it might have been possible to track her, but the footsteps had disappeared fifty feet distant from the wall.

Still, Bayard had been tempted to continue the search, and Verdun had pressed for it. However, the night was bitter cold with wind that had begun to spit cutting flecks of ice, portending a new day wrapped in white. As its descent could prove dire for any caught out in it, they had turned back, all of Bayard roiling with certainty that if the witch had been long gone before Elianor was found, she stood a good chance of surviving the weather. And if she lived, she would try again to visit her plague upon the Boursiers.

Crossing the hall whose sleeping occupants would not rouse for another two hours, he silently cursed the one who had aided Agatha. Keys had been used to release her from the cell—keys her savior should not have possessed since there were only two sets that accessed the underground, the cell, and the manacles. Two *known* sets, including the one he had taken from Agatha the night he had traded places with her. Since the steward had produced both that had been entrusted to him prior to Bayard's departure for Castle Mathe, there had to be a third set. That, or someone inside Adderstone betrayed the Boursiers. Someone with ready access to the steward's coffers.

As Bayard neared the stairs that would return him to Elianor, he glanced at Verdun and wondered as he had done often this night if Constance could have gained the keys. Though he preferred to believe a known betrayer had simply betrayed again, it was hard to fit her into the circumstances. True, it would have been no stretch for her to guess the steward kept the keys, but it would have been nearly impossible for her to negotiate the keep without drawing attention, especially since her chamber was without access to the inner walls.

Aye, empty-handed, Bayard acknowledged again. *Appallingly so.*

The two men ascended the stairs and traversed the corridor over which Boursier and Verdun men stood watch. But rather than return to his chamber, Bayard's unwelcome guest halted before the solar. Ignoring the men-at-arms on either side of the door whose hands were on their hilts, he looked to Bayard and said, "She shall ever be my niece longer than she shall be your wife."

It was only the fear of awakening Elianor that kept Bayard from asserting that, with the speaking of vows, she had become his alone and would ever be no matter how many days of her life others might lay claim to.

Grudgingly, he inclined his head and opened the door.

The chamber was warm and bright, the fire well fed.

Rising from a chair that had been placed alongside the bed, the physician glanced at Verdun, fixed his gaze on Bayard. "My lord, your lady wife rests well."

Bayard came alongside him and studied Elianor's countenance. "Her injuries?"

"I first stitched and bandaged her head, then reset, splinted, and bandaged her arm. Blessedly, the break is a clean one, and 'tis fair certain she will regain full use of her arm."

Bayard silently thanked the Lord, reached down, and touched her cheek. "Has she awakened?"

"Twice, and for that and the pain, I gave her a sleeping draught. She will not likely rise before the nooning hour."

Bayard turned to Verdun who watched from the foot of the bed. "Are you satisfied?"

"As much as is possible." The man turned and strode from the solar.

"If there is naught else you require, my lord," the physician said, "I shall leave you to your wife."

Bayard inclined his head. "I thank you."

Moments later, the door closed behind the physician.

Bayard looked long upon Elianor, and each time the question arose as to why he was so gripped with concern, he excused himself with the reminder that not only was she his wife and, therefore, his responsibility, but he yet suffered from a weakness for beauty. That was all this was.

He caught up the coverlet, began to draw it over her arm, and stilled. The wedding band she was ever turning about her finger was gone. Had the physician removed it while tending her?

Bayard looked to the table, but no gold glinted upon it, and he was fairly certain the man would have set it there had he been the one to slip it from her finger. Had Elianor removed it? If so, for what reason? Even when she had been shown to be an impostor, invalidating the first vows they had spoken, the ring had not left her hand. Had her aunt's presence at Adderstone caused her to eschew it?

He should not be so bothered, the same as he should not be overly concerned for Elianor's wellbeing. After all, he had not wanted her for a wife, certainly had not coveted her as he had coveted Constance Verdun.

Assuring himself his ring would soon be back on Elianor's hand, he lowered the coverlet over her.

Dismissing the chair as a poor excuse for a bed and reasoning he could do Elianor no harm by stretching out on her right-hand side, he removed his boots and weapon-heavy belt and slid beneath the covers.

As he waited for sleep to quiet his mind, regret slipped beneath the doors he had closed against it—regret that he had cared too much that Constance was near, that he had not joined Elianor at meal as she had entreated him to do, that he had not been here when voices sounded through the walls. All would be different. Elianor would be uninjured and the threat of Agatha put down.

Not that he begrudged Father Crispin his good and worthy counsel or the Lord His prayer, but both had been as much a matter of seeking peace as an excuse to distance himself from emotions steeped in memories of what had happened here all those years ago.

If there was any hope for Elianor and him, he must forever put that night behind him. And he would. Somehow.

25

It was a dull throb, but insistent, as of an anxious child tugging at her arm.

El resisted until the little one dug nails into her flesh. She caught her breath, opened her eyes, and turned her head to see who had hold of her. There was no one to her left, but though her eyes were slow to focus, she placed herself. She was in Bayard's solar, in his bed, and on the night past...

She recalled the torchlit Agatha, heard the pronouncement that she was of no use, felt the fall. And the landing. And the pain.

She flexed her left hand. Though the movement sent an ache up her forearm, the pain that had consigned her to darkness was mostly absent. Meaning her injury was not dire?

"Merciful Lord," she whispered, then lowered her lids and drew her thumb across her ring finger.

She opened her eyes, felt again for the band of gold. Where was it? And why this panic constricting her chest?

"Bayard?" She turned her head opposite and winced at the pain above her left ear. Though she was the bed's sole occupant, she felt sweet relief when she saw the coverlet was folded back to reveal deep impressions in the pillow and bottom sheet. He had been in *their* bed.

"The Baron of Godsmere attends to more pressing matters," a voice sounded from across the chamber, then Lady Maeve rose from a chair before the hearth—she who said it was the devil who gave breath to Agatha, who made no attempt to hide her dislike of the one her stepson had wed, who had good reason to feel as she did.

Wincing at how dry her throat felt, El said, "Where is my husband?"

The thick-waisted lady moved toward the bed. "As told, he attends to matters of the demesne."

Matters more pressing than his injured wife, Bayard's stepmother would have her believe. And yet some time during the early morning hours, he had lain with her. Had his hand been upon her again?

The lady halted at the foot of the bed.

"Did Bayard find Agatha?" El asked.

"He did not, for certain hopes she met her end in a snow bank."

El frowned. "Has it snowed again?"

"So much it may be days ere we rid ourselves of your kin."

Venom, but though El knew it was a challenge, she was not of a mind—or a body—to rise to it.

Lady Maeve pressed a hand to the left-hand post. "Whilst my husband lived, this was our bed."

El suppressed laughter born of irony at having so recently acknowledged the bed as belonging to Bayard and her. It was not only Constance who had prior claim to it.

"And as you are aware," Lady Maeve continued, "it was my father and mother's before that."

So it had been, until Denis Foucault had betrayed his earl, causing his demesne to be divided into three lesser baronies to award those who had, in turn, stood against him. And among the betrayers was Archard Boursier. Following Baron Foucault's death, he had wed the man's daughter in what was believed to be an act of atonement.

Lady Maeve nodded as if to herself. "Here I birthed a daughter for my husband. Here I should have birthed sons." She dropped her hand from the post. "But there was only Quintin, and by your actions, the one person who is mine as much as I am hers, is stolen from me."

El did not feel threatened. Still, she did not like being flat on her back during their exchange.

Beneath the coverlet, she raised her splinted arm. The ache made her sink her teeth into her lower lip, but once she settled her arm across her abdomen, the discomfort was tolerable.

Next, she pressed her right elbow into the mattress. As she levered to sitting, she returned her gaze to Lady Maeve who watched her struggle with interest. And satisfaction?

After arranging Bayard's pillow and her own behind her, El eased back and took the opportunity to run her gaze over the bedside table. Her ring was not there. Did Bayard have it?

Feeling the weight of being watched and the expectation of a response, El said, "I am sorry about your daughter, Lady Maeve. Never did I intend her harm—"

"Did you not?" Flecks of saliva leapt from the lady's mouth. "Had you succeeded, she would be as destitute as my stepson would have been."

El could not argue that. "You are right. I was foolish. And selfish. And afeared."

"Afeared?"

"That The Boursier would choose me over Thomasin de Arell."

Once more, the lady stared, but this time there was a softening about her face. "You believed Bayard abused your aunt and would do the same to you."

El inclined her head. "Though I know it does not absolve me of wrongdoing, already I had..." She paused. Why did she feel compelled to confide? Guilt over Lady Quintin's imprisonment? Aye, that. The longing to be understood by one who could make her life difficult? That, too.

"Speak, Lady Elianor," Lady Maeve said.

"Having suffered a bad marriage, I could not bear the thought of another."

After a long moment, the woman murmured, "Murdoch Farrow."

El startled. "You know of him?"

She averted her gaze. "Insofar as hearing you had wed him."

There was falsity about her words, and El guessed Bayard had shared her past with his stepmother—a trespass she resented.

"Though my stepson chose Thomasin de Arell for his wife," the woman said, "still you stole him from his bed. Why?"

"All had been set in motion. Thus, I determined not only would I save Lady Thomasin from an abusive marriage, but my uncle from a Boursier."

"My daughter."

It was not a question, and so El waited out the indignant silence.

Finally, the lady said, "Methinks you no longer believe Bayard capable of abuse. Am I right?"

Was she? Despite all that was told of him, despite every threat he had made, Bayard Boursier had proven himself honorable. How recently honorable, she could not know, but he was more honorable than she who had upset all that was to have been.

"I have tested him," she said, "so much that even one who does not raise a hand to a woman might do so, but Bayard has done me no harm. Thus, he is either much changed or much maligned."

Lady Maeve snorted. "Much maligned. I may not have birthed him, but I have known him since he was an infant. Never would he or did he abuse that harlot." Her jaw shifted. "Though I almost wish he had, for it would have saved—"

She drew a whistling breath between her teeth, closed her hands into fists.

Secrets at Adderstone, just as Castle Kelling had secrets. El doubted she would ever know all that twisted in and out of the Boursiers' lives, but if she gained a measure of acceptance, she might learn enough of what they hid that she would not feel as alone as she had in Murdoch's home.

Lady Maeve cleared her expression, opened her hands, and crossed to the chair the physician had drawn near the bed on the night past.

"I do not like you," she said as she lowered herself, "and I am not apt to give you cause to like me. But as we are to dwell within the same walls, I shall strive to tolerate your company providing you afford me the same consideration."

The pact was so unexpected El could think of nothing to say.

Lady Maeve leaned near enough to reveal that her brown, otherwise unremarkable irises, were edged in gold. "Of course, should ill befall my daughter, all changes."

It would be the same for Bayard. "I understand," El said and turned back the coverlet. "I would like to go belowstairs."

Lady Maeve raised an eyebrow. "The physician has said you are not to exert yourself."

It was an injured arm, not a leg. It ached, but not enough to compel her to remain abed all day. Slowly, she opened and closed her fingers. And stilled. "Do you know what has become of my wedding ring? Did Bayard remove it?"

The lady swept her gaze to El's hand, looked to the bedside table. "I suppose he must have."

El touched her thumb to the base of the finger around which she had turned the loose ring. "Else 'twas lost when I fell."

"I am sure it will soon be returned to your hand," Lady Maeve said, then added, "after the swelling goes down."

Though El's fingers were swollen, she thought it likely the ring would fit better now.

"Your chemise is ruined," the lady said.

It was. From wrist to elbow, its sleeve had been cut away, leaving a ragged edge above her bandaged and splinted arm.

"I will have to borrow one until my garments are delivered from Castle Kelling," El said. Unfortunately, with such weather upon them, that could be a long while.

"Neither mine nor my daughter's would be a good fit," Lady Maeve said, "but we have cloth aplenty, and one can be fashioned for you."

Obviously, not by El's hand. And, again, it could be some time before her maid was sent to her. In the meantime, her outer gown would have to cover all ills.

"I am done resting." She lowered her feet to the rushes.

Lady Maeve sat back, making no move to assist though El swayed where she rose beside her.

Once El found her balance, she measured her steps to the wooden chest against the far wall. She lifted her folded cotehardie from atop the lid, and only then realized it would be difficult to dress without aid. Too, the numerous buttons that closed the tight-fitting sleeves would have to be undone to fit her splinted arm into it.

"You will need help with that," Lady Maeve said.

El turned and found the woman had moved to the center of the chamber. "I thank you." She held out the cotehardie. "If you will unbutton the left sleeve and hold the gown open over my head—"

"I am no maid."

Thinking she jested, El nearly smiled. But Lady Maeve had no lightness about her, she who had been exalted as a Foucault when the Boursiers, De Arells, and Verduns were mere vassals to her father.

El lowered the gown. "Forgive me. I misunderstood."

Lady Maeve turned away. "I shall rouse my maid and have her assist you."

She is tolerating me, El reminded herself, the better to accept the snub, and lowered herself to the chest to await the lady's maid.

26

An hour later, El had been put to order as much as was possible. Hulda, who appeared to be of an age near that of her mistress—and had likely served her since Castle Adderstone was the Foucault residence—was gentle and courteous. However, upon her lady's return to the solar, the maid went silent as if for fear of appearing disloyal.

"Presentable," Lady Maeve said, circling as Hulda knotted the sling supporting El's left arm. "You were even able to do something with her hair."

El fingered the thick braid that had been pinned around her head. Though Hulda had cleaned away the dried blood, her hair was in need of a wash. Not for the first time, she wished she had rallied her courage when she had been given the opportunity to bathe at Castle Mathe. Never had she gone so long without immersing herself in a tub and soaking and scrubbing until the water lost its heat. Still, she was passably clean, Hulda having stripped and sponged her with perfumed water.

Though the damaged chemise beneath the cotehardie into which El had been carefully buttoned was also in need of washing, it would have to wait.

"My husband expects me, Lady Maeve?" El asked.

"I have not been belowstairs to inform him you have awakened," she said.

El frowned. When Hulda had come alone to the solar with a tray of food and drink, El had assumed Lady Maeve had gone to the hall. She must have withdrawn to her own chamber, finding the prospect of watching her maid attend to El's ablutions as unsavory as attending to them herself.

"But as told by the din in the inner bailey," the lady continued, "methinks Bayard has moved himself and his men out of doors."

El had heard voices and the push and scrape of shovels from beyond the shuttered windows, but had assumed they were of servants set the task of clearing paths through the snow. "For what did my husband take his men outside?"

"The more able-bodied there are to clear the snow, the sooner 'tis done. And as Bayard's men failed him in allowing my daughter to be taken by De Arell, they are not exempt. Not that they often are, but certainly not this day. And providing the sky does not loose more of its misery upon us, Godsmere's garrison will soon enough find themselves practicing at arms." Her mouth curved toward a smile. "I believe you will find you have wed the worthiest of those whom King Edward has commanded to take a wife. Such a pity you do not deserve him."

The words were unkind, shaking their pact, but El knew the woman had cause to believe she was undeserving of the one she had raised as her own son.

"If my husband and his men have left the hall," El said, "I shall also require a mantle."

The lady gave a short laugh. "Bayard will not like that you are out of bed, but he will like it even less if you expose yourself to the cold."

"Hence, I shall don a mantle."

Ignoring the annoyance that rose on Lady Maeve's face, El looked to the maid who had stepped alongside her mistress. "I thank you for your aid, Hulda."

"You are welcome, milady."

El returned to the wooden chest and reached for the fur-lined mantle of finest wool that Bayard had sent his squire to fetch her when she had spoken vows with him as Thomasin de Arell. She paused, savored the warmth that swept her as she recalled that act of kindness. And it was only the first of many he had shown her.

Behind, Lady Maeve sighed. "Fetch my mantle, Hulda."

Keeping her smile to herself, El drew out her husband's mantle. Unfortunately, as heavy and voluminous as it was, it was no easy thing to don with the use of only one arm, and twice she dropped it to the rushes.

Bayard's stepmother made an impatient sound, crossed the chamber, and took the mantle from her. With jerks and tugs, she fit it to El's shoulders, then frowned over the simple brooch. "Not this one," she said and stepped to the chest. When she returned, she fastened the mantle with a gold, beautifully worked brooch. "There. Though the mantle is too large for you, you look more a baron's wife."

El felt a rush of gratitude that was all the greater since the woman had earlier refused her assistance, but before she could voice it, Lady Maeve added, "Now let us see if you can behave better than your aunt did."

The hated Constance.

Tolerance, El told herself, then asked, "Where is she?"

"She remains abovestairs, and I think that is wise. Do you not?"

Under the circumstances. "I would like to see her."

"Now is not the time. Hulda tells me she is in the chapel at prayer."

"You keep watch over her?" El asked sharply.

Gaze unwavering, Lady Maeve said, "Suffer offense if you must, but this is my home, and I will not allow your aunt to move it to madness as she and that foul woman did years ago."

"You think 'twas she who released Agatha from the underground?"

The lady's mouth tightened. "It matters not what is thought but what was done. For all the days the witch was imprisoned here, she found her release only when Constance Verdun once more entered these walls. It more than gives one pause."

El wished she could argue that it had not been Constance, but her words and beliefs would carry no weight. So who had been with Agatha in the inner walls? Who had not cried out when El was knocked down the steps? Who had remained silent when Agatha noted a broken neck was a good end to one who had been her mistress?

Head beginning to ache anew, El pushed the pondering aside, stepped past Lady Maeve, and crossed the chamber. In the corridor, she found an armed man on either side of the door and Hulda hastening forward.

Once Lady Maeve was arrayed in her own fur-lined mantle, she ordered one of the men-at-arms to hold watch over the solar and the other to accompany them belowstairs.

However the first one, a larger man girded with sword and four daggers, thrust a hand to the chest of the other man-at-arms and stepped forward.

Lady Maeve glowered, but grumbled, "Oh, very well."

Curious, El considered the big man-at-arms who eyed her out of a square face, then he grunted and led the way down the corridor.

The descent of the steps was more difficult than expected, and El had to pause once to steady herself and assure Lady Maeve she did not need to return to bed.

The great hall was empty except for servants, as was the inner bailey when they ventured outside onto the landing.

It was cold, though not breathtakingly so. The overcast skies that had emptied a foot of white now brooded, taunting the frail beings below with the possibility of more snow that would return the recently cut path to its former state.

"And so to arms," Lady Maeve said of the clanging metal and crack of wood that rose above the inner walls.

El pitied those who had not been allowed to first warm themselves before the blazing fire in the great hall. "It seems heartless. Surely Bayard's men are chilled through."

With a snort that was becoming as familiar as her disdain, Lady Maeve said, "Be assured, Bayard is among them. As for the chill, if his men are exerting the effort expected of them, they welcome the cold."

El had not considered that, and it was hard to do so with her nose, cheeks, and ears beginning to sting.

Lady Maeve started to turn away. "Let us await them in the hall."

"I would like to go to the outer bailey."

"For what?"

"Methinks I would benefit from the fresh air."

"You will break your neck is what you will do. Now come inside."

She might have been convinced to do so, and the prospect of sitting before the hearth held appeal, but the sooner she asserted herself, the easier for all to accept her as the new lady of Castle Adderstone.

El slid her right arm from beneath the mantle and extended it toward the man-at-arms. "I shall require your assistance in descending the steps."

He reached to her, paused, and frowned at Lady Maeve.

"With all respect to my...mother-in-law," El said, supposing that was the proper title, "I am Baron Boursier's wife. Thus, you require no one's permission to do my bidding."

Lady Maeve's resentment stirred the air. "In that you are right, Lady Elianor—with one exception." She returned her regard to the man-at-arms. "Baron Boursier." Then she pivoted toward the doors and the warmth of the hall.

The man-at-arms stared after her, and when she was gone, muttered, "Baron Boursier first. Ever first." He nodded, and as El pondered his behavior, took hold of her arm. Deftly, he supported her down the steps and over the white, dirt-strewn path.

"By what name are you called?" El asked as they neared the inner portcullis.

He looked down at her, his face so still and emotionless that she startled when a grin slashed open his mouth to reveal missing incisors amid great, yellowed teeth.

"Why, I be Rollo, milady. I do thank ye for askin'." His was a coarse, thick voice, as if spoken over a mouthful of food, but it was friendly.

And El liked friendly, something she had not known as Murdoch Farrow's wife. Still, there was something more to the man. Or was something missing—the same as his teeth? If he was on the simple-minded side as his manner suggested, surely he would not be trusted with weapons. Too, that other man-at-arms had readily acquiesced when Rollo had insisted on accompanying the ladies belowstairs—

Rollo. El knew the name. When Bayard had dragged her into the hall on the eve he had freed himself from the underground, he had been angered to learn his sister had gone in search of him without the aid of one named Rollo. Could this be the same?

"I may call ye Lady El..." His grin lowered. "Eli...?"

"Lady Elianor."

"El...ianor." He jerked his head as if shaking off a fly. "That be a long name."

True, and she had made it longer by pronouncing it with four notes the same as Bayard did.

The man shrugged. "I shall learn it."

"I am pleased to be your lady, Rollo."

He gave a curt nod. "I hope ye be a God 'un."

First, she faltered over his reference to God, wondering if he but pronounced *good* in a strange way or if he truly meant *God*. Next, she faltered over his boldness. Was her aunt behind it? Had he served in Bayard's household when Constance was its lady?

Telling herself it did not matter, El said, "I shall endeavor to be. May I ask something, Rollo?"

"Aye, milady."

"Have you also served as Lady Quintin's guard?"

His brow bunched. "For years and years, but she did go to Castle Mathe without me, and now she be stuck there."

"I am sure she thought it more important that you attend to your mother. She is doing better?"

He nodded and said no more as they entered the outer bailey through which paths had also been cut, leaving the snow banked against the walls of the buildings. Buildings that were silent amid the din of men practicing arms. Doubtless, if not for the snow, they would be peopled by those who supplied the castle with all manner of needs, including ironware for their lord and his garrison, candles, dyed cloth, and ale. Instead, the castle folk were likely enjoying their role as spectators, happily gathered around those who fought mock battles in preparation for mortal ones.

Rollo guided El around the stables, and the training field came into view. It was thronged by castle folk interspersed with knights and men-at-arms. Indeed, it was so well attended that the many whose swords sent up a song of steel on steel, and quarterstaffs a beat of wood on wood, could only be glimpsed.

But the glimpses El was afforded of a large figure with auburn hair revealed Bayard was among those at practice. As she and her escort neared, they remained unnoticed by the others who seemed not to feel the cold though they exerted no effort to warm themselves.

When a shout of "Godsmere!" went up, strengthened by the voices of the garrison upon the walls overlooking the outer bailey, Rollo said with pride, "It be Baron Boursier who drew blood."

El knew the way of things, that even at practice, soldiers were not averse to bloodletting. Still, it disturbed her, and for that she mostly stayed away from the training field.

To her surprise, the big man moved his right hand from his sword hilt and patted her arm that he held to. "Worry not, milady. Yer husband will put down that other 'un."

He was so certain that she pitied whoever that other one was. Absently noting that the sound of steel and wood had ceased, she said, "I thank you, Rollo."

She had not believed he could show more teeth, but he did—rather, their absence farther back in his mouth.

Once more, steel sounded, but this time it seemed of two swords only. They were quick, successive strokes as of two fighting in close proximity, followed by a moment of silence, a collective gasp, and a far less represented shout of "Emberly!"

As El tried to make sense of it, Rollo returned his hand to his hilt and pushed a path for them to the front of those who had gathered before the entrance to the training field.

A score of knights and men-at-arms stood upon the field they had muddied so thoroughly that few patches of snow remained. The reason they had lowered their own weapons immediately apparent, El's breath stopped.

Bayard stood in profile twenty feet distant. Hair darkened by perspiration, teeth bared, gaze hard upon his prey, he was a terrible sight. And more terrible was the way his great body moved quickly and fluidly—against her uncle.

Magnus was also transformed, though he looked less of a beast than Bayard. And more bloodied.

Bayard swung his sword down. Though El's uncle deflected the blow, the tip of his opponent's sword scored his lower jaw.

"Godsmere!" the bulk of spectators roared.

Finally, El found her breath. "Halt!" she cried and wrenched free of Rollo.

Twice more she called out as she ran forward, but she went unheard, for Magnus did not falter in countering with a slash that came close to adding the blood of her husband's left arm to the dirty snow at his feet.

Bayard recovered from the side lunge that had spared his flesh, bellowed, and charged his opponent.

"Bayard!" El shrieked. "Do not!"

This time he heard her, snapping his head around to bring her within sight of his singular gaze.

Magnus also wrenched free of the bloodlust that had made him deaf to her beseeching and blind to her approach, but though his gaze fell upon her, the sword he wielded did not yield its momentum, catching Bayard high in the chest and carrying its point toward El.

Just as she registered that she, too, would bleed upon this field, an arm slammed around her waist and swept her to the side.

Barely hearing Rollo's thick-tongued voice above Bayard's roar, she stared at the sight of her warrior husband that turned more terrible as his blade deflected Magnus's.

Her uncle fell back a step and fended off the next assault.

El's struggle against the one holding her back jostled her splinted arm, but she ignored the pain and cried amidst the spectators' din, "Pray, cease!"

Grunting and shouting, Bayard drove Magnus toward the side fence, causing those who stood upon its rungs to scatter. Then her uncle was against it, fending off the next blow, crossing and locking swords with his opponent above their heads.

Now it was a contest to see which man could first bring to hand the dagger upon his belt—a contest won by the one whose greater bulk should have slowed him.

"Bayard!" El beseeched as he pressed his blade to Magnus's throat.

Chests heaving, the opponents stared at each other, both surely aware that a sweep of the hand would be the end of Magnus. However, the slightest of nods—a grudging acknowledgment of defeat—ended the match.

Bayard pushed off his opponent. As the cry of "Godsmere!" sounded again, he thrust his sword and dagger into their scabbards and pivoted. The gaze he landed on El was so fiery it might have been colored red rather than blue.

"Never!" he thundered as he strode to where Rollo held her. "Never place yourself between men who are as dogs at each other's throats! Do you understand?"

Not in all the days since she had become his captive had he so closely resembled the man who had first laid hands on her in the underground cell. But though fear ran through her, she exclaimed, "You were trying to kill each other!"

"Kill!" He halted so near that the scent of his labor wafted heavily between them. "We are at practice, Elianor!"

She glanced at the bloodied material near his collarbone for which Magnus was responsible. "'Tis more than that. It looked as if—"

"You feared I would slay your beloved uncle? Nay, despite the temptation, never did I forget he is your kin. Just as, methinks, he shall never forget *I* am your husband now."

Those vicious, blood-seeking swings and thrusts were practice? El leaned to the side and looked to Magnus.

He watched them, as did the castle folk who eyed their lord and lady whilst chattering amongst themselves.

"Elianor!" Bayard barked.

She straightened. Without regard for their audience, his thunderous expression remained fixed on her, and it made her own anger bloom. Over and again she had been humiliated before Murdoch's people. She would not silently suffer the same at Adderstone.

She peered over her shoulder and met Rollo's frowning regard. "Release me!"

He moved his gaze to Bayard. A moment later, his arm around her eased, but not enough to allow her to escape.

"Say it, Elianor!" Bayard demanded.

"What?" she spat.

"I want your word that never again will you go near men who are at arms or fists or angry words, whether it is but practice or the purposeful spilling of blood. Say it!"

The onlookers' voices growing louder, she once more considered them—resented their curious regard, detested the smirks of men who approved of her humiliation.

Narrowing eyes upon her husband, she saw he had followed her gaze. When he returned to her, she hissed, "How dare you speak thus to me!"

His jaw bulged, but he put his face near hers, and this time his voice did not carry. "How dare you nearly get yourself stuck!"

"Had I, would you care?" Immediately, she regretted how childish she sounded—more, that in this there could be no argument. Bayard did not want to care, but he did, as time and again, day in and day out, he proved.

Lord, what a tongue I have loosed, she silently bemoaned. *If I am not care-ful, it will draw more blood than did his sword this day. Grant me calm.*

She moistened her lips, but before she could apologize, Bayard drew her from Rollo's grasp and into his arms. "Too much I care," he spoke into the hair atop her head. "God knows, too much."

Vaguely aware of the spectators of whom she had been painfully mindful moments earlier, El mused that this must be how snow felt when the sun came out, causing it to sparkle bright as diamonds while it slowly and beautifully melted and became one with the earth.

"Woman," Bayard groaned, "you seem determined that I should lose you ere we even begin our lives together."

Cheek to his neck, slung arm pressed against his abdomen, she breathed him in. His scent was far from pleasant, but she was not repulsed as she had been with Murdoch who, because of the amount of fat carried upon his person, had often caused her gorge to rise. Especially when—

You will not think there whilst you are here, she told herself. *And one day, God willing, you will not think there at all.*

She dropped her head back to look upon *this* husband's face. "Forgive me. When I saw the two of you at swords, I did not think. I but wanted to stop it. I was so afeared."

"As was I when you near ran yourself onto Verdun's sword."

El stared. What did this man who hardly knew her feel for her?

"Still, I will have your word, El."

El. Not that she minded the affectionate form, but how her heart fluttered when he spoke her name with breath and length as if to keep it long upon his tongue.

She nodded. "My word you have, Husband."

He looked to her mouth, and she thought he might kiss her as she wished to be kissed—gently, deeply, breathlessly. But as if remembering they were not alone, he looked around. Then he set her back and shouted for the castle folk to go about their duties and the garrison to practice at arms.

When he returned his attention to her, she nodded at his bloodied collarbone. "You are hurt."

"But scratches, whereas you…" He parted the heavy mantle, considered her sling. "For what are you out of bed, Elianor?"

"My head is much improved, and 'tis just my arm—"

"A *broken* arm, which could have been your neck."

His reminder of the death Agatha had planned for her caused the bile in her belly to burn a path up her throat, and she had to swallow hard to keep it from her mouth. "So it could have been, but it was not."

"By God's grace."

Was it? This time, unlike the others before she had become apathetic about calling upon Him, had He been here for her? Or had she simply fallen well?

"You know the witch escaped, aye?" Bayard said.

She nodded.

"I will flush her out of whatever hole she has gone down. Until then…" He looked past her, called, "Rollo, my lady wife is in need of rest. Escort her back to the solar and—"

"Nay." El said. "I am rested."

"You are not."

Anger once more stirring, she stepped nearer him. "I am hardly fragile, Bayard Boursier. If there is one thing you have learned about me, surely 'tis that."

His eye began to darken, but he closed it and drew a deep breath. When he lifted his lid, his still, blue-green gaze told that he had pulled his emotions back from the edge. "That I do know," he said, then once more addressed Rollo. "See Lady Elianor back to the keep, and remain near that you might render whatever services she requires."

For her protection, he would have her believe. And she did believe it, but was it also a means of keeping watch over her as watch was kept over Constance?

It would be easy to be offended, but El determined she would not provide more fodder for any who yet watched. As it was, she had shamed Bayard enough by entering the training field that was no place for a woman, and then to have tried to end the contest between Magnus and him…

Rollo stepped forward and halted alongside El. "But milord," he rasped low, "milady did shame me—did not allow me to protect her as you did give me to do. I be not worthy."

"There is none worthier," Bayard said. "I am to blame for not warning you that my lady wife must needs be watched as closely as my lady sister." He shifted his gaze to El. "Had I known Lady Elianor would so soon abandon her sickbed, I would have."

"But she were almost stuck, milord."

It was said with such misery that El felt more wretched for the shame she had scattered this day.

"Almost," Bayard said, "but you kept the blade from her as is your duty. There is no shame in that." He clapped a hand to the man's shoulder. "Now, I would ask that you do as bid."

"Aye, milord." Rollo took his charge's right arm. "Come, milady."

As he turned her away, El's seeking thumb reminded her something was missing. "You have my ring, Bayard?"

His brow grooved. "I do not. I thought you had removed it."

"'Twas loose. Methinks I must have lost it in the fall."

"Then the passage will be searched."

She nodded and allowed her escort to guide her from the training field.

"Elianor!"

Rollo halted, and she looked around.

"*I* will search the passage," Bayard said. "You are not to venture there again."

She had not thought to with her injury, but she could not begrudge him the warning. "Aye, my lord."

Bayard pivoted and strode toward Magnus whose gaze moved between husband and wife.

"Milady." Rollo urged her forward.

Neither spoke until they began their ascent of the keep's steps.

"Ye did shame me, milady," Rollo said, mournfully.

Wondering at the puzzle of him, she said, "I did not mean to. I am sorry."

A smile rose upon his face. "I am glad you are." The smile fell. "Hence, I shall forgive you—later."

El would have laughed if not for fear of offending this brute into whom had been breathed what seemed a good-natured soul. She liked Rollo, and as with each time she compared her experiences with Murdoch to those with Bayard, she found herself in the grip of gratitude. Indeed, in that moment, she wished it were a chapel she entered rather than the hall—a peculiar longing she had not felt in years. If ever she had felt it.

Dear Lord, once again, I am bewitched by a beautiful woman. Once again, I have but to look upon her face and form to know desire that could undo all I have struggled to become—that could return me to all I should not have been.

From where he had halted inside the doors of the great hall, Bayard stared at the one he had not wanted and who had certainly not wanted him.

She should be resting abovestairs. Instead, Elianor of Emberly—

Not of Emberly. She was now and would evermore be of Godsmere, as further evidenced by the role of lady of the castle she appeared to have taken upon herself.

Musing that he preferred her hair out from under the modesty afforded by the veil she had donned upon her return to the keep, he looked from where she stood upon the dais with the cook on one side and the steward on the other, to where Lady Maeve sat before the hearth. His stepmother's gaze awaited him, and a bitter smile. She did not like yielding her place to Elianor, just as she had not liked ceding it to Constance all those years ago. But she had stepped back to allow Elianor to step forward.

Judging by the state of the hall that bustled with more activity than usual for late afternoon, it seemed his wife had everything well in hand. Servants tended the fire, spread cloths upon the high table, arranged trestle tables and benches for the evening meal, and picked debris from the rushes. Of odd note, was the ungainly lad who usually kept to the kitchen. Evergreen branches draped over an arm, he moved about the hall, setting and hanging his greenery as should have been done much earlier with Christmas Day a sennight away.

"My lord!" Elianor called and stepped to the edge of the dais where Rollo aided in her descent.

Regretting that he had not made straight for the solar so she would not further suffer the sight and scent of him that had not improved these past hours, Bayard strode forward to meet her. As they neared the center of the hall, he saw the hair visible on either side of her veil was damp.

She had bathed? The thought disturbed him, for it was rooted in the dirt of carnal things.

She halted before him, and Rollo drew up short several feet behind her.

"Your bath has been made ready," she said.

As he had sent Squire Lucas to arrange an hour past. He glanced down at himself. "As you can see, I am much in need of a long soak and scrub."

She smiled apologetically. "I hope you do not mind that I asked Hulda to wash my hair in your bath water."

He raised his eyebrows.

"Be assured, I had her use plain soap."

"I do not mind." He leaned near and said, "Even were my bath water scented, I would not be bothered, providing my lovely wife waited there for me."

She caught her breath, and when he straightened, he saw her face was flushed.

It was a pity he could not ask her to tend his bath. Not only would it be difficult for her to do with her injured arm, but the temptation she presented might preclude him from moving slowly with her.

Hoping to alleviate the discomfort provoked by teasing that had surprised him perhaps more than her, he said, "I did not expect you to so soon take to managing the household, but I am pleased you are at ease doing so."

She inclined her head. "I am not without experience, for I did manage my uncle's household."

No mention of managing her first husband's household. Why? From what he knew of her relationship with Farrow, something told him he would not like the answer.

"And Lady Maeve was most gracious in allowing me to take my place in your household," she added.

"I am glad." Catching the scent of his labors made all the more potent by the hall's warmth, he said, "Now methinks I should remove my filth from your hall."

"My hall?" It was said so softly, as if with wonder, Bayard was not certain he had heard right, but her face reflected the same.

"Yours, Elianor." His as well, but as he had the entirety of Godsmere with which to concern himself, the running of the household would be her responsibility. And he did not doubt she would prove quite capable.

"I thank you," she said.

He inclined his head and crossed the hall.

Abovestairs, Squire Lucas awaited him, but when the young man hastened forward to aid in the removal of his lord's garments, Bayard waved him away and retrieved a torch to light the hidden passageway.

It took little time to ascertain that El's ring was not upon the steps down which she had plummeted, nor upon the landing below that bore the stain of her blood.

Bayard was bothered, for it seemed the only explanation for its absence was that Agatha had descended the steps to gloat over what she had believed to be Elianor's corpse—and then taken the ring from his wife's hand. The thought of it churned the ale with which he had slaked his thirst before leaving the training field.

Vowing he would end the threat of Agatha of Mawbry, he returned to the solar. When he came out from behind the tapestry, he noticed the dressing table and chair set between the shuttered windows, a place that had been absent such furnishings since Constance had left Adderstone. It was there his first wife had seen to her ablutions, combed and braided her hair. And now Elianor would do the same.

Bayard gave himself into Squire Lucas's hands. Shortly, he lowered himself into the water. And wished it were Elianor who scrubbed his back and neck, whose fingers pushed soap to the roots of his hair.

Slowly, he told himself, *and one day she shall do so without fear and trembling.*

Lord, he silently beseeched, *let me not make the mistakes with Elianor that I made with Constance. Help me to help my wife welcome my touch.*

27

SHE HAD BEEN certain it was safe to enter, that Bayard would be done with his bath. He was not.

Having halted just inside the solar after closing the door on Rollo's watch outside it, El stared at her husband where he reclined in the tub before the hearth. Head back, he slept. Thus, it was not too late to withdraw and summon his squire to ready him for supper that would be served an hour hence.

The best course, she told herself, and yet she wavered. It stank of fear to beat a retreat from one who had thus far shown he was nowhere near the man Murdoch had been.

Could that one even be called a man, she silently amended. Her first husband had in no way resembled her second despite her fear the latter would prove worse.

She put her shoulders back and stepped toward the hearth whose fire crackled and cast golden light around the tub.

He is unclothed! warned the voice within. *Dangerous!*

"He is not Murdoch," she breathed.

Still, he is dangerous!

Aye, but to me?

She halted at the foot of the tub. Though she kept her eyes from all but Bayard's face, she did not have to look lower to know the bath water

— 241 —

was clouded enough by soap that not even the shape of his body would be known to her were she to look close upon it.

She supposed the best way to awaken her husband was to call his name, and she meant to, but his face was so peaceful that not even the black eyepatch could reconcile him with the man she had faced in the underground cell. And so, again, she fell to observing him while he slept.

She liked the thick column of his throat, bit of cleft in his chin, firm, bowed mouth, lightly lined brow. And his hair…

It had been raked back off his brow as if with impatient fingers. Though dark with moisture, firelight showed its auburn cast.

She did not mean to move from observation to imagination, but she went where it led and envisioned pushing her fingers through the damp strands, gripping the back of his head, drawing it down to her, holding his mouth to hers.

I too much like his kiss.

The silent admission pulled her back to reality, and as she shook her head to clear its imaginings, Bayard's chest rose with a deep breath. Then a smile lifted his mouth.

El sought his gaze, but his lid remained lowered.

"No matter how long you stand there, dear wife," he drawled, "this fouled water will not reveal that which you have yet to know of your husband."

She retreated a step. "I was not…I did not…" Her cheeks grew so heated she felt lightheaded. "'Twas your face I looked upon!"

His smile lowered, eye opened. "You find it unsightly?"

His lost eye. The diagonal scar visible above and below the patch. The weight of his question that made an invulnerable man near vulnerable.

Hurting as she would not have believed she could do for one better known as The Boursier, she said, "I do not find it displeasing. Indeed, I…"

His brow began to smooth. "You what, Elianor?"

Elianor—four notes, as she would have it ever spoken by him. "I find it pleasing," she said, then turned before he could see how much brighter her face could become.

At the dressing table Rollo had obligingly delivered to the solar, she lowered to the chair. As she one-handedly unpinned the hair veil, she cast her thoughts elsewhere to keep them from wandering to the man behind. They landed on the woman to whom he had once been wed.

Shortly after returning from the training field, El had gone to Constance's chamber to assure her she was well, for she had not been unaware of her aunt's appearance outside the solar in those early morning hours. However, the guard who had slipped inside to announce El had told that Constance could not receive her. And that was all. No explanation from the woman who clung to her vow of silence.

The slosh of bath water made El tense with imaginings of Bayard emerging from it.

Lest he think to grow her more accustomed to him in his unclothed state, she said across her shoulder, "You ought to summon your squire. The supper hour is soon upon us."

His lack of response tempted her to look around. Instead, she set aside her veil and pulled her hair over her shoulder. Trying not to think about the sound of him dragging a towel over his wet limbs, she retrieved the comb—one of several items Lady Maeve had provided until her own could be delivered to Adderstone—and began to work the ivory tines through the lowermost tangles. It was not easy, having only the one hand to accomplish it, and as she tugged and jerked and winced over snapped strands, she wished Hulda were here to assist her.

When Bayard came alongside, she peered sidelong at him. Confirming he was clothed, a robe belted about his waist, she lifted her gaze and thought him most attractive in a hard-bitten way. Indeed, the only thing soft about his face was that which framed it—slightly waved, towel-dried hair that brushed his shoulders.

He raised an eyebrow, then a hand.

She stared at his palm, thinking it could not mean what it seemed, then laid the comb across it.

Bayard lifted her hair from her shoulder to her back, moved behind her, and began to work the comb through the tangles.

"I have no experience with a woman's hair," he said, "so you must needs be patient."

Then, in this, Constance had not been first.

Silly, petty, El silently chastised, even as she relaxed beneath his ministrations. Closing her eyes, she lowered her chin to better experience the pleasurable sensation of being so lovingly—

Lovingly? It could not be that. Still, it was wonderful that it should feel that way.

Dear Lord, is Your hand in this? Did I well enough pay the price of being wed to one beast that I might now know kindness and consideration from one who only appeared to be a beast? For whom I feel—

She jerked her thoughts aside, certain she could not feel that for Bayard. Were it even possible, such emotions could not so soon come upon her.

I am needy, that is all, she told herself. *Too long in the dark of Murdoch's cruelty. Too long in the healing light of Magnus's generosity. Too long waiting to feel the slightest breath of girlhood dreams of a love like that of Tristan and Iseult...Abelard and Heloise...*

She caught her breath, surprised her thoughts had gone to fanciful tales she had scorned and buried deep once the reality of married life had closed its fingers around her throat.

"Elianor?"

She opened her eyes, looked past her slung arm to her clenched right hand in her lap, heard her breath move quickly in and out.

Bayard moved to her side again. "Are you pained?"

Not as he thought. She met his gaze. "Nay. Not an hour ago, the physician prepared a draught that eased my discomfort."

"Then?"

She searched for something other than the truth, shrugged. "'Tis just my thoughts. So much has happened that they chase one another hither and thither, disturbing me as I should not allow them to do."

"You must needs leave them in the past."

She blinked. "Can you, Bayard?"

"'Tis that for which I pray."

Much maligned, Lady Maeve had told, and it made El's throat tighten. "Then I shall also pray."

He inclined his head, returned to her back, and once more worked to put order to her hair.

"I did not find your ring in the inner walls," he said as she began to relax.

She glanced over her shoulder. "It must be there."

"It is not."

She touched her bare finger. "Do you think Agatha—?"

"I think you require one that better fits," he said. "Worry no more on it." Then he asked, "Are you well with Rollo's watch over you?"

El was only momentarily offended by his change of subject, for it was in keeping with what was becoming his tendency to protect her. "'Tis disconcerting to have him so close upon my heels, but I do not feel amiss with him, and he...Despite his size and the numerous weapons he carries, he seems a gentle soul."

"He is—providing he is not riled. Rest assured, should any try to harm you while you are in his keeping, his gentle soul will turn brutal. Indeed, had he been present at Castle Mathe when my sister leapt upon De Arell, much blood would have been shed ere she could be made his prisoner—if made a prisoner at all."

"He is a most curious person. How did he come to be in your service?"

"By way of Lady Maeve. Though she refuses to acknowledge him as her half-brother, my father was certain Rollo was Denis Foucault's baseborn son."

Then Archard Boursier had made further atonement for the betrayal of his liege by taking Rollo into his household?

Bayard paused to work through a tangle at the crown of her head. "As you have surely noted," he said, "he is a bit simple-minded. However, upon discovering the youth exhibited an unusual facility with weapons and fighting, my father trained him up into a man-at-arms. He has served our family well."

A secret made known to her.

"The comb runs smooth down to the ends," he said. "And that is as capable as I am of setting a woman's hair to rights."

As neither could she manage a braid, it would have to hang loose about her shoulders, but the veil would provide the modesty required of one who was wed and should only be seen "in her hair" by her husband.

Before she could thank him for his aid, he lifted its mass, causing cool air to brush her nape.

"You have beautiful hair," he murmured, and when she looked up, he lowered his face to it and breathed deep.

A quiver went through her. "It has taken years to grow it long again."

He went still, as she did when she realized what path she had led him down.

"He cut it?" Bayard growled.

Though relieved she was not the recipient of the anger pulsing from him, she longed to speak of anything but *that*.

'Tis too late now to take another path, El. Tell him and be done.

"Nay, I cut it."

His brow darkened further, and now it seemed his anger moved toward her, as if he thought she lied.

"'Tis true," she hastened. "And I did not do a good job of it." She reached to the back of her neck, ran a finger across the scar. "The knife was dull, though not so much when it slipped."

He touched the place she indicated, so lightly it felt like a feather.

"Why did you cut your hair?"

"Rebellion. He was always wrenching at it to control me when I... fought him. Too, he was fond of my hair, and I decided to take it from him as he had taken so much from me."

"And were punished for it." It was so darkly said El knew that were Murdoch alive, his days would number only as many as it took Bayard to root him out.

"I was, but never did I regret doing it, for it made me feel I was not lost, that I was still in here somewhere." She laid a hand to her chest.

"Often cowering—though I refused him the satisfaction of knowing just how much—but still I was not so lost I could not find myself if I looked very hard."

"You never stopped fighting him?"

It was not really a question. Despite such short acquaintance, Bayard knew her. "Only when it gained me something I badly needed, such as mercy upon a servant, a walk in the garden, a chance to meet Agatha so she might gift me with her powders."

Gaze darkening, Bayard let her hair fall and took a step back.

She shifted around on the chair to face him. "I am moved that you are concerned with my plight, but 'tis in the past—"

He slammed his hands to the back of her chair and dropped his head between his outstretched arms. "Miscreant," he choked. "Knave! Swine!"

Now he was the one breathing sharp and fast, the wood beneath her quaking as if it might not long resist being reduced to a pile of sticks.

El touched his hand. "Bayard—"

"'Twas not enough that so depraved a being rendered you untouchable, but to make you a prisoner in your own home!"

El nearly protested being untouchable. After all, she near—nay, not near—craved Bayard's kisses. But, as was his right, he wanted more.

As do I, she silently acknowledged. *I want to know it can be different, that even if it is not pleasurable, it will not hurt or humiliate. I want to lie in his arms, my head on his chest, his heart beating beneath my ear.*

Bayard jerked his chin up, startling her out of her imaginings. "When we arrived at Adderstone and I told that you were home, you near asked if ever you would be allowed outside its walls. Am I right?"

She moistened her lips. "Aye."

"You thought I also meant to make you a prisoner."

"I hoped you would not."

"Then Murdoch Farrow is *not* in the past, is he, Elianor? Whatever I do, you think first of what he might do and clothe me in his sins. Almighty! Were he not already dead—"

The chair quaked more violently, making her long for his hands in her hair again, for him to untangle her strand by strand. But on the matter of Murdoch, she must defend herself, and not angrily as she would have done days earlier.

"I do compare you to him, though far less now than when first we met." Remembering the night she had unmanned Bayard and felt his hand at her throat, she momentarily closed her eyes. "I gave you cause to rouse your wrath, just as you gave me cause to believe I ought to fear you—threatening me with ill, telling me I should cower and tremble for what I had wrought."

He raised his head higher, and she was encouraged to see some of the blue returned to his gaze and feel the quake become a tremble.

"I now believe they were but words," she continued. "But I had no reason not to believe it then." She settled her hand upon his, felt the ridged veins beneath his flesh. "You are right. Murdoch is not as much in my past as I would have him be, but neither is Constance in your past."

A frown bunched his brow. "'Tis hardly possible with her once more beneath my roof!"

"This I know, but even were she not here, still you would compare me to her, just as you did when first we met."

"With good reason! Six days you imprisoned me in that godforsaken cell that I might forfeit all!"

She could not argue that. "You had reason to despise me, and I have only the excuse of having believed the same as my uncle did of what Agatha told of your relationship with my aunt. Just as I feared you might make of me a prisoner, I near lost my breath at the thought of once more suffering the cruel attentions of a beast."

He stared at her.

"Bayard," she said softly, "when I laid plans to see your lands forfeited, it was for fear of what you would do to me if you took me to wife. By the time I learned you intended to wed De Arell's daughter, I had already enlisted Agatha and all was set in motion. Thus, she reasoned—and I with her—that if we stayed the course and your lands were forfeited, we would save Lady Thomasin from an abusive marriage and my uncle from wedding the sister of the man I believed you to be." El's throat tightened so suddenly, it hurt. "A man you have not been to me."

Blessedly, his continued silence seemed born not of anger but of thought, for the chair stilled and the color in his face began to recede. Then he straightened and stepped near again. "We are both of us haunted," he said, "just as we have both made mistakes—as when I pressed your aunt into a marriage she did not wish—but I believe you and I can make a good marriage. Do you, Elianor?"

A *good* marriage. It was greedy to want better, but she did. "I believe we can."

He drew his hand from beneath hers and laid it to her cheek. "I am sorry for what he did to you, and not only because his brutality holds you from me." He slid his fingers to her neck. "And I am sorry I frightened and hurt you."

Then he also remembered her attack upon him that had ended with his hand spanning her neck. She shook her head and struggled for words to assure him it had been nothing compared to—

Leave me be, Murdoch, she silently pleaded. *Go away—so distant, so dark, so deep that never can you find your way back to me. To us.*

"Elianor?"

Bayard wavered above her as if she looked at him through water. And she did, unable to keep tears from her eyes.

"Pray, do not," he groaned.

How she wished she could obey, but things inside her were breaking free. "Forgive me," she gasped and, feeling her face crumple, gripped a hand over it.

Bayard lowered beside her. As a sob loosed itself from her chest, he drew her into his arms and gently pulled her hand from her face. He kissed her nose, her brow, pressed her head to his chest, and held her near as a keening sound rose from her.

El hated herself for it, that it was loud and ugly, but all the pain and terror and sorrow would not be put back in its bottle—a bottle she had not realized was so full when she had flung it to her depths.

Bayard cradled his wife, and as she wailed and wet his chest with tears, thought there was nothing he wanted more than that she never again suffer such hurt. And if that meant he could not ever truly have her—

Never have her? Never be man and wife as it was ordained? Impossible. He sought God, but not so far as to don a monk's habit. He wanted this woman, to fall asleep in the night with her tucked against his chest… awaken in the morn curved against her back…for her to be mother to his children.

It shall come to pass, he assured himself as her cries began to ease. *I will be patient, and she will grow accustomed to my touch.*

"Milord?"

Bayard jerked, for though he immediately identified the voice, he did not yield up his guard so completely that one had to call to him as if to rouse him from a deep sleep.

He peered over his shoulder at the one in the doorway. No matter how loud Elianor's cries, only Rollo would dare enter unbidden knowing his lord was within. But that was because he did not truly dare. He simply acted on protective instincts.

"Is…?" The big man's shoulders twitched with a nervous shrug, and he put his head to the side as if that slight movement might enable him to see more of Elianor. "Is my lady well?"

"Fear not, Rollo. I am tending her."

The man-at-arms bobbed his chin. "That is God," he said, replacing the word *good* with *God* as he often did, and taking a step back.

As Bayard started to return his attention to the one who continued to empty her grief as if unaware of anything beyond it, he caught movement that brought his head back around.

A woman pushed past Rollo and would have flung herself across the solar if not that the man-at-arms clamped a hand on her.

It was Constance, doubtless roused by Elianor's cries, and coming behind her were the men Magnus had set to watch over her chamber. Rollo dealt with the first by thrusting an elbow up and back into the man's face, and before the confrontation could get out of hand, Bayard dealt with the second by calling, "Release her, Rollo!"

He did not want that woman here—by all that was holy, he did not—but more, he wanted Elianor to remain ignorant of her audience. Fortunately, her uncle had not also come running, meaning he was not abovestairs.

Though freed, Constance stood unmoving and stared at Bayard, while in back of her, Rollo braced to defend the solar where he now faced her second guard.

The woman who had first shared this chamber with Bayard stepped forward, and his anger began to uncoil.

"Leave," he growled, wishing he could shout it.

She faltered, but continued forward. And he had no choice but to let her come.

Halting alongside him, she shifted her gaze to Elianor whose face was pressed hard to his chest and right hand clenched on the lapel of his robe.

Bayard nearly repeated his command, but in her eyes saw what he did not want to be concern lest it soften him toward her.

He tensed further. What he did not want was what was needed were she not to come between Elianor and him. As Father Crispin had once more urged on the night past, God would have him see, feel, think, be, forgive—

Jaw aching with the meeting of his teeth, he told himself that even if Constance and he could not forgive each other, what was hard in him could bear softening.

He drew a deep breath. "Be not anxious. I have her."

Eyes shifting between Elianor and him, she pulled her lower lip between her teeth.

"Constance," he tried again, "You know I will not harm her."

A despondent smile turned her lips, and she inclined her head. She did know, for he had never given her cause to believe otherwise. She turned and, moments later, the door closed.

Bayard rubbed Elianor's back, stroked her hair, and murmured things he would have thought only a desperate man would allow to pass his lips.

And Elianor quieted and came back to him.

"Forgive me," she whispered. "I did not know that much was inside me—not after all these years."

"'Tis good it is out."

She drew back and lifted her face toward his. Her cheeks, nose, and eyes were red, the latter swollen, but though she had never looked less beautiful, he thought her lovely. And dear.

He cupped her face in his palm. How was it possible they could be so changed? How had they moved from fury, hatred, distrust, and fear to dear? And after Constance, why did he allow himself to be so moved? He had vowed to never again fall under a woman's power, yet here he was thinking first of the one in his arms.

"It is good," she said. "Still…"

"Aye?"

"I am sorry I am"—her voice caught—"broken."

He frowned. "I do not believe that of you, Elianor. Were you, we would not be here like this."

She smiled sadly. "If not broken, then bent."

He pondered that and thought there could be no better word to describe his own state following the failure of his first marriage. "All are bent, Elianor, some more than others. The good of it is that something bent can often be pushed back into shape. Perhaps a better shape." Such was that to which Father Crispin had applied himself to pull Bayard back from the brink. Had he gone over it, the feud would surely have escalated, possibly resulting in death. The priest's patient counsel and instruction in humility and prayer had been a means of unbending Bayard and easing him into a shape more pleasing to God. Though the work was hardly complete, there was enough progress that a Boursier and a Verdun stood to spend the remainder of their lives together. And not as enemies.

"I hope 'tis so," Elianor said, "for I do not wish to be untouchable."

He nearly assured her she was not, for she had allowed him to more than touch her, but it was as he had named her when his anger had boiled in light of the abuse she had suffered at that knave's hands.

A breath shuddered out of her. "After what he did to me—"

Bayard slid his thumb to her lips, gently pressed them. "Unless you truly wish to speak of it, no more need be told."

Slowly, she nodded.

As he lowered his hand, he let his gaze linger upon her mouth and told himself there would be other and better times to kiss her.

But Elianor did not think so, sliding her hand to his shoulder, pulling herself up, and placing her mouth so near his that when she whispered, "Not untouchable," her lips brushed his.

He stared into her green eyes, saw the uncertainty that made them waver, realized she did not breathe as if for fear he would gainsay her.

Though roused by her admission that she wished his touch, he kept control over his body by telling himself consummation was more than skin on skin, more than the easing of an ache. And yet, he did not understand how he knew that, for he had not known it with Constance, and it was not something discussed with Father Crispin. If anything, it was sensed, and only now with Elianor.

"Bayard?" Again, her lips brushed his, his name upon them beseeching him to concur she was not untouchable, to confirm she was not broken.

He slid a hand around the back of her neck, felt the scar that evidenced her defiance of Murdoch Farrow, and nearly slew the moment with an oath.

Elianor, he told himself and drew her closer. He kissed her lightly, and that should have been the end of it—for now. But as if unaffected by the discomfort she must surely feel with her slung arm pressed between them, she leaned into him, returned his kiss, and deepened it with such hunger Bayard's body longed for the bed and the shedding of clothes.

Not hunger, he silently corrected. It was what he wished her to feel, but he did not think it was that. More likely, it was desperation. Perhaps even the hope that their joining would erase Murdoch. He hoped it as well, but if she was not truly ready, she might, instead, liken him to that miscreant.

He pulled back, and she opened wide, questioning eyes.

With all the regret of a body taut with want, he said, "Not untouchable, Elianor. Indeed, you are so touchable you tempt me beyond good sense. I want you, but after all you have suffered of a man, I would be a fool did I not let you become more used to me."

Was it uncertainty that flickered across her face? Hurt?

He brushed his mouth across hers. "Years. Time aplenty to know each other."

She delved his gaze, then lowered her head to his shoulder and was silent so long he began to think she slept.

"Bayard?"

"Aye?"

She tilted her head back, looked to his eyepatch. "Will you not show it to me?"

All that had been light in him began to darken. "For what?"

She reached up, and he tensed, but it was his jaw to which she laid a hand. "You know more of me than I thought ever to tell anyone. This I would know of you."

He stared at her.

She pressed her lips inward, and her chest rose with a deep breath. "The night we put you in the underground, your eyepatch went askew. I set it aright, but not before I saw your scarred lid."

Bayard struggled to push down anger. It nearly sickened him to imagine himself weak and defenseless beneath Agatha's regard and that of this woman who was now his wife. This woman whom it was now his duty and desire to protect from such things.

He felt the quake of muscles gripped tight, the ache in his teeth.

Pride. That was what Father Crispin would name that which smoldered and aspired to flame, that which, if loosed, might undo what had been done this day as he had held Elianor amidst the pain of her own past brought to light.

As he wavered, wariness crept across her face, and she dropped her hand from him. "Forgive me. I thought…"

"The eye is unsightly, Elianor. Are you sure?"

Her eyes widened. "I am not afeared. I vow I am not."

"Then I will show you."

She intercepted his hand, pushed it down, and lifted the eyepatch.

She did not startle or catch her breath as she gazed upon the opaque eye that could not even distinguish light from dark, that fiendish thing that caused the few who caught sight of it to cross themselves as if the devil were in their midst.

"Oh, I am sorry," she breathed, then turned her hand around his neck and urged his head toward hers.

Hardly believing what she intended, he closed his eyes and felt the touch of her lips upon the scarred lid.

"As told," she said, "it does not frighten me."

A strain in his chest that had only ever before been so full with the dark emotions of jealousy, anger and grief, Bayard felt strangely vulnerable, a state he did not like. Repositioning the eyepatch, he said gruffly, "It portends well for our marriage," then eased her off his lap, stood, and drew her to her feet. "Now, lest you have forgotten, the supper hour is upon us."

"I did forget," she exclaimed. "Indeed, I am so unpresentable, the meal will be late in being served to your guests."

"*Our* guests can wait," Bayard said. "Now I must needs dress."

While he donned his garments, Elianor crossed to the basin of water. After washing her face, she returned to her lady's table, all the while keeping her back to him.

It would not always be so, he assured himself. Just as she did not fear his blinded eye, she would become comfortable seeing him unclothed— and with him seeing *her* unclothed.

He dragged his boots on, belted on his sword, and returned to where she struggled to pin the veil in place. It was another thing with which he had no experience, but he took the task upon himself and secured the veil as best he could.

Leaning past her, he retrieved the hand mirror. "Acceptable?" He held it before her.

She considered her reflection, then looked up, and he was pleased that though her face still evidenced the strain of spilled emotions, her color was nearly normal and eyes less swollen.

"I thank you," she said.

He lowered the mirror, offered his arm, and led her from the solar and onto the stairs up which the sound of restless retainers and guests climbed.

Feeling her tense, he paused. "All is well?"

"Do you think your people will truly accept me after what Agatha and I did?"

For certain, they would be wary for a time, but he said, "I accept you, and they shall follow where I lead."

Mention of the witch calling to mind a question that did not need an answer if he understood Elianor as he was beginning to think he did, Bayard wavered between whether or not to ask it.

If you understand her…

"I need to know, Elianor, do you still believe you owe Agatha for her aid with Farrow?"

Her eyes widened, and the indignation there was also in her voice. "I cannot comprehend why she should hate you so—and now me—but whatever she plays at, I will no longer dangle from her fingers like a puppet whose strings must needs be yanked."

Her choice of words called to mind the chess match with King Edward, in the midst of which Bayard had felt like a playing piece moved at his liege's whim. And more so when the self-satisfied knight errant, Sir Francis, had lent his sardonic opinion to the discussion.

"Then we are in agreement," he said. "She must be rooted out and made to never again work ill upon our families."

This time, Elianor hesitated.

So there could be no misunderstanding, Bayard said, "If necessary, death will be her end."

She jerked her chin. "If there is no other way."

For his wife's sake, he hoped it would be enough that the witch was imprisoned without cease, but something told him that would not be enough for Agatha of Mawbry.

28

⎯⎯⎯∞⎯⎯⎯

THE MEAL HAD been tolerable. For the most part, Bayard's retainers had contained their curiosity over the woman whom all but those who had accompanied Lady Quintin to Castle Mathe had believed to be Thomasin de Arell. Now that it was known Elianor of Emberly was the one who had imprisoned their lord, they were surely piqued over the missing pieces of the tale.

Blessedly, just as Bayard had assured her, they followed his lead, striving to behave as if nothing untoward had made him take to wife the wily woman at his side.

Emberly's men were a different matter. They did not hide their discontent at seeing the one who had served as lady of Castle Kelling now sit at the high table as lady of Castle Adderstone, wife of the Baron of Godsmere. And Magnus...

There was no disguising his concern for his niece who had come late to the hall with a face that evidenced she had been far from laughter prior to her appearance. From one of two tables set perpendicular to the high table, he watched her and her husband.

Thus, when Bayard called an end to the light meal and escorted El from the dais, she was not surprised by Magnus's approach. Regard fixed on his host, he halted before them. "Should I be concerned that my niece has been shedding tears, Boursier?"

Bayard's hand upon El tensed so minimally she knew he had antici-
pated the question. Doubtless, he had also been aware of Magnus's
observation throughout the meal.

He looked to El. "As I must confer with my steward, I shall leave you
to answer your uncle."

Pleased that he did not concern himself over what she might say, she
inclined her head. "So I shall."

As he strode toward the immense fireplace before which others had
gathered, El saw the nod he gave Rollo who stood at the foot of the stairs.

The big man-at-arms was among those who had kept watch over
the hall throughout the meal. Now he grinned and hurried toward the
kitchen where he would surely be well fed.

"El?" her uncle said.

She winced over his creased brow. "Ease your worry, Magnus.
Providing Agatha is, indeed, gone from Adderstone, all is well."

"And yet you came to the hall with a face that evidenced you were
at tears."

"So I was, but Bayard is not to blame." She wished for a better place
to hold this conversation, but as it seemed it was to be had before the
dais, she glanced around to be certain none listened. "The blame falls
upon the one to whom I was yet a maiden when we wed." The evils of
which Magnus knew only by way of Agatha's loose tongue, for it had
been shame enough that he knew without El also speaking of it. "I vow,
my new husband was patient and understanding."

His face brightened as if slapped. "You told Boursier what that…"
The tic at the corner of his right eye started up. "…*poltroon* did to you?"

There was something endearing in his struggle to find the right
word to besmirch Murdoch Farrow. Like Bayard, he was not at a
loss for names but, rather, ones mild enough to be spoken in a lady's
presence.

"He knows enough," El said, "as he should, for he is the one who
must live with the ills of my first marriage."

Magnus stared so long she knew she would not like the words form-
ing on his tongue. "Tell me you do not imagine yourself in love, especially after so short an acquaintance."

It did not seem possible to the El she had been, but to the one she
was becoming...

He grunted. "More to the point, tell me you do not have such feelings for one who has long been our enemy."

She understood his disbelief, but it did not change that something
immovable had moved within her and continued to move when she was
near Bayard, be it in body or thought. "I cannot yet name my emotions,
but I am as surprised as you that they have changed."

He stepped nearer. "Do you forget what he did to my sister? Or have
you determined to no longer believe he ill-treated her?"

His question returned her to the inner walls when Agatha had
concluded El had ceased to believe Bayard capable of having abused
Constance—and had, therefore, pronounced upon El what was to have
been a death sentence.

"Elianor?" Magnus pressed.

She marveled that her name spoken in full should sound so sweet
only upon Bayard's lips. And not merely because he made of it four
parts, the first being little more than breath. Because it was *he* who
spoke it.

"Magnus, do not be angry with me, but after all I have *not* suffered
at the hands of a man said to use his fists on a woman, I do not see that
in Bayard. I—"

She caught back the declaration that she did not believe he was simply a changed man, but that he had never been such a man. Though a
heart that had been too long in hiding urged her to speak it, she was no
longer the gullible young woman whom Murdoch had quickly set right
when she had tried to tame the devil in him with kindness and understanding. Too, never would Magnus credit her wholehearted defense of
Bayard.

"What do you see?" he said.

Though she knew it would make her seem inconstant, she compromised. "It becomes increasingly difficult to believe Bayard was ever that man."

As his handsome face hardened, she touched his sleeve. "You told that my aunt never spoke of what happened when Bayard found her with Serle de Arell."

"One had but to look upon her bruised face to know what had passed. And when I cursed Bayard Boursier for the abuse done her, she did not gainsay me. Despite her vow of silence, she could have done so by written word or gesture."

A thought struck El. Was it possible Constance had willfully allowed such ill to be believed of the man who had taken Serle's arm, gained an annulment, seen her confined, and had her lover sent on pilgrimage?

"Lest you forget," Magnus continued, "when Agatha returned to Castle Kelling, she told that Boursier had ousted her because of her protests against his callous treatment of my sister."

She had heard it from Agatha herself when Magnus had sent the woman to El after the first of two years as Murdoch's wife. And believed it. But now...

"Bayard told me the reason he cast out Agatha was because he discovered she was providing powders that Constance slipped into his wine to keep him from their bed," El said. "The same ones Agatha gave me to taint his drink so we could imprison him."

His eyes widened.

"Magnus," she entreated, "did not you, yourself, warn me against Agatha?"

His jaw shifted.

"Was she not the one who revealed I had left Castle Kelling while you appealed to King Edward to overturn his decree?"

"Aye," he begrudged, "and you lied in telling 'twas to Ellesmere you had gone."

Doubtless, his search for her at the abbey had revealed the falsehood. "I am sorry for that, but you should know Agatha broke my confidence

because I insisted on accompanying her to Adderstone to release Bayard.
I am certain she hoped you would keep a better watch on me, giving me
no choice but to allow her to go alone. And she did—after rendering me
unconscious."

He jerked. "She has struck you before?"

"Aye, though death was not her intent then."

A muscle spasmed in his jaw. "I warrant she is deceitful and dangerous, but that does not mean she lied about Boursier's brutality."

El dug fingers into her palms. "You are so determined to believe he
did wrong that though it was at Agatha's hands I near met my death, you
continue to lend credence to her words—she who has shown she hates
the Verduns as much as the Boursiers."

The anger in his eyes flared. Guttered. Died. "I no longer know
what to believe."

Silently, El marveled that she was fairly certain of the truth. In her
bid to convince him to give little or no weight to Agatha's tales and consider Bayard might not have done what was believed of him, she had
moved herself nearer her husband's side—so near it seemed a nudge was
all it would take to declare him innocent.

"But even if 'tis true he did not abuse Constance previous to finding
her with Serle," Magnus said, "what of the blows she received that day?
One can hardly begrudge him his anger over being cuckolded, but it
does not excuse him for beating her."

"It does not. *If* he beat her. Thus, that I might know the truth, I
would like to speak to my aunt."

He frowned. "Am I to understand that the man whose character you
so eagerly defend has not shared with you the events of that day?"

There seemed both gain and loss in her answer. Gain that it was
Bayard's actions, not mere claims of innocence, that made her argue his
case. Loss that for all her leanings toward him, he had not confided that far.

"Though he maintains he never abused her, he has revealed very
little of that day. Thus, I have tried to speak with Aunt Constance, but she
will not admit me. If you would ask her—"

"As you are inclined to believe Boursier is innocent," Magnus said sharply, "what gain in allowing you to drag my sister back to that horror?"

El felt the snap of her own anger. "If there is any responsible for returning her to that horror, it is Constance. *She* had you steal her into Adderstone. As for what gain there might be, though my husband's first wife is no longer physically present in our marriage bed, she is yet between the sheets, as is Bayard's anger for what was done there. Thus, just as I must be free of Murdoch if my marriage is to be more than the striving to make heirs"—*if you can do that,* whispered doubt—"Bayard and Constance must be free of each other. If there can be peace between them—"

"Peace?" he scoffed.

"Had my aunt not willingly entered these walls, I would have little hope of it. But she is here, and I do not think she came only that she might suffer further torment."

He stared at her, then loosed a sigh that took the stiff out of his back. "Forgive my unbelief. Just as I am disposed to expecting the worst to alleviate the sting of disappointment, I am unaccustomed to seeing you in a state of hopefulness." He nodded. "I shall speak with Constance."

She momentarily closed her eyes. "I thank you."

When the silence between them became uncomfortable, she glanced at the windows high in the walls and noted no moonlight penetrated the oilcloths. "I heard tale it may snow again."

"'Tis more than tale. Ere I left the training field, more had begun to fall."

"Then you will stay another day."

"Were Constance not in our party, we would have set off this morn, and now it may be days ere we depart. God willing, we will not still be Boursier's unwelcome guests come Christmas."

Six days hence. "You are my guests as well, Uncle."

His smile was short-lived, for something drew his regard from her. "I will leave you to your husband," he said and strode opposite.

"All is well?" Bayard asked as he came alongside.

"I cannot say my uncle is happy."

"What, besides being snowbound at Adderstone, burdens him?"

Though tempted to tell him she had confessed it was increasingly difficult to believe Constance had suffered abuse at his hands, she feared speaking it too soon—of exposing so much of her heart.

"I told him I wish an audience with my aunt that I might learn what happened the day you…found her with Serle de Arell."

His jaw tightened as if the tender man who had brushed out her hair and held her while she cried had returned to a place from which he had escaped. "For what purpose?"

"I believe there is more to it than what I have been told—more than Magnus knows."

"And if there is?"

"Perhaps what is wrong between you and my aunt can be made right."

He lowered his face near hers. "You make it sound as if 'twas a mere disagreement, as if that—" Like her uncle, he seemed to struggle for a less offensive name with which to besmirch the one under discussion. In the end, he did not name her. "The marriage bed was defiled, blood was shed, and let us not forget the maiming."

Something with which he lived every day, as did Serle de Arell.

"Forgive me for not better choosing my words. I understand it can never be completely right between the two of you, but surely I can seek peace enough so that what haunts you will not forever haunt our marriage?"

He drew a strident breath. "I would not begrudge you your peace. But should you not ask me of that day? Or do you not trust what I would tell?"

She caught back a protest, once more shied away from a heart that sought to twist her—

Twist, El? whispered the memory of Bayard's assurance that she was not broken. *Mayhap your heart is but trying to bend you into a better shape.*

Too soon, she silently defended her right to exercise caution.

"Do you not?" Bayard pressed.

"I did not think you would wish to speak of it." Only partly true, the defense so weak she winced.

"'Tis not something I choose to discuss," he said, "but if you must hear of it, it would be better learned from your husband."

El could almost feel the opposing walls of the corner into which she was being backed. "Magnus," she said, "he will more likely believe what his sister—"

"I did not ask after him, Elianor."

She swallowed. "I wish to trust you, but…" She did not know what more to say that would not further offend him. And in the growing silence, she keenly felt his pale, singular gaze.

At last, he said, "You are right not to trust me, Elianor. We hardly know each other."

There was no solace in his resentful assent. Indeed, it threatened all hope. Stepping nearer, she said, "I would know you better, Bayard. *Will* you tell me of that day—share with me as I have shared with you?"

"That you might compare my tale to your aunt's?"

"I—"

"Good eve, Elianor." He turned and strode to the stairs.

Was the chapel his destination? Would he pray again? Would he come late to their bed and once more be gone when she arose?

Regretting her part in shaking the bridge that had begun to span the distance between them, she motioned the servants to set the hall to rights and crossed to the hearth where she lowered into a chair near Lady Maeve to await what she was not sure she wished to be a summons to her aunt's chamber.

29

~~~

As yet, no summons. And throughout the wait, few words were exchanged with Bayard's stepmother who mostly stared into the fire and made mischief with the purse on her girdle—stroking it, causing its coins to clink, occasionally gripping it so hard the contents clattered.

As El considered the castle folk who had begun to position their pallets about the hall in anticipation of an end to their long day, Lady Maeve said, "How fares your arm, Lady Elianor?"

El glanced at the sling. "Owing to your physician's ministrations and draughts, I am mostly unaware of my injury except in light of its limitations."

The lady nodded. "I did not expect you to so readily take to your new role as mistress of Adderstone—injured or nay."

Might that be a compliment? "As the running of my uncle's household was entrusted to me, I am accustomed to all it entails."

"Would that it disposed me toward approving of you as my stepson's wife," Lady Maeve bemoaned, "but under these circumstances..."

Which need not be enumerated. Nor did El believe it wise to apologize again for being the reason Lady Quintin was held captive by the man who would be her husband. "I understand, my lady."

"Not as much as you believe." Bayard's stepmother returned her gaze to the fire, and once again the contents of her purse grew restive.

Thinking their conversation at an end, El eyed the stairs in the hope Magnus would appear.

The jangling ceased, and Lady Maeve said, "Though Bayard is not of my body, I have had a care for him since he was born. Did you know his mother died birthing him?"

Surprised by the conversation's turn, El said, "I did not."

"Aye, while these lands were yet whole and my father was baron of all of Kilbourne."

Denis Foucault, the betrayer and the betrayed.

"When I was Lady Maeve Foucault."

El hesitated over words she knew few dared speak, but as Bayard's stepmother had opened the door to them, she ventured, "Methinks it must be difficult being a Foucault *and* a Boursier."

A bitter smile scratched itself into the lady's face. "Certes, it has been no easy thing, especially since Archard was lost to me."

"You miss him?"

Sorrow softened Lady Maeve's mouth. "Nothing so small as that. I ache for him."

Realizing she was in the presence of great love, albeit mourned, El's heart convulsed. "Then you forgave him for..." *Betraying* was too harsh a word to wield against one for whom the lady's heart still beat. "You forgave him for revealing your father's true allegiance?"

Wariness crept across the woman's brow, and El knew she regretted having allowed their talk to trespass upon such private matters, but she said, "More easily than I forgave my father for refusing to allow us to wed."

Then Archard Boursier had wished to marry his liege's daughter? Another thing El had not known.

"Indeed," Lady Maeve said, "I never completely forgave my sire. Had he not denied us, had he been true to but one of his promises to award Archard the keeping of a castle, I do not believe his most esteemed knight would have moved against him. And without Archard, neither would the De Arells and Verduns have rebelled."

She made it sound as if her world would not have been knocked off its foundation. "Still, your father and his liegemen might have lost all once the earl learned his vassal did not support the baronage's cause."

"If ever he had learned of it." Lady Maeve sighed. "But that is in the past. Now I must needs look to what the future holds for my Quintin."

"Marriage to De Arell."

Lady Maeve gave a huff of disgust. "That whelp?"

El nearly smiled to hear the imposing, well-seasoned Griffin de Arell called such. Though his father was the only living one of the three who had turned against Foucault, the son was many years distant from being of an age or disposition to warrant such disparagement. Of course, the last time Lady Maeve had seen Griffin was likely when his father yet served hers—when he had, indeed, been a whelp.

"Nay," Lady Maeve said, "I do not think so."

El frowned. Did she truly believe she could prevent her daughter from wedding De Arell? If she succeeded, such defiance could cause the barony of Godsmere to be torn from Bayard as surely as if he, himself, had refused the decree. "I do not see how you can thwart Lady Quintin's marriage without risking all of Godsmere."

The woman blinked, shrugged. "A dream only—wanting it to be for love Quintin weds, just as I did."

El did not doubt the sincerity of the lady's love for Bayard's father. Still, it bothered her how certain she sounded that Griffin de Arell would not wed her daughter. Just as El had been given no choice when her scheme against Bayard had failed, neither could Quintin say with whom she would spend the rest of her life. "My lady—"

"Do you think you are favored by God, Lady Elianor?"

The change of topic was so abrupt El could not think of a response.

"Not even a full day since taking a fall that could have been the death of you"—Lady Maeve flicked a hand toward El's splinted arm—"and you claim your place at Adderstone."

El inclined her head. "It is a blessing, and perhaps your daughter will also be blessed when she weds De Arell."

The lady's mouth tightened.

"During our stay at Castle Mathe," El continued, "Baron de Arell was mannerly and respectful whilst in your daughter's company."

Lady Maeve snorted. "Like Bayard, you seek to assure me of that which cannot be assured. And just the same, you have failed. De Arell is no fool to mistreat my daughter in her brother's presence. No matter the odds, Bayard would not have tolerated it. But now that De Arell has no one to answer to…"

Before El could point out her daughter had appeared to suffer naught in the days before her brother's arrival, Lady Maeve added, "And even if that whelp lays no hand upon her, his vile father might."

"'Tis said Ulric de Arell is incapacitated," El argued, "so much he no longer ventures belowstairs—does not even leave his chamber."

"So I have heard, but with a Boursier beneath his roof, mayhap he will find the strength to do so."

Though frustrated, El knew she could not begrudge the lady her worry over her only child. After all, El had feared Bayard to the extent she had tried to see him ousted from Godsmere so that neither she nor Thomasin de Arell would suffer him. And though it would seem Griffin de Arell was no more a beast than Bayard, all knew that while Ulric de Arell had ruled the Barony of Blackwood, most often he was the one to instigate trouble between the three families—whether moving against the Boursiers and Verduns, each in their turn, or rousing Verdun against the Boursiers. Doubtless, he had never risen above the disappointment of his failed bid to replace Denis Foucault as Baron of Kilbourne, and it had surely cut deeper to lose Castle Adderstone to Archard Boursier.

"Elianor?"

El looked up and found Magnus stood alongside her chair.

"Not this eve," he said with a glance at Lady Maeve.

"I thank you, Uncle."

He inclined his head and pivoted.

"Your aunt?" Lady Maeve said as El followed his progress to where his men had gathered near the dais.

"She keeps to herself, of which I am sure you approve."

"There are few things I desire more than to never again share air with that woman." A muscle in her jaw spasmed. "And here she is once more at Adderstone, flaying wide open the scars she inflicted."

In that moment, the night past and the day gone rushed at El, and there was nothing she wanted more than to be distant from such bitterness, her mind calmed by sleep.

She stood. "I wish you good eve, my lady."

Once more, Lady Maeve began to shift her purse.

Upon reaching the solar, El was not entirely disappointed to find Bayard absent. She would not have what had passed between them in the hall spill over into their chamber, especially considering what had last transpired here when the arms of the one she had once believed to be the basest of men had become a haven. Bayard Boursier, on whom she had gazed that day in the market in preparation of his imprisonment, had provided yet more evidence he was not merciless, not kin to the night, and that he possessed a soul far from black.

And yet still you do not trust him, a small voice reminded her.

"I want to," she whispered, and determinedly cast off thoughts that would deny her the rest she needed.

It was difficult to negotiate her splinted arm, but she soon disrobed, slid beneath the covers, and fell down into sleep.

This eve, it was not voices that trespassed upon her sleep and opened her eyes upon the dark. What was it?

El listened, and when she did not hear the breath of one who should be abed, when she slid a leg across the mattress to confirm she was as alone as when she had laid down, she thought that must be what had awakened her—wanting the one who was not with her. Wanting Bayard.

"Cease," she whispered, but that did not keep her from remembering the night he had pulled her atop him so she might become accustomed to him, nor his hand upon her shoulder and hers upon his.

As she turned onto her side, away from his absence, the dull ache that moved elbow to wrist sharpened.

Gingerly, she stretched her splinted arm atop her side down to her thigh, then closed her eyes and told herself to sleep—to not dwell on the empty place beside her.

She did not sleep. She did dwell on that emptiness. And regretted that Bayard and she had come so far only to have Constance's continued silence swing like a sword between them.

But does it do so because I am the one who allows her silence its keen edges? she wondered. *Because I am afraid to trust though trust may be due?*

Considering all she had endured with Murdoch, it made sense to hold back that part of her, no matter how true Bayard might seem. But was there not wrong in allowing fear, more than faith, to dictate her actions—and to such an extent she turned her face from the something hopeful it seemed Bayard was placing within her grasp?

She closed her eyes. And there fear awaited her. Ever quick to offer a solution, it assured her a cautious life was better than a happy life, the latter being but a dream ripe for dashing upon the rocks. Indeed, the tales she had embraced in her younger years—the love of Tristan for Iseult and that of Abelard for Heloise—had not ended happily.

In that moment, it would have been easy to embrace caution if not that Bayard's presence in her life was so deeply felt. Feeling him now, she was once more drawn toward that something hopeful. And so she stepped through fear and fingered her faith.

Lord, she silently prayed, *I am at sea. Despite what I wrought against Bayard, and for which he had good reason to be angered, time and again he shows forbearance, even kindness. Indeed, had Agatha not convinced me he was abusive and Magnus not himself believed it, never would I have thought Bayard capable of such. Surely they are wrong about him. And if Constance would only speak of that day, it could be proved. If she would but tell me—*

Abruptly, El sat up, causing the bedclothes to slip to her waist and let in a chill that rippled across her limbs. She stared at the hearth across the chamber, lowered her feet to the floor, and by the stingy glow of the fire's remains, donned her husband's robe. Cinching the belt tight to take up the excess length and width, she crossed to the door and opened it.

Rollo straightened from where he had lowered to his haunches against the wall. Though he had been at rest, the light of torches in the corridor showed there was no sleep about his eyes.

"Milady? Ye be needin' something?"

"My husband. Do you know—"

"The chapel." He jutted his chin toward the far end. "There he be. You wish me to fetch him?"

"Nay, I shall go to him."

"Then I go with ye."

Holding back a protest that would likely have no effect other than to offend, she followed.

As they neared Constance's chamber, Rollo grunted in acknowledgement of the sleepy-eyed man-at-arms positioned in front of the door.

The man grunted back.

"I should wait here?" Rollo asked, halting alongside the chapel door.

Pleased that in this, she had a say, she said, "I think that is best, Rollo."

"Ye remember my name!"

His delight made her smile. "How could I not? You have been most gallant."

Ruddy cheeks darkening further, he said, "And ye are a God lady."

A *God* lady. El hoped it was not an affront to the Lord to like the sound of that.

Rollo eased open the door, and she stepped into a chapel faintly lit by a dozen candles at the far end. As the door quietly closed behind her, she picked out the dim figure of the one prostrated before the altar.

Did Bayard realize he was no longer alone? Or was he too taken with prayer to hear or sense her presence? Would he begrudge her interruption?

Pulled between continuing forward and retreating, she strained to catch the murmurings of voiced prayers. Nothing. It was as if he were as absent here as he was from their bed. She wavered, then advanced in her stockinged feet.

When she drew alongside him where he lay with arms above his head and forehead to the floor, he did not rouse, nor when she knelt near.

"Bayard?" She touched his shoulder.

"Once again, you wander about in the dark of night," he reproached, his voice gritty and dull as if fatigue pressed him to the floor.

"I am not without escort. Rollo is outside the door."

He drew a deep breath. "For what are you here, Elianor?"

"I do not know what hour it is—if it is before the middling of night or after—but 'tis late and surely you ought to be abed."

He turned his face toward her, and she caught the glitter of his gaze amid the hair fallen over his brow. "With you?"

Grateful for the shadows that would provide less evidence of the color in her cheeks, she said, "Aye, your wife who lay down alone and awakened to find the other side of the bed still empty."

"A state in which she does not wish it to be?"

Tempted to push the hair off his brow, she sat back on her heels. "She does not."

"You have spoken with your aunt?"

The question should not have surprised her, for that was where they had left their relationship—her unwilling to trust what he had to say of accusations he had borne all these years—but she was not yet ready to speak there. "I have not," she said and changed the subject. "Are you done with your prayers?"

He gave a short, humorless laugh. "I am far from done."

She frowned. "You have only recently come to the chapel?"

"Nay, Father Crispin was long in taking me to task, and then I was to pray. And I did—until I began to feel every hour of every day since first I gazed upon you."

El felt her throat tighten, but though she longed to apologize for all she had caused him to endure, she said, "You have been sleeping here on the floor?"

"Hardly godly, but perhaps for this I am oft out of favor with God, hmm? Unable to dwell long in His presence and show the respect due Him."

Recalling the early months of her first marriage when, day after day, hour after hour, she had exhorted God to right the injustice done her, El did not believe the Lord was moved by how much time one spent in His presence. *If* He was going to bring one out of darkness, it seemed He did so only when He was ready.

"I must return to my prayers," Bayard said. "Go, and I will join you within the hour."

She brought his face back to focus. "For what do you pray?"

He hesitated, said, "For more things than a man who has struggled long to be near God should have to pray. But this eve, I pray that the mistakes of our first marriages will not continue to bleed into this one."

El's heart constricted. So spoke the man she feared to trust despite all evidence he was not and had never been what was believed of him.

Though tempted to return to the solar and bundle herself back beneath the covers, she said, "I shall add my beseechings to yours," and set the palm of her uninjured arm upon the floor and eased down beside him.

"Your injury, Elianor!" He moved to rise.

"'Tis no strain." She turned her face to his. "And I wish to be here. With you."

He frowned. "You are certain?"

"Of being here with you, aye. Of prayer..." She smiled apologetically. "I do not speak much to God other than, in passing, to send prayers and pleadings His way—just in case He is near enough to catch what I cast and, for once, inclined to act upon it."

"Murdoch," he growled.

It was not the direction she wished to go, but Bayard deserved to know. Holding his gaze, she said, "I prayed as long as I could. Over and over, I called upon the Lord to deliver me, but there was only silence— as if He condoned what was done to me."

Bayard's hand closed over hers. "Never would He condone such evil, Elianor."

"I do not wish to believe it, but then what am I to believe? That He did not hear my cries? That——" Hearing her voice rise, she said more measuredly, "That He was not there? Ever?"

"He was there, Elianor. He heard your prayers." It was said with such certainty she could almost feel his arms that had earlier held her while she cried. "Though I sometimes fail to remember in the midst of trial, as when I feared Godsmere was lost to me, He is not ours to command. We must wait on Him, even though we be mired in the pain and anger of injustice for what could amount to many years."

"It seems too simple an explanation for His silence."

"It does," Bayard conceded, then asked, "Do you feel He has yet to answer the prayers you gave unto Him while wed to Farrow?"

She swallowed. "I was freed—finally—but how am I to know that was the work of the Lord?"

"You cannot, but if He did not intervene, perhaps it was because, in knowing what would come to pass, He instead set to preserving you through the waiting." He gently squeezed her hand. "And do not doubt you were preserved, Elianor, for are you not here with me this eve? A night distant from all those other nights?"

Far distant. Here was hope—on the chapel floor with this man who had once been her enemy.

"A night distant even from last eve when you could have been lost to me?" he pressed on.

How sweet that there was someone who might feel the loss of her. Sweeter yet, his words were laced with sincerity not unlike when he had spoken of his fear of losing Godsmere.

She relaxed into the smile his words coaxed from her. "I wish to believe it."

"Do, if not from my lips, then Father Crispin's. 'Tis as he oft counsels, much to his frustration."

Within El arose a memory of the priest on the morn they broke camp to ride on Castle Mathe. He had said Bayard deserved better than her, and it seemed he was right. "Father Crispin has a care for you," she said.

"He does. We have long been friends—since I was a boy of six and he served as a stable boy to the Foucaults."

Another Foucault connection. Another family intimacy revealed. More hope. "I am glad."

Bayard drew her hand to his mouth, kissed her fingers, and turned his face to the floor.

30

THIS TIME, ELIANOR was the one who gave herself over to sleep during prayer.

Having been too absorbed in his meeting with God to hear her breathing deepen and feel her hand slacken in his, Bayard stared at her profile and was tempted to run a finger across the tips of her lashes, down her small nose, over her bowed upper lip.

That was not all he wished to do, and not merely because she was lovely to look upon. Despite the near ruinous beginning to their relationship, and that she refused to trust him despite his struggle to exercise control over anger and frustration, he felt more for her than he had for Constance who had been just as comely when he had made her his bride. Though alarmed to feel so much so soon for his second wife, there had to be redemption in that he was drawn to her for more than her outward beauty. Indeed, he thought that even were he to lose all sight, he would be no less attracted to Elianor.

Dear Lord, he once more turned his thoughts heavenward, *I would not ask that there be love between us, for I would not venture again to such pretentious depths of emotion, but I beseech that Elianor and I find mutual contentment in our marriage.*

In the chapel that was spared darkness only by the fortitude of the few remaining candles, Bayard raised himself from the floor. Careful to avoid jostling his wife's splinted arm, he gently turned her onto her back.

She murmured, but did not rouse when he lifted her and straightened.

Musing that he was making a habit of carrying her to bed, grateful this night was different from the night past when he had found her broken within the inner walls, he traversed the chapel and worked the door.

As expected, Rollo was alert where he stood in the corridor.

"I thank you for keeping watch over Lady Elianor," Bayard said low. "She is my responsibility now. Gain your rest."

The big man eyed the woman whose head rested on his lord's shoulder. "This 'un will stay, milord?"

The question was not unexpected, for Rollo had once been fond of Constance, her betrayal and removal from Adderstone having caused him to become morose for months thereafter. Of course, that aura had been well seeded by Bayard and Quintin who had suffered more deeply and longer as a result of Constance's faithlessness.

Bayard looked to Elianor. "She will stay and be mother to my sons and daughters."

"Wee ones," Rollo said with a crooked smile.

God willing, once their marriage was consummated. But now, with her injury...

Bayard assured himself there was time aplenty, said, "Good eve, Rollo," and stepped forward.

The man's ability to quickly maneuver his great bulk always something over which to marvel, he reached the solar first and opened the door. "God eve, milord," he rasped and quietly closed the door behind his lord and lady.

As Bayard crossed the chilled, shadow-draped chamber, he set his mind to kindling the fire once he had Elianor abed. But when he lowered her to the rumpled sheet, her softly parted lips moved him to an inopportune awareness of his body, and moved him further when he recalled her responses to his mouth upon hers.

He did not doubt that she wanted him more than Constance had wanted him. But was it desire only? Could it be something more?

"Bayard?"

He raised his gaze to Elianor's half-opened eyes. "Aye, 'tis me," he assured her. "Rest easy." As he drew back, she swept her uninjured arm up and curled a hand around his neck.

"Stay," she whispered.

"Worry not, lady wife, I shall be here when next you awaken."

"That is not what I mean. I would have you more than stay. I would have you..." She drew a deep breath. "I would be your wife in full."

"Your arm," he reminded her in a voice so strained he hardly recognized it.

She pushed her fingers through the hair at his nape. "Surely it is not needed?"

It was not. Imagining the taste of her mouth so near his, he said, "You truly wish this, Elianor? This night?"

"I do."

"Out of obligation?"

"Nay."

Feeling the pound of his heart, he gave her one last opportunity to reconsider. "To make children?"

He knew the moment she took hold of that one, for though the space between them remained constant, he felt her lurch away.

"There will be a better time," he said and would have withdrawn if not that her hand gripped his scalp and he caught the glitter of her tears. "Elianor?"

"When you thought I was Thomasin, you told that among the reasons you had not taken Elianor of Emberly to wife was because she had not provided her first husband with an heir."

As understanding moved through him, she continued, "Though often enough he—" Her breath rushed out and back in. "Many were the times I could have grown round with child, and I did not. Perhaps because ever I prayed I would not birth a child made to suffer him for a father, perhaps because he was incapable of sowing children, or perhaps because my womb is barren." A sob escaped her. "You want and need an heir, Bayard."

Her anxiety—and the pain behind it—was so sincere he felt his heart strain against the walls he had fortified on all sides of it.

Elianor eased her hand from the back of his head, drew it down his jaw, dropped it to her chest. "A far better match I would have made for Griffin de Arell who already has his heir. Had you wed Lady Thomasin, she would likely bear you children, and your sister..."

Bayard tensed.

"Any sons born of her union with De Arell will be of less consequence than the son his first wife gave him." She searched his face. "Had I not imprisoned you, your sister would have wed Magnus and been the mother of his heir."

Bayard did not want to think about Quintin who, despite what Elianor believed, could prove better wed to De Arell. He did not want to ponder the need for an heir that, in that moment, seemed of little consequence. And he certainly did not want any woman other than this one in his bed.

And with that last silent admission, he realized that what he felt for Elianor was like—and yet not like—what he had felt for Constance.

Impossible. But if possible, foolish. And if foolish, dangerous.

Not impossible, he accepted, and though he knew he ought to be ashamed, there was only the truth. He had not dared pray for there to be love between Elianor and him, and perhaps there was not. But it was present on one side of them.

Lord help me. Once more I am a fool. I love this woman.

"I fear I have ruined all, Bayard. Could I change what I did—"

"I would not have you change it," he said gruffly.

"But—"

"It is in God's hands." He lowered his head toward hers. "Let Him do with it as He wills." He touched his mouth to hers, and when she allowed that small intimacy, angled his head and deepened the kiss.

She was still so long he feared she would not be roused again, that though he might share the bed with her, their backs would be turned to each other. But then, tentatively, becoming bolder with each replenishing breath, she gave back. And when he moved to her ear, she whispered, "I so like your kisses. They are far different from…"

He nearly growled her first husband's name, but he would not have the knave any more present than already he was. "My word I give, Elianor, what comes after the kisses will also be far different—not merely payment of the marital debt."

Her answer was nearly all breath. "Show me, Bayard."

He straightened, drew off his tunic, and dropped the garment to the rushes.

Wide-eyed, she lowered her gaze from his face to his throat, lingered. Considered his shoulders, drew a deep breath. Moved her eyes down his chest to the waistband of his chausses, swallowed hard. But as he started to join her on the bed, she said, "Pray, would you add to the fire?"

It was as he had meant to do when he had carried her inside, but he did not think it was only the cold she wished to allay. The shadows were likely of greater concern—her wish to see clearly it was he who came to her.

He crossed to the hearth, and when he returned minutes later, light ran up the chamber's walls and flickered across the ceiling.

Wordlessly, Elianor scooted to the center of the bed.

Bayard lowered to the mattress, propped himself on an elbow, and peered into her face.

She slid her tongue over lips that tentatively rose toward a smile, face flushed so deeply there was no masking the color of her discomfort.

He brushed the backs of his fingers across her heated cheek and, feeling her startle, asked, "Are you sure you are accustomed to me, Elianor?"

Her smile softened. "Speak my name again."

He raised an eyebrow. "Elianor."

She momentarily lowered her lids. "No one has ever spoken it the way you do. And never have I liked it better."

Why the revelation should make him desire her more, he did not know, but he put his mouth to her ear and said more slowly, "Elianor, wife of Bayard Boursier of Castle Adderstone upon the barony of Godsmere. Elianor."

She turned her face to his. "I am accustomed," she murmured, and loosened the belt and parted the robe.

The gesture was so beguiling—so sensual—he was grateful for the chemise beneath that aided in keeping his passion in check.

Slowly, he reminded himself. *There is only one first time, and if she is to leave Farrow behind, you must be Bayard to her. Only Bayard.*

He claimed her lips, and later, when she softened and whispered his name and returned his kisses, he slid a hand inside the robe.

She allowed it, and he ventured further.

Knowing that never again would he don the robe without remembering this night when the woman who was not yet ready to trust him in full, had trusted him enough to yield the gift of her body, he began to unclothe her.

First, the robe—momentary tension, barely perceptible startles. Next, the chemise—prolonged tension, evident startles.

He kissed her eyelids. "I can stop, Elianor. You have but to speak."

She opened her eyes. "I do not wish you to stop. I want to know it can be like your kisses."

"That is not asking much," he said, then hoped he had not spoken too loosely. Despite the intimacy of giving one's breath unto the other, it did not compare to what happened when two became one—providing she could be moved to feel something near what he was certain he would experience with her. More, providing she did not feign to feel what she did not, as Constance had done.

Bayard nearly cursed to find that other woman here, resented that she and Farrow conspired to deny Elianor and him their long-awaited wedding night.

Determined to shut them out, he said, "My word I give, I will not hurt you."

She smiled. "This I know."

He moved his gaze down her, next his hands. Pausing often to allow her bouts of tension to ease, he lingeringly touched her throat, chest, and abdomen—all the way down to the soles of her feet. He lightly caressed her ankles, thighs, and hips—all the way up to her fingers that meshed with his. Restrainedly, he kissed her neck, jaw, and ear—all the way in to her soft mouth.

And when her body asked it of him, he made her his wife in full.

"It did not hurt."

El gasped, but it was too late to catch back words that were childishly full of wonder, for already they were in her ears, meaning they were in Bayard's—unless he had been taken by sleep.

It was hope without merit. Against her back, where he had drawn her into the curve of his body after making love to her, she felt a break in the rise and fall of his chest.

Closing her eyes upon the chamber that the slayer of shadows—the fire Bayard had kindled—refused to yield to the night, El prayed her thoughtless words had not spoiled what they had shared. Unlike with Murdoch, from whom she had learned how sensitive a man could be regarding his prowess upon the sheets, she had not spoken in hopes of dousing Bayard's desire. It was relief-induced contentment that had set her thoughts upon her tongue.

He lifted his hand from her hip, brushed her hair aside, and swept her ear with his breath. "I am glad, Elianor. But there is more to joining one's body with another's than merely the absence of pain. I would have you also enjoy it."

Warming in remembrance of how patient he had been, of the places he had touched, of her name upon his lips—and his upon hers—she said, "Pray, forgive me. Though I know I did not feel what you did, you awakened in me things heretofore unknown. Things most... pleasant."

He parted his body from hers, turned her onto her back, and leaned over her. "'Tis I who should beg forgiveness." His husky voice warmed the space between them. "I did not stay the course."

She moved her gaze from his patched eye to the one that reflected light. "What course?"

"To go slowly. And I did, for as long as I could, but you are much too desirable. Had I waited—"

"I did not wish you to wait any longer." She laid a hand to his stubbled jaw. "You promised it would be different from..."

Memories, unlike those made this night, slipped through, seeking to splatter their darkness upon this moment.

"Elianor?"

She returned Bayard's face to focus, slid her thumb across his lips in the hope he found her touch as pleasing as she found his. "It *was* different, but not only in that it did not pain me. I speak true when I say I was moved. Indeed, were I never to feel more than that with which you gifted me, I would ever be content to share this bed with you."

Against her palm, she felt the release of his breath, next the kiss he pressed there. "Contentment may be the destination," he said, "but it is the journey that determines how content one truly is. In future, I shall exercise more patience so your journey may be as sweet as mine and your contentment greater."

She believed him, just as she believed he was as distant from Murdoch as happiness was from sorrow. "I am certain I will like it even better the next time," she said. And, perhaps, once she learned how to touch him as he had touched her, his enjoyment would also be greater.

His mouth settled on hers, and as she returned his kiss and felt the quickening of her heart, she wondered if he meant to journey with her again this night. But then he said on a sigh, "Patience," and lay down beside her.

If not that her injured arm could not bear her weight, she would have turned into his arms and pressed her face to his chest. Instead, she gave him her back in the expectation he would once more draw her against his body.

He did, and settled his hand atop hers where she set it on her thigh to support her injured arm.

Thinking that never had the prospect of sleep seemed as attractive is it did with Bayard so near, she closed her eyes.

"You do know that this night you yielded to me, Elianor?"

It seemed an odd thing to say in the moment, and yet not, she realized as a memory freed itself from her languor. "So I did," she said warily.

"And did you not say you would yield only to a man you loved?"

She had. But had she been wrong? Or very right? Though she had told Magnus she could not yet name what she felt for her second husband, perhaps she could. It was certainly what Bayard asked of her. But what of his response that night?

"I said it, just as you said that if ever I claimed to have such feelings for you, you would reduce them to ashes."

He groaned, a sound so boyishly abashed it began to loosen the worry in her chest. "In my defense," he said, "your actions pushed me to anger of a depth to which I had not descended in a long time."

Relieved to move away from the weighty question of love, she said, "And in my defense—if I may beg it—I was made to believe The Boursier was a beast."

When he responded, the boy was no longer in his voice. "What do you believe now?"

The cautious side of her told her to wait, but the other side that had urged her to join her prayers with his in the chapel, sent forth words. "You are not a beast. Never were you."

The muscles of his chest bunched against her shoulder blades. "You said you had not spoken with your aunt."

This time it was she who pulled away, turning onto her back to peer into his face. "I have not."

"Then?"

Glad for the firelight that allowed her to gauge his reaction, she said, "By way of your behavior and deeds—and lack thereof against one who terribly wronged you—'tis I who have determined the truth of you. Thus, I give you what I earlier would not. My trust."

He searched her face, and when he spoke, it was with uncertainty at odds with the man known as The Boursier. "Even ere you know my side of the tale?"

"Even ere. I yield to my heart that it might bend me into a more pleasing shape."

His eyebrows rose. "Your heart?"

Strange that it was easy to speak of it, but with Bayard, less and less she feared expressing herself. "'Tis so," she dared. "Does that please you?"

He slid a hand up her neck, cupped her jaw. "It does. But you do know such talk returns us to the question of whether or not you would yield only to a man you love."

Of course it did. But though it was Murdoch who had made the language of her heart foreign to her by rendering it mute, even with Bayard it was difficult to move from speaking of those things that moved the heart to speaking of that which moved it most deeply.

Trust, she reminded herself, but still she hesitated—and came upon an easier means of answering. "'Tis you who made it a question, Bayard, not I."

He was silent a long moment, then surprised her with a laugh that seemed equal parts elation and relief. "So I did."

And, as ever, she had given him cause. "It seems hardly possible," she said, "and *entirely* impossible that it be so soon, but you have done something to me I only thought could be done before I became the property of a man eager to dissuade me of the notion there could be great feeling between husband and wife."

The slight curve to Bayard's mouth spread warmth to the places in her that not even the most vigorous fire had reached. "You have done the same to me, Elianor."

She stared, certain she misunderstood, for this was at greater odds with The Boursier. But then, how many more times must he prove that was not who he was—at least, not with her?

"You do not believe me?" he said.

She pulled her lower lip between her teeth. "I wish to, but mayhap you are merely content after..."

He lowered his head, kissed her. "I knew it ere I made love to you."

She caught her breath. "Truly?"

"I am also amazed, Elianor."

Though neither had used the word *love,* it was there. The new, hopeful Elianor—she of four notes—was certain of it.

Bayard sighed. "But now, with day soon upon us, we ought to seek whatever rest can be had."

"I am tired," she said, "but I am almost afraid to sleep lest when I awaken, you are not here with me—that I find this was but a dream."

He considered her, then put a leg over her and lowered to the mattress on her opposite side. Mindful of her injury, he drew her into his arms, pressed her head beneath his chin, and said, "As I am here with you now, so will I be come morn. I give you my word."

She melted into him. "How did you know this is where I wish to be—tucked against you, your heart beneath my ear?"

"Because it is where I wish to be with you." A chuckle rumbled from him. "For two people given to great grievance against the one who ordered them to wed, we are most compatible, my lady wife."

She closed her eyes, murmured, "Mayhap we ought to thank King Edward."

"Mayhap, though I am more inclined to thank God for bringing light into our darkness."

"Then I shall as well."

He kissed the top of her head. "Sleep, Elianor. I will be here when you awaken."

31

No Bayard. His promise forgotten. Or, perhaps, never made.

Preferring the former that would prove last eve was no mere conjuring of the mind, El tried to console herself that if it had been a dream, at least it was not so far removed in time that she found herself in Murdoch's bed. There was hope in that it was Bayard's bed, that *he* was her husband. And one day, she might awaken to his kiss—

She gasped. He had been here before dawn had taken him from her. Kissing her eyes, nose, and mouth, he had softly called her name. And when she had spoken his, he had said, "See, I am here, Elianor."

She had pressed nearer, thinking he wished to know her again.

"Regrettably," he had whispered, "my squire is within, and I have duties to which I must attend."

She had opened her eyes just enough to know it was wasted effort, the solar too dark to make out his features.

"Return to your rest," he had said and moved away.

As she had hugged to her the kept promise that she would not awaken alone, she had heard his lowered voice and that of his squire's, the rustle of clothing and creak of leather boots, the thump of logs and crackle of a fire. And just before his departure returned her to sleep, his breath had swept her face and he had said, "Rollo will be outside your door."

El eased her splinted arm from her side and laid her palm to the mattress where Bayard had embraced her throughout the night. His impression and warmth were gone, but she felt his presence. More, she felt gratitude of such height and breadth it strained her chest.

Is this You, God? she put to the heavens. *Your doing? Or is it but the turning of one season into another—this one landing right side up?*

Though more often inclined to believe that last—a mere upending of the dice—what had been spoken upon the chapel's floor made her recoil from this being mere happenstance.

He instead set to preserving you through the waiting, Bayard had said. *And do not doubt you were preserved, Elianor, for are you not here with me?*

"I am," she breathed and tucked her chin beneath the coverlet's edge. "Dear Lord, I thank You that this is not a dream, that as night gives unto day, dark gives unto light." She slid her hand to her lower abdomen, pressed her palm to that barren place. "It seems wrong to ask for more, but I beseech You to further bless our union. Pray, open my womb."

It was a pittance of a prayer, but it was a start atop that made on the night past, and as she had learned with Murdoch, the Lord was unmoved by an effort to more greatly number one's words.

El turned back the covers and lowered her feet to the floor. Grateful Bayard had seen to it that it was warm air upon her skin, she stood.

The robe she had parted for Bayard hours past, and which he had gently removed, was neatly folded upon the foot of the bed.

Such consideration he showed the woman he had rejected in favor of Thomasin de Arell, the same who had tried to steal all from him. Thus, she was not to doubt he felt for her as told. But though the knowledge thrilled her, it was frightening, for it placed her so near happiness that even if she never laid hands to it, she feared she might lose a vital piece of herself were it removed from her sight.

"Lord, be with Bayard and me," she whispered and smiled at the realization she was at prayer without consciously seeking it.

Her injured arm making her long for the loan of Lady Maeve's maid, she donned the robe and began to sort herself. A half hour later, dressed in her tired, loosely-laced gown, her hair's ills hidden beneath a veil, she determined she would ask Magnus to send her maid to her once he returned to Castle Kelling—whenever that might be, for when she had peered past the shutters, she had seen more snow had fallen throughout the night.

Opening the door, she found Rollo on the other side.

He smiled. "God morn to ye, milady."

"God morn to you, Rollo. I suppose you are to accompany me to the hall?"

"Wherever ye wish to go, milady, though I am to tell you that 'un"—he jerked his head to indicate a chamber down the hall—"sent word she would speak with ye."

El lowered her smile. Though fairly certain he would not refer to Lady Maeve so derogatorily, she said, "Lady Constance?"

"Aye, that 'un who worked ill upon my lord and his sister."

Recalling that Bayard had said Lady Quintin had also been injured the day he had found Constance with Serle de Arell, she wondered if her aunt was directly responsible for that injury—had dealt it herself. El almost asked, but seeing something like regret tighten the man's face, she guessed he had not meant to reveal that.

He wrinkled his nose. "Will ye go to her, milady?"

Though it was what El had sought on the day past, she no longer needed to hear Constance's account of that terrible event. But since Magnus had secured an audience with her as asked of him, she could not now turn aside. Nor could she, in good conscience, delay the meeting. Having arisen hours after the morning meal was served, her presence in the hall was not required.

"I shall go to her."

Mouth pressing tight, Rollo turned and led the way to Constance's chamber.

The man-at-arms outside it was different from the one who had watched over it on the night past, but he was just as familiar.

El halted alongside Rollo. "Horace, would you tell my aunt I have come?"

He shifted his gaze from Rollo to her. "She waits on you, my lady," he said and opened the door onto a chamber illuminated more by a brazier heaped with glowing coals than the snow-bright light squeezing through the shutters' seams.

There on her knees beside the bed was Constance, her face in profile where she raised it heavenward.

El took a step back, whispered, "She is at prayer."

"Enter!" Constance called in a voice more likely to sound from a crone, then looked around.

At twenty and seven to El's twenty and one years, Constance had aged as all must, her face lightly lined and grooved. Still, her beauty was mostly intact, and if not that years of longing and sorrow had caused her sparkling eyes and radiant smile to fall into disuse, El thought she might be nearly unchanged.

"Come," Constance beckoned.

El stepped forward.

"Not you," Horace snarled.

El looked over her shoulder into Rollo's face that reflected none of the lightness with which he had greeted her this morn. So narrow-eyed and hard was the countenance he thrust at Horace that she caught her breath.

"Where milady go, I go. Or she go not at all."

Movement drew El's gaze to the fingers Horace wrapped around his sword hilt. Rollo's hand returned the warning.

"You can await me out here, Rollo," El said. "I am safe."

"Not with that 'un." He jutted his chin at the woman beyond El. "That 'un will cut ye."

"There is no cause to speak ill of my aunt, Rollo."

"He may also enter," Constance called.

"But my lady," Horace protested, "your brother—"

"—did not set you outside my door to shield me from my niece, nor my old friend, Ro—" Constance's voice broke, and she cleared her throat. "Let them in and await my summons."

The man hesitated, and El knew he warred over worry of what his lord would have him do. But then he said, "I can allow it only if the door remains wide, my lady."

Constance's eyes flashed, but she jerked her chin and Horace stepped back to allow Rollo to follow his charge.

As El approached her aunt, aware of Rollo's presence over her shoulder and Horace's battle-ready stance in the doorway, Constance stood and clasped her hands at her waist. Though during El's visits to the abbey, her aunt's gaze most often sought the floor, it was direct and searching.

What was this woman, known to Bayard before he knew El, looking for? El pondered. The same heartbreak Constance had felt while wed to The Boursier? If so, she would not find it upon her niece's face.

Though El knew she ought to embrace her aunt, despite such displays of affection having been stiffly received during their silent visits at the abbey, the air about Constance was more strained than usual. Thus, El halted several feet distant.

Her aunt continued to search her, but just when El feared her inner turmoil might make itself seen, Constance said, "As Magnus insists that I speak with you, I have asked the Lord to release me from my vow of silence." That last word was so hoarse it was almost unrecognizable.

She coughed, patted the base of her throat. "Forgive me. These past years, my voice has been used only for whisperings when I could not otherwise make my needs known." A slight smile turned her mouth. "And, I am told, sometimes I mutter while at sleep."

El inclined her head. "I am grateful you have granted me an audience, Aunt." She winced. As a little girl, on the occasions of her visits to Emberly, it had not seemed strange to title the older girl *aunt*, but as the years had moved El toward womanhood, lessening the six-year gap in maturity, it had begun to feel peculiar. And more so now that they were both women.

"Your arm?" Constance looked to where El clasped it across her abdomen.

"Mostly discomfort. Either I tolerate pain well"—and she supposed she must, having been wed to Murdoch Farrow—"or the break was not so bad."

"I am glad." Constance moved toward the chairs before the brazier. "Let us sit, and I will make known to you the man you now call husband."

El did not follow. "I thank you, but 'tis no longer necessary."

Her aunt came back around. "Something has changed between you?"

El knew she need not be ashamed, but that did not keep heat from rising to her face.

"Ah, the patience of Bayard," Constance murmured. "I am not surprised, for 'tis who he is—that is, when he is not moved to jealousy and anger."

El tensed, felt an answering tension from Rollo.

"On the night past, hmm?" Constance nodded. "*Our* Bayard can be all consideration."

El's stomach lurched, then came the bile of jealousy—an emotion with which she heretofore had little experience. But had Constance intentionally laid claim to the man she had never wanted? In their younger years, she had been likable enough despite an imperious air, and the worst El's mother had spoken against her much younger sister was that she was overly indulged. However, with the passing of years, El had come to realize that the strain emanating from Odile in Constance's presence went beyond disapproval—perhaps as far as dislike.

"Do you not think him considerate?" Constance pressed.

In that moment, also privy to dislike, El determined she would not be subordinate where Bayard was concerned. She put her chin up. "I wished to speak with you, Constance," she eschewed the title of kinship, "that I might learn the truth of what you suffered at *my* husband's hands. But that truth is now known to me—and would have been sooner had I not feared it, for far better than you, I am acquainted with the cut and color of abuse. And that is not a garment Bayard wears."

The woman's lids fluttered. "On such short acquaintance, you believe what he tells of that day?"

El squared her shoulders. "He has yet to give an account, and if he never does, still I will not believe he beat you as Agatha told and you allowed Magnus and others to believe."

Constance caught her breath, then asked with what seemed mock wonder. "Do you think yourself in love?"

El kept her chin up, held her gaze.

"Ah, dearest niece, you should not be quick to gift something so precious, especially to one who has yet to prove himself worthy and capable of returning your feelings. Trust me in this, for there is no greater pain than that born of a heart longing for what it is denied."

El startled when Rollo's hand touched her shoulder. "Do not listen, milady. That 'un be bitter."

His protective gesture causing her throat to constrict, El said tightly, "As told, I am no longer in need of an audience, nor will I be dissuaded from what I know to be true." She turned and started toward Horace in the doorway.

"Elianor!"

El paused, peered over her shoulder.

Emotions—uncertainty, frustration, fear—etched Constance's countenance, but when she sighed, her face returned to its beautiful planes.

"You stand in the presence of a woman whose years pass with excruciating leisure, leaving her in no doubt God does not look kindly upon her." She blinked against tears. "No matter how often she falls to her knees, no matter how long she clasps her hands, no matter how hard she beats her fists against her brow, He is silent."

El longed to ignore the tug upon her heart, but she was too intimate with the silence of the Lord to not feel for her aunt. She turned back.

"Thus," Constance continued, "this woman is so desperate she would use her niece to gain what has long been refused her."

The admission set El back on her heels. "Use me? For revenge?"

"Forgiveness." Constance gave a brief, sorrowful smile. "Bayard will not pardon me. Is that not right, Rollo?"

El glanced at him, but a scowl was his only answer.

Constance gestured to the chairs angled close to one another. "Pray, sit."

El's curiosity was up, but no more than wariness. She did—and did not—wish to be here.

"Methinks we ought to go, milady," Rollo rasped.

Constance took a step forward. "I beseech you, Elianor, stay."

El let her feet carry her forward, and though Rollo's grumblings followed her, he did not. As she and her aunt settled in the chairs, the big man positioned himself to the right of the door.

A glance at Horace confirming Magnus's man was more at ease with his rival distant from the one under his protection, El returned her attention to her aunt.

Constance stared at the glowing coals, hands restless in her lap as she squeezed one, then the other. At last, she met El's gaze. "You are right about Bayard. Never did he abuse me—no matter how I angered him."

The only relief El felt was in hearing the truth affirmed. "Why allow that ill to be believed of him? Do you hate him that much?"

"Hate him?" Her laughter was clipped. "Certes, I wanted to hate him for stealing me from the man I love. But that is no easy thing, as you have learned. Indeed, had I not given my heart to Serle, I could have loved Bayard." She sighed. "And it would have been me in his bed last eve."

Jealousy once more jabbed El, loosing words she should not speak. "Instead, you cuckolded him."

Constance's startle seemingly genuine—as if she only then realized to whom she spoke intimately of the man who no longer belonged to her—El silently vowed she would conquer her jealousy.

"Forgive me," Constance said, "such words I should not speak. But neither should you judge me. Though you may know the stirrings of love, you cannot comprehend what it is to feel so deeply for another that all of you brims over, making their absence a physical pain that claws at your emptiness—one you would do *anything* to relieve."

It was true. El did not love Bayard to that extent, but she did not envy her aunt. Though she believed her capacity for love would grow, she would not have it be so boundless it caused her to break marriage vows and men to lose eyes and arms.

Constance sat forward and gripped El's hand. "Heed my advice. Be not quick to gift your love. Better yet, do not gift it at all. Once you cast it before you, once it is returned and allowed to blossom, your life is no longer your own."

"Is that not as it is ordained," El said, "that two become one?"

Once again, her aunt startled as if returned from an unseen place. "In that you are right, for you have the luxury of marriage to one for whom you feel. As did I—until Bayard." She curled her nails into El's palm. "Did he not covet and take what belonged to another? Did I not warn him I would never feel for him what I felt for Serle?" She nodded. "Bayard is as much—if not more—at fault for my faithlessness. Indeed, one might say he asked to be made a cuckold."

A growl reminded El they were not alone, and she glanced at Rollo from whom the disgruntled sound issued, then Horace.

Acknowledging there was some truth in what Constance said, El felt almost sick with sorrow for the lives ruined by the hurts Bayard and her aunt had inflicted upon each other.

Constance released El and sat back in her chair. "If I could change what happened that day, I would."

"You would be faithful to Bayard?"

She shook her head. "Too late for that."

"I do not understand."

"That day was not the first that I was intimate with Serle. It was the last, and ruined by the wrath and blood in which it was steeped. Woe that I did not do as Agatha instructed."

This time El was moved by surprise, as much for the revelation Constance had previously cuckolded Bayard as tidings that her maid had contributed to those terrible events. "What had Agatha to do with that day? Did not Bayard oust her two months earlier?"

"He did, but she loved me too much to abandon me."

Had Agatha not twice struck El, the last time with murderous intent, still El would not have believed the maid's devotion had anything to do with love. It was something self-serving, even if only to feed a twist in the woman's soul.

"You are saying she stayed?" El asked. "Hid herself within Adderstone's walls?"

"Nay, that would have been dangerous. Instead, she continued to use the underground—"

"Continued to?"

"Aye, though only as a means of carrying Serle's messages to me and mine to him."

"And before that?" El pressed.

"Ere Bayard tossed her out, she arranged for Serle and me to meet there every other month," she said, then hastened to add, "only that we might be near each other—to talk."

Again, El's stomach protested. Not only had Agatha stolen powders into Bayard's drink to prevent him from being intimate with his wife, but she had aided in replacing that lost intimacy with intimacy outside of marriage—even if only by way of brief meetings and words on parchment that kept Constance and Serle's yearn for each other alive.

"You said Agatha gave you instructions that day, meaning 'twas she who arranged it."

Constance nodded. "Has ever a servant been more devoted to her mistress?"

Who, exactly, was Agatha? And why was she so eager to tug and jerk and sever the strings of others' lives? Unfortunately, as enamored as Constance was with the woman's friendship, it was not a question she was capable of answering.

"When Serle came for you that day," El said, "what were Agatha's instructions?"

"I was to flee with him as soon as Bayard departed for London, and I meant to. But there my beloved was in my bedchamber, and there my husband was not. Though we did not intend it to happen, we had not been intimate since before I wed, and so..." Constance momentarily closed her eyes. "Bayard, who was to have been gone a fortnight, returned and found another man in our bed."

Though reason had told El it would be a terrible blow for a man to learn he had been cuckolded—worse, to witness it—only now that she was wed to Bayard was she able to sympathize. The mere thought of happening upon him with another woman pierced her. And she was glad of it, for she had been grateful to the women servants who had tempted Murdoch to stray. The reprieves had been short-lived, but priceless.

"Tell me, how did Agatha learn of the underground passage?" El said. "And who provided her with keys?"

Constance shrugged. "I know only that she did not gain the knowledge, nor the means, from me. Nor did I care how she came by it." She narrowed her lids. "If you are also asking if I freed her from Bayard's prison, I did not, though had it been possible, I would have."

El stiffened. "Surely you know she pushed me down the steps, that it was a broken neck she wished upon me?"

With an air of patience, Constance said, "In all my years with her, never did she show herself capable of such ill. Nay, Elianor, methinks you have interpreted what was an accident as being of foul intent, influenced as you are by Bayard's hatred of one who put my needs ahead of others'."

El sat forward. "There is naught to interpret, Constance. Agatha struck me down, and ere I lost consciousness, I heard her tell whoever was with her that a broken neck was a good end to a Verdun."

Uncertainty crept up Constance's features, but she shook her head. "I am not saying you lie, only that you are mistaken. 'Tis true Agatha is a difficult woman, but I know her best, and I know her to be good."

Never before had El so longed to shake sense into someone. "It was not the first time she struck me unconscious."

Constance expelled an air of disgust. "Cease, Elianor!"

"Does a good woman pave the path toward infidelity? Does she drug a husband to keep him from his wife's bed?"

Constance thrust forward in her chair, jutted an anger-dimpled chin. "You would condemn her for that? You who benefitted from the absence of your first husband's attentions when he was at his worst?"

El blinked. During her one-sided conversations with Constance, she had tried to offer comfort by letting her aunt know she was not alone in suffering a husband's cruelty, but no details had El given of her own abuse, nor had she told of the relief provided by the powders slipped into Murdoch's drink.

"Agatha visits you at the abbey," El said.

As if suddenly fatigued, Constance sank back in her chair. "Only thrice has she come to me, but she told of the aid she gave you when Magnus sent her to you. Thus, dare not look ill upon her for keeping Bayard from my bed unless you look ill upon yourself for accepting her aid in keeping Murdoch from yours."

Once more, El longed to shake her. "Perhaps I should not have taken the relief she offered, but my circumstances were different from yours. I *was* abused, and never did I—nor would I have—asked for her aid in cuckolding my husband."

Constance flicked a hand as if to sweep aside the words, confirming she was not open to reason where Agatha was concerned.

Grudgingly determined to leave the matter be, El asked what had yet to be answered. "Earlier, you said you would have used me had I allowed it. How?"

Her aunt eyed her, and El wondered if a lie—or delusion—might next spring from her. "When I convinced Magnus to bring me into Adderstone, it was so I might speak with Bayard as he has denied me all these years."

Surprised, though she probably should not be, that Constance wished an audience with him, El said, "For what would you speak with him?"

"As told, I wish his forgiveness. But though I thought he would seek me out—he did so love me once—he has not come. But after he found you in the inner walls, and I saw the way he was with you, and yesterday, when I saw how you were with him while you wept..." Constance trailed off.

El had glimpsed her aunt in the doorway the night Bayard had delivered her out of the inner walls, but had been unaware of her presence when she had poured out her grief over her first husband while her second husband held her.

"There seemed another way to reach Bayard," her aunt continued, "that through you, I might gain forgiveness."

"Me?"

"Aye, before I knew you were so enamored of him that you would reject what you have held to be true about my marriage to The Boursier."

Though suspicion crept over El, all the more sure-footed for her having earlier considered her aunt had willfully allowed Bayard to be falsely accused, she was not ready to set her imaginings adrift on that current.

Once more leaning toward her, Constance said, "I thought to bargain with him—to ease whatever misgivings you have about his character by revealing the true cause of the injuries I sustained that day."

There it was. Though El had not allowed herself to be fletched and fit to the bow aimed at Bayard, it made her feel dirty. "All these years," she whispered, "you held hostage the truth behind your vow of silence."

Constance snatched her niece's wrist and pulled her from the chair and onto her knees before her. "If you had one narrow hope of happiness," she hissed, her sour breath a poor fit for her loveliness, "only one chance to fix what impatience and carelessness had broken, would you yield it up to the man whose covetousness began it all?"

The hypocrite in El longed to proclaim she would not compromise her morals, but it slunk away with the reminder she had done just that in attempting to see Bayard divested of Godsmere. And her resentment over being carelessly handled also stole away when her aunt's anger turned to grief, as evidenced by a flood of tears.

El sighed. "As you say, I have never loved as you have, Aunt Constance," she once more acknowledged their kinship, "so I cannot know the lengths to which I would go to preserve such a love. I only hope I would do what is right and good, even at the loss of my heart."

Shoulders easing, Constance released El. "I know what I sought to do is not in God's will, but what is one more wrong in a world brimming with wrongs?"

As El did not believe she wished an answer, she held her tongue, but her aunt pressed, "Tell me. What is one more wrong?"

El gently squeezed the woman's arm. "To one person, it can be everything, just as Bayard's one wrong in taking you to wife was everything to you."

Constance's gaze shuddered, and she groaned, "So many wrongs, Elianor. That day, I called him *Serle* while we—" She shook her head. "I felt so terrible that I could not stop crying, and he was so angry he departed Adderstone hours earlier than planned." Her breath caught. "And returned far earlier than expected. Do you know what he said— rather, *shouted*—when he found us abed?"

Refusing to allow her mind to tug toward imaginings of anyone other than Bayard and herself there, El held her aunt's gaze.

"That he had resolved to find a means of releasing me from our miserable marriage, and for that he had turned back—to tell me. It may have been a lie, it may have been the truth." She squeezed her eyes closed. "But it no longer mattered."

Silence descended, and as El waited for it to lift, she glanced across her shoulder at Rollo. He listened, as did Horace where he stood just outside the door, but as if aware they witnessed something intensely private, both men studied the lay of the floor.

El returned her attention to Constance, but it was some minutes before her aunt raised her moist lashes. "Ere the shedding of blood, all was forfeit. So you see, Elianor, I had naught to lose by returning to Adderstone." She raised her eyebrows. "And everything to gain."

Those last words were not benign, as told by her aunt's tone.

El understood. "Tell me," she said, "had Bayard accepted your offer to reveal to me he was never abusive, what besides forgiveness would you have asked of him in return?"

A smile moved Constance's lips. "Love."

El drew back.

Her aunt gave a sharp laugh. "Not Bayard's love. Serle's love, for therein lies true forgiveness—your husband granting me the happiness he, himself, stands to enjoy if all is well between you and him."

"But how—?"

"At last, she speaks," growled the one of whom they spoke.

32

FOR THIS, BAYARD had not come abovestairs after hours in the saddle that had seen him and his men traversing new-fallen snow as they rode village to village.

It was for Elianor he had mounted the stairs. Imagining her yet abed, thinking to shed his damp garments and curve his body around hers in place of the great hall's warming fire, he had faltered at the sight of her uncle traversing the corridor ahead of him toward the man-at-arms who beckoned from outside Constance's chamber.

A sense of something ill had made Bayard eschew the solar, and as he overtook Verdun, he had caught the sound of Elianor's voice and recognized another voice despite its scratch and rasp.

From the doorway, he had seen Elianor at that woman's feet. Elianor's comforting hand upon Constance's arm. Elianor who had proclaimed she alone had determined the truth about her new husband. And yet, in his absence, she sought confirmation of that truth despite her claim he was so fully in possession of her trust she need not hear his side of the tale.

He shifted his gaze from the wide eyes she had turned upon him, to Constance who sat with her back to him on the edge of her chair—utterly still, as if she were prey, fearful the slightest movement might cause him to pounce.

Trying to calm his roiling—to control himself as Father Crispin would have him do—Bayard drew a long breath, then turned to her brother whose brow was weighted with questions his silent sister had allowed his imagination to answer all these years. "It seems you guessed wrong, Verdun," he said and entered the chamber.

"Milord," Rollo said, having come to attention the moment his liege appeared in the doorway.

Bayard glanced at him. "You may leave us."

The big man leaned near, in a loud whisper, said, "Would that I had not delivered the message, milord," and turned away.

Though tempted to demand Rollo give substance to his words, Bayard pushed his mantle back off his shoulders and continued forward. Behind, he heard Verdun dismiss his own man-at-arms, then the crush of rushes beneath the man's booted feet.

Halting near the chairs that faced the brazier, Bayard answered the pull of Elianor's gaze. "In answer to your question, Wife," he said, "allow me to share with you and your uncle the terms of forgiveness repeatedly offered by the woman I first took to wife."

He jutted his chin at Constance. "Every year, she sends a missive in which she promises to forgive me and restore my good name by revealing the truth of all she suffered at my hands."

Elianor's eyes widened further, the wariness in those green depths turning stricken.

"And what selfless thing does she ask in return?" He recalled the tersely written parchments Father Crispin had finally convinced him to put to the flame. "Forgiveness. But not godly forgiveness. Nay, forgiveness that requires I seek to lift the penances the Church levied on her and her lover, thus allowing them to once more *love*."

Constance thrust to her feet and swung around to face Bayard. "What?" she snarled, eyes moist, teeth bared. "Only I am to forever pay the price of the wrongs we inflicted on each other?" Her voice broke, and she clapped a hand to her throat, then jabbed a finger toward Elianor. "While you happily bed my niece and get her with children, I am to pass lonely night after lonely day, knowing no ease, no hope, nothing at all?"

Bayard stared at her. Though her features had matured, she still appeared very much the woman he had wed five years past. She was not. And, unexpectedly, he felt something like regret at the changes wrought in this beautiful, caged bird—but only for that moment before she stepped toward him between the chairs and spat, "Four years of my suffering is not enough to satisfy The Boursier? What is it you want? *More* blood for blood?"

She should not have said that last, for it thrust Quintin to mind, the innocent in all this, causing words of accusation and anger and all things foul to hurtle toward his tongue. But as was Father Crispin's habit, even when not present, he spoke to Bayard.

Act as God would have you act. Be as God would have you be. Forgive as—

In once more rejecting that last, so heightened was Bayard's resentment that he might have rejected all if not that Elianor rose behind her aunt and leveled beseeching eyes upon him.

If naught else, for her, he told himself. *And, perhaps, she will truly come to trust you.* And if he and Constance found some kind of peace, then all the more blessed it would be.

Ache in his hands alerting him to the fists he had made of them, he opened his fingers and determined he would act and be as God wished. Hopefully, forgiveness of Constance—godly forgiveness—would one day follow.

He returned his gaze to her. "You are right."

She stared, then blinked rapidly as if to assure herself she was still of this world.

"We must both bring that day to a close." He shifted his aching jaw. "But I make no promises, other than that I shall try."

She dragged her teeth across her lower lip. "And Serle?"

"No promises," he repeated and reached to Elianor. "If you are done here?"

She stepped around her aunt and slid her hand into his.

As he turned her toward the door, he was struck by how Elianor and he must appear and surprised by a pang of sympathy for Constance's plight that he would not have expected in light of the price Quintin had paid and might pay the remainder of her life. But there it was, accompanied by guilt that he might look forward to each day and night that lay ahead.

As they neared Verdun, Bayard saw his long-time adversary's gaze was fixed on Constance, though it did not seem anger with which he regarded her. Disbelief? Disappointment? Regardless, there were things that must be spoken between brother and sister.

And husband and wife, Bayard allowed, glancing at Elianor as they exited the chamber. From what he had heard of her conversation with Constance, she was perceptive in guessing there was more to what was required of Bayard beyond words of forgiveness, but she had not truly believed him innocent of abuse as claimed on the night past.

They traversed the corridor in silence, and when he led her into the solar and closed the door, she turned to him and said, "You are displeased with me."

Though he knew it made one vulnerable to be so easily read, a part of him was gladdened that she sensed his emotions. "I should not be, for 'twas foolish to believe you trusted me enough that you would not pursue an audience with your aunt."

Hurt flashed in her eyes. "You think I sought to verify your innocence."

"Did you not?"

Now anger, and when she spoke, her voice was sharp, though its edges did not cut as deeply as when first they had met under circumstances so dire there had seemed no hope for them. "The only thing of which I may be accused is heeding the summons Constance delivered by way of Rollo."

Bayard frowned a moment ahead of understanding. *That* was the message the man-at-arms regretted delivering.

"Having previously asked to speak with her," Elianor said, "I could not then ignore her. But I would have you know I went to her only that I might tell her I no longer required an audience—that I well enough knew the man I had wed."

Did she speak true? Or only what she knew he wished to hear? Bayard delved her gaze that was without waver, but not righteous rancor.

"And that, *Husband,* is what I did. Had my aunt not admitted she had hoped to use me against you, I would have departed. Thus, you happened upon us conversing of things past and present and thought first to believe the worst of me."

Bayard silently berated himself. And more chastisement was due, since what she told made more sense than that Constance had willingly confirmed his innocence. Whatever words had passed between the two before he had come unto the chamber, honesty had been forced upon his first wife by Elianor's refusal to believe that with which Constance had hoped to bargain.

Bayard sighed. "So I did."

He heard the catch of her breath and guessed she had not expected him to so easily concede to her innocence. "Then you also..." Now her gaze wavered. "You also see 'tis *you* who are not ready to trust?"

He settled his hands to her taut shoulders and drew her toward him. "I do, and I am sorry for it." He lowered his forehead to hers. "Pray, forgive me. If not now, later."

As she stared up at him from beneath the edge of her veil, the green of her eyes began to yield to the dark of her pupils. "'Tis done," she said. "And, I suppose, it will be done time and again on both sides, since we have not much experience with trust. But we shall learn it, aye?"

Bayard's heart expanded in his chest, and once more he was stirred with pity for Constance. Pushing aside thoughts of her, focusing on the one before him now, he said, "So we shall."

She laid a hand to his jaw. "I thank you for awakening me this morn."

Not how he had wished to awaken her, but during their lovemaking, she had been all startles and quakes and tremblings, and often he had sensed her responses were as much born of fear as pleasure. Thus, it was too soon to pursue further intimacy.

He lowered his gaze to her mouth, decided a kiss would not be amiss, and pressed his lips to hers.

Whether oblivious to the damp and dirt of him, or that she did not mind, Elianor sank against him, and when she rose to her toes to deepen the kiss, he pulled her nearer.

"My arm!" she gasped.

He drew back, grimaced. "Forgive me. To hold you is so sweet, I forget what Agatha has wrought." And for which she would pay in full. Indeed, rooting her out was uppermost in his mind such that he and his men had lingered at each village long enough to learn if the witch had been sighted. Fortunately, so memorable a figure was she that those who had never laid eyes upon her would know her from the description. Unfortunately, none had claimed to cross paths with her.

"Bayard," Elianor said with urgency. "There are things my aunt told of Agatha that you must needs know."

He inclined his head. "Let us speak of them while I change my clothes, for if you have not noticed, I am near wet to the bone and most foul."

"You were moving snow again?"

"Nay, that was left to others while my men and I visited the villages."

She tilted her head questioningly.

Unfastening the brooch that held his mantle closed, he strode past her toward the hearth and said over his shoulder, "Even if we suffer no more snow, what has fallen will likely prevent those from the outlying villages from journeying to Adderstone for the Christmas celebration five days hence." He draped the mantle over the warming frame, bent, and removed his splattered boots. "Hence, now that their needs are known to me, I shall send supplies and foodstuffs and gifts so they will yet be blessed on that joyous day."

When he straightened, Elianor stood before him, something like wonder on her face. "'Tis hard to believe it was not so long ago I first looked near upon you in the market."

He hearkened back to it. "I remember the day. And the woman who gave her wrathful gaze to me from beneath a shawl too heavy for such uncommonly warm weather."

Her mouth curved. "I thought a merciless heart beat in your breast, was certain you were kin to the night—a beast."

"A one-eyed beast." He said it lightly, yet still it grated.

Her smile drifted away. "I am sorry for that."

"Neither have my words always been kind, and for that I apologize. Should we not put it behind us?"

She nodded.

He dragged his tunic off, and she took it and placed it on the warming frame. When she came back around, he handed her his chausses. Though he yet wore his long undertunic, she blushed prettily and turned away. While she arranged his chausses on the frame, he retrieved his robe from the bed and belted himself into it.

As he had known he would, he remembered all of Elianor when it had been her body warmed by the garment. But it was better not to think there. Not now.

Shifting his thoughts to that which held no appeal other than finding an end to the depravity, he returned to the hearth and settled into the chair opposite the one he gestured for Elianor to take—grudgingly, since he preferred her in his arms.

"Now, Agatha," he said.

33

———◦∞∞◦———

Constance.

El looked to where Bayard had lowered into the chair beside hers. Like others who had paused in the midst of settling down to an early supper, he had gone still. And as evidenced by the diminishing din, more were taking note of the woman who had stepped off the stairs into the great hall.

Seeing her husband's nostrils flare, El said, "Bayard?"

The gaze with which he followed Constance's progress shifted, but rather than toward El, he looked to his left where his stepmother sat. Face lowered, intent on her hands, she slowly slid the fingers of the right over the left—as yet, oblivious, but not for much longer now that the hall was silent except for whispers and murmurs.

It was the loud scrape of a bench that lifted Lady Maeve's head and carried her gaze to Magnus. As he strode the length of the lower table from which he had pushed back, she frowned, then blinked as if slowly awakening.

The moment she caught sight of the woman who advanced on the dais, she drew a sharp breath, and on the exhale hissed, "What does she here?"

Bayard remained unmoving, and El wondered what he warred over. He had said he would try to make peace with his first wife, but was this too much too soon, especially in light of his stepmother's reaction?

Dear Lord, El silently prayed, *let not words or actions further wound those present.*

Magnus came alongside his sister, put his arm through hers, and drew her to a halt two strides from the dais. Though his face was as grimly set as Bayard's, he said as if nothing untoward had occurred, "Baron Boursier, my sister and I thank you for your hospitality."

After a long moment, Bayard said, "I am glad we could accommodate you, Baron Verdun...Lady Constance."

The wife who no longer was raised her chin higher. "I am welcome in your hall, Baron Boursier?"

He inclined his head. "You are welcome to join your brother at table."

It seemed as close to a welcome as she would get. But restrained though it was, it was not well received by Lady Maeve whose pale face colored and fingers dragged their nails over the tablecloth.

Though both Magnus and Constance surely witnessed the woman's agitation, they turned and started toward their table.

Once they were seated, Father Crispin rose, beseeched God to guide all in thoughts and words and actions, then blessed the meal. Barely had he regained his seat than the servants surged forward.

With the resumption of the din of those who hungered for conversation as much as food, El leaned toward Bayard.

However, his stepmother captured his attention ahead of her.

"Bayard!" the lady protested. "God's mercy, what do you?"

He covered her restless hands with his much larger one. "God's mercy," he gave her words back to her. "That is what I do. It is time."

Bitter laughter. "Because *your* life is righting itself? What of my life? More, what of Quintin's?"

"My lady—"

She snatched her hands free. "'Tis one thing to forgive that woman for what she did to you, another to forgive her for what she caused to be done to my Quintin. *That,* you have no right to do, Bayard Boursier."

El glanced around the hall at those who carried on as if the happenings at the high table did not warrant their interest. Not even her uncle and aunt sought to satisfy their curiosity.

Ignoring the servant who appeared and reached a pitcher to his lord's goblet, Lady Maeve continued, "No right at all, especially whilst you are content to allow your sister to remain De Arell's prisoner."

Once wine was poured for all and the servant moved away, Bayard said in a tight voice, "I have told you, had I feared Quintin was in danger, I would have done whatever was required to bring her out of Castle Mathe. But not only did she assure me Griffin de Arell had done her no harm despite her attack upon him, I did not find the Baron of Blackwood to be without honor—disagreeable, aye, but I believe she is safe and suffers no discomfort in the quarters given her. Too, not only is Sir Victor with her, but lest you forget, De Arell is to be her husband."

Lady Maeve stood so suddenly her chair rocked, causing the serving girl who had placed a trencher of stew between Bayard and El to hasten from the dais as if for fear she might be the recipient of her lady's wrath.

In a voice that trembled with nearly as much violence as her body, Bayard's stepmother said, "No matter your assurances, my daughter is not safe there."

An ache in El's hands alerting her to how tightly she clasped them, she loosed her fingers and, guessing Bayard was as aware as she of the lessening din, waited to see how he would respond.

"As promised, Lady Maeve," he measured out his words, "when the weather warms sufficiently to allow a day's journey, I shall seek my sister's release that she might abide at Adderstone until she weds."

The lady showed her teeth. "If anything happens to her, never will I forgive you." She pointed at the lower table where Magnus and Constance dined. "Just as I shall never forgive that one."

Bayard stood and in a firm voice, said, "I will escort you to your chamber, my lady."

His stepmother jerked back. "I would not think to inconvenience you, Baron Boursier." She turned and marched across the dais.

Bayard remained standing. In contrast to the others who clearly struggled to keep their eyes from straying amid muted conversations, he watched her cross the hall and ascend the stairs.

"I am sorry," El said when he resumed his seat.

He drew the trencher between them, handed her a spoon, and nodded for her to choose the first morsel. "You wish to ask me about Quintin."

She scooped up a piece of venison drenched in a sauce that wafted the scent of rosemary. "You told that she was also injured the day you found my aunt with Serle de Arell."

He inclined his head. "That is but the start of the tale."

"Then I shall trust you to tell me when you think I should know."

He considered her as she slid the spoonful in her mouth. "You should know, Elianor, but our chamber is not the place for the telling."

Because that was where it had happened? Just as it was where he had lost an eye and Serle de Arell an arm?

"After supper, we will speak of it," he said and dipped into the trencher. "Certes, you will require my fur-lined mantle."

A surprise, but not an unwelcome one, for there was something appealing about once more being out of doors with him on a chill, starry night. And she knew what it was—his kiss in the wood following her attempt to escape him en route to Castle Mathe. A kiss when the man she had feared him to be would have used a fist to subdue her.

She smiled. "I will be ready, Husband."

It was not starry, but it was, indeed, chill. And blessedly still—not even a breeze to make the freezing air more deeply felt.

As El huddled in Bayard's mantle, she was warmed not only by its fur lining, but memory of his first kindness when he had sent for the garment in response to the chill she had taken while speaking vows in Thomasin's name. Now here Elianor Boursier contentedly stood with her husband upon Adderstone's outer wall, face tilted up to watch the slow-moving clouds filter moonlight.

"To tell of Quintin," Bayard finally said, his words changing the shape of the mist he breathed out, "I must begin with that day."

El turned toward him and, by the light of torches spaced along the wall, saw his expression had gone grim.

"Nay," he said, "further back so you may judge me accordingly." There was regret in his voice as if wary of that judgment.

Seeing his gloved hand curl into a fist on the iced embrasure before which they stood, El stepped nearer and laid her gloved hand atop his. "'Tis in the past, Bayard, and after the tale is told, there it will return. And stay."

He considered their hands, loosed his clenched fingers, and set his gaze upon the bordering wood with its snow-frosted evergreens and leafless, skeletal oaks. "I was the one who made that day possible, but so angered was I by Constance's betrayal and all the bloodshed and loss, it was long ere I was able to accept the greater portion of responsibility."

He returned to silence, but did not linger there. "When Serle de Arell and Constance were betrothed as children, their union was not deemed a threat to the Boursier family. However, as the conflict between all our families grew, on the few occasions the Verduns joined with another, they chose the De Arells over the Boursiers, doubtless because of the betrothal. Increasingly concerned that the permanent joining of De Arells and Verduns would be detrimental to our family, my father decided something must be done."

Archard Boursier who had led the way in betraying their liege, Baron Denis Foucault.

"Shortly after he began to ail, he offered Rand Verdun a better match for his daughter—marriage to the Boursier heir. I resisted, more for my interest in another lady whose beauty had captivated me than the wrong of it." He looked sidelong at El. "Beauty is a weakness of mine."

It was one of the reasons he had given for choosing to wed Thomasin—an attempt to combat that failing.

El smiled lightly. "Obviously, you had not yet laid eyes upon my aunt."

"Nay, but one glimpse of her changed all. Though she discouraged me by making no secret of her love for Serle, I ignored that her heart lay elsewhere, justifying my pursuit of her with the certainty I would make a better husband and she would come to feel for me as she felt for Serle. Though it took effort to convince her father that marriage into the Boursiers was more desirable than honoring his agreement to wed his daughter to De Arell's landless second son, especially as Magnus was opposed to breaking his sister's betrothal, I gained my prize."

Another long pause. "On our wedding night, I discovered Constance had given her virtue to Serle."

As Constance had earlier revealed to El.

Bayard captured El's gaze. "I was angered, but I raised no hand to her. I stayed away for days, and once I cooled, I determined I would give her time to forget Serle. For over a month, we were not intimate again, not only to ensure it was I who sired any child she bore, but that we might begin to know each other."

Our Bayard can be all consideration, Constance had said.

"When she took me to our bed again, I knew her desire was distant from mine, that she but paid the marital debt, but I thought it possible we would grow content together."

Of a sudden, he seamed his mouth, and it was then El glimpsed what he had sensed—the man-at-arms making his rounds of the wall walk. When the guard passed by with a nod at his lord and was many yards distant, Bayard continued.

"I should have heeded my sire. He warned that Agatha exerted more influence over Constance than a maid ought to and was too often in her lady's company, making it difficult for my wife to form attachments with Lady Maeve and Quintin. He told me to watch Agatha, and I did, but not closely enough, and less so when the duties of the barony fell fully upon me following his passing."

Feeling Bayard once more form a fist beneath her hand, El was not surprised when he loosed a growl. "It was almost a year ere I discovered Agatha had been drugging my wine so my wife would suffer fewer of my attentions, and I do not doubt Constance used those opportunities to meet with Serle in the underground."

As El had earlier related to him of what her aunt had revealed of Agatha's role in destroying their marriage.

"I expelled Agatha," he continued. "Calling hell down upon me, the termagant left Adderstone—or so I believed." His grunt was more weary than bitter. "Though no greater regret had I than that of wedding a woman who longed for another, I knew the Church would grant an annulment only at great cost that could empty Godsmere's coffers. Thus, I endeavored again to make the marriage right, and Constance agreed she would try. For the two months she was free of Agatha's influence, she warmed toward me, and I thought we could make something good of my error."

He looked out across the darkened land before Adderstone. "The day of my departure for London, I lingered abed and made love to my wife. Never before had she been so responsive." He released a billowing mist. "But it was not my name she put in my ear. It was his. Afterward, she fell to sobbing and begged my forgiveness. I could not give it, and so I left Adderstone earlier than planned, and it was hours ere my ire eased sufficiently to allow me to think clearly—and accept my wife would never stop yearning for another. Determined to find a way to release her from marriage, I turned back to Adderstone to tell her of my intentions and send her home to her brother to await the undoing of what should not have been done. You know what I found."

"I know," El whispered.

"My shouts hastened Father Crispin to the solar, and as he pleaded for me to sheathe my sword, Serle gained the time needed to bring his own sword to hand. We clashed, and it was soon apparent my opponent was deficient in wielding a sword and would pay the highest price for bedding another man's wife."

Bayard shifted his jaw. "I was not expecting Constance to do more than cry and plead, but she came at me with a meat dagger, so desperate to save the man she loved that she stepped into the midst of our bloodlust. I thrust her aside, so though I am responsible for the bruises and abrasions she allowed your uncle to believe were caused by my fists, it was her fall upon the hearth that marked her—and may have preserved her life."

Of course, El thought. It could be no other way.

"It was to my detriment," Bayard continued, "for I left myself open long enough for Serle's blade to seek my neck. Blessedly, my reflexes caused his blow to fall across my face, taking my eye rather than my life."

El ached for this man she had once thought unworthy of ache in any measure.

"It was that scene Quintin came upon—my raging, my blood. Just as Constance gave no thought to the danger of coming to Serle's aid, Quintin gave no thought to coming to mine. Near blind and unaware of her presence, I defended myself against Serle's next attack, and it was the sweep of my sword that cut my sister."

"Oh, Bayard," El breathed, realizing here was the reason he had been so angry when she had placed herself between his sword and Magnus's on the training field.

"Aye, 'twas I who wounded her. And as she cried out, all I could think was to avenge whatever ill had befallen her. That is when I took Serle's sword arm."

El recalled Lady Maeve's ill-spoken wish that Bayard had, indeed, abused Constance—surely so her aunt would have been sufficiently cowed that never would she have cuckolded Bayard. Hence, her daughter would not have suffered as she must have done. Fortunately, it could not have been too terrible an injury with which she was afflicted, for the woman had seemed entirely in possession of her sour-tempered self when El had been in her presence at Castle Mathe.

Not until Bayard pulled her against his side did El realize her teeth were chattering.

"There is more snow upon the air," he said.

Was there? No sooner did El question that which could further delay Magnus and Constance's departure than she felt the air quiver as if it gathered together its stores of ice.

"We should return to the keep," Bayard said.

"Not yet," she protested.

He wrapped his arms around her. Only when her teeth quieted and his warmth had soothed away her shivering, did he speak again. "I would have killed Constance's lover had Father Crispin not taken me to the floor moments ahead of the arrival of my men. And so Serle's life was preserved, and when he recovered sufficiently, the Church sent him on an extended pilgrimage to atone for his sins, while your aunt was sent to live out her life at Ellesmere Abbey." He drew back to meet her gaze. "Do you think the punishment too grave, Elianor?"

El recalled her aunt's desperation to also be given a second chance as Bayard had been given. "It seems that just as all are at fault to some degree, all have suffered long enough. I know it was wrong of Constance to try to use me to force you to act on behalf of Serle and her, but the ill is in the past, is it not? Done."

His jaw clenched. "'Tis not done. At least, we cannot be certain of it."

"I do not understand."

"That is because you have not asked after Quintin's injury."

El blinked. "Although she and I are of brief acquaintance, I assumed her injury could not be so dire that it yet afflicts her as do the injuries Serle and you sustained."

"Her injury is unseen, Elianor. According to the physician, it may afflict her all the days of her life."

El waited.

"My blade pierced her lower abdomen," Bayard finally said, "and if she is able to conceive at all, a pregnancy could prove fatal once her womb grows large with child."

"I am sorry," El said. What he told explained much, not only Lady Maeve's hatred of Constance and Quintin's chill reception of the woman's niece, but it accounted for Bayard's struggle to forgive his first wife. And, likely, he also struggled to forgive himself.

He groaned. "Do you know how many times I wished I had not turned back to Adderstone that day?"

A thousand times, El guessed.

"Thus, it was no great feat for Quintin to convince me to break her betrothal years ago, determined she would not wed. And now King Edward requires that she make a marriage."

To Magnus had El's actions not changed the course Bayard had set. "I see," she said. "Though 'tis good she is to marry De Arell, for he already has an heir, the danger is not past. If she conceives…" She shook her head. "Still, it is not certain a pregnancy could end wrong."

"Certain enough to fear for my sister's life, and so you understand Lady Maeve's distress and why she cannot bear to keep company with Constance."

"And the reason your tolerance of my aunt is intolerable to your stepmother."

"She believes I betray her and my sister."

"Then you are to allow her desire for revenge to supplant forgiveness that is good and right?"

"It is a hard place in which I find myself, Elianor. I wish an end to these tainted years, but at what cost? Lady Maeve may not have bore me, but she raised me, and well. And I care too much for my sister to not consider how my choices affect her."

El raised her hand to his cheek, felt his cold flesh through her glove. "I am here with you in that hard place, as I will be here with you no matter whether you turn right or left."

He searched her gaze. "I believe you are, though I yet marvel how it can be."

She smiled. "Methinks Father Crispin would explain away your confusion with one word—rather, name. God."

Bayard slowly nodded.

"And now is the tale all told?" El asked.

"The largest pieces. A good beginning."

El rose to her toes. "My lips are cold. Will you not warm them, Husband?"

He hesitated, and she feared she had erred in inviting an intimacy at such a time as this, but he lowered his head. And when he drew away, the heat of his kiss had moved down and down again, all the way to her toes.

This eve, he will make love to me again, she told herself. *And perhaps the pleasure will be greater than the absence of pain. Perhaps I will feel something of what he felt with me. Perhaps.*

34

CHRISTMAS EVE, AND still there was no break in the weather long enough to allow Magnus to safely journey home with his sister. And until he did, Lady Maeve made it clear with her self-imposed seclusion that she would not return belowstairs.

Though El wished the woman did not continue to be so deeply affected by what had befallen her daughter years past that she could not bear to be in Constance's presence, she understood. If the physician was correct, Lady Quintin's arms would ever be empty of children born of her and there would be no grandchildren about Lady Maeve's skirts.

El had not realized she pressed a hand to her own abdomen until pain shot up her healing arm. Turning her thoughts off the path they warily tread, she chose instead the path of gratitude.

Though she would not have Lady Maeve keep to her chamber, there was good in it. Her withdrawal from the household allowed El to more firmly establish herself as Godsmere's new lady without servants first seeking their former lady's permission. Thus, the efforts of those who had done El's bidding these past days had set the room aglow.

Standing at the end of the hall opposite the raised dais, El gazed upon those things she had called into being in preparation for the morrow's celebration of God becoming man.

At Castle Kelling, Magnus had allowed her a free hand in transforming the comparatively drab hall into a festive place, but it was more easily accomplished at Adderstone, an extravagantly constructed and furnished castle meant to reflect Baron Denis Foucault's status. Now it was a reflection of Bayard Boursier—and his new wife.

Fragrant boughs of pine fashioned into swags draped the enormous beams and shuttered windows. Arrangements of ivy, mistletoe, and holly decorated the heavily embroidered cloth that covered the high table, the immense cupboard whose shelves brimmed with silver platters, plates, and goblets, and the intricately carved sideboards that boasted pewter bowls and tankards.

More tapestries had been hung, as well as banners displaying the red and gold of the Boursiers. A fearful variety of weapons—swords, maces, daggers, a ceremonial pike whose grip boasted jewels—had been cleaned and polished and remounted upon the back wall of the arched alcove immediately visible to visitors upon entering the keep. But perhaps most beautiful were the stately iron candleholders that stood in the four corners of the hall and on either side of the high table. Fit with clusters of candles whose wicks burned bright, it was almost magical.

El gave a soft, disbelieving laugh that she was mistress of this. More, that its master felt much for her—Elianor of four notes, not three. She could not be happier.

The breath went out of her, but she drew it back in and tried to direct her thoughts to something that would tempt her toward a smile rather than the nibbling of her lower lip.

It was no use. Though it was selfish to want more, she *could* be happier. Each morn that moved the castle inhabitants nearer Christmas, Bayard awakened her with a kiss before leaving the solar. But kisses and embraces were the only intimacies they had shared since the consummation of their marriage four nights past. And with the passing of days, El worried all the more for his lack of interest in collecting on the marital debt.

She hoped it was not anything she had done, such as blurting that his lovemaking had not hurt—or anything she had *not* done, such as being unable to feel what he felt. But though she told herself it was surely a result of Bayard's concern over his stepmother's refusal to leave her chamber and his frustration over the weather preventing him from retrieving Quintin and making this season of joy difficult for the villagers in the outlying areas, she always came back to Elianor Boursier. Another Verdun whose passion for her husband was surely seen as lacking.

Tasting blood, El released her teeth's hold on her lower lip. She would broach the matter with Bayard—this eve when he lay down with her.

As she stepped forward, further stirring the scents of herbs cast upon the rushes, the doors to the great hall opened, admitting chill air that rippled her skirts, fluttered the banners and tapestries, and caused the candlelight to jump.

Alarmed that both doors had been thrown wide without a care for the loss of heat, El turned toward the porter. And halted when she saw the man had stepped aside to make way for those who struggled beneath the greater part of a tree.

"We've the Yule log, milady," said a scrawny fellow who appeared to be contributing to the effort as much as the three others whose bodies were obviously better suited to the task.

El inclined her head. "I thank you."

Relieved when the porter closed the doors, causing the cool air hastened in by the gray, lowering day to settle, she eyed the log as it was carried past. Bayard had promised to send one of a size that would sustain a fire from Christmas Eve well into Christmas Day until it was entirely consumed as was tradition. And this one surely would, for it was no green thing, likely seasoned for months for this occasion.

A memory rose of Murdoch raging over the smoke of a Yule log too recently cut, but she pushed it away. Watching the men who cleared a path through the rushes down to the floorboards as they moved toward the stone floor of the hearth, she wished it were as easy for Bayard to push away her increasingly visible aunt.

Sitting to the right of the hearth as she had done for several hours while El worked around her to prepare for the evening meal, Constance lifted her head from her embroidery to consider the log that would be lit after a supper that would be simple compared to the morrow's feast.

Reminded of the menu over which she and the cook had labored days past, El determined she would confirm the man had acquired all the foodstuffs needed to make the Christmas meal feed all, including those who lived in the town outside Adderstone's walls. Certes, it would be crowded in the great hall, but joyously so.

Once the log was lowered before the fireplace, into which it would be rolled, El invited the chill-dampened men to follow her to the kitchen to revive themselves with drink.

The imposing Rollo close on her heels, she led them down the corridor and into the room that was so heated by preparations for the evening meal she felt her cheeks redden and knew her garments would soon cling.

While a kitchen lad ladled up mugs of hot cider for the men, the cook assured El all was in order for this eve's supper and the Christmas Day feast.

When she and Rollo returned to the hall, it was not as she had left it. Into it had come more chill air, doubtless ushered in by the score of men who stomped their feet and rubbed their hands, the majority having gathered at the hearth from which Constance was now absent.

As Rollo came alongside El, she noted the reason he had turned more protective. Not all the men in the hall were Bayard's and Magnus's. A half dozen or more were unrecognizable.

"What goes, milady?" Rollo rumbled.

Tamping down alarm with reason—that Bayard's men would be on alert if the strangers posed a threat—El sent her gaze around the hall and saw her aunt and uncle stood alongside the alcove with its display of weaponry. And to the right, at the sideboard upon which goblets and pitchers of wine sat, was Bayard. Mantle pushed back off his shoulders, hair flecked with moisture, he took the goblet of wine a servant had poured and handed it to the man before him. A welcome visitor, then.

"All is well," she said.

Rollo nodded and, having also noted his lord's presence, did not follow her across the hall.

As she approached Bayard, she considered the man with whom he conversed. Though the visitor stood inches shorter and the hair bound at his nape was gray, he was broadly built, though that might be illusion, draped as he was in a thick mantle.

"My lord husband," El called. "I see we have visitors at Adderstone."

Bayard gave her a smile far from genuine. "Aye, come in from out of the cold," he said and reached to her.

As she took the last steps to his side, the other man turned and she nearly startled at the sight of his ruined visage. But though tempted to avert her gaze and look anywhere but upon the burn scars that violently puckered his neck up to his cheekbones, she held steady and was grateful for the comfort of Bayard's hand enclosing hers.

"Sir Francis Cartier"—Bayard returned his attention to the visitor—"I present my wife, Lady Elianor Boursier."

It was impossible to tell if the man's smile was more genuine than Bayard's, for his mouth did not move in any natural way, his lips further evidencing the tragedy that had befallen him. "So The Boursier chose a Verdun over a De Arell," he said.

The words were so unexpected—and contrary to the actual events—El once more struggled to contain her startle.

"Lady Elianor," Bayard continued, "Sir Francis is a mercenary who serves—"

"Knight errant," the man sharply corrected, then chuckled as if to make light of his reaction. "The king of England's most loyal sword."

"I met Sir Francis the day King Edward decreed that our families wed one into the other," Bayard said tautly. "Sir Francis thought the king too lenient in his dealings with us."

"He is a more tolerant man than I," the knight said.

El stretched a smile across her mouth. "You are welcome at Castle Adderstone, Sir Francis. With night upon us, and this the eve of our

Lord's birth, I hope you and your men will accept our hospitality and pass the night in our hall."

The knight raised his eyebrows. "You are all generosity to share your beautiful abode, my lady."

There was nothing generous about it. Though she had no cause to dislike him as much as she sensed Bayard did, she cared not for the air of arrogance that rose from him like an odor. Of more concern was the subtle breath of guile and the way his dark, gold-rimmed eyes moved down her.

Pausing upon her splinted arm, he said, "I see your means of dealing with a reluctant wife have not changed, Boursier."

Danger. El sensed it as surely as if swords had been drawn. And for a moment, Bayard's grip on her hand was as firm as one would expect of a grip upon iron. Understanding his reaction over the persistence of sins he had not visited on another, but eager to ease the tension, she said, "I thank you for your concern, Sir Francis, but you are mistaken. My arm was broken in a fall of my own doing." No need to bring Agatha into the tale.

"I see," he said, "but what I do not see is a wedding ring."

El glanced at the hand she held at her waist. "Sadly, 'twas lost in my fall, but if you doubt the verity of my marriage to the baron, Father Crispin will attest to the vows spoken between us." Again, no need to tell more than need be told—that she had originally spoken vows in Thomasin's name.

Sir Francis put the goblet to his lips and considered her over the rim as he drank. Lowering the goblet, he transferred his gaze to Bayard. "A fortunate man you are that so beautiful—and loyal—a woman was among the choices given you."

El glanced at her husband whose attention was entirely on the other man, as if he thought it a poor idea to let him out of his sight.

"Sir Francis was sent by the king to ensure the first of his decrees was honored," Bayard said, "and when he departs on the morrow, he may deliver tidings that this barony is to remain in the hands of the Boursiers."

The man who was offended at being named a *mercenary* sighed. "I shall, and I cannot tell you how pleased I am, Boursier, that you so value this bit of dirt that my men and I are saved the trouble of ousting you."

Bayard's grip once more turned firm.

"Soon we shall sit down for supper," El said. "Until then, you and your men are welcome to make yourselves comfortable, Sir Francis."

"That we shall, my lady. I thank you."

"Excuse us," Bayard said, drawing El away, "there are matters to which I must attend ere the day is done."

"You cannot spare your wife's company?"

Bayard halted.

Sir Francis shrugged. "I am certain the king would approve of my becoming further acquainted with the wife of one of his barons—all the better to assure him he was right to give you a chance to retain…" He frowned. "What is this little barony of yours called? Ah, Godsmere."

Danger once more pulsing from Bayard, El hastened to say, "Of course I would be happy to know you better, Sir Francis."

"Then I shall leave you two to it," Bayard said and released El's hand and turned away.

Hoping his ire toward Sir Francis did not bleed into her, El met the knight errant's gaze.

He returned it—once more, over a long drink.

As he lowered the goblet, Rollo appeared at her side, doubtless sent by Bayard. Brow weighted, lids narrowed upon Sir Francis, he said, "Milady."

Hoping he was well enough versed in propriety to say nothing of the other man's disfigurement, El said, "Sir Francis Cartier, this is Rollo. Rollo, Sir Francis Cartier is the king's man and our guest."

If any lacked propriety, it was Sir Francis. As he raked his gaze over Rollo, the sneer tugging up the right side of his mouth enlarged. "Rollo," he muttered with a dismissive lift of the eyebrows.

Aye, mercenary, El silently agreed with Bayard. *Knight errant* was too honorable a title for such a man.

"I was briefly introduced to your uncle, Lady Elianor," he said, jutting his chin in the direction of Magnus whose head was bent toward Constance as if to catch words spoken low. "Is that Boursier's half sister with whom he converses?"

El was momentarily surprised that he knew of Quintin, but it made sense he would be somewhat versed in the three families since the king had given him the task of verifying the first of the marriages was made.

"Nay, that is Baron Verdun's sister, Lady Constance—my aunt."

There was no mistaking the confusion upon the man's brow. Though that part of his face had escaped the damage done the lower half, it capably expressed emotion his mouth could not.

"Boursier's first wife?" he said. "As the king told it, she was committed to a convent following the annulment of their marriage."

El stared. He was not *somewhat* versed in the three families as she had assumed. He was *well* versed.

She cleared her throat. "She was and remains. My uncle was bringing her home to Castle Kelling for Christmas when the snow caused him and his entourage to seek shelter here." Once more, the less told, the better.

Of a sudden, the mercenary laughed. "So civilized!"

El frowned.

"Forgive me, Lady Elianor, I but marvel over the miracle of a first and second wife peaceably sharing the home of the man to whom they were—and are—wed. And nearly as stupefying is that they are related to each other. For that alone, I would have expected Boursier to have chosen the misbegotten De Arell woman to wed."

So Bayard had. Struggling to keep dislike from her face and voice, El said, "As you say—civilized."

"And yet..." Sir Francis lifted his face toward the ceiling, breathed deep. "...the stench of discord is upon the air."

El's jaw began to ache, and she thought that if he could, indeed, sense discord, it had to be her own. Granted, he was no Murdoch, but it was no pleasant thing to be in his presence.

"Forgive me, Sir Francis," she said briskly, "but I must return to the kitchen to ensure this evening's meal is equal to our guests whom the king holds in high regard."

Before he could respond, she dipped her chin and pivoted. And gnashed her teeth when her ears caught his chuckle.

"That 'un," Rollo said, quickly coming alongside, "I do like even less than that other 'un." He jerked his head to indicate Constance.

"I fear Sir Francis is one of those who is content only if he can make the lives of others as miserable as his own," El muttered.

"Best stay clear of him, milady."

"Certes, I intend to."

When the low-burning fire was the only light that remained in the chamber, Bayard crossed to the bed, disrobed, and lay down beside his wife.

As he drew the covers over him, she said, "'Twas not as bad as feared."

She referred to Sir Francis and his men. Though the mercenary had been seated beside Bayard throughout the meal—a place of honor, though in Cartier's case, a means of keeping him in sight—the king's man had been as near to pleasant as he was likely able to manage.

Of course, the turn in his demeanor was surely a result of the delight he had taken in Bayard's French wines. Fortunately, he was not one whose behavior turned belligerent and dangerous the more he imbibed. Nor had his men, a surprisingly reserved bunch, caused trouble among the celebrants. Thus, the meal was happily concluded, the Yule log lit, hymns that praised the miracle of Christ sung, and wassail pots filled with hot spiced cider and slices of roasted apples passed around.

Better yet, Sir Francis and his men had declined the invitation to attend the midnight service known as "Angel's Mass," preferring to bed down in the hall so they would be rested for their departure following the Christmas Day feast. Hopefully, the weather would not take a turn for the worse and delay their departure.

Bayard pulled himself back to the present that was not yet an hour into Christmas Day. If not that Father Crispin was taking ill such that he had not been present at meal and his midnight mass had been half as long as usual, they would be well into the second hour of the day celebrated for bringing the light of salvation into the dark of humanity.

"I wish I could say I am sorry you found Sir Francis to be an unpleasant sort," he said, "but I am pleased your instincts are sharp enough to allow you to see past his charms."

Elianor laughed. "Charms? If he has any, he keeps them well hidden. Thus, you give my instincts more credit than they deserve. Though I know my prayers should not be so self serving, this eve I spent several upon requests that the weather continue to improve so he might sooner depart."

Bayard chuckled. "As did I." He closed his eyelid and began to drift.

"Bayard, are you still pleased I am your wife?"

Her voice was so small and uncertain that he pulled back from the edge of sleep. Turning his face toward hers, he caught the sparkle of her eyes. "You know I am."

"Then why do you not make love to me? I thought..." He heard her swallow. "...you did not find me displeasing the night we first loved."

There it was—what he had been waiting to hear. "I found you most pleasing, Elianor. 'Tis just that I am not willing to risk you."

"I do not understand."

"As told, no matter the desires of the flesh, I would go slow rather than risk making another bad marriage."

"But I no longer wish you to go slow."

She was so vehement he almost laughed. Turning onto his side toward her, he levered onto an elbow and laid a hand to her cheek. "That is what you think, but your body is not in accord, and as I am determined our marriage will be different from what both of us have known, I am willing to wait so that one day you might soar with me."

"Soar," she whispered.

"Aye, but first you must better trust my touch."

After a long moment, she said, "I do trust it. Indeed, I find it and those other things most pleasant. I just cannot quite forget..."

He brushed his mouth across hers. "This I know, Elianor. And in time, you will be free of the past and fully mine."

"Not if you continue at this pace," she countered. "You go much too slow, Husband."

"Do I?"

"Most certainly." Her hand found his and drew it toward her. "And now I require another lesson. Slow? Very well. Just not too slow."

She laid his hand to her belly—her bare belly, he realized, her skin warm and soft beneath his calloused palm.

When had she shed her chemise? While he had completed his ablutions at the basin? Extinguished the candles?

"You, dear wife," he said, "are unclothed."

"Calculated, I vow. But is it enough to tempt my much too considerate husband?"

"Certes, it will suffice." He lowered his head and kissed her sweet mouth.

Sometime later, when she had tempted him well beyond a single, slow lesson and it was his name she spilled into his ear, he knew her again. And she began to know him.

35

———

LAMB STEW, POACHED fowl, peppered venison, wine-marinated pork, white bread, all manner of pies, plum pudding, and more. Such was the Christmas Day menu, and an ambitious one since the celebration included many of the town folk and the weather had made it difficult to procure the abundance required to feed all.

Not surprisingly, the warmth within the great hall was as much due to the Yule log's hearty flames as the vast number of adults that crowded the tables and their little ones who sat upon blankets on the rush-covered floor.

As Father Crispin was no better for a night's sleep, it was Bayard who praised God for His son's sacrifice that gifted humanity with salvation and asked for a blessing upon the bounty. When he signaled the servants to begin pouring drink, excited chatter arose.

Settling back in the high seat, ignoring Sir Francis on the one side of him—as most of those present aspired to do, though for the more obvious reason of the mercenary's frightening visage—Bayard looked to his wife on his other side.

El smiled, letting her feelings show amid relief that all was in order. Though in the rush to make ready for the day, few words had been spoken between them since the hour past midnight when Bayard had made her feel things yet more promising, there seemed no need for words now. She guessed he felt the same, for he reached to her, and when she set her hand in his, turned his gaze forward.

She would have done the same if not for Sir Francis. His face was mostly in profile, but his sidelong gaze that Bayard's unseeing left eye did not catch, was fixed on the clasped hands of the lord and lady of Godsmere. A moment later, it shifted to her eyes.

His burnt smile briefly showed teeth, then he leaned near Bayard and said, "For one bitterly opposed to marriage, Boursier, it seems you owe your king much gratitude."

Bayard looked to him.

"I wonder, though, if your sister will be as pleased with that whom your choice of Lady Elianor has left to her."

"Though I shall ensure De Arell makes her a good husband," Bayard said, "whether or not she is pleased is of no consequence, is it? What King Edward wants, he shall have."

Sir Francis lifted his goblet. "Ah, the price of dirt."

As Bayard's hand tensed upon El's, the mercenary took a drink without spill or dribble despite the awkwardness of what was so simple a thing for others who had not come through whatever tragedy had befallen him.

"Once more, I disturb you mightily, Boursier." He shrugged. "That seems my lot—collecting adversaries as bountifully as a beautiful woman collects suitors." He looked to the lower table nearest the dais, and El was certain it was Constance he regarded. "But worry not, the sun shines, the snow melts, and the air is still. Thus, this day you shall be rid of me and my men."

As bowls of fragrant stew were served, Lady Maeve stepped off the stairs, emerging from her chamber for the first time in five days. That she had chosen to reappear on Christmas was a gift El hoped would lessen Bayard's worry and guilt.

The crowded hall blocking a direct approach to the high table, Lady Maeve moved along the wall and ascended the dais on the side nearest El.

Bayard stood as she neared, greeted her, and spoke something low that made her smile faintly, then frown.

He turned her toward Sir Francis who had risen from the chair she usually occupied, but before formal introductions could be made, the mercenary stepped forward, caught up her hand, and sharply bowed his head. "Sir Francis Cartier, in service to King Edward. And now yours, dear lady."

When he raised his face, she startled and made a sound between a gasp and a gulp.

"Lady Maeve, is it not?" he said, then, "Pray, forgive me. I should have been more gentle in presenting myself." He released her hand and gestured at his face. "Such a sight is disturbing. But, alas, there is no means of hiding the devilish visage that was cruelly dealt me years ago." Of a sudden, he laughed. "That is, short of walling myself up like a pitiable anchorite, and of such religious bent I am not."

Lady Maeve blinked, as did El who would not have expected such an outpouring from the man. Might he be entranced? Bayard's stepmother was attractive, a noblewoman, *and* a widow.

"My apologies," she said, her words barely perceptible above the din. "'Twas impolite to react so, especially since I was not unprepared." She glanced at Bayard, and El guessed that, in addition to his greeting, he had forewarned her of the introduction to come. "My only excuse is that I have not been well these past days."

Sir Francis's brow rippled. "I am sorry to hear that, but pleased you feel well enough to attend the feast." He stepped aside and gestured at the chair he had vacated.

She pressed a hand to her chest, and the smile that moved her mouth quaked as if wrought of nervousness. "It is not necessary——"

"I insist." He glanced at Bayard. "As I am sure the Baron of Godsmere would wish."

"I thank you for the consideration shown my stepmother," Bayard said.

"'Tis naught, especially as your other guests at high table will surely be as generous and make room for me."

Stiffly, Bayard gestured for the knight seated beside Sir Francis to move down. Thus, all those to the left were displaced, though none lost the honor of sitting upon the dais since the last three occupied a bench rather than chairs, allowing another to squeeze among them.

Exhibiting unexpected gallantry, Sir Francis guided Lady Maeve to her chair and lowered himself into the one yielded to him.

Throughout the courses that followed and revelry that grew with each pour of ale and hot elderberry wine, Lady Maeve picked at the foodstuffs and was mostly unreceptive to Bayard's attempts to draw her into conversation. However, despite her initial shock over Sir Francis's countenance, it appeared she was not immune to the attention paid her. Angled toward the man with whom she shared a plate, she exchanged words with him that several times caused the mercenary's eyes to light and mouth to attempt a smile.

After a time, Bayard's stepmother made no further show of sampling the small portions that would gorge no bellies on their own, but which, combined with portions of other courses, would be the cause of discomfort for many. Though she continued to grace Sir Francis with her attention, she began to worry the purse on her girdle as she had done the night El had sought an audience with her aunt.

When she looked to Constance, and the clatter and clink that had heretofore been muted by the din increased, Bayard leaned toward her and murmured what El imagined were words of comfort.

Lady Maeve's expression seemed one of gratitude, but also desperation, then she turned back to Sir Francis.

El touched Bayard's arm and asked low, "Lady Maeve?"

He dipped his spoon in a pudding that wafted cinnamon and cloves and offered it to her. As she sighed over what her full belly would not enjoy as much as her tongue, Bayard said, "Though I would not deny her a chance to once more know close companionship, in this instance, I am grateful she so loved my father that she is unreceptive to that snake's charms."

El inclined her head, offered a spoonful of pudding to Bayard.

Though the festivities to come would be of a more simple nature than those enjoyed during temperate Christmases when minstrels and traveling players were hired for entertainment, anticipation grew as all lingered over bellies full of food and drink. Thus, those in the hall were quick to quiet when Bayard stood.

"Now to make merry!" he pronounced.

Chairs and benches scraped as guests hastened from tables that would be cleared by servants who had relieved the first group partway through the meal.

Bayard assisted El out of her chair, but when he turned to his step-mother who waved away Sir Francis's attempt to help her to her feet and offered his own hand, she said, "I am content to watch the festivities from here."

"Alas, the lady spurns me," the mercenary bemoaned. "But 'tis for the best, as my men and I must depart for…" His mouth bent upwards. "I cannot say, only that it is a matter of such importance that were I to neglect it, I might be the cause of harm falling where it ought not."

"Then we will not further delay you," Bayard said.

Sir Francis raised an eyebrow, returned his regard to Lady Maeve. "A pleasure it has been. I look forward to when next we meet."

She inclined her head. "Good day, Sir Francis."

He bowed and strode the length of the dais, at the far end of which his men had gathered.

"It appears you have gained an admirer," Bayard said.

Lady Maeve did not respond until the mercenaries had exited the hall. Then, eyes brimming with resentment, she said, "Be assured, I have less a care for that man than you do."

Bayard slowly nodded. "You are certain you do not wish to join us before the hearth?"

Once more, she took her purse in hand. "What right have I—has anyone—to make merry when my daughter has no occasion to do so?" She put her chin up. "And do not tell me again she is in no danger, nor that De Arell will make her a good husband."

"Lady Maeve, I—"

"Do not!" That last was said with such vehemence that several of those moving toward the opposite end of the hall looked around. Pressing a hand to her chest, she said, "Go. Take your new wife and sing and dance and worry naught for what your sister suffers for having come to the aid of a brother who does not regard her as fondly as she regards him."

"My lady—"

She shoved back her chair and rose. "As I am the only one who has a care for Quintin"—the contents of her purse jangled—"I shall no more regret placing my faith in one other than you, Bayard Boursier."

He stepped near her. "I am sorry you are distraught."

"You know not how distraught I am! Enough to sell my soul—"

Like hard rain upon metal, the contents of her purse spilled to the dais.

"Ah, nay!" She dropped to her knees and began sweeping the coins together.

Bayard lowered beside her, but she slapped his hands away. "Leave me be!"

Not daring to move, certain her assistance would be even less welcome, El shifted her gaze between the two and caught the glint of something beneath the high seat.

She looked nearer upon it.

A gold band. And it was set with a dark stone upon which a curious symbol was engraved.

36

"My ring!" El swept it to hand, looked to Bayard.

He frowned. Then came realization, and he turned his regard upon his stepmother. "What did you do, Lady Maeve?" he asked in a voice El had not heard since before his threats and warnings to the woman he had believed to be Thomasin was replaced with tolerance, coaxing, and kisses.

Suddenly still, Lady Maeve stared at the ring. Then, as if all the air went out of her, she folded over her bent knees and clasped her head in her hands. "Nay. Ah, nay."

"Tell me!" Bayard growled.

El glanced around the hall. Most had gathered before the hearth, and those who were near enough to heed the happenings at the back side of the high table were busy clearing away the feast's remains.

El set a hand on Bayard's shoulder. "Methinks Lady Maeve is in need of rest, Husband."

He drew a deep breath, inclined his head, and slid an arm around his stepmother's waist. "Come, my lady, I will assist you to your chamber."

"Aye," she whispered, and leaning heavily against him, got her feet beneath her. "I am so very tired, Bayard."

As he guided her across the hall, El following, others hastened forward to offer assistance and were assured his stepmother was merely fatigued. Only Rollo, visibly distressed over Lady Maeve's state, ignored the order to return to the festivities and accompanied them abovestairs.

Inside the chamber, Hulda rose from a chair before the brazier, dropped her mending onto the seat, and hurried forward. "My lady?"

Bayard lowered his stepmother to the edge of the bed, lifted her legs onto the coverlet, and eased her back against the pillow.

"She is ill?" Hulda asked.

"She is tired. Worry not, Lady Elianor and I will tend her."

"But—"

"If you are needed, Hulda, I will summon you."

Something that might have been resentment rippled across the woman's face.

Holding fast to what remained of his patience, Bayard said, "'Tis Christmas Day. Go enjoy the celebration."

Feet dragging, the woman crossed the room and glanced back as she stepped past Rollo who hovered near the door.

"I can stay?" the big man asked.

"Nay!" Lady Maeve cried. "Send him away!"

Bayard saw no harm in permitting her half brother to remain, but he could not risk Rollo's presence preventing her from speaking. "Return belowstairs, Rollo. Once Lady Maeve and I have talked, I will bring word of how she fares."

With a low, mournful groan, the man backed into the corridor and pulled the door closed.

As Bayard shifted his regard to Elianor where she stood at the foot of the bed, Lady Maeve said, "Pray, leave me, Bayard."

He settled to the mattress beside her, noted that she continued to clutch at her chest. "Should I send for the physician, my lady?"

"I but wish to be left alone."

"Would that I could, but I must know what you know."

She turned her face opposite. "Not now."

Struggling to keep his anger from her, he said, "You were the one who took the keys from the steward to release Agatha, the one who replaced them ere they were discovered missing. 'Twas you in the walls with her, there when that woman pushed my wife down the steps."

She whimpered. "I wish it had not been me there."

Lord, brace me, he silently prayed. *May my words and actions be worthy.*

Lady Maeve jerked her chin around, set her gaze upon Elianor. "I vow, I did not know what she intended, and when I saw, I thought it was too late—that your neck was broken."

"You could not tell she yet breathed when you took the ring from her hand?" Bayard demanded.

"I did not! Only when the ring was discovered missing did I return to the passageway. I found it on the steps. You must believe me!"

In light of her betrayal, he must do no such thing.

"What about the ring is so important you had to retrieve it?"

She shook her head.

"Why did you release Agatha?"

It seemed she would not answer, but finally she said, "For Quintin. As you would not keep her safe, I had to turn to Agatha." Pleading brightened her eyes. "I vow, I am no friend of that woman's. Indeed, I had hoped her imprisonment would be the end of her."

"Why?"

"I hate her—how she makes puppets of us all."

Her vehement words brought to mind those she had spoken after he had brought Elianor up out of the underground—her declaration that Agatha was of evil bent.

"What has my sister to do with that witch's release?" Bayard asked.

"Everything. Hence, time and again I have bowed to Agatha's demands in order to keep my daughter safe."

Bayard felt as if he had entered a labyrinth. Deciding to leave be the matter of Quintin's involvement—for the moment—he said. "Time and again?"

"Since she accompanied Constance to Adderstone and showed herself for what she is."

"What is she, Lady Maeve?"

She scrabbled at her chest, causing the material of her gown to bunch between her fingers. "Though 'tis true Archard was dying, he was not meant to leave me so soon."

Bayard felt fire lick upward, singeing his throat on its way to his tongue. "Tell me!"

"He did not know what Agatha was, but he sensed the evil of her." Her lashes fluttered. "He warned you about her. Remember?"

Not easily forgotten, for that warning had visited him often after his father's passing when he had discovered Constance's maid had been drugging him.

"She killed him," he said and looked to Elianor who leaned against a bed post as if for support. Like Constance, she had believed the woman an ally. Unlike her aunt, she had learned that was not so—and nearly paid the price to which his father had been subject.

A sob escaped Lady Maeve. "She hastened his death with one of her powders, though I did not know it until we buried Archard."

Bayard pushed his ire into his fists, waited.

She swallowed hard. "I felt darkness prick me, slide beneath my skin. Whence it came, I did not know, but when I looked up, she was there among the trees. And when the dirt struck his coffin, she smiled. 'Twas then I recalled that just before I found Archard dead, I met Agatha on the stairs as she was descending and I was ascending." Lady Maeve splayed her hand on her chest. "That evening, I confronted her with my suspicions. Do you know what she did?"

Bayard held his tongue that was fit only for wrathful words that would frighten her into silence.

"That evil thing laughed and said it was good I knew what she was capable of, for she intended to use me well."

"You told no one?" Elianor asked softly.

Lady Maeve's frantic gaze shifted between her audience of two. "I had no choice. You must know I did not, Bayard."

"I do not know that, and so I await an explanation with all the patience of one who has just learned his father was murdered and his stepmother did naught to see justice served."

She took hold of his forearm. "She said she would do the same to Quintin if I did not aid her. And so I did—and have continued to do when called upon."

Bayard shuddered over the effort required to contain the emotion trying to break his surface. "Had you revealed her sin, she would have burned for what she did to my father."

"You do not understand!"

"Because you do not make sense!"

"What she does, she does in the name of the Foucaults!" The words spilled from her like water from a breached dam.

Bayard drew a sharp breath. "How do you know that?"

Her eyes darted to Elianor. "The ring."

Elianor opened the hand she held protectively at her waist, revealing her wedding band.

"It was my father's. I knew it the moment she presented it to me. Ever he wore it upon his little finger until—" She winced, shook her head.

"This symbol," Elianor said, "it is the letter F inside a D, is it not? For Denis Foucault?"

Before Lady Maeve could answer, Bayard demanded, "Surely you do not say your father lives?"

His stepmother dragged her teeth over her bottom lip. "I can tell no more."

For a moment, it seemed a wind had come into the chamber, but it was only the force of his breath. "So Agatha seeks revenge. Why? Is she a Foucault?"

"Already I have told too much. Quintin's safety depends on my silence."

Bayard thrust to his feet, crossed the room, came back. "All these years, you have maintained contact with her."

"Pray, believe me, I had no choice."

"It was she," Elianor said.

Bayard looked to his wife whose gaze was fixed on Lady Maeve, who was surely fitting together pieces of her years with Agatha.

She nodded. "'Twas not Bayard who told you of my first husband's abuse. It was Agatha. Did she also reveal my plan to imprison Bayard that he might forfeit Godsmere?"

"Nay, I knew naught of that."

"Then who gave her the keys to the underground?" Bayard demanded.

Lady Maeve struggled to sitting. "I did, but it was years ago, while she served as Constance's maid."

"Used for the passing of missives and meetings between my first wife and her lover," Bayard said. "Most recently, used to imprison me."

"I did not know of those plans!"

Not trusting himself to draw nearer, he ignored the hand she stretched to him.

She made a pitiful, pained sound, wrapped her arms around her knees. "I have her word she will keep my Quintin safe."

"Her word!" Bayard snarled. "You believe one such as that will keep it?"

"Though one side of Quintin is Boursier," she said with desperation, "there is safety in the Foucault blood I passed to her."

"What present danger do you fear my sister faces, Lady Maeve?"

Her nostrils flared with a long breath. "Agatha is not alone in this, Bayard."

He thought on it, and it was as if a ray of light shone across the darkness, pointing him toward something he had thought he understood. He had not. Nor had the De Arells and Verduns.

"The burning of crops and villages," he said, "the slaughtered cattle. It was not always one of our three families striking at the other, was it?"

"I cannot know for certain, but I believe many of the sins that roused our enmities were dealt by those who wish to restore what was torn asunder—to take back all of Kilbourne."

Though he had not yet thought of Agatha's foul deeds as a means of piecing the barony back together, that was, of course, the goal. "These others, are they at Castle Mathe?"

"At least one, and for that I fear for Quintin."

"Tell me who they are, Lady Maeve."

"I know very little, but what I do know, I cannot say——"

"How am I to aid my sister if you insist on playing games?"

His stepmother leapt off the bed and once more took hold of his arm. "'Tis no game, but life and death, as surely you must know now that 'tis told murder was your father's end, just as it was nearly Lady Elianor's end."

Bayard longed to thrust her aside, but as prayed, he remained in control.

"A bargain!" Her voice pitched high. "That is what I will make with you."

He glowered. "What say you?"

"Bring Quintin home, and I will tell all I know of Agatha and the others." She nodded vigorously, and Bayard glimpsed a light in her eyes that possibly shone from the edge of madness.

He breathed deep. "I will ride to Castle Mathe on the morrow and bring her home. Then you will tell all."

She fell against him. "I know I am weak, but I only did what I had to do." She dropped her head back. "Promise you will not tell Quintin. I could not bear it if she hated me."

Bayard looked to Elianor, and the compassion on her face eased his roiling. "Come." He guided his stepmother toward her bed.

Elianor reached it first and turned back the covers.

Once Lady Maeve was settled, she said, "You have been a good son to me." Tears spilled from her eyes. "But it is not enough."

"Enough for what?"

"The blood needed to piece Kilbourne back together does not know your veins." The coverlet drawn up beneath her chin rustled with the movement of her hand upon her chest. "I do love you, Bayard, and no matter what comes to pass, I pray you never doubt that."

He knew she cared for him, and though he railed against her being the witch's pawn, he understood her need to keep Quintin safe from one who had proved she was capable of murder—just as he now understood the reason she had never sufficiently recovered from his father's death and had further deteriorated following the confrontation between Serle and himself. The aid she had given Agatha made her culpable of the horrors all had been dealt that day.

"I do not doubt it, my lady," he said and laid a hand over her restless one beneath the coverlet. "I shall summon the physician."

She shook her head. "'Tis fear for Quintin that tightens my chest. Pray, bring her home to me."

"I shall. Rest now."

As her lids fluttered closed, he turned to Elianor.

"It explains much," she whispered.

He took her arm and led her across the chamber. "What it does not tell is how many years the Foucault avengers have sparked the strife between our families—surely, at least as far back to when Agatha first became Constance's maid." He opened the door.

At the end of the corridor, Rollo turned from the stairs and faltered when he saw them step from the chamber.

Guessing he had been pacing, Bayard pulled the door closed. "I instructed you to return to the hall."

Rollo lumbered forward. "I woulda, but I was great worried over Lady Maeve."

"She is resting now."

He halted before them. "I should keep watch outside her door?"

It would be good for someone to be near should she need something. "Only until Hulda returns."

Rollo nodded and took up position.

Once Bayard and Elianor began their descent of the stairs, Elianor said above the sound of revelry that wound upward, "You will tell Magnus what we have learned?"

"I shall, and when I go to Castle Mathe on the morrow to bring my sister home, De Arell will also know."

And stronger than the bonds of marriage forced upon the three families might be the bonds of uniting against a common adversary—one who wore only the face of Agatha of Mawbry. For now.

Humming. But not familiar as she would have expected. Still, there was naught comforting about it. If there was music to that which rose from a throat that sounded as if afflicted with the pox, it was not of any world Maeve Foucault Boursier wished to inhabit.

The droning—aye, it was better named that—portended ill. And so she feigned the sleep she had come up out of, which was all the easier to do in the dark of a chamber that had succumbed to night. What hour it was, she did not know, for though she had slept fitfully, her awakenings had been so brief that she could not remember if anyone had been here to witness them.

But someone was here now. And wished her to know it.

The humming ceased.

"Maeve."

Though the voice did not surprise her, her body reacted as if it did, betraying her with a jerk and a sharp breath that roused a throaty chuckle.

"I thought you had awakened."

As she raised her lids, the light of the brazier's remains gave little more than form to the shadow whose substance caused the mattress to dip on her right side. Not that she required further proof of who had come to her.

A sigh. "I believe you have failed me, Maeve. And if I am wrong… Well, methinks it only a matter of time ere you make me your enemy."

She swallowed.

"All these years, I have protected you and your daughter, and this is how you show your appreciation." Now the click of a tongue. "I am so disappointed, I would ache had life not taught me such feelings are for the weak."

Realizing she was trembling despite the warmth the covers trapped against her living, breathing body, she drew a hand up from her side and pressed it between her breasts. Beneath it, her heart beat hard and fast.

"Naught to say, Maeve?"

"Pray, believe me," she rasped, "I have not—will not fail you. Everything asked of me I have done. Everything!"

That one bent low, pressed a cool forehead to hers. "Would that I could trust you, but I believe you are a traitor to your blood. And that means…" Another sigh, this one filling her nostrils with rank breath that made her stomach turn and throat close. "…you are in my way, little Maeve."

Little. How long since she had been named that? Though she had every reason to be terrified, the word was strangely soothing.

A dry mouth brushed her brow. "Now go quietly, hmm?"

"Why?" she whispered.

"For your daughter—unless you wish her to go loudly."

She caught back a sob. "You will continue to protect my Quintin?"

"I give you my word."

"There is still a place for her?"

"She has only to accept it."

"But—"

"Shh, Maeve. Quietly, remember?"

She whimpered, dragged her nails across her chest, and as her heart strained toward another beat, told herself, *Quietly, little Maeve, as if you never were. So quietly, only Quintin will prove you once lived. And loved.*

Oh, how she had loved! And been loved. Of that she was certain, even if Archard Boursier, who had taken her to wife to atone for his sins, had not known how deeply he felt for her.

Hence, go quietly, she silently entreated. *For the beautiful child Archard gave you. For Quintin who is everything. Everything…*

37

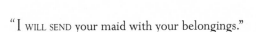

"I WILL SEND your maid with your belongings."

El smiled up at her uncle where he sat in the saddle against a crisp blue sky on the morn after Christmas Day. "I thank you, Magnus."

He inclined his head, looked to Bayard. "I am glad much of what was unresolved between us is now put to rights, Boursier, and that we are not only allies by way of a common enemy, but through marriage."

That first referred, of course, to what had been revealed of Agatha's dark workings.

"I am confident," Magnus continued, "that together we can end the Foucault threat, whatever form it takes."

"I will send word of De Arell's response to the tidings," Bayard assured him, "and whatever else can be learned from my stepmother once my sister returns to Adderstone." He stepped back. "Godspeed, Verdun."

"And you."

It was no idle blessing, for Bayard would ride to Castle Mathe this same day.

"Bayard," Constance called from where she sat on her dun-colored palfrey behind her brother, "I would speak with you."

He inclined his head and reached to Elianor. When she took his hand, he drew her with him to her aunt's side.

"I would have you know I forgive you," said the woman whose lovely visage was framed by her mantle's fur-lined hood, "even if you do not seek forgiveness. And I pray one day you will forgive me."

Though slow to respond, he said, "I do seek forgiveness, and I thank you for gifting me with yours, just as I gift you with mine."

She momentarily closed her eyes. "And Serle?"

El heard her husband's teeth grind, but he said, "I will do what I can for both of you."

As a radiant smile transformed her aunt's face, El curled a hand around the purse beneath her mantle that held the ring which had made this peace possible.

Constance, previously eager to defend Agatha, had been slow to realize how the revelation of her maid's duplicity might affect her. But when she had come around to it after Bayard revealed to Magnus what was learned from Lady Maeve, Agatha became the evil one, just as Bayard's stepmother claimed her to be.

Thus, it was Agatha who had encouraged Constance to consummate her love for Serle and maintain contact with her lover following her marriage to Bayard. Agatha who had stirred Constance's discontent with her husband and encouraged the lovers to pass missives between each other. Agatha who had convinced Constance it was excusable to cuckold a man who had stolen her from her true love. Agatha who had arranged for Serle and her to flee Adderstone.

Though Constance's enlightenment was self serving in its own way, El knew it must have been difficult, if not impossible, to turn aside the temptations Agatha must have served up like the tastiest sweetmeat. Her aunt may have been a willing victim of the forces that sought to avenge the Foucaults, but her weaknesses had been exploited.

Smile softening, Constance shifted her gaze to her niece. "Elianor loves you, Bayard, as I should have and wish I could have. Truly, I am happy for you."

"I thank you," he said gruffly. "And now I wish you Godspeed."

Shortly, from atop the gatehouse, El and Bayard watched as Magnus and his party appeared beyond the town's walls and struck out across the thawing land that caused their mounts' hooves to kick up clotted earth.

"And so I shall soon leave you as well," Bayard said as he guided her toward the steps.

"You are certain you do not wish me to accompany you?"

"I do wish it, but with your injury, 'tis best you remain within these walls."

It would be difficult to handle a horse, El conceded, and the journey would be slowed if he took her up before him. Too, the Christmas celebration would continue for many days, and if the baron could not preside over it, his lady wife ought to. "Then I shall await you here."

As they descended to the outer bailey, Bayard said, "Providing De Arell cooperates and the weather as well, I should be gone only one night."

"I shall pray he cooperates." Which was more likely once he knew what Lady Maeve had revealed.

Upon entering the great hall, a mournful cry reached them.

At the foot of the stairs, Lady Maeve's maid was on her knees. Surrounded by a half dozen servants, two of whom had drawn near and placed hands on the woman's shoulders and back, she hugged her crossed arms to her chest and wailed.

A pall descended upon Bayard, and though he demanded, "What goes?" as he strode from Elianor's side, he knew.

Hulda's head came up. Tears coursing her bright cheeks, she cried, "Oh, my lord! She is gone. My beloved lady has left us."

An ache opening within him over his sister's loss that would be felt all the deeper for her not having been here—and his own loss, Lady Maeve being the only mother he had known—he took the stairs two at a time and called over his shoulder, "Send for the physician." Not that he doubted Hulda, for she was well enough aged to be acquainted with the face of death, but the man should be able to determine the cause.

When he entered his stepmother's chamber, Bayard saw she lay upon her bed just as he had left her on the day past. Or nearly so. The coverlet he had drawn up to her shoulders was at her waist, revealing her bunched hand upon her chest.

Her heart, then?

He halted alongside the bed, and as he stared down into a face that, despite its gray cast, looked peaceful, he ached all the more. Ignoring her protests, he had sent the physician to her, and though the man had reported her heart troubled her as it often did when she was over-wrought, he had assured his lord that his draught had calmed her sufficiently to allow her to sleep. There had been no warning she would not rise again, that her fears for Quintin would not be quieted, that she would take to the grave those secrets that could mean the end of Agatha and the others—if there truly were others—who conspired to reassemble the pieces of Kilbourne.

Hearing footsteps, Bayard looked over his shoulder.

"I did return to my lady early yestereve, my lord," Hulda said as she entered alongside Elianor. "I vow I did, and she told that she felt much improved. Had I known she was so unwell, I would not have gone back to the festivities as she said I should."

Bayard's thoughts went to Rollo whom he had instructed to remain outside Lady Maeve's chamber until Hulda's return. When the maid had reappeared, he would have departed, unaware Hulda would not stay long. Thus, if Lady Maeve could have called for help, the man-at-arms would not have been present to defend her.

A sob escaped Hulda where she had halted in the center of the room, her eyes averted from the woman upon the bed. "I should have been here for her. My wee Maeve ought not to have died alone."

"You could not have known." Bayard glanced at Elianor who had put an arm around the maid, then looked back at his stepmother. Wondering if it was too convenient for her to have passed away before revealing what she had determined to hold close until her daughter was returned, now armed with the knowledge his father had not died of what had appeared to be natural causes, he slowly picked his gaze over the scene.

All seemed in order—no signs of struggle or distress, other than Lady Maeve's hand clutching her chest.

"You said you came to her early eve, Hulda."

"Aye."

"And later?"

"Not again until this morn that I might make her ready for the day."

"Then you did not sleep on your pallet?" He nodded at the stuffed mattress against the wall.

"After the games and singin', and more mead than I ought to have had, I fell asleep in the hall."

The same as many celebrants had done, as evidenced by the great scattering of bodies that had made it difficult to negotiate the hall this morn in order to see Verdun and his party away from Adderstone.

"Do not blame yourself," Bayard said. "Were you here, 'tis not likely you could have changed the outcome."

"But she died alone!"

Bayard looked one last time upon his stepmother and turned away. "There is naught to be done here. Elianor, take Hulda below while I summon Father Crispin."

"Oh, Lady Quintin!" Hulda bemoaned as she was guided from the chamber. "The poor lamb!"

All the more reason to bring his sister home. For certain, De Arell could make no argument against releasing her now.

An hour later, the ill priest having arisen from his bed to attend to the death at Adderstone, Bayard was so set on retrieving Quintin that it was Elianor who reminded him he no longer must shoulder burdens alone. Having followed him to the stables where a dozen of his men and horses were being readied for the ride to Castle Mathe, she pulled him aside and stepped near. "I will be waiting for you."

Her softly spoken words and unwavering gaze lightened him enough to be with her in that moment—to breathe her, to feel her touch all the way through, to strengthen his hold on the hope she had brought into his life.

"You are my light, Elianor," he said. "Despite this day's sorrow, were it a dream, I might be selfish enough to refuse to awaken from it."

"As I might myself." She rose to her toes and kissed him.

When he rode from Adderstone a quarter hour later, over and again he heard her parting words, "Godspeed, my love."

Death changed all. There were no grumblings and only a mild air of discontent when the celebrants were told the festivities were at an end now that Castle Adderstone was in mourning for Lady Maeve Boursier.

Still, knowing the days of Christmas might be the only bright spot during the bleak, soul-shaking winter, El ordered the cook to send prepared foodstuffs and drink to the town folk and those who dwelt in the outlying villages.

Having had little appetite for the midday meal, her thoughts time and again flying to Bayard who had departed two hours past, El sat back from the trencher she had invited the mournful Rollo to share with her. "You may finish it, if you like," she told the man-at-arms she had earlier coaxed out from behind her chair where he had watched over her as Bayard had ordered him to do.

"I thank ye, milady," he said, "but I am not much hungry."

Understandable. Lady Maeve may not have embraced him as her misbegotten brother, but he was affected by the severance of that bond.

"More wine, milady?" asked the serving woman who ascended the dais.

El nodded. "I thank you, Anne."

The woman poured, eyed Rollo's cup and, at El's nod, refilled it as well.

"Father Crispin?" Anne asked.

The priest, who had arranged for Lady Maeve to be laid out in the chapel after the physician concluded her heart had failed her, set a hand over the top of his goblet. "I have had enough, thank you."

It did not seem so to El, for he had sipped at it as much as she had picked at her food, but his red-rimmed eyes and persistent sniffling evidenced he was still unwell.

"Indeed," he said and looked to El, "if you will excuse me, my lady, I will return to my chamber and try to sleep away this evil in my head."

"Of course."

As he trudged along the back of the dais, El lifted her goblet and drank. When the priest mounted the stairs and went from sight, she moved her gaze over Adderstone's retainers who solemnly occupied the lower tables. Not only had yesterday's cheer been drained from them by the passing of Lady Maeve, but they were a fatigued lot, many slumped on upturned hands. One knight had even laid his head on the table.

A great yawn brought her chin around and she was granted an eyeful of the interior of Rollo's mouth.

Even as she winced, his yawn prompted one of her own. She lowered the goblet and pressed the back of her hand to her mouth. When she opened her eyes again, all seemed blurred, and she blinked to sharpen her vision. However, it remained unfocused and began to waver and darken around the edges.

She shook her head, felt her body begin to sink into itself.

"What?" she said, or thought she did, for her ears caught no sound other than that of another yawn.

Surely this is not...Nay, she could not have. Could she?

Her head was lowering, narrowing vision registering that more were making beds of the trestle tables.

She could. She had.

And in the midst of a celebration that entailed a multitude of comings and goings between the town and castle, it had been easier to do than when El had been her accomplice and stolen into the kitchen to drug The Boursier.

"Bayard," she said, and again heard nothing. Nor when she cried out his name.

38

LADY THOMASIN WAS in a temper. But then, Bayard *had* nearly run her to ground. More than that, her anger seemed roused by the discovery she had a protector—one of De Arell's knights who had appeared to defend her.

Bayard was not in the habit of making prey of women who had done him no ill. However, when he had gone to relieve himself while the horses took water from a iced-over stream he and his men had cracked open, he had heard something not of the wood. At first, he had thought it imagining—a play of the mind resulting from the nearly sleepless night spent holding Elianor following Lady Maeve's revelation—but it had come again.

Humming, and not of just any song. Agatha's song.

Struggling to contain the fire within, lest it be loosed only to be doused with blood, he had tracked the source and caught sight of a hooded figure moving briskly among the trees, a basket swinging from her arm.

He would have caught her unawares if not for De Arell's knight whose shouted challenge had caused Bayard's prey to spin around, hood to fall, bright eyes to grow large, firm jaw to drop—no Agatha of Mawbry, this. No quick end to the woman who had murdered Bayard's father, had nearly murdered his wife, and would murder again were she not stopped.

There had been no time to demand answers from De Arell's daughter, for though Bayard had drawn his sword during his pursuit, her protector was fast upon him.

Fortunately, the knight who had descended the steps to do De Arell's bidding when Bayard and Elianor had been admitted to Castle Mathe, had recognized Bayard and a meeting of swords was averted.

Now the man, for all of what Bayard guessed were his efforts to keep his lord's daughter safe during her much-rumored wanderings, was the recipient of the lady's wrath.

"That ye dare!" she lapsed into the rustic speech that evidenced she was only recently elevated to nobility. "That ye trespass upon me privacy!" She took a step toward the knight.

"My lady, I was only—"

"Only what, Sir Otto?" She threw the basket at him. Empty of whatever it had held, it fell short of the man by several feet.

"I was honoring my lord's orders—that I follow and watch from afar to ensure your safety."

"Enough!" Bayard bellowed.

Silence fell, the only sound that of dry, withered leaves that rattled where they continued to cling to branches that had wearied of spring's finery months ago.

Then the young woman snapped around. "And ye?" she demanded. "Pray, for what does The Boursier lurk in me father's woods?"

"I ride on Castle Mathe to bring my sister home," Bayard allowed, though his patience was almost frayed through. "We but paused to water our horses."

She scoffed. "I warrant me father knows naught of yer intent."

"There was no time to send word. Lady Quintin's mother has died."

Her eyes widened further, and she sucked a breath. "Oh, I did not know!"

"Nor would I expect it of you. As for your father, if he is not honorable enough to release my sister so she might bury her mother and properly mourn her, I will take her by force—which your presence here makes all the easier to do." Was it divine intervention that this time he had the real Thomasin with whom to bargain?

She frowned, glanced at her protector whose sword had come up again.

Bayard considered the man who looked as if he might foolishly risk what he ought not. "I would not fault you for doing your duty, Sir Otto, but let there be no doubt the outcome will be the same. I *will* use Lady Thomasin regardless of whether or not I must relieve you of that blade."

"There need be no bloodshed," the young woman said and quickly stepped toward Bayard, bringing herself within reach. As her protector growled with frustration, she lifted a staying hand toward Bayard. "I am sorry for yer family's loss, and if you must needs use me, I grant ye—" She cleared her throat. "I grant you permission. Not that it will be needed, for I am certain that in this matter, me—" Her jaw shifted, and this time when she corrected her speech, it was with anger seemingly directed at herself. "In this matter, *my* father will bend."

"Let us hope you are right," Bayard said, then to Sir Otto, "Sheathe your sword, Sir Knight. I vow no harm will befall your lady. At worst, she will be traded for my sister."

Grudgingly, the knight slid the blade into its scabbard. Bayard did the same.

"There, not a drop of blood," Lady Thomasin said. "Now, let us hasten to my father who, I vow, will prove he is not the knave some believe him to be."

"We shall soon know for sure," Bayard said. "First, though, I must ask you—"

"Of course, Lady Quintin may not agree with me."

Though it had been Bayard's intent to question her about that which had caused him to pursue her through the wood, he demanded, "What say you? Does or does not my sister fare well?"

She gave a funny, slanted smile. "She does well, though still my father keeps knives from her—indeed, takes it upon himself to cut her meat when she deigns to join us at meal. I probably do not have to tell you his thoughtfulness does naught for her disposition."

She did not. Relieved he had not misplaced his trust in Griffin de Arell, he said, "The song you were—"

"Strange, that," she mused. "Lady Quintin may hate my father, but 'tis an uncommon sort of hate. And so I often imagine hatin' Magnus Verdun the same, and all I can think is it would be better to simply kiss the man. Thus, I wonder if your sister ought to as well."

Bayard stared at this young woman whom he would have wed if not for Elianor's deception. And more than ever, he was grateful for the healing wounds upon his wrists that had begun the story of Elianor of Emberly and Bayard Boursier. The woman he had grudgingly wed twice was enough of a handful for him. Magnus Verdun, a man whom other men could not deny was overly blessed of face and form, would surely pale beside Thomasin de Arell who, despite being plain of face, was almost offensively vivacious in expressing herself.

"Ah, but…" She winced. "The time for that is past, eh? What I mean is…" She shrugged. "'Tis now a time of mourning, not kissing."

Bayard looked to Sir Otto. His stance had relaxed somewhat and there was a smile in a corner of his mouth. Though he must be accustomed to Lady Thomasin's singularity, it obviously remained a source of amusement.

"Lady Thomasin," Bayard said, "what caused me to give chase was the tune you hummed."

Frowns did not become the lady, for they were exaggerated, as if learned from a foul-tempered father. "Aye?"

"I know the tune and some of the words, but it is most familiar to me by way of the person from whom I first heard it."

She raised her eyebrows. "'Tis a pastorela that tells of a nobleman trying to talk his way up a peasant woman's skirts with all manner of flattery and deception. Naturally, I find it interestin' since…" She shrugged. "As you know, I am the result of something similar." Then a laugh, slightly bitter at the edges. "Forsooth, Magnus Verdun cannot be pleased I am the only one left to him."

"From whom did you learn the song, Lady Thomasin?"

She blinked. "My friend."

Bayard's muscles bunched. "Who?"

"Why?"

"Tell me!"

A sharp *tsk,* but she said, "Her name is Aude."

He frowned. "Not Agatha?"

"As I said, *Aude.*"

Bayard's mind wrenched him back to when he had brought a bleeding, broken Elianor up out of the passageway. She had muttered something about Agatha saying it was not Agatha, then posed a question with one word—rather, name. Aude. As Elianor's consciousness had begun to slide away, her need for reassurance that she would come back to him had kept him from pursuing her meaning. And he had not thought again on those strange words as, it seemed, neither had she.

"You do not believe me, Baron Boursier?" Lady Thomasin said.

Bayard returned her to focus, but before he could further his inquiry, she looked to Sir Otto and said, "Is that not right?"

Amusement no longer evident about the man's mouth, he said, "How would I know—?"

Lady Thomasin made a sound of disgust. "You think me so fool to believe this is the first time ye've followed me, Sir Otto?"

With a sheepish dip of the head, he said, "I do not, my lady," then looked to Bayard. "'Tis true, Lady Thomasin has an acquaintance named Aude—not Agatha—though I cannot say I have heard her sing."

"Well, it is of some comfort my privacy was not entirely trampled," the lady said, "that you were not listening at doors and through cracks."

Bayard stepped nearer her, laid a hand on her shoulder. "Tell me of this Aude. What does she—?"

"Baron Boursier," Sir Otto said, "surely we waste time speaking of a simple woman when we ought to start for Castle Mathe so your sister might sooner learn of her loss and see her mother buried."

"He is right." Lady Thomasin hugged her mantle closer. "It grows colder, and it will not be long ere day darkens."

True. The sun's position told five hours had passed since his departure from Adderstone. Less than two hours of daylight remained.

Bayard jutted his chin at the knight. "Sir Otto, lead the way to the stream."

With obvious grudging, the knight turned aside.

As Lady Thomasin hastened forward to retrieve her basket, Bayard followed and returned to the question burning a hole in him. "Aude," he said, shortening his stride so they might stay abreast.

"A simple woman, as Sir Otto said." She nodded at the knight who was far enough ahead that he would have to strain to be privy to their exchange, then flicked Bayard a frown. "I hope you do not think to make Aude's life any more difficult than already it is."

Only if she is not the one I believe her to be, he silently qualified. "I do not. I am merely curious."

"Hmm," she murmured. "Aude is a wanderer, though she mostly keeps to the three baronies."

What had once been the barony of Kilbourne.

"And since she moves place to place, I mostly happen upon her, and when I do, she is kind enough to aid me with..."

"With?"

"Distributing to the poorest among us those things not needed at Castle Mathe."

"Pilfered goods."

She snorted, so loudly he would have thought it a man who made the sound had both his eyes been blinded. "Since the lord of Castle Mathe is my father, they can hardly be called that. Too, as he has set Sir Otto upon me, 'tis obvious he knows what I do. So let us call them *alms*." She smiled. "Of which our heavenly father approves."

"When did you last see this Aude?"

Her mouth lost its curve, brow furrowed. "Was it a sennight past?"

Bayard held his breath. A sennight would make it impossible for Aude to be Agatha, for Lady Maeve had only just released her. Even if the woman had a worthy horse, with the poor weather—and her broken hand—she could not have made it to Castle Mathe on the Barony of Blackwood.

"Nay," Lady Thomasin shook her head. "Five days past."

Agatha, then.

De Arell's knight halted, came around. "Is my pace too fast for you, my lady?"

Another snort. "I wager all yer sneaking around after me has tired you out more than it has done me. Pray, lead on!"

His lips thinned, but he resumed his course.

The distance between them having narrowed, Bayard caught the man's disgruntled muttering. Ignoring it, he said, "Lady Thomasin, where did you see Aude?"

"At Castle Mathe, and 'twas strange to see her there, for she keeps to the villages—when she is not keeping to herself."

When Lady Maeve had enlisted the woman to protect Quintin, had it prompted the termagant to venture where she did not openly go? If so, what had she thought to accomplish by entering the castle walls? If it was true she had Foucault supporters there, what had passed between them?

"Did she tell you for what she came?" he asked.

"I did not talk to her. I was passin' into the outer bailey when I caught an eye of her coming in with other villagers. I called out, but lost sight of her, and though I looked for her, I did not find her."

Because she had not wished to be found.

"So she might yet be within Castle Mathe's walls."

Lady Thomasin made a face. "Certes, in all the days past, I would have seen her again."

If she had wished to be seen.

"Too, this day when I distributed *alms* in the village of Cross, I did ask after her. The blacksmith's son said she passed through several days ago and had one of her horse's shoes replaced."

Then she had obtained another horse, and not from Adderstone following her escape, for Bayard had confirmed all horses were present in the stables, including the ones Agatha and Elianor had used in the course of his imprisonment.

"Did the blacksmith's son say which direction she went?"

Lady Thomasin's lips quirked with what seemed satisfaction. "I did ask, and he told that Aude looked to be heading toward Godsmere."

And here he was upon the barony of Blackwood. He took Lady Thomasin's arm to hasten her along.

She gasped, but stretched her legs longer to accommodate him. "Why are we in more of a hurry? Surely ye—you—do not fear Aude? She is a good, harmless soul, I vow."

A vow she would be unable to keep, for she would soon learn, as had Constance, that there was nothing harmless or good about Agatha of Mawbry.

"She only wishes to be left in peace," Lady Thomasin continued as Bayard's men came into sight. "Indeed, she has likely set in for the winter in that hovel of hers."

"Hovel?" he snatched up the word.

"Aye, and you have no right to bother her there, it being this side of the border between my father's demesne and yer's."

An extensive border. Bayard halted and pulled the lady around to face him. "I do not fear this Aude, but I do fear for her, Lady Thomasin. Thus, I need your help."

She blinked. "Is she in danger?"

Mortal danger. "She is. Tell me, where is this hovel?"

Bayard glanced at the knight who had come around and gripped his sword hilt—a warning that regardless of whether or not he would prevail, he would defend his charge.

"I ought not to know its whereabouts," Lady Thomasin said, "since Aude caught me the first time I tried to follow her and took me to task, but I did discover it." She winked. "I am most curious, at times annoyingly persistent."

The knight stepped nearer.

"Stand down," Bayard said. "The lady and I but converse."

"Fear not, Sir Otto," the lady said, then continued, "Early last spring, I accompanied my father on a hunt, and the chase brought us near the border between the demesnes. After the deer was brought to ground, we paused to eat and rest before starting back, and while the men were slumbering, I slipped away."

She looked around. "Did you follow me then, Sir Otto?"

"Not on that occasion, my lady. I was not among the hunting party."

"Forgive me, I did not recall." She returned her regard to Bayard. "That is when I caught sight of Aude, and this time I more cautiously followed."

"Where?" he asked, patience close to snapping.

"A small lake formed by the stream that flows from a ravine." She frowned. "And so heavily treed you are nearly upon it ere you realize 'tis there."

Bayard was fairly certain he knew the one, though it was not exclusive to Griffin de Arell. Much of that murky lake, in the absence of sufficient rainfall, was better called a bog. It lay near the center of what had been the great barony of Kilbourne before it was apportioned into Godsmere, Blackwood, and Emberly, and it was at that place the three lesser baronies converged. Thus, all families could lay claim to a portion of the lake. And how obscenely fitting that the woman who worked revenge in the name of the Foucaults had made a home there.

"I know it," Bayard said, and looked past her to Sir Otto who raised his eyebrows, then to his men who watched and waited.

Bayard knew what must be done. Fortunately, it would not benefit Quintin to be told of her mother's passing this day as opposed to delaying until the morrow or the day after. It might even be kinder to permit her the extra time in which to be free of the weight of that heartache.

In contrast, it would be of great benefit to all if Bayard could put an end to Agatha's evil reign.

"It seems, Lady Thomasin," he said, "my visit to Castle Mathe must be postponed a short while."

"Then 'tis quite serious, this ill that befalls my friend?"

Struggling to keep distaste from his face, he said, "You will have to trust me to explain it all later."

Annoyance began to line her brow, but a bob of her eyebrows cleared it. "What of your sister?"

"I would ask that you share with your father the news of Lady Quintin's loss so he will be prepared to release her to me when I return to Castle Mathe—and have him apprise my knight, Sir Victor, of the situation. As for Quintin, 'tis best she hears the tidings from me."

"Very well." She looked to her father's knight. "It seems, Sir Otto, 'twill be just you and me again."

"Your journey all the sooner completed astride." Bayard nodded toward his men. "I shall lend you my sister's horse."

"We shall say naught of it," Lady Thomasin said before Bayard could caution her against doing so. Flighty this little bird might be, but she was not without wit that gave color to her otherwise unremarkable plumage. Hopefully, for Magnus Verdun's sake, she had a greater store hidden away somewhere.

"I thank you," Bayard said.

A quarter hour later, the two parties went their separate ways, Bayard's backtracking and swinging east.

Providing the skies remained clear and the air continued to stir itself to no more than a whisper, the two-hour ride would deliver them to the lake shortly after nightfall. And that could be a good thing, for the dark would more easily make Agatha the prey she deserved to be.

39

A LOUD, SHARP breath, as of someone too long under water surfacing and desperate to confirm he still lived.

Realizing it was she who made the sound, El exhaled and tried to bring her chamber into focus.

Not her chamber, her sense of smell revealed. It was too earthen— of damp dirt, moldering leaves, wood. And hovering over all was the scent of the fire felt against her back.

Where was she? Why did her jaws ache? Why would her eyes not focus? She could see light, but—

Something was over her head, and through its loose weave she glimpsed a wall of wattle and daub. As she frowned over it, she realized the ache in her jaws was from a gag wet with saliva, and the pain throbbing through her broken arm was due to her wrists being bound in front of her where she lay on her side.

Fear tightening its grip, she scrabbled back through her memories and placed herself in Adderstone's hall. She had been drinking wine before being overcome with fatigue, had been struck by realization before all had gone dark. Agatha.

Dear Lord, she sent heavenward, *I am in the midst of evil. Pray, let Bayard's people be unharmed. Keep watch over my husband and his men. Help me.*

"Worry not," a woman said low, as if from the other side of a door, "we shall take The Boursier the next time."

Aye, Agatha. And she was surely speaking with one of those who supported her quest to avenge the Foucaults.

Whatever her companion's response, all El could discern was that his tone was far from subservient—as if Agatha answered to him.

Be still, El counseled as she began to quake. *Think.*

She would no longer be within Castle Adderstone. For no good purpose, she had been delivered somewhere quiet and removed. Past the wattle and daub wall was no other wall that would indicate a sizable structure. Rather, the wintry outdoors lay beyond, for though her back was warmed by fire, the air slipping through the woven wall and past her hood nipped at her face.

"Castle Mathe," the man's voice came through, but the rest of what was said eluded her.

Careful of her arm lest it had suffered further injury, El bent her knees and struggled to sitting. Though constricted by something wrapped around her and an ache in her bones likely caused by her journey over the back of a horse, she made it upright.

Through the hood's weave, she saw the fire beside her was set in a pit at the center of the hut, its smoke wending toward a hole in the roof. And over her right shoulder was the door that muffled the voices.

El raised her joined wrists. Ignoring the ache in her arm, she fumbled with the hood cinched at her neck. Blessedly, the ties were easily loosened, and she soon threw off the hood. Noting it was a blanket in which she was wrapped, she worked the gag from her mouth, then peered around the hut. It was furnished with two stools, a chest, a stack of wicker baskets alongside a straw pallet, and a crude table whose top was littered with items similar to those with which Agatha had occupied herself at Castle Kelling.

Grateful the muted conversation allowed her to monitor her captor's whereabouts, El turned her attention to her bound wrists and was relieved to find the splints continued to hold the broken bone in place. As for the rope, it had been knotted with little care, secure as her captor had been in her being unable to resist in her drugged state.

She put the knot between her teeth and began to pry at it. She had nearly worked it free when a horse whinnied. She peered over her shoulder. Certain the muted words were ones of parting, she more viciously applied her teeth to the knot.

Shortly, there came the sound of a horse departing.

"Please," El whispered and gasped when the bindings loosened. Before she could free herself, the door opened. Lowering her barely bound hands to her lap, she looked around.

Against a blue-black sky lit by a generous moon and striped with the trunks of barren trees, Agatha considered her. "I see you have made yourself comfortable, Lady Elianor," she said and stepped inside and closed the door. A hand upon the long dagger at her waist, she walked wide around her captive. Confirming the rope yet bound El's wrists, she visibly relaxed and moved a stool near the one she no longer called mistress.

She seated herself, sighed. "Only a broken arm. I hoped for more."

Forcing down bile, El bit, "A broken neck. My death."

Agatha harrumphed. "You think to be offended? You who deserve such a sorry end?"

Because her grandfather had broken fealty with the Foucaults. "You pretended to be my friend," El said.

She gave a bark of laughter. "Hardly. But I will admit to misleading you—not that you minded being yanked about on my ratty leash."

It was true, the price of reprieve from the worst of Murdoch's cruelty being blind trust. "What of the others you drugged at Adderstone?" El asked. "Did you harm them?"

"Of course not. They were in my way only insofar that they might interfere with acquiring you and—I had hoped—The Boursier. By now, only those who made gluttons of themselves by imbibing too much yet suffer the draught's effects."

Seeing no reason why she would lie, El took comfort in that and swept her gaze around the hut. "I do not understand why you removed me from Adderstone—why you have not rectified your failed attempt to murder me."

"Certes, I would have been done with you, but 'tis believed you know things, and I must discover what they are."

"I do not understand."

"What did Lady Maeve reveal before her…" She smiled darkly. "…*convenient* death?"

El stared, and when understanding dawned, gasped. "'Twas not her heart. You killed her."

She shook her head. "I did not."

Her accomplice, then.

"But in one thing you are right. Her heart was not her undoing. It was a pillow."

If not for the need to maintain the appearance of being bound, El would have hugged her arms to herself.

"Thus, what I need from you, Elianor, is an accounting of what Lady Maeve revealed."

El increased her frowned. "I know not of what you speak."

Agatha leaned forward, wagged a finger. "I think it possible you lie."

It was then El noticed the other hand upon the woman's knee—the one she had broken to free it from the manacle. Thickly bandaged, the ends of the splints just visible, it offered hope beyond the loose rope about El's own wrists. Nearly as broken as her captive, Agatha of Mawbry was vulnerable.

"What did Lady Maeve tell of me when you and The Boursier assisted her to her chamber after the Christmas feast?"

Either her accomplice had been present in the hall, or talk of Lady Maeve's near collapse had reached the one with whom Agatha conspired. "Naught. We put her to bed, and that is all."

Agatha searched her face so long, El feared she would find the lie there. Finally, the woman sat back and fondled the dagger's hilt. "Then I might as well be done with you."

It almost sounded as if El's fate might be different were she forthcoming, but regardless of whether she sealed up the truth or spilled it, her life was forfeit—unless she could catch Agatha unawares.

"What do you fear Lady Maeve revealed?" El asked, as much to understand the woman's motives as to delay her.

Agatha pulled the dagger from its sheath, and as she slid her gaze down its silvery length, murmured, "Things hidden in the dark far too long."

"What things?"

The woman lowered the dagger toward a finger at the end of her bandaged wrist, a moment later, showed El the drop of blood suspended from the blade's point.

El moistened her chapped lips. "Why did you aid me with Murdoch?"

"And The Boursier," Agatha reminded and smiled. "Your uncle sent me to serve you. Thus, I earned not only his gratitude and trust, but yours." She smiled wider. "'Twas me you turned to for help in imprisoning The Boursier."

So she had, placing trust in Agatha ahead of trust in Magnus who would never have allowed his niece to do so foolish and ill a thing.

"Too," Agatha said, "there was great satisfaction in seeing Murdoch succumb to my powders, for he was easy to hate—so much I sometimes felt for all you suffered at his hands."

"Then…" El fit hope upon her face, the crushing of which would surely appeal to whatever twisted thing pulsed inside the woman. "…you also aided me because you had a care for me."

Agatha laughed. "You think much of yourself—you, the grand-daughter of a man whose only success was had by way of another's generosity."

Foucault, though El could not say it, for it was Lady Maeve who had revealed the woman's motivations.

"Nay," Agatha said, "I have only ever had a care for my loved ones, Elianor. And, alas, you are not one of them."

El was stunned by her choice of words—that she had loved ones at all. Meaning the ill she worked on the three families was personal? Might she be a Foucault?

Of a sudden, Agatha stood.

Desperate to widen the gap between death and herself, El said, "Why did you lie about Bayard beating my aunt?"

"Because I could. Because I found it amusing. Because those false tales roused Serle de Arell to save his beloved. More, because it served my purpose."

"What purpose?"

She moved her gaze from El to the table on the other side of the hut. "To make the lives of those deserving of my hatred miserable, and to ensure their hatred for one another continued to burn."

El tensed in readiness to throw off the rope, but when Agatha moved, it was around the fire pit. The table was her destination, and peering at the woman across her shoulder, El saw her dip the dagger into a pot. When she withdrew it, amber coated its tip. Honey.

As El eased her hands from the rope, Agatha lifted the blade before her. "As often as I dared, I drugged The Boursier to keep him from your aunt's bed, encouraged her love for another man, and when everything came together—when I delivered Serle de Arell into his beloved's chamber at Adderstone—it turned out better than expected. Rather than merely discover his wife had fled him, The Boursier returned and witnessed the act of being made a cuckold." She sighed. "I would have liked to see that, but I had departed." She licked the honey, turned the blade, licked again.

El knew she needed a weapon, but the only thing close at hand was wood that fed the fire. Fortunately, having recently been set amidst the flames, only the uppermost portion of the piece nearest her was alight. Still, that which she would take hold of would be very warm, possibly hot.

El returned her gaze to Agatha, and finding the woman watched her, asked the only thing she could think of, and to which she genuinely wished to know the answer, "Who are you?"

Agatha raised her eyebrows. "The better question is: *What* am I?"

Her rewording made El shudder. "Very well. What?"

Outside, an owl hooted, and Agatha glanced at the door. Then she shrugged, once more dipped her dagger in the honey, and began to hum.

Thinking the tune the only one she had ever heard from the woman, El looked sidelong at the piece of wood that would serve as her weapon.

"What am I?" Agatha raised the blade again. "To Boursier, Verdun, and De Arell, I am plague, pestilence, and righter of wrongs." A distant look in eyes that were no longer upon El, she drew a finger through the honey, sucked it. "I am eater of light, darkest of night, lover of the fallen, mother of the risen."

Was she, perhaps, more mad than evil?

It did not matter. Regardless of the state of Agatha's mind, she meant to kill.

El kicked off the blanket wrapped around her legs and lunged. Blessedly, the wood was only very warm. Unexpectedly, it was heavy.

She leapt to her feet, and raising the weapon between her and the advancing woman, almost laughed. Given the opportunity, she would knock her makeshift torch upside Agatha's head the same as the woman had done her in the inner walls.

"Come no nearer!" She swept the flaming wood before her, wished her injured arm could share its heft.

Wielding her dagger, Agatha halted four feet distant. "Well played, Lady Elianor. Once more you prove you are more of a survivor than I believed."

"I have much to live for."

"Ah, you think yourself in love with The Boursier." Her mouth curved, causing her expression to turn almost friendly. "That pleases me, for the more you have to lose, the better I like it." She charged.

El swept her weapon high. The impact with the dagger loosened her hold, but she tightened her grip in time to counter Agatha's next swipe and to move nearer the door.

She deflected two more assaults, one that almost caught her in the side, but the next time she swung, her grip failed and the piece of wood flew toward Agatha.

The woman jumped aside, causing El's weapon to hit the wall and drop to the straw pallet in concert with Agatha's tumble to the earthen floor.

El turned and wrenched open the door. As she went through it, out of the corner of her eye she saw the pallet catch flame.

Agatha's screech followed her as she pressed her injured arm against her waist and ran into a chill night she did not recognize—one surely much removed from Adderstone. Fortunately, the light of the moon enabled her to find a path among the dense, barren trees. But it also benefitted the one who came after her, who called to her, who shouted warnings that she went the wrong way.

Meaning it must be the right way.

Dear Lord, pray let me be—

The pound of hooves. Of many horses. Of Agatha's allies. Ahead.

El turned hard right. Registering the slap of a low-hanging branch across her cheek, she plunged between skeletal trees, over hard ground, through soft ground that smelled of rotting leaves, toward a shaft of brilliant light.

She wrenched to a halt and, teetering on the edge of a low bank, stared at the opaque, glass-like surface across which moonlight shone. A frozen lake. But how frozen? Enough to bear her weight?

She glanced over her shoulder. To her right, the hut burned, flames beginning to eat through the wattle. Behind, Agatha came for her. Beyond, those who rode to the woman's aid would soon appear.

The frozen lake, then. Though Agatha might venture out upon it, the riders would not risk themselves and their horses.

Heavenly Father, El prayed, *let the ice hold that I might find my way back to Bayard.* She drew a breath, descended the bank, and set foot on the hard, slick surface. Nothing, not even a crackle to warn her off.

"Elianor!" Agatha cried, revealing she was much too near.

El ran. And slipped and dropped to one knee. Biting her lip to keep from voicing her pain, she thrust upright and advanced more cautiously, assuring herself that anyone who followed would have to do the same.

When Agatha called again, El looked around. The woman stood at the edge of the lake, a moment later descended the bank, dropped to her knees, and began driving her dagger into the ice—attempting to crack it open and send El into the icy water. And past Agatha, visible between the trees, came the riders. As many as a dozen.

Shivering, as much from fear as the biting cold, El looked forward again. Though the opposite side of the lake was distant, it was her only hope. As she resumed her trek, the pound of hooves drew nearer, a shriek split the air, and there came the terrifying, thunderous crack of ice.

Feeling the tremor of fissures traveling toward her, El peered over her shoulder. Agatha was on her feet, stumbling as she moved toward El on the very ice she had weakened—braving it as if it was her only hope as well. Was it possible she fled the riders? That they were not allies?

It matters not! El told herself. *Move, else the question is moot.*

She had advanced a half dozen more steps, all the while praying for God's aid as the ice popped and cracked and reached its spidery fissures toward her, when a man shouted her name. Making of it four notes.

40

EL CAUGHT HER breath. As if God had dropped Bayard in this unknown wood, her husband was here.

She whipped around. Past Agatha, who drew near and whose blade flashed moonlight, were the shadowy figures of those who dismounted near the shore. "Bayard!" she cried.

"Down!" he shouted. "Lie flat! I am—"

Whatever else he said was trampled beneath a sound that tore across the air and caused black gashes to open in the ice and race toward her and Agatha.

"Get down!" Bayard bellowed.

El jumped to the side away from the fissures, lowered to her knees, and spread herself upon the ice.

Still Agatha came, so near there was no mistaking the ferocity in eyes that revealed her one objective—to sink her dagger not into ice, but flesh.

She was three strides distant when she jerked to a halt, still holding aloft her dagger when the ice shattered around her and the piece upon which she stood tilted, opening the water wider as if to spoon Agatha of Mawbry into that gaping black mouth.

The woman shrieked and flung herself toward El. Though the lower half of her body went into the water, she drove the dagger into the ice upon which El lay and, clinging to the hilt, struggled to keep her upper half from going under.

It was then El saw the feathered shaft protruding from the woman's shoulder. Bayard or one of his men had made his mark.

Convulsing, teeth chattering, Agatha reached her useless, broken hand toward El. "Help me!"

Strangely, El longed to pull her to safety, but more than fear for what might befall her should she draw near to Agatha, reasoning prevailed. Not only did El also have only one hand with which to defend herself, but the ice continued to break, and one crack was inching toward her— that most recently opened up by Agatha's blade.

El scooted back, away from the entreating hand.

Scrabbling against the ice's edge, Agatha tried again to drag herself up onto it. "Help me, Elianor!"

Continuing her retreat, El muffled a sob, shook her head. "I am sorry."

The woman pared back her lips. "Sorrier you shall be," she spat through crimson teeth that flecked the ice with blood. "Upon my word, you will suffer tenfold—"

The dagger betrayed her, causing the ice into which it had been planted to break free. With a great gasp, Agatha went under.

El stared at where she had been, imagined the icy water swallowing her down its gullet, wondered why she should now so deeply feel the cold.

"Elianor! Do not move!"

Slowly, she raised her head. She could see the figures of men and horses on the shore and the torched hut behind them, heard urgent voices. But where was Bayard? How long until he came for her? Would he reach her ahead of the cracks she could yet hear above the tapping of her teeth? Or would she join Agatha in her watery grave?

"Oh, I am cold…" She opened and closed hands she could hardly feel, whimpered at the pain shooting through her injured arm. Longing to hug it to her, she rolled onto her back.

"Be still, Elianor!"

He sounded near. Wrapping her arms over her chest, tucking her hands in her armpits, she tilted her head back. She expected to see

Bayard striding across the frozen lake, but he was not there. Perhaps the ice was too precarious. But still, he would try. And for it, he might go into the deep dark with Agatha.

She closed her eyes against the bright moon, called out, "Leave me, Bayard."

"Never."

She caught her breath, turned her head. He approached from the far left, cautiously moving toward her on his belly across ice that appeared unaffected by the great shattering alongside which she lay, gaze intent on her, eyepatch askew.

"Go back," she beseeched. "The ice—"

"I am here, Elianor."

And he was, his clouded breath mingling with hers, his body alongside hers radiating heat.

"Bayard!" She reached to him.

"Be still," he said again and, wasting no moment on kisses or embraces, shifted onto his side and unknotted the rope at his waist. Quickly, he worked it beneath her and bound her to him. Then, chest to chest, her injured arm pressed between them, he turned onto his back and wrapped his arms around her.

"Now!" he shouted, and his men slowly began to pull them back across ice that creaked and groaned with their passage over it.

Despite the heat of Bayard's body and his warm breath upon her scalp, El's teeth clicked when she asked, "How did you know I was here?"

His arms tightened around her. "I did not. I knew only that Agatha might be found in this place. Though I saw two running from the fire, it was too dark to know you were the one pursued." Beneath her ear, she heard him swallow. "But when you went out upon the lake and she called your name..."

El shuddered. "I thought you and your men were of Agatha—that there was nowhere else to go. I was so afeared, Bayard."

"As was I." He said it with such anguish, it was as if he grieved the loss of a loved one.

But I am not lost to him, nor is he lost to me, she told herself and began to pant, as if she were hot rather than cold. But that could not be. Could it?

"When you are warmed," Bayard said, "you will have to tell me how you came to be here."

She nodded—rather, jerked her head, along with the rest of her body. "While at meal, our drink was drugged, and I-I awoke here. Agatha wanted to know what L-lady Maeve told—"

"Later, Elianor. It can wait."

It could not. There were things he needed to know. "Another was here—methinks the one who t-took me from Adderstone. I heard him speaking w-with Agatha outside."

"Hush," Bayard urged as the frozen lake continued to pop and crack around them. "There will be time aplenty to talk once you are safe."

Would there be? What if—?

Cease! she commanded her frantic thoughts. *Bayard is here. He has you. Will ever have you. Ever.*

She sipped breaths of air, whispered, "And then you will take me home?"

His arms held her nearer yet. "Aye, beloved, I will take you home."

"It seems, dear wife, you are partial to setting things afire."

Elianor, whom he had held close this past hour where he sat against a tree facing the burning hovel that had warmed away her chill, lifted her head from his shoulder and turned her face toward the glowing remains. "Only once with intention," she said, "and 'twas because I feared you as I should have feared Agatha."

Though Bayard had thought to lighten the conversation now that each had shared their side of the tale—that which Elianor had learned of Agatha during her captivity, and what Thomasin had told of the woman known to her as Aude—the one who had perished beneath the frigid lake persisted. But then, it was not likely Foucault vengeance would die with Agatha, who had made games of their lives.

As told by Bayard's stepmother and confirmed by the one Elianor had overheard speaking with the witch, there were others. And just as they were responsible for the deaths of Archard Boursier and Lady Maeve, they would not be content until the Boursiers, Verduns, and De Arells fell at their feet. But if the men Bayard had sent to track Agatha's accomplice succeeded, one more would be in hand and would, with the proper incentive, reveal what Lady Maeve and Agatha had taken to their graves. However, if the man escaped...

Should King Edward's forced marriages fail to unite all three families, their shared enemy would make of them strong allies. To root out those who sought to piece together the barony of Kilbourne with violent acts and murder, Boursier, Verdun, and De Arell would have to stand together.

"Bayard?"

He focused on his wife's face, saw concern in the draw of her eyebrows. Determined to keep the conversation from returning to the one who had boasted she was *the eater of light* and *darkest of night*, he said, "Most assuredly, I will have to watch you closely around fire."

"You fear I will set our bed aflame?" Though innocently spoken, realization quickly cast color upon her cheeks and lowered her eyes.

Bayard lifted her chin and touched his lips to hers. "*That* you already do, Elianor. And, I vow, I will return the favor." Indeed, he believed he had almost done so the last time they had made love. She had been more receptive to his touch, had mostly gasped and trembled with good reason.

"I know," she said against his mouth. "Soon, I hope."

One more reason to return to Adderstone this night, though of utmost importance was ensuring the wellbeing of those who had succumbed to Agatha's sleeping draught.

"Are you certain you are well enough to make for home?" he asked, knowing it would be past midnight before they reached the walls.

She nodded. "I am well with it, so long as your arms are around me."

"Ever," he said and, a short while later, lifted her atop his destrier, swung up behind, and put his arms around her.

EPILOGUE

———◦◦◦———

Barony of Godsmere, Northern England
Spring, 1334

SHE WOULD EVER be amazed that so much could change in so little time—
that what presented as white could be black, that kindness and consideration could prove wrong the ill believed of another, that the wall around
one's heart could be beautifully breached, that the marital debt could
be anything but, that one day she would share the man she loved with
another. Or so she hoped.

"Do you think we have made a child?" she asked.

Bayard halted in the market beside a stall brimming with trinkets
that shone and winked and tempted one to touch. "If we have not"—he
pulled her around to face him—"'tis not for want of trying."

Feeling herself grow warm on this cool spring morn, she determined
she would not succumb to self-consciousness. He had kept the promise
made her, and if she was now too forward...too bold...too brazen...it
was more the fault of the one who had known what his patience and gentle
touch would awaken within her. Thus, had she brought to their bed a pen-
chant for setting things afire, he could hardly complain that he did not get
enough sleep or was late to begin his day. She certainly would not.

Liking the way the sun at his back lit his auburn hair, wishing it did
not remind her of that autumn day in this same market when she had

sought his ruin, she lifted the arm that had healed well and laid her hand to his cheek. "Still, we should make more of an effort."

He drew her hand away and kissed the backs of her fingers. Her new ring, a delicate gold band set with a ruby, sparkled. Fashioned for her three months past, it had been well settled upon her hand before the arrival of the king's missive that had granted approval of their marriage despite what Edward called *troublesome circumstances*, and which had caused him to offer Bayard condolences for being bound to such a woman as Elianor of Emberly.

"More of an effort," her husband mused. "That I will not argue, but methinks we should first attend to the task for which you requested my assistance."

Smiling, she looked over her shoulder at the market that grew more crowded toward the nooning hour and caught sight of Rollo before a stall that was hazy with the heat and scent of freshly baked pies. At his side was El's maid, sent to her at Adderstone as promised. Of late, something lovely seemed to be happening between the two, slowly shaping itself into what might be a future together. And El could not be more pleased.

Shifting her gaze to a table piled high with cloth, she said, "I am thinking darkest blue."

"The color of Verdun," Bayard said with mild censure.

Blue *was* flown by the Baron of Emberly, but that was not the reason she proposed it. "Though dark green would suit your sister equally well, I do not think she is of a mind to wear her betrothed's colors." And had not been of a mind since De Arell had delivered her home to Adderstone the day after his daughter had revealed to him the death of Quintin's mother.

During the reunion of brother and sister, Lady Quintin had seemed more approachable than when El had encountered her at Castle Mathe. Too, she had been less disagreeable toward the man who had held her prisoner. But when told of her mother's death, all had changed. If it was true what Lady Thomasin had alluded to regarding Lady Quintin's attraction for Griffin de Arell, it seemed true no longer. The Baron of

Blackwood was to blame for her not being with her mother whose murder, she believed, might otherwise have been prevented.

"I question whether Quintin is of a mind to wear any color other than black," Bayard said.

As did El, but the delay granted his sister in wedding so she might mourn her mother would soon end. King Edward wanted another marriage, and unless Lady Thomasin and Magnus accommodated him, it was Quintin and Griffin de Arell who would next find their lives pledged to each other. And it did not portend well to wed in black.

"If it is possible to persuade your sister to shed her mourning clothes," El said, "methinks the darkest, loveliest blue will do it." Among her discoveries about Quintin, who had become fairly receptive to her sister-in-law, was the woman's ability to be moved by beautiful things.

Bayard arched an eyebrow. "Certes, your uncle would not object."

That bothered El as well. Magnus had visited Adderstone a fortnight past to discuss the Foucault threat that had yet to raise its head again—though the man who had taken El from Adderstone had escaped those sent to track him down. During her uncle's stay, Lady Quintin had been aloof, and yet El had also sensed an attraction between Magnus and her. It did not bode well.

"Unfortunately," Bayard continued, "though your uncle might prefer to take my sister to wife, and she would take him to husband, there is nothing for it. The Verduns must make a match with the De Arells."

El nodded. That joining of families could happen if Bayard's efforts on behalf of Constance and Serle were successful, but such a union would not likely satisfy the king who had decreed that the barons themselves wed into one another's house.

"King Edward," Bayard growled. "He is hardly better than Agatha, making pawns and puppets of us all."

El stepped nearer him. "For us, that proved a good thing."

Glower easing, he peered into her face. "Only because you defied the king. Had you not, Thomasin would be a Boursier, and you would be a De Arell."

"Ah, but who can say we would not have been as surprised to make a good match with them as we were surprised with the match we did make?" she teased.

Mouth beginning to curve, he lowered his head. "I say it." His lips brushed her ear. "Whether or not we were destined for each other, there is no better match for me, Elianor of Godsmere."

"Lianor," she murmured into his ear. "Have I told you how I love the way you speak my name?"

He drew back, and his smile made her heart flutter. "Just last eve. Have I told you how I love you?"

"Just last eve." She slid her arms around his neck. "But, pray, tell me again."

Excerpt

BARON OF EMBERLY

—⟶⟵—

The Feud

England, 1308. Three noblemen secretly gather to ally against their treacherous lord. But though each is elevated to a baron in his own right and given a portion of his lord's lands, jealousy and reprisals lead to a twenty-five year feud, pitting family against family, passing father to son.

A Warrior Dangerously in Control

England, 1334. In the second book of *The Feud* series, Baron Magnus Verdun is a warrior whose handsome face gives little indication of the darkness he struggles to contain. While pursuing the murderous brigands who plague his lands, he becomes the unwitting savior of the woman the king has decreed he wed—the reckless Lady Thomasin, whose very presence threatens his carefully ordered life. And more so when she proves outspoken beyond what is required of a dutiful wife. Can he tame this woman whose willful ways ought to offend, but instead captivate? More, dare he allow her near and risk exposing the secret that could push her away?

A Lady Perilously Improper

Despite efforts to make a proper lady of her, the illegitimate Thomasin de Arell knows she is no match for the Baron of Emberly. Though she expects her new husband will think her beneath him, she is unprepared when he insists on separate chambers. When he also demands she control her behavior, the spurned Thomasin rebels—and unknowingly becomes the pawn of forces determined to further the feud. But upon finding herself in Magnus's arms, she discovers he is not as indifferent as he would have her believe. And when she glimpses his torment, she is determined to shine light on his darkness. Will he let her in? Or will their enemies use the distrust between husband and wife for their own ends?

In this sequel to the bestselling medieval romance, *Baron Of Godsmere*, join Baron Verdun and his lady as they discover that true love seeks first the soul, and is as easily seen in the dark as in the light.

2

⊷

THOMASIN CONSIDERED THE great edifice rising above the town laid out
before it. There she was expected to live out her days titled Lady of
Emberly, she who was to have aspired to no higher than a chambermaid.
Or so the steward of Waring Castle had believed, just as he had thought it
his right to pursue the girl she had been four years past. But she had possessed something his other prey had not. Beyond the temerity to defend
herself, she knew how to use the glistening ink at the tip of a quill—a
skill hidden from those who would not have approved, and known only
by the one who had made it possible. She who was no more.

Swallowing sorrow, Thomasin glanced over her shoulder to confirm
no others had happened upon this portion of the wood. All was still. Too
still?

When she had shed Castle Mathe this morn, she had not intended
to venture this far, but impulse had struck as she moved through the village of Cross distributing bread. Prompted by the knowledge she would
leave her father's lands five days hence, and the galling presence of the
one who kept watch over her, she had borrowed a horse from the miller
and put heels to it.

She did not doubt that the one who followed her, likely Sir Otto, had
also obtained a mount, but not before she had gained a league or more
on him. Had he known her destination, he could have overtaken her due
to her fair horsemanship, but she had bested him. As he deserved to be.

Aye, he who skulked after her outside the castle walls, who had little to do with her inside them, who had looked too long and often upon her father's betrothed, Quintin Boursier—

"Fie on ye, Thomasin," she rebuked. Jealousy benefitted her naught. Had she the beauty of Lady Quintin, therefore a chance to catch the handsome knight's attention, perhaps it would be worth churning up her insides and risking disdain. But as her mother had oft said—one of few remembrances of that woman Thomasin had not abandoned as she had been abandoned—one ought not wish where wishes were prey.

She caught back a laugh. She *had* wished, as well as prayed, though not for a man to look well upon her. A better life was what she had longed for, away from orders she resented, given by those who pinched and prodded her as if she were freshly baked bread to be granted no more thought beyond satisfying a man's immediate hunger.

Miraculously, her wishes and prayers had been answered, and chafe though she sometimes did over her father's control, a far better life he had given her. Rather than dirtying her hands amid the foul things others left behind, she was a lady whose hands were to be kept busy with the offices of sewing and weaving and resting prettily in her lap. And now…

She returned Castle Kelling to focus. Now her half-noble blood would become intimate with the full-noble blood of a baron—of handsome note, she understood. More handsome than Sir Otto?

Though she told herself she did not care what her husband thought of her and that marriage to her was more than a traitorous Verdun deserved, she felt a nervous flutter. Regardless of what his face revealed and what words he spoke when first they met, she would not flinch. She would clasp to her the blessing in being bereft of beauty—that one did not have to struggle to match what was inside to what was outside. And if he ill-treated her, he would discover she was noble enough of mind to retaliate.

"I shall not be afeared," she whispered and looked to the sky in the spaces between the canopy of brilliant leaves. From the village of Cross, it had taken two hours to reach the home of her betrothed. Thus, two hours back to return the horse, and another hour on foot, would see her at Castle Mathe by late afternoon. Though it was possible she would not be missed, her father confident she was in the care of his knight, it was also possible the knight had returned home to report she had evaded him.

Averse to starting back, she pondered what Griffin de Arell would do if he learned she was missing. It had been quiet of late upon the three baronies, almost as if the threat of last Christmas had never been.

Almost, for murder had come. It was not known for certain who had killed Lady Maeve Boursier, but the woman Thomasin had thought was her friend—Aude to her, Agatha to others—had been involved. And though Aude was now dead herself, it was believed there were others who wanted what the woman had failed to deliver—revenge against the De Arells, Verduns, and Boursiers whose betrayal had caused the once immense barony of Kilbourne to be divided into lesser baronies to reward the three vassals who had exposed their lord's treachery.

Aye, all was quiet, so perhaps the threat no longer existed. Perhaps any left behind to stir the longstanding feud between the three families was forever gone.

She wanted to believe it, especially in that moment, for it would mean the difference between starting back now or later.

Later, she decided. She had come this far and been this long missing, so what were a few more hours that could be spent exploring the demesne she would eventually traverse as she did Blackwood? Even if her sire responded by increasing her guard such that she could go nowhere unescorted, she would not suffer it long.

"Five days, Magnus Verdun," she said, imagining him somewhere inside those walls. "Then you will be my problem. As I may prove yours."

The *lady* could not have made it much easier, mused the one who had watched her since this morn when she had stolen out of the castle.

The plan had been to take her to ground after she departed the village of Cross, but she had borrowed a horse and headed opposite—here, to the home of the one she was to wed. *Was.*

Throughout her ride, there had been opportunities to bring her to ground when she veered off the road into the wood to avoid travelers, and he had been tempted to give the signal. But a need to scratch his months-long boredom had made him linger over her fate. Thus, he had allowed her to draw near Castle Kelling, though only because the one who lorded it had two days past gone to the village over the eastern border of the barony of Kilbourne—this portion of which the grasping Verduns had named Emberly.

Bile surged, and he let it bathe his teeth before spitting it out.

Emberly. Blackwood. Godsmere. By those names and the actions of the three who had betrayed Baron Denis Foucault, Kilbourne was debased. But it would rise again once he dealt with those who did not know they were dead men—and women.

Singing returned his attention to the lady, and he tensed in recognition of the pastorela that told of a nobleman who pursued a shepherdess with flattery and deception to convince her to lie down with him—a not uncommon pursuit, though it was sometimes the shepherdess who convinced the nobleman to lie with her.

This was not the first time he had heard the song from Griffin de Arell's misbegotten brat, it having been taught her by the woman who had befriended her years past.

Fear not, Aude, he silently assured the presence that had fastened itself to his back after her passing. *Her end will be as cruel as yours.*

Seeing his prey turn her horse aside to follow the road from the cover of the bordering trees, he signaled the others to hold. They would assist the *lady* in dismounting once she went deeper into the wood where none but judge and jury would hear her cries—of which there would be a goodly amount since he was not the only one bored with waiting.

Soon, he told himself, for she had not yet watered her mount and it must be done. But as they trailed her, she did not stay the road that led back the way she had come. She took the one branching left toward the village just over the border, the same Magnus Verdun visited once and twice a month.

Pleased to know that baron's secret, the watcher narrowed his eyes on Thomasin de Arell. He did not think she had lost her way, having observed her often enough to know she had a good sense of the land and made use of the sun's position to guide her. Thus, she was not done with her venture—else she had no intention of returning to Castle Mathe, this being her escape from marriage.

That gave him pause, but he shook it off. To her detriment, he would have to insist she accept his aid to ensure no marriage was made between the houses of Verdun and De Arell, for he could not risk failing as Aude had done in the marriage between the Boursiers and Verduns. Too, he could not resist the possibility that suspicion for the death of the low-born woman would fall on Magnus Verdun. Not necessary, but it would be a pretty boon—of which Aude would approve.

He sighed over memories of the woman who had sung the pastorela and had once tempted him to intimacy, that same dead thing he had fished from the frozen lake following her failure. Ah well, she had served her purpose. Mostly.

3

---⚬⚬⚬---

A VILLAGE LIKELY LAY in this direction, as evidenced by the occasional footprint in moist earth, a partially-hidden trap awaiting a creature destined for the pot, and scraps and threads that thorns and rough bark had snatched from the garments of those who passed too near.

Thomasin once more looked around and decided to venture farther east another league. If the village did not come into view, she would begin the journey home.

She stepped to her mount and patted its neck bent low over the stream it had been necessary to venture deep into the wood to find. "Enough?" she said.

It continued to drink, and she rebuked herself for not sooner leading it to water. Just as she had much to learn of handling horses, she must become better versed in their care.

Her own thirst satisfied, she swept her gaze over the ground. She should not bother, and yet she began searching for a walking stick worthy enough that her grandfather would give his weight unto it.

A dozen paces from the stream, she found one whose lower reaches were sunk in the loam. Of good size, she determined as she freed it. She brushed the soil away and was pleased with its character—of a golden color from its bulbous hilt that would fit well the palm, to its thick tip that required little shortening and would not skitter out from beneath one who leaned on it.

Smiling, she swung around. And the breath went out of her.

Two men, wearing the garb and arms of warriors, stood before her mount. And beyond them, on the other side of the stream, another was seated on a great stallion between two riderless horses. Had she time to look nearer at one who was likely of the nobility with such a mount beneath him, she did not think she could have made out his features owing to the distance and the tree's immense shadow falling over him. But that could not be tested, for the two men this side of the stream advanced.

Though she longed to flee, on foot it would be a token resistance. "What do you want?" she demanded.

Neither gave an ugly, knowing smile like that which the steward had often slanted at her, but she was not so fool to think they were different. She was a woman alone in a wood, and this time, unlike when she had come face-to-face with *The Boursier*, Sir Otto was not here to protect her.

"I am..." She swallowed. "...Lady Thomasin of Blackwood. My father is Baron de Arell." She hated vaunting her status, but other than teeth, fingernails, and a stick that would prove a pitiful defense, it seemed her only weapon.

"Aye, you are," the bearded one rasped.

He knew? Or was this mockery? She jerked her head in the direction from which she had come. "I am betrothed to Baron Verdun of Castle Kellin'."

"Kellin', eh?" said the bald, stubble-faced one, exaggerating the commoner's turn of word into which she had lapsed.

Was that her heart in her throat, so large it felt as if she would choke?

Quiet thyself, she silently counseled. *Watch your words and behave the lady, else this could go worse than wrong.*

She set the stick's tip to the ground. "Five days hence, I am to wed the Baron of Emberly upon whose lands ye stand."

They halted ten feet distant, and she felt a flush of relief.

"Wed?" one said. "We think not. Now all you must do is decide how unpleasant you wish this."

Dear God, she silently beseeched, *help me.*

"What say you?" the bearded one asked.

Thomasin shot her gaze to the one who watched from afar. "Sir Knight," she called, "if ye see me safely returned to my father, ye will be rewarded."

He remained unmoving.

She looked back at his companions. "All of ye will be rewarded."

"Alas"—the bald one jerked his head toward the one who remained astride—"I answer to another." Then he and his companion strode forward.

She had just enough time to jump aside and raise the stick. Gripping it with both hands, she used it to stir the air between them. "Come no nearer!"

"Pity this must be so unpleasant," the bearded one said and lunged, ducked beneath her next swing, and came up in front of her.

She stumbled back, gaining enough space to swing again. This time, she landed a blow, but not to the one at whom she aimed. The stick caught the bald one alongside the head, and she glimpsed a slash of crimson near his left eye as he wrenched the weapon from her.

The rough wood tore across her palms as it left them, and she knew there would be blood and stinging pain, but before either was seen or felt, her assailant turned the stick on her. The first strike caught her on the shoulder and finished its arc against her ear.

She screamed—or tried to, for if she had voice, she could not hear it above the ringing in her head.

Then she was dealt a hit to the ribs.

She loosed another scream, and as all began to blur, doubled over. Or was she already down? Curled on her side? All she knew for certain was that hands were on her, and no matter how she struggled, her only gain was more strikes and punches to the face and ribs.

Then weight fell upon her, and in the breaths drawn between screams, she inhaled the odor of a long-unwashed body.

As she continued to bite, claw, and kick, the men began shouting, and there was distant satisfaction in knowing that even in defeat, she could mark them for their sins—their flesh bruised, blood beneath her fingernails, soft places pained.

Amid a pounding of hooves, their shouts rose, and she became aware of the weight lifting from her and removal of the hands that had touched where they should not. But as her senses struggled to right themselves, she felt warm air upon her legs before the yank of her skirts that surely preceded the first sensation.

Dear Lord, preserve me, and by my words and actions I shall aspire higher, she silently vowed, and opened her eyes.

"Cur!" she shrieked at the one who loomed over her, though not as near as when she had last looked upon him. "Miscreant!"

His words were harsh and forceful, but the only one she made sense of was, "Cease!"

Attempting to keep her consciousness above dark waters, she saw enough of his wavering face to realize the one reaching for her was neither of the two who had beaten her to the ground.

This, then, the one who had watched from astride his horse. Now he would take what his men had gained for him. But she was not done fighting. And suddenly she had an abundance of means to defend herself.

No longer pinned, her arms were free to reach and rake, legs to kick. Though her head was too pained to allow her to look clearly on her assailant, when her knee struck hard muscle and she sank nails into stubbled flesh, there was no mistaking the baring of his teeth and tightening of a face too handsome to be fastened on a devil.

"Fie on ye!" she spat, and again reached with hooked hands.

He caught her wrists together and lowered his face near enough for the steel gray of his eyes to be told and the strangely pleasant scent of his body to be breathed.

"Me father'll kill ye!" she shrieked over whatever threats he made. "Gut ye like the pig ye are!"

As the spit of his angry response flecked her face, she strained her back upward, then dropped to the ground and thrust her head toward his descending one.

There was a crack as of lightning near enough to burst one's ears, and like the clouds through which it sounded, it dimmed her world.

"Pray, do not," she whimpered as she was swept deeper and darker. "I am to...wed."

Magnus Verdun knew it was possible to be angrier than he was in that moment, but not outwardly so—at least, not easily.

As he filled his lungs and slowly exhaled to bring his mind and body under control, he watched the woman's lashes flutter and lips part on a sigh.

She had been beaten, this one who appeared to have ventured alone to the wood, her sullied and torn garments the least of her worries. The greater concern was the injury to her head, and not just the one he had shared with her when she believed him a party to her attack. Beneath scratches and smears of dirt were swellings and bright spots likely to present as bruises. Of further concern was whether or not her assailants had wrested from her what she had obviously refused them.

The one holding her to the ground had been the first against whom Magnus struck when, having followed her screams, he thundered his mount onto the scene. It had been no easy thing to allow to flee the one who watched his companions seek to ravish the young woman. But Magnus had granted it all the sooner to stop the one who had her skirts up.

The thrown dagger had served, though only just, for his mark had not been the shoulder into which the blade stuck. His horse's movement had denied him the center of the back that would have laid down the bald man and allowed Magnus to give his full attention to the second one drawing a sword.

Guiding his horse with the press of his thighs, Magnus had veered away, those extra moments giving him time to bring his own sword to hand and counter the bearded one's thrust. Thrice he had come around, and twice his blade let crimson that also marked him. But death was not to be for that one any more than the other. The bald man had made it astride and spurred toward the woman as if to trample her.

Magnus had sent his own mount into that one's path, saving her, but gifting the bearded one with time in which to gain his own saddle. Then he and the other had set off after their companion who had first fled.

Now Magnus had an injured and unconscious woman on his hands. And the sooner she was tended, the better. But he could not convey her to Castle Kelling, not because it was more distant than the village he had departed this morn, but because of the one he had hidden in the undergrowth before answering this woman's cries.

He gathered up the seemingly slight woman and found her firmly built. Not that she was weighty. Rather, she lacked the fragile, fine-boned frame he expected. Whatever work she did, it put muscle on strong bones.

He lifted her onto his horse, draped her over its neck, and swung up behind her. As he drew her limp form back into his arms, his gaze fell on the flecks of blood staining his tunic. They were not his own, and it took effort to move his senses elsewhere, but he did and frowned over the scent of violets wafting from hair of lightest brown. She was no common laborer, as further evidenced by garments that, though simple and now near ruin, were far from worn. Too, whatever her destination, she had not come on foot. A merchant's daughter or wife, he guessed.

He nudged his mount toward the horse by the stream—an animal far from fine—caught up its reins, and setting it to a gallop, guided it back the way he had come.

Minutes later, the one he called forth poked his head above a tall shrub. "Who is that?" asked the wide-eyed boy of seven and some.

"I know not, but the sooner you show me you know how to mount a horse"—Magnus jerked his head toward the riderless one—"the sooner your mother can tend this woman's injuries."

As the boy emerged, he raised his strung bow over his head and settled it diagonally shoulder to hip. "Who did that to her?"

"Again, I know not, Eamon. I but stopped them from doing worse." It was true he could not name her attackers, but the boy need not be told of the suspicion that the months-long respite following the death of the woman he now knew to be named Aude as well as Agatha, could be at an end. He prayed not, but that lone figure watching his lessers from astride a fine horse boded ill.

"Did you kill them?" Eamon asked, flushing with excitement as his gaze took in the blood upon Magnus.

"I did not, but they are done for—will surely seek other lands upon which to work their ill. Now make haste. We shall continue our hunt another day."

It proved a challenge for the boy to mount the woman's horse, for what the animal lacked in beauty and youth, it made up for in height. But shortly, Eamon accepted the reins. "May I lead the way?"

Magnus might have allowed it if not for those who were yet somewhere in this wood. "Another day. This day, stay near."

About The Author

—⁂—

Tamara Leigh holds a Master's Degree in Speech and Language Pathology. In 1993, she signed a 4-book contract with Bantam Books. Her first medieval romance, *Warrior Bride*, was released in 1994. Continuing to write for the general market, three more novels were published with HarperCollins and Dorchester and earned awards and spots on national bestseller lists.

In 2006, Tamara's first inspirational contemporary romance, *Stealing Adda*, was released. In 2008, *Perfecting Kate* was optioned for a movie and *Splitting Harriet* won an ACFW "Book of the Year" award. The following year, *Faking Grace* was nominated for a RITA award. In 2011, Tamara wrapped up her "Southern Discomfort" series with the release of *Restless in Carolina*.

When not in the middle of being a wife, mother, and cookbook fiend, Tamara buries her nose in a good book—and her writer's pen in ink. In 2012, she returned to the historical romance genre with *Dreamspell*, a medieval time travel romance. Shortly thereafter, she once more invited readers to join her in the middle ages with the *Age of Faith* series: *The Unveiling, The Yielding, The Redeeming, The Kindling,* and *The Longing*. Tamara's #1 Bestsellers—*Lady at Arms, Lady Of Eve, Lady Of Fire,* and *Lady Of Conquest*—are the first of her medieval romances to be rewritten as "clean reads." Look for *Baron Of Blackwood,* the third book in *The Feud* series, in 2016.

Tamara lives near Nashville with her husband, sons, a Doberman that bares its teeth not only to threaten the UPS man but to smile, and a feisty Morkie that keeps her company during long writing stints.

Connect with Tamara at her website www.tamaraleigh.com, her blog The Kitchen Novelist, her email tamaraleightenn@gmail.com, Facebook, and Twitter.

For new releases and special promotions, subscribe to Tamara Leigh's mailing list: www.tamaraleigh.com